# The Awakening of Fate
## Becca Anne

# Dedication

*For Amber*
*A beautiful light gone from this world too soon.*

# *Author's Note*

First, WELCOME BACK to a world full of Nordic Magic in the land of Osera! Thank you so much for picking up book two in my debut fantasy series! I'm thrilled to be given another chance to borrow your mind for a few hours. As always, I hope you can find a home in this story, and love and friendship within these characters.

Before you continue, I deem it important to mention that a good portion of this book is very heavy. For my more emotionally inclined readers, I want to give you a fair warning that if you know you are sensitive to any of the <u>themes</u> in the content warnings (*as I am and struggled myself writing it*), please feel free to reach out to ask for a spark notes version of the more difficult chapters. Take breaks if you need to, and know that, I too, cried way too hard at some of the things discussed. I may be overreacting and once you've read it you might think '*That wasn't that bad. What was she talking about?*" and I hope that is the case! But I wanted to stress a bit more on the content warnings because if this was something I had read without them, I know I would have struggled mentally outside of this story.

Additionally, I want to briefly remind readers going forward that this story is based off Norse Mythology but will not be one hundred percent accurate to Lore and Legend, as I have used the stories of the Old Gods to help form and create the lore and magic systems you will learn about and experience throughout '*The Bargain with Fate Series*'. However, through my research, my intention is to keep the stories, magic, and history of Norse Gods as accurate as possible with fantasy flair bestowed upon the less-godly aspects. Not that this matters much, but I want you to know I have tried my best at keeping the Gods' stories accurate.

*The Awakening of Fate* has been through the hands of five different beta readers, six different sensitivity readers, as well as a copy editor, and a line editor.

My goal for this series is to harbor a safe space for all who enjoy reading, and although I feel as I have put forth a hundred and ten percent of my effort and intentions on making that a reality, I understand that things can still be missed. If you do find something harmful, hurtful, or otherwise, throughout this story, please respectfully reach out to me through my author website: beccaannebooks.com.

# Content Warning

This book contains sensitive content and may not be suitable for minors and should be read and purchased with discretion. *The Bargain with Fate* series is intended for New Adult and Adult audiences and contains adult language, violence, and sexual situations and is intended to be sold to adults 18+. This book and others in the series may contain scenes triggering to readers and should be read, purchased, and gifted with caution. If you have any questions or concerns on specific triggers, please reach out to me on social media @beccaannebooks or through my author website. The trigger warnings are as follows:

*Graphic Violence*

*Adult Language*

*Sexual Situations*

*Themes of Depression*

*Themes of Anxiety*

*Themes of Suicidal Ideation*

*Themes of Survivor's Guilt*

*Suicide Attempt*

*Negative Self-Talk*

*Death*

*Mentions of Slavery*

*Blood and Gore*

*Mentions of Violence towards Children (off-page)*

*Child Death/Murder (Hinted at briefly through a vision/Non-violent)*

## My Books Are Not For You If...

If you are Racist, Homophobic, Transphobic, Xenophobic, Queerphobic, Fat-phobic, Evangelical Far-Right Conservative, or hold prejudice and discriminate against people who struggle with mental illness, the content in my books is not intended for you. The content in my books will be extremely triggering for you. Unless you will be reading these stories to expose yourself to a diverse world where love is love and you are not judged or treated differently for the color of your skin, how big someone's body is, who someone loves, or who someone has sex with, TO LEARN, DO NOT invest your time and money here.

OSERA
SKADI MOUNTAINS
THE NOTCH OF SISTERS
SYLPH MOUNTAINS
KINGDOM OF SOL
MOUNT EIR
LAKE LAGOM
FRITH
WILLINGMAN WOOD
KRON CASTLE
NÓTT FOREST
LYKKE VILLAGE AND PORT
EXRIS
PORT SISU
STILLRIDGE
REACHING RIVER
LAKE KYNDA
RÁN SEA
PORT REISA
KINGDOM OF SKIRRA

# One

Death is inevitable. Some might think it honorable, sought out in the final journey to Valhalla, … but what happens when death is sudden? Unexpected? Unfair? What happens when it shadows you? Taunts you? Reaches its outstretched hand for you at every corner of conflict. How should we live when death consumes our reality?

Time passed, as did my muted thoughts, while the rain settled into a steady drizzle upon my entrance into Exris. Once in the safety of the city, I dug around in the travel pack I had thrown together in the royal barn, looking for anything to clean and bandage my wound. The rain washed away most of the blood as I was making my escape out of Sol's town.

I grabbed a small vial of healing paste and applied the mixture to the arrow wound from one of the royal archers. It did more damage than I initially realized. The underlying muscle was exposed, and as I continued to tend to the wound, blood began seeping from it. *Dammit.* I pulled my knife from my back pocket and cut the excess end of my tunic, tying it around my arm. *That should be enough until I get back and Bryn can ...*

With muddled thoughts, I pulled Arvak to a stop. My eyes burned from the strain of tears against my eyelids. *Is this what life is going to be like now?*

*Coward. He would've died for you.*

I shook my head and urged Arvak forward. As we turned down the road leading to Jerrik's shop, an explosion erupted. People began screaming and running in every direction. As I looked on in confusion, I realized with dismay whose shop was engulfed in flames. I pushed Arvak into a sprint down the road, leaping off her and smacking her back end to make her run from the danger.

"JERRIK!" I screamed into the roar of the flames but heard nothing. My mind flew to Brax. I had left him here with Elias. My eyes widened in horror, and my mind went blank as I barreled through the splintered front door.

I waved my hand frantically, attempting to disperse the thick smoke before me. The walls were covered in flames that danced toward the ceiling.

"BRAX! ELIAS! JERRIK!?" I screamed for them, hoping at least one of them would respond.

"Over here!" Jerrik shouted from the back. "They are back here!" I ran behind the counter, feeling the heat of the flames press heavily against the side of my body. I turned my back to the wall of fire as I leaped through the doorway to the storage room. I began to cough from the dense smoke collecting in the air. That's when I heard someone else coughing, too.

"Jerrik?!" I called out, looking between boxes and shelving.

"Veronica? Veronica! Go right from the doorway!" He instructed between heavy coughs. I did as I was told and found Jerrik standing over a row of fully stocked shelves blown over by the explosion. I fanned away the smoke in the air with my hands and bent over to find Elias trapped underneath. Jerrik was frantically throwing boxes off to free him. I didn't hesitate to grab ruined supplies and toss them to the side. I then picked up a box and, through the smoky air, made out a paw. My heart skipped a beat, and I shoveled debris off Brax. Enough that I could grab his back legs and pull him out from under the shelf. He whined at the sudden movement, and I breathed a sigh of relief. I took off my cloak and threw it over him, instructing him to wait so I could help Elias.

"That should be enough boxes. We can lift the shelf together!" I yelled across the room. The fire roared louder as flames began to lick through the doorway behind me. "On three!" I yelled. Jerrik nodded, coming around to take his place next to me. "One! Two! THREE!" We both grunted from the effort to lift the half-stocked shelf, even with our adrenaline fueling us. Luckily, Elias managed to wiggle himself out from underneath. Once he was clear, we dropped it.

"We need to get out of here!" Jerrik yelled, hauling Elias from the ground and guiding one of his arms over his shoulder so he could help him walk.

"The back door," Elias croaked as he pointed to the back of the store. I carried Brax in my arms as we hurried towards it. I gently placed him on the floor as I went to open the door, but it didn't budge. I rammed my shoulder into it. Nothing. I looked to Jerrik, who handed me Elias so he could try ramming it open, but still to no avail. He tried one last time, and it barely cracked open, allowing him to see what was blocking the door.

"Someone parked a wagon in front of the door. We will have to go out the front," Jerrick instructed. He took hold of Elias again, and I looked around, eying a leathery cloak spilling out of an abandoned box. I grabbed it, throwing it over the men's shoulders and patting them on the back.

"The fire has gotten worse! The front door was blown open. We have to run like hel to get out of here!" I shouted as I bent down to Brax, wrapping him thoroughly in my cloak and heaving him into my arms. I nodded at Jerrik, and they disappeared past the blazing doorway, and I followed suit. Dense charcoal smoke filled the store, and flames now hung from the ceiling, forcing us to crouch towards the floor so we could reach our exit.

Jerrik and Elias disappeared in front of me for a moment before I was blinded by the light reflecting off the clouds. I spilled out of the front door, tripping off the small front porch, turning to catch the brunt of the fall on my back so I didn't crush Brax. Jerrik came up from behind and grabbed me under my arms, dragging me along the muddied ground until we were safe on the opposite side of the road, and sat me next to Elias, who was close to coughing out a lung.

He looked at me, distressed. "I'm so sorry! I don't know what happened. One second, I was looking for an item for a patron, and the next thing I knew, we were trapped underneath the shelf," he explained frantically. He eyed Brax, then returned to look at me.

"He will be okay," I assured him, placing a supportive hand on his leg. "Are you okay?" He nodded and moved each body part, one at a time, to double-check. I looked past Elias and noticed Jerrik slumped over and breathing heavily as he watched his shop burn in disbelief. The townspeople had gathered and were helping run buckets of water over to douse the flames. "I'm so sorry, Jer. ..." He shook his head in response.

"Everyone is okay. That's all that matters," he stated, looking over to Elias, who offered him a hand that he took immediately. We sat there and waited for the blaze to die down and smolder. The rain gradually slowed to a stop, and the shop looked like a charred pile of rubbish. I continued pouring water over Brax to cool him off when Jerrik guided Arvak, who was pulling his wagon, in front of us. He helped me wrap Brax up in my cloak again and get him situated on a comfy bed of hay in the back before we went to assess the damage. The Exris patrol guards were finishing questioning Elias. I kept out of sight behind a neighboring building until they left.

"So, you said there was a patron inside when the explosion went off?" The patrol guard asked.

"Yes, Ma'am," Elias answered.

"There were no signs of a body found in the aftermath."

"I did hear the bell chime from the front door, but the explosion happened right after it went off. I didn't have time to process much."

"Alright. We will make a report of the incident. If anything comes up, let us know." Jerrik and Elias nodded, and the guards mounted their horses and headed down the road. I stepped out from my hiding spot and was going to speak, but Jerrik cut me off.

"Someone parked that wagon at the back door, so we couldn't escape," he hissed under his breath as he moved closer to me. "This wasn't an accident, but I don't want to talk about it here." I nodded and turned to Elias.

"Are you coming with us?" I asked. He looked over to Jerrik, who raised an eyebrow at my question.

"I would be honored to," he stated but didn't move. I turned to Jerrik.

"Do you trust him?" I questioned, looking past his eyes to try and read whatever thoughts were going through his head. He nodded curtly.

"I do. I also think it might be safest for him to stay in Lykke for a few days." He turned to Elias, "if that is something you would be open to." Elias let a slight hint of a smile play at the corner of his mouth.

"I would appreciate a room if there is one to offer."

I smiled grimly and placed my hand on his shoulder. "Alright, boys. Let's get the last bits of salvage loaded, and we can be on our way." They both nodded, and we worked in silence. Elias volunteered to be our guide for the night and lit the lamp that hung from the side of the wagon.

Meanwhile, Jerrik stepped in front of me, his face filled with sorrow. He then pulled out a cloak he had been concealing behind his back. It was the sable coat from his and Sylve's recent hunt. The fire had slightly singed the cloak on the ends, but it was still beautiful. "I wanted to gift it to you for the summer solstice, but … time is never guaranteed." My lip quivered at the harsh truth in his words, the weight of reality crushing me. I accepted it and threw it over my shoulders. "It's a winter cloak, but you need one for our ride to Lykke anyway. I know you don't have the heart to take yours from Brax."

I turned to look at Brax, curled up on his makeshift bed, sleeping peacefully amongst all the activity surrounding us. "Thank you," I offered solemnly.

He pulled me in and hugged me tight. "I'm so sorry," he whispered onto the top of my head. I wrapped my arms around him and returned the gesture, tucking my head into his smoke-covered clothes to hide the tears that had escaped and rolled down my face. I shook my head and leaned away from him, pulling the hood over my head.

"Let's get going. It's going to be a long night," I urged, clearing my throat. Jerrik insisted that I sit in the wagon with Brax while he took watch next to Elias, keeping his bow ready to use if he had to. The methodical rocking of the wagon over the gravelly trail helped quiet my mind and relax next to Brax, allowing sleep to creep its veil over my eyes.

# Two

Elias brought us to a stop outside the Inn. Jerrik hopped out first, throwing his bow across his back before helping Elias off the front of the wagon. He required assistance since his leg was badly injured from the explosion, causing shooting pain when he bears weight on it. They paused briefly, and Jerrik looked back and offered an outstretched hand. I shook my head.

"I need a minute," I stated, looking away from the building, away from where I expected Bryn to run out to make sure I wasn't hurt. My heart felt as if it was going to explode just being near it.

"I'll send someone to help you and Brax in a few minutes," Jerrik promised, leading Elias inside. I heard the voices quiet as the door opened and closed, leaving me to myself.

I stroked the back of Brax's neck slowly, rhythmically. He moved his head to lay in my lap, licking my hand resting on my leg. *What do I do?*

*Coward!*

How can I walk through that door and face the people closest to me without breaking into a million pieces?

*It should've been you!*

What do we do now that he is gone?

*Useless!*

I closed my eyes and tried to breathe. I could feel the warm, tingling sensation growing and creeping up my neck. My chest started to constrict the longer I kept my eyes closed, so I forced them open. *Focus on your breathing, Veronica. In. ... One, two, three. Hold. Out. ... One, two, three.*

There was still darkness. The warm light from the Inn illuminated the small area just before the dirt road. Everything was quiet, lifeless even, in comparison to most nights. The crickets refused to perform their nightly symphony. The ocean was calm after the storm, sweeping onto the shoreline instead of doing its usual dance along the rocks. No dogs barked. No goats bleated at each other. No wind whistled through the night. The trees didn't whisper tales of another life. Still. Silent. Lifeless.

"Penny for your thoughts?" a soft, honey-filled voice asked beside me. Sindre had been so quiet that I hadn't even heard the door to the Inn open. I shook my head and went to scoot off the end of the wagon when he put a hand on my shoulder. "I'm not here to rush you. You don't have to go inside if you're not ready." I nodded and let myself continue to sit on the edge instead. "Would you like me to leave you alone?" he asked softly. I looked up and met the warmth in his brown eyes. There was no pity. Only honest concern tinged with sadness.

"I'm sorry," I croaked. My throat was sore from the inhalation of smoke. "Stay, ... please." He nodded and walked around, finding a seat next to me. He didn't speak, just listened—listening to the silence that had befallen the town and the Inn.

"Jerrik told us what had happened at his shop. I'm glad you all are okay." I nodded, looking back at Brax. *If I had lost him tonight as well. ... * I shook my head and looked up at the sky. The moon was full. *That explains a lot. The full moon seems to have an odd effect on people.*

"What happened to your arm?" he questioned, moving the cloak further off my shoulder. I looked down at my wound. I had forgotten about it entirely.

"An arrow grazed it," I answered plainly. From the corner of my eye, I saw his expression harden.

"A what?"

"An arrow," I reiterated, pulling loose the scrap of the tunic I'd used to cover the injury to show him through the ripped sleeve.

"An arrow from what?" he asked, gently holding my arm up to examine it.

"The Royal Archers." His arms fell limp in his lap, my arm following suit.

"Veronica ..." I looked at him numbly, waiting for him to finish what he was going to say, but he was looking at me, waiting first for my response. When I didn't, he took a breath. "Why did a Royal Archer shoot an arrow at you?"

"It wasn't just one. I'm pretty sure it was all of them." His eyes widened, and I knew he wanted to reprimand me, but he kept his composure.

"Did you kill someone?" he asked cautiously.

"Almost."

"Gods, Veronica. I told you not to do anything stupid," he muttered into his palm as he ran it down his face.

"I didn't *kill* her," I mentioned under my breath.

"Her? Her who?" He leaned over to catch my eyes, but I avoided him. "Erikka? Her, Erikka?" I nodded. He stood quickly and bent over, running his hands through his locs. "You attempted to *kill* Erikka? The Princess? Calder's only heir?"

"YES! But I DIDN'T! Okay?" I blurted, voice cracking again.

He stared back at me, his lips pursed tightly. "You need to tell Ragnhild. He's waiting inside to speak with you about funeral arrangements," he urged softly. "I can bring Brax inside if you would like."

"No. I got him." I hopped off the wagon and bent over the edge, reaching for the corner of my cloak. I pulled it and slid Brax along the length of the cart closer to me, picking him up. He felt significantly heavier than when I carried him at the shop now that my adrenaline had subsided. My knee buckled under his weight, and Sindre caught me under the arm. I looked up at him sheepishly. "Maybe I don't have him." He smiled softly and bent over to take Brax from me, lifting him with ease. "Thank you."

He nodded, and I walked over to face the door of the Inn. I took a deep breath before stepping inside. I let Sindre walk around me and place Brax next to the small couch where Sylve waited. Ragnhild sat on the chair closest to the hearth and looked up from his mug. I stood awkwardly in the middle of the room, looking around to see where everyone had gone.

"They have all retired for the night," Ragnhild reassured. He patted the back of the chair next to him. I politely shook my head to refuse his offer, and he nodded in understanding.

"I know you need to speak with her about certain things, but something has come up that Veronica needs to tell you. Sooner rather than later," Sindre announced, patting me on the shoulder as he passed to enter the kitchen. Ragnhild didn't look up from his drink while I pulled off my cloak and laid it over the arm of the couch.

"Did you kill her?" he asked plainly. My eyes widened in shock as Sylve whipped her head to look between Ragnhild and me.

"You already know?"

"I expected *some* sort of event to arise from this," he explained gently, leaning back in his chair.

"Um. Hey there. What are you guys talking about?" Sylve cut in, looking between us for clarification. Sindre came out of the kitchen with two mugs in his hands, passing one to me before sticking his free hand in his pocket and drinking his, raising his eyebrows at me. I sighed.

"I ... attacked Erikka, ... but I didn't kill her," I assured, hurrying to deliver the last half of my confession. Sylve didn't say anything. She just looked at me through narrowed eyes.

"What *else*?" she pushed curiously. I cursed inwardly; she knew me too well.

"I set my room on fire as a distraction so that I could break into her private quarters via her balcony." Sindre spat out the contents of his drink, and everyone looked at him. Ragnhild laughed to himself while Sindre swiped at his face with a sleeve.

"You kind of left that part out," he choked, looking at me in disbelief.

"Did anyone identify you?" Ragnhild questioned seriously, setting his mug on the small table beside him.

"Mazen and Erikka did."

"Did they compromise your identity amidst all of the chaos?" I contemplated his question, running through the event quickly. Mazen stopped himself from calling out my name as more guards made their way to Erikka's quarters.

"No."

"What about anyone else? How did you leave the castle?"

"I jumped out of her balcony and rode off. I had the hood of my cloak up when the archers noticed me, so I doubt they could tell who I was," I explained, still holding the mug in my hands.

"This is what I was waiting for," Ragnhild started, "I needed confirmation on any ruckus you may have caused at the castle."

I lowered my gaze to the floor; the feeling of guilt and shame blanketed my shoulders. "I'm sorry," I muttered defeatedly under my breath. He stood and walked over to me, putting his hands on my shoulders.

"Child, you misunderstand. You are my blood brother's kin and take after him in all the best ways. This is not an inconvenience to us, nor was it *unexpected*." I looked up at him through teary eyes to find him smiling at me softly. "Do not add an unnecessary burden to your shoulders. I have already started to spread the word in Exris as we passed through for those who would want to attend that we would be holding Brynjar's funeral tomorrow at sunset." I looked down again, unable to absorb the honest and raw emotion Ragnhild held in his eyes. "The Lykke townspeople have been made aware as well, dear. Your actions only affect how soon we leave for Frith."

"What about those in Frith?" my voice was barely a whisper. "The other elders? The Frithians?" I thought about Ylva. She has no idea. ... I clenched my jaw and looked back at Ragnhild. He shook his head regretfully.

"Time is the one thing we don't have much of to work with. We can't take him to Frith either. The funeral has to take place in the Kingdom for the news to make it back to Calder." I nodded and stepped around him, picking up his mug from the table.

"Is there anything else I need to know?" I asked the room, my back now turned as I walked to the kitchen.

"You will need to go through his belongings ... tonight," Sylve informed quietly. I froze to the floor. "We will also all need to gather an item to send with him." My chest shrunk. Tighter. Tighter. *Am I even breathing?*

"V?" Sindre cooed from behind me. His breath was warm on the back of my neck, and his fingertips caressed the sides of my arms, coaxing me back to my body. I pulled in a quick breath and stepped away from him.

"I need a moment," I announced, sliding into the kitchen and placing the mugs in the wash basin. I braced my hands on either side of it, hanging my head down. *Is this really happening? Do I really have to do this?* Go through his belongings? Take what I can with me and decide what must be left here?

*It's your fault!*

*Coward! Pathetic!*

I felt the weight of a hand grace the center of my back. I looked up quickly to find Sylve. "I can help you go through his things," she offered gently, moving me out of the way so she could pour out my mug and wash the two I had placed in there. I didn't respond right away. I didn't want to feel like a burden, but the company might be nice. "I could just pack them up for you. That way, you could take your time going through them in Frith ... if you aren't ready yet." She placed the mugs back on their rack along the wall, then turned around to lean on the counter. She didn't say anything else or look at me for a response. She just offered her presence. Sindre stepped into the kitchen a few moments later.

"Ragnhild is going to bed. Do you need help with anything?" he offered solemnly. I looked between the two of them. Both had the same longing look on their faces. I know they wanted to be supportive, but they were mourning as well, and I didn't want to burden them. With the way they've been carefully glancing at me, I feel like all I've been doing is burdening them with my presence. *You need to control your emotions.* Keep myself together so I can fill his role. *Stop being a liability.*

"No, I can handle it. Thank you both." I nodded at them. "Goodnight," I announced quietly as I walked past them and entered Bryn's room.

Once I locked the door, everything stilled. His bed was still unkempt, and some of his clothes had been strewn across the floor. I decided that was where I was going to start. I picked up his clothes and began to pilfer through them with a heavy heart. I figured I could donate most of it. That is what he would have wanted to do with it anyway. I sectioned through his tunics and decided to keep my favorite ones to sleep in.

I held a blue one in my lap and felt the material between my fingers. I loved it when he wore blue. *It always brightened his brown eyes.* Jerrik would always swoon over how handsome he looked in that color. The memories forced a twisted smile onto my face. I held the tunic to my chest, taking in the lingering scent, hoping I would never forget it—forget him.

I placed the tunic on top of a now full crate I'd just filled with his clothes I wanted to keep and moved on to his other belongings. Bryn never cared much about material items. He always made it a point to pass things on to those who could find a better use for them. However, he did keep a few things for himself.

All his keepsakes were secured in a relatively small wooden box, no wider than my shoulders and no taller than my knees. It had an intricate carving of a raven spreading its wings with the Valknut symbol—three intertwining triangles all pointing up in the same direction—in the center of its chest. I ran my fingers along the weathered wood. My grandmother had crafted this as a gift for him sometime after the war, knowing there might be something precious he might want to keep for himself one day. I never met my grandmother. She passed from an illness that quickly consumed her body and mind when my mother was a young child. At least, that's how Bryn had told me her story. When I opened it, a puff of aged dust filled with an earthy scent—somehow a cross between Bryn and forgotten treasures—tickled my nose, causing me to sneeze.

The first item that sat on top must have been the most recent thing he added because it was ... my axe? The axe that recently impaled me on our most recent raid. He had cleaned and polished it, wrapping it in scarlet fabric. What a weirdo. I smiled fondly at this surprising find. I had been looking everywhere for this. I didn't even think to ask him if he had it.

The next item occupied most of the space in the box, and I would recognize it anywhere. It was my mother's would-have-been wedding dress made by my grandmother. As a child, Bryn let me play around in the simple fabrics. My grandmother was a master of her crafts. How she conceived and constructed every aspect of this gown still amazes me to this day. It was folded neatly. The top part of the dress was gray, cut just above the breast line and tied together at the shoulders. From there, the sleeves draped off the shoulders, dissolving into the long orange train I remembered flowing endlessly behind it. Somewhere around the waist, it gradated into a bright orange, as if representing the fire forging the iron at the ensemble's top. As gray blended into orange, a loose belt folded over itself at the hips and cascaded down the front while the rest of the beguiling gown flowed freely to the floor. It wasn't tight, nor did it puff out with extra material. It simply caressed the legs as it melted into a trail of fire meant to blaze the path my mother walked. She had embroidered a beautiful design of interlocking rings and triangles that decorated the bodice, which met and flowed down the middle. The dress is more beautiful than any of the elegant gowns and dresses Erikka wears every day. It would have been an honor to wear this. I banished the thought from my head. Matrimony—which Bryn especially loved—is not for me. He always told me he would rather worry about the amount of fighting and killing I would do than deal with any man or woman that might come seeking my hand.

I didn't want to be responsible for folding the precious dress back correctly, so I lifted all the layers and ran my fingers along the bottom for what I knew he kept there. I heard it scratch along the bottom of the box before I pulled it toward the center of my hand. I held my palm out and admired, again, another piece of Bryn's life that he held dear—his wedding rings. His, a black band of steel, interlocked with my grandmother's, a bright silver, secured at either end to a leather string meant to be worn as a necklace. Bryn didn't want to send these rings with my grandmother during her funeral. He wanted them here as a reminder of a life that once existed. Their love had been real, no matter how much time passed. Instead, he opted to send his blood with her, hoping his spirit might be reunited with hers in the afterlife.

*Fuck.* Tears welled in my eyes, and I blinked them away. I don't have time to mourn him. There are more important things at risk that I need to be preparing for, things I need to give all my effort and attention to. A rebellion that will happen, with or without the help of the citizens of Sol. I *will* kill The King, with or without an army behind me. I *have* to.

I knotted the leather string that held the wedding bands behind my neck, wearing it as a necklace and tucking them under my shirt before closing the box with the rest of the items and moving it into the pile that goes to Frith. The rest of his extra clothing can be donated to the Frithians, just like he'd have wanted.

When I had finished filling the boxes, I walked over to his side of the bed and stood there, wondering what had happened. I noticed a wooden mug on the floor, peeking out from just under his bed. The small table it had presumably been sitting on was slightly askew, so I pushed it back against the wall. When I bent over to pick up the mug, I accidentally pushed it further under. I groaned in annoyance as I got on all fours to secure the runaway item. As I shimmied my shoulder under the bed to reach for it, I noticed a crumpled piece of parchment. I grabbed that, too, and retreated, sitting myself up on my knees with my newfound items. I was going to dispose of my findings without a second thought, but something, perhaps curiosity, tugged at me to open the parchment.

My mouth dropped open, and I covered it in case my body failed me and screamed out in anguish.

### RaT aMOng De ravOns

I was on my feet instantly and swung my door open to find Sindre and Sylve talking quietly in the main sitting room. I walked over, grabbed both their wrists, and pulled them into Bryn's room with me, closing the door and grabbing a pillow to stuff into the crack. I held out the piece of parchment, and Sylve took it. Looking at me blankly, she shoved it into Sindre's chest for him to examine.

"What is that?" Sylve asked quietly.

"I found it crumpled up under his bed," I whispered. "His side table had been displaced, too, and his mug was on the floor."

"Do we think they jumped him when he was asleep?" Sindre growled through gritted teeth.

"It's possible." My anger started to claw underneath my skin, distracting me from thinking clearly. The thought of him being attacked as he slept makes me want to kill someone. "Someone told Calder ...," I stated in disbelief, shocked at the idea that a Raven would turn on us. What is there for any of us to gain by doing that? I looked up at the twins to gauge their reactions. Sylve seemed more in thought than feeling her emotions, but Sindre looked as if he would explode any second. I stepped closer to him and wrapped my arms around his waist, pressing my forehead into the center of his chest. He did not return the gesture. "I know." It was all I could think of to say under my breath as I held myself to him. Sylve came over and put a hand on both of our shoulders.

"We need to get some sleep." She hesitated to say more as her gaze drifted to me. "Are—Are you okay with sleeping alone? Because I can sleep with you if you want company."

I shook my head. "I've got Brax tonight, so there is no need for us to squeeze in next to each other." She held my forearm for a moment. I placed my free hand over hers. "I'll be just fine." I nodded towards Sindre, who still seemed lost in his thoughts. "I'm more worried about him." Sylve looked over at him before shaking her head at me.

"I'll just knock him over the back of the head or something, and he will go right to sleep." She smiled, nudging her elbow into his ribs. I snorted a laugh before clearing my throat due to the unamused eyes that found mine.

I walked out into the main sitting area to get Brax and paused, realizing I wouldn't be able to lift him again to move him into Bryn's room. Before I could even think to ask, Sindre walked past me, picked Brax up, and brought him in for me. He placed him gently on the bed, and I snaked past Sindre's arm to pull the blankets over him, fluffing his pillow so he could be nice and comfy tonight. I turned to them and thanked them with a nod, and Sylve walked over and kissed my forehead before hugging me, as did Sindre, saying their goodnights.

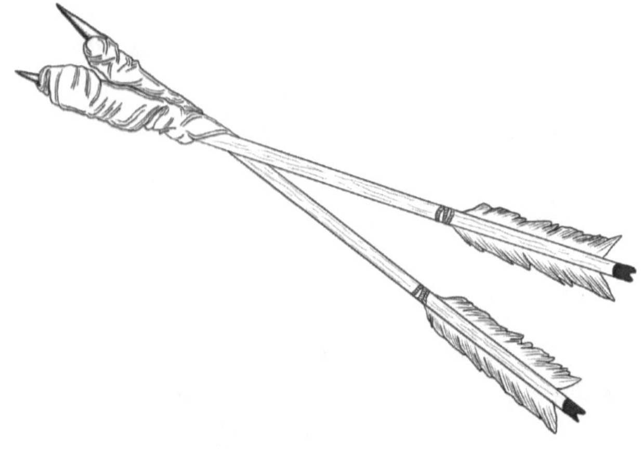

# Three

The sky was on fire again: a familiar scene. I felt as if I had been here before, but I couldn't quite pinpoint the memory I was hoping to find. I turned around to find an army of Draugr running towards me.

I looked down into my hand, and Bryn's axe appeared.

As the Draugr passed me, I followed them, running into battle against warriors made from translucent light. I spared no life that dared jump in my path. I knew where I was going. I knew what I had to do, even though I could not quite form the goal in my mind.

When the final warrior fell, the Draugr disappeared. The fiery sky had now darkened with heavy smoke. I began to choke on the air as I headed toward a shadowed figure. I stepped forward and heard a squelch under my boot, a puddle. Upon closer examination, it wasn't a puddle of water but blood. My eyes followed a trail of flames only to find Sindre's dead body, and past him lay Sylve, with Jerrik just beyond her. A rush of despair brought me to my knees, but I fought against the urge to collapse entirely. Screams of agony clawed at my throat for release. I looked up at the shadowed figure that stepped into the light of flames that now surrounded us. My friends' bodies had disappeared. It was a masked man with eyes of silver light, gleaming with a vicious desire to kill.

*The mask was blurry, as were the details of his face, but he was a large man, bigger than most I'd ever seen. As he stalked forward in my direction, I noticed him dragging someone along by the back of their shirt. Once he stood before me, he threw a man to his knees between us. Brynjar.*

*Bryn was mangled, beaten, and bleeding, but as I moved to run to him, I slipped on ice and fell on all fours. Ice shards wrapped around my extremities, cementing me in place. I tried to scream for him, but the ice crept up the side of my neck and covered my mouth. I tried to pull myself free, but the frozen shackles didn't budge an inch. Tears blurred my vision further as I watched the man transform into a wolf, larger than any I had ever seen, and stalk over toward Bryn. I thrashed against my restraints, but they only constricted further, sending shooting pain up my limbs, threatening to break them.*

*The wolf strode over to stand behind Bryn and paused, looking at me with malice in its eyes. I looked at Bryn and tried to tell him to run, my screams muffled by my icey mask. He looked at me, his brown eyes pleading. "Help me, Veronica."*

*My eyes widened in horror at his words, the clarity of his voice, and at the wolf whose mouth had opened unnaturally wide, grabbing Bryn's head before ripping it from his body. My body went cold as those starlight silver eyes seized mine after tossing the decapitated head to the side. He stepped over Bryn's body, advancing with predatory determination, blood dripping from his teeth—teeth that were bared at me. Snarling.*

*He leaped for my throat.*

My door flung open, slamming into the wall behind it. "Veronica! Are you okay? VERONICA!" I felt pressure on my shoulders, then a sharp, stinging jolt to my face before everything quieted. I blinked my eyes open a few times, rubbing my throat with my hand. It felt like I had just attempted to swallow a hot iron brand. I pushed my damp hair from my eyes and looked up at Sylve, whose eyebrows were raised with deep concern.

"I'm fine," I croaked, surprising myself at the hoarse voice that enshrouded my words.

"The *hel* you are!" she retorted, rubbing the sides of my arms. "You were screaming as if someone was trying to kill you! Are you okay?" she repeated herself, this time with a hint of panic.

"Someone must have sent me another mare," I joked tiredly, "I'm fine. Really," I reassured, running my hands down my face. Sindre knocked on the door frame, leaning against it coolly.

"I've convinced the Inn to go back to sleep. Are you okay in here?" he asked, watching me rub my throat. "Water?"

"Please," I begged with my eyes, and he nodded, stepping out of the room.

"What was your dream about?" Sylve asked, unconsciously massaging my leg in a soothing pattern.

"Nothing. Don't worry about it," I answered quietly. The side of my face started to burn as time passed, so I rubbed it to work out the sensation. She shot me a dirty look as Sindre walked back in with some water, handing it to me and tilting his head.

"Damn, Syl. Were you trying to disconnect her head from her body?" he commented, shoving her shoulder playfully. I flinched at his words, earning me a confused look from both of them.

"Well, ... she wasn't waking up."

"I'm fine. I needed help anyway. I didn't want to stay in my head any longer than I needed to." I laughed to myself, and the two of them stared at me. "What?"

"Nothing," Sindre cut in as Sylve opened her mouth to speak. "It's almost sunrise. Are you going to go back to sleep? Because I could use some help cleaning up the port for this evening," he offered nonchalantly. I looked at Sylve, who was watching me closely, analyzing—which irritated me.

"Or you can try to go back to sleep. I can stay with you this time?" she asked.

I shook my head. "I can help at the port," I answered tightly. "I'll just need a second to get ready." Sindre nodded and walked out of the room while Sylve stood and followed, but instead of leaving, she closed the door and turned back to me with a worried look.

"I know what you're doing."

"I'm not doing anything," I reassured as I whipped off the oversized tunic and walked over to grab a yellow one and brown tights from my bag.

"I'm really worried about you, Veronica. We all are." She motioned towards the door with her head. I went to braid my hair back but got annoyed when my arms started to burn, and my fingers began to tangle strands into knots, so I abandoned all efforts to finish and threw it up into a bun.

"I'm fine," I reiterated numbly.

"You are always expressing your emotions. Besides attempting to kill Erikka, there has been an *understandable* lack of emotion from you. It's okay to—"

"I will grace the world with my emotions once I'm holding Calder's head in my hands," I stated coolly. I turned to catch her reaction. She only offered me a concerned pout.

"You can talk to me …" she pleaded quietly.

"Calder. Dies," I answered firmly.

She nodded tightly. "Well, … you two can have fun cleaning the port, but I'm going back to bed. I'll stay here with Brax." She passed me to flop into the spot I had been lying in and cuddled up next to my fluffy soul-dog, who only groaned as she adjusted him.

Cleaning the port with Sindre had begun as an overwhelming task, but as more people started to arrive in Lykke, more help was offered, and we were able to move the Ravens' longships further down the coastline. They had just moved Bryn's funeral boat to the end of the dock, tying it off and preparing it to lay his body down in a few hours. It was simple yet elegant—something he would have appreciated if he were here. *It's your fault!*

*Coward! He would've die—*

"Veronica!" Ragnhild called from beside the vessel and waved me over to him. I complied, and when I got there, an elderly gentleman was wiping the sweat from his brow while inspecting the carvings on the boat. "You know Arlan?" He motioned to the man who remained focused on his work, and I nodded. "Well, he needs to be told, again, that the boat looks perfect," he joked as he jabbed the man in his side, causing him to groan in discomfort.

"Oi! You know I'm an old fucker now. You can't be poking and prodding me like that anymore," he grumbled, rubbing his side.

"It truly is beautiful, Arlan. My Afi would be honored to sail to Valhalla in a vessel as pristine as this one," I declared sincerely. The woodwork along the exterior was, in fact, the most detailed I had ever seen. A dragon's body stretched along the length of the vessel, its wings out in flight, curved enough to make it look like Bryn's body would be nestled between them. The wings had various runes inscribed in them, and the body was detailed with scales all throughout. Arlan placed his hand over his heart and bowed deeply.

"It just needs its final touch." He stepped into the boat, grabbed a massive dragonhead, and heaved it onto his shoulder. He then placed it over the stern and completed the effect he was hoping for. The ship was a dragon, ready to take Bryn home. As tears welled up, I blinked them away the best I could.

"Thank you, Arlan. ... It's breathtaking."

"You are very welcome, Miss Veronica." He bowed his head once more. "I did the best I could to honor him. I owe him this, at the very least. You know, he fought alongside my wife in the war, and their group had gotten ambushed in the middle of the night. These Skirrian warriors invaded their camp quickly, causing chaos and killing at random to do as much damage as possible. They abducted my wife as they fled. ... Everyone knows war comes with casualties, but he refused to give up on her. Despite being ordered to relocate his camp immediately, he went after them without any delay. He killed all six warriors on his own, freeing her and killing a few more together on their way back to their camp. Once ALL his warriors were safe and accounted for, only then did he relocate them. Anyone else would have let them take her, ... would have prioritized their mission at the time, especially in the heat of war. But he didn't, and I will be eternally grateful for his actions." Arlan held out his hand, and I grasped his arm in a firm warrior's handshake. He patted my shoulder and nodded before he walked up the pier. I watched as he approached his wife, who was pulling out some overgrown weeds between the wooden pier near the shoreline. She was crying and would pat her eyes with the sleeve of her dress every so often. He placed a supportive hand on her back as he bent over to help her with her chores. I felt a hand on my shoulder, and I turned around.

"You will find that Brynjar has touched many people's lives tonight. If at any time it gets to be too much, feel free to step away. We will all understand," Ragnhild offered kindly as we stared at the boat together.

Sindre had walked up behind us, stopping to admire Arlan's masterpiece. "There are about two hours until the ceremony begins," he reminded. "We should get cleaned up and changed." I nodded and turned to Ragnhild, and without another word, we all walked back to the Inn.

As we were crossing the road, a horn sounded from a few houses down the street, and a lone mounted royal warrior trotted down the dirt path toward us with a message. There were already hundreds of people roaming the streets, beginning the mourning rituals for Bryn 's funeral, so the messenger had to maneuver his way through the crowds to reach us. Sindre stepped in front of me, keeping me hidden behind his immense frame. Although significantly shorter than Sindre, Ragnhild stepped in front of him and stood his ground, waiting for the announcement.

"Ragnhild Hall!" called the royal warrior. Ragnhild stepped forward, partly because he had been summoned and partly to keep him from coming any closer. "I presume you will be taking over as Lord of Lykke? As you are next in line?" Ragnhild nodded and straightened his posture. "Then you are responsible for ensuring this information is given to all Lykke citizens after I make the announcement." The warrior turned his horse and took in a breath as he prepared to speak, but Ragnhild cut him off.

"If I may, what is your announcement? The people here are in mourning, and if it is solely unimportant information and can be discussed individually, I would rather do that." The man looked down at him with a twisted expression of annoyance.

"They are mourning a traitor to the Kingdom. I will make the announcement as it has been ordered by King Calder himself," he retorted and turned away from us completely. My jaw tightened, and I felt anger encompass my limbs. Sindre's shoulders tensed, and he stepped back, lightly pushing up against me, his arms slightly extended backward, attempting to keep me hidden but also preparing to push me out of sight if this went poorly.

"Attention, residents of Lykke! This is a Royal Announcement from His Majesty King Calder! There has been another attack at the castle with Her Royal Highness Princess Erikka Kron as the attempted target." I held my breath, and I felt Sindre do the same. "The attacker has been described as male, with scarlet red hair, presumed to have been the same attacker as the one who made an attempt on the King's life earlier this month." Sindre relaxed, but my mind was spinning. *They didn't tell the King the truth; ... Erikka didn't ...* I didn't hear the rest of the announcement and was only pulled out of my thoughts when Sindre grabbed my arm and hurried me into the Inn.

When the door closed, I looked at him in confusion, and he stared back. "You said they saw you."

"Oh, they did. I made sure of it."

"Then why didn't they give you up?" He crossed his arms over his chest as if I should know.

I shook my head. "I don't know, ... but that gives us one less thing to worry about. I'm going to get ready," I remarked and left him standing in the hall.

I stood in Bryn 's room, staring blankly at my few available clothing options. A black or blue dress, leggings, and a brown tunic I didn't particularly like. I don't want to underdress, but I'm not wearing a dress that hinders my ability to move if I need to. *Gods, help me.* Someone knocked on the door. "Who is it?" I called out.

"I think I've got something you could wear," Jerrik called from the opposite side of the wooden door. I hurried over and flung it open to find him with a folded piece of blue fabric. I stepped to the side for him to enter and closed the door behind him. He turned and held it up for me—a blue dress. I turned my gaze up to him with my eyebrows raised.

"It's a dress. ..."

"Yes, it's technically a dress. BUT I have been working on crafting a dress more practical for our female warriors. Look," he laid the end of the dress up against his leg, "both sides have slits up to the middle of the thigh, connected by leather strings in a criss-crossing pattern. The strings pull the fabric together at the top of the legs but then loosen to fall and really make a strong statement. It also makes it easier to move your legs and, if necessary ..." He drew out the last word and raised his eyebrows several times in my direction. "You can always run a blade up these strings, which frees you completely while still keeping you covered." He smiled proudly. The dress was a stunning shade of light blue, similar to the one Jerrik loved seeing Bryn in. "And on top of all this, you look almost as good as Brynjar did in this color." *There it is.* "Try it on at least." I nodded and took the dress from him, and he turned around. After I slipped the dress on, I cleared my throat, and he turned back to me, twirling his finger, signaling *me* to turn around. I did as he asked, and he fastened the dress in the back. "Here." I looked back, and he was handing me an under-bust corset. When I took it, I recognized the stitched tear caused by my axe.

"You repaired it?" I asked, surprised.

"Do you doubt me?" He feigned offense, then shrugged it off. " I added two additional layers of leather on the inside. Any more than that would ruin the fit," he explained confidently.

"Thank you, Jerrik. I love this corset; it's my favorite gift from you." I smiled halfheartedly. He cleared his throat and held it out, offering to tie it for me. I turned around once more and let him fasten the corset around my waist. I looked down and ran my fingers along the repaired leather at my side, then the outline of the raven at the center. "Did you—"

"I ran another layer over the raven to enhance the design. There is no reason to be subtle about it anymore." He smiled proudly and hugged me from behind, wrapping his bear-like arms around my shoulders. "I'll be out there waiting for you." He patted the top of my head and headed towards the door. "Love you."

"Love you, too." I took a deep breath and started to braid the hair on either side of my head. *I can do this.*

*No, you can't. This is your fault. You are the reason for all this pain. All of their suffering. You could have stopped this.*

*I can do this.*

I braided two plaits until they met the tops of my ears and tied them off, letting the rest of my hair fall down my back, another breath in.

*Useless.*

I secured my weapons belt around my waist, my sister swords at my hips, and a knife at my lower back. I added a knife at my ankle and one at my thigh.

*Why have so many weapons if you won't use them to save those closest to you?*

I left the room, and when I opened the front door to the Inn, Jerrik was there waiting. The crowd for the funeral had grown and was a mere few feet away from the door. Tonight, the sky was painted a watery mixture of purples, pinks, and oranges. A few clouds streaked across its expanse as the moon waited in the sky for the sun to extinguish itself into the sea just beyond its view.

Jerrik cleared his throat, bringing my attention back to him. He extended his arm and I quickly took it. And that's when I felt it—the stares. The tears that weren't mine.

As we walked through the gathered crowd, my skin burned from the heat of the collective gazes. Each step felt heavier and heavier as I noticed the sound of stifled sobs. *You did this.* I looked up and was met with many red, teary, and swollen eyes. The energy became suffocating as we passed through the sea of emotion. Jerrik squeezed my hand and coaxed me forward. *Coward!*

Sindre, Sylve, Ragnhild, and the other two elders stood patiently at the edge of the pier, waiting to start the ceremony. Ragnhild stepped forward and hugged me tightly. "Stay strong, child," he urged softly. I nodded and moved over to greet Bergunn and Thora. I noticed they had tethered two smaller boats to Bryn's that had already been filled to the brim with parting gifts—keepsakes, memories. I looked back at the grieving landscape and saw the expanse of Bryn's impact, all the lives he touched. My breath caught in my throat, and my eyes stung. I can't do this. I turned back to Ragnhild and shook my head, clenching my jaw tight as ragged breaths pulled their way past my teeth, making my chest hitch rapidly as I attempted to stifle a sob. He put a supportive hand on my shoulder.

"There were more people in attendance than we had anticipated," he smiled softly. "I hope you don't mind, but we went ahead and let people say their goodbyes and place their offerings in the boats prior to this." I shook my head.

"I don't mind at all. It's best they had their time without me here anyway." Ragnhild cocked his head thoughtfully but didn't comment as I continued. "Who all is left?"

"Just our group, ... but I will make an announcement one more time just in case someone hasn't had a chance to place their offerings," he explained quietly.

"Okay, you all can go first. I can wait," I offered, stepping out of their way. *Delaying your goodbyes won't change the fact that he is dead because of you.* Ragnhild nodded and ushered the others to form a line in front of him. One by one, they stepped aside after their farewells, and within what felt like a few minutes, I was back to standing in front of Bryn. He was placed on his back on a bed of straw, a woolen blanket folded over him. All that was visible was his bruised face. Tears stung my eyes as they escaped and streaked down my face. I brushed them away quickly and pulled out my knife, leaning over the edge of the wooden carved boat to be closer to him. I laid the blade in my palm, feeling the cold steel break through the warmth that had made them sweat, and closed my fist around it, pulling it free from my grasp. I felt the warmth of my blood pool in my fist, the relieving bite of the cool blade swiftly dulling as I sheathed the knife and pulled away the blanket that kept his hands hidden. I brought my closed fist over his folded hands just below his chest and allowed my blood to drip onto them.

"In hopes of being reunited in the next life." My voice was wobbly, so I cleared my throat and quietly recited the Raven's oath. I put my bloodied fist over my heart. "By the Gods, I have so sworn. By my honor, I have so sworn." I stood and stepped back in line with the others, letting my still trembling hand fall to my side, blood steadily running down my fingers and onto the wood beneath my feet.

Ragnhild turned to the mourning crowd. "Before we bring the ceremony to a close, if you missed the opportunity to bid your final goodbyes and offer your parting gifts, feel free to spend the next few minutes doing so." Movement rippled through the mass of people as families met with Bryn to bestow their gifts. It seemed as if every other family was taking the time to stop and share their condolences and tell me stories of their experiences with him.

"My dear Freyja had gotten herself stuck in one of these elms a few years back, and Brynjar didn't hesitate to climb up that tree and coax her down," an older woman told me. "Freyja had to have sensed the good in him because she hates everybody, but she walked right down that limb and over to your Afi and curled herself around his neck as he climbed down. Every time he would walk by, she would greet him, and he would give her a loving pat. But if anyone else dared try that with my Freyja. Ooooo! You would've been guaranteed to lose a finger." It took most of my energy to smile at the story. "He was a special man." She patted my arm as she walked off, and the next person came forward to shake my hand. I took in a deep breath as the woman sobbed into her husband's chest. Sylve braced her hand on my back. *This is your fault! Look at what you caused!*

*All of their pain is on you!*

"Thank you," she cried, "for allowing all of us to be here with you." Her husband rubbed her back as she tried valiantly to speak clearly through her emotions. "Brynjar," she cleared her throat and reached out to hold my forearm, "he saved us." I looked up at her, and from the look in her eyes, I knew what she meant. I nodded. "I will forever be indebted to him and now to you." She looked up at her husband as tears streamed down her face. "I would never have had this life or met my husband." He kissed her forehead as his own tears trickled down his cheeks. "If he hadn't been brave enough after the war." She shook her head. "Thank you."

I nodded as they walked off. I looked down at the ground where I stood, in front of the overwhelming crowd, and closed my eyes to recenter myself.

*Am I really here right now? Is this really happening?*

*It could have been avoided had you stopped them from killing him.*
*But you let this happen!*
*Your body should be the one lying in that boat!*
*What use are you to these people?*
*What have you done for them?*
*Nothing!*

I opened my eyes with the intent of keeping my mind far from the scene before me. Maybe this way, I could maintain a strong facade and fool everyone into thinking that I am able to fill Bryn's role as a solid base for our people to build upon. Be someone they could rely on and look to when things are difficult, … to save them all from a fate they have no idea looms in the future. … I was lost in thought when the edge of a silken black dress flowed to a stop before me and broke all delusion of composure. My eyes snapped up in fury, assuming it was Erikka from the silk, only to realize it was a stranger.

A woman, a few inches shy of Sindre and Sylve's height, with scarlet red curls draped over her chest from under the hood of a muddy green cloak. Her eyes were a familiar bright green that looked even more luminous under the shadow of her hood, but I couldn't figure out where I had seen her before. She looked at me almost as if she was utterly uninterested in being here, but she was breathtaking. We both stood there momentarily contemplating each other until Sindre cleared his throat and nodded toward the line that had formed behind this woman. She didn't acknowledge anyone else besides me as she reached out to grab my hands, pressing a cold, ovular object into my palm as she held onto me. I looked down at our hands and noticed she had scars on top of hers. Raised and lighter in color than the surrounding skin, the runic shapes seemed almost as if they were branded into her skin. When she pulled her hands away, I noticed that the scars were also on her palms. My eyes shot up to hers in confusion, but she was already walking away without a word.

I looked down to find a golden amulet the size of my palm in my hands. As I studied it, I noticed it was shaped by two snakes, intertwining with each other to form an 'S' shape. As I flipped it around, a delicate golden chain unfolded and fell through my fingers. I gasped at the rarity of the relic I was holding. I can only imagine what it might be worth. I quickly scanned the crowd, but she had disappeared. Something deep in my gut was pulling me back towards Bryn. I slowly turned around and, as if in a trance, passed the line of people who had stopped to speak with the twins and Ragnhild in place of me. As I came to the side of the boat and knelt down, I could have sworn the emblem started vibrating, almost like a purring cat.

Although the woman had given me no instruction, I knew what I was intended to do with it. I pulled back the blanket from Bryn's hands once more and placed the golden amulet in them, wrapping the golden chain around his wrists and placing the blanket back over his chest. It hit me then, as Ragnhild ushered people from the pier so we could prepare to send him off, that this would be the last time I would ever see him. I looked at his face, forcing each softened feature to burn itself into my memory. Despite the bruises, he seemed at peace.

*I can only hope.*

*You did this! This should have been you! You are useless!*

"I love you, old man." Tears fell from my eyes and rolled lazily down my cheek as Sindre came over and helped me to my feet.

The Elders and my friends untethered the accompanying vessels loaded with gifts from the dock, and I steadied myself beside Bryn's boat. Once the elders launched the other two, Ragnhild and I took our places next to Bryn and launched him out towards the open sea. Sylve, Jerrik, and Bergunn stepped back and drew their bows, each notching an arrow in place. Thora walked over and wrapped an oil-soaked cloth on each arrow just below the arrowhead, then lit them on fire. Sylve looked over to me, tears streaming down her face, and I nodded, giving her the go-ahead. All three aimed their flaming arrows high into the darkening sky and let them fly. Tears of acceptance fell from my eyes as I closed them. When I opened them again, the arrows had struck home and lit all three ships ablaze as they sailed away from Lykke. I watched as Bryn sailed away from me and into the day's final moments filled with light.

I stood and continued watching numbly until night blanketed the horizon. I remained on the pier as the crowd dwindled to nothing, as they all started their journeys home, going back to their normal lives, back to their daily paces, without knowing or worrying about what is to become of Sol. What will happen to everyone's lives now that Bryn is gone and we don't have him directing us? I was upset that Ragnhild had refused to tell all of the townspeople about Calder's plans tonight. It would have been a perfect opportunity to get that information out to so many people at once, but no, everything I suggested was met with—*'we need to meet with the elders, we need to get the verdict on the Frithians' decisions, we need to remain peaceful with Calder'*—even though we have lost our "in" on Kingdom secrets. I'm sure they won't welcome me back with open arms. I don't have a room to stay in, and Erikka, ... it would be a risk to even try. Ragnhild doesn't trust I could withhold myself from making a daily attempt at the King's life, which is understandable.

I was still standing there, my legs and feet aching as the flames died out, and I could no longer see a few feet past the pier into the water. *You deserve the pain. Look at all the pain you caused today. You could've stopped him.* I felt a presence beside me, and when I turned to look, I found Sindre, his arms clasped behind his back, his eyes focused into the distance. I didn't greet him. I turned my gaze back into the shadowy abyss, and we stood there for a few moments longer.

"Even though you are not wanted for the attack on the Royal Family, Ragnhild wants to get to Frith as soon as we can." I nodded. "We already packed all of his belongings onto the travel cart. ... We will leave in the morning." I nodded again, and he turned to face me. "Let's go inside." He offered me his hand, but I turned away from him and led the way back to the Inn for the night.

*Goodbye, Bryn. I'm sorry.*

# Four

"Aren't we coming back?" I asked from across the room. The three elders looked at me with confusion.

"What do you mean?" Thora responded, placing the extra clothing, blankets, and supplies into a crate from the armoire near the front door.

"Why are you packing *all* of the extra supplies? Aren't we coming back at some point? Won't we need it?" I looked around at all of them. They looked between each other before Ragnhild put down the quilt he was folding and walked over to me, placing an arm around my shoulder and ushering me out the back door. Brax was already outside, trying to make friends with the horses as if he had forgotten about being caught in a fiery explosion only a day ago. I brushed his arm off my shoulder and stopped walking, turning to face him. "What are you not telling me?" I demanded.

"I thought you would have understood ..." he trailed off, but nothing was making sense to me. I waited him out. "We can't come back to the Inn, dear."

"*Can't?* Of course, we can. Why couldn't we? It's no different than before, Ragnhild," I protested, crossing my arms across my chest. His violet eyes softened as he took in a breath.

"Without Brynjar operating the Inn, without his daily presence, we won't be able to maintain what we have established here. The raids will have to be halted for a while until we iron out a plan to move forward."

I stared at him blankly. "So—so—you—we just abandon it? The Inn? The thrall in Skirra?" He shushed me and reached out in an attempt to placate me, but I brushed him off and backed away. "I'll stay here! *I'll* keep the Inn running!" I protested, tipping toward the edge of panic. The increasing volume of my outcry drew the attention of Sindre and Jerrik, who were in the barn.

"Veronica, you are not ready for such a task. This is bigger than just keeping the Inn running, and you know that. I'm going to need you to calm dow—"

"Calm down!? Ragnhild, you are packing up EVERYTHING in my home! Removing it all! I already went through Bryn's things! Wasn't that enough? Won't that be good enough?" I was furious. I yelled at him as if he was the cause of this, when in reality ... *You caused this! Why are you surprised?* I clenched my jaw shut as Sindre and Jerrik walked over. Ragnhild held his hand up to them, and they stopped walking just before they reached us.

"We can't travel frequently between our ... destinations." He looked around for any stragglers who may be working on the farmland nearby. "You cannot stay here, not after what the Crown did to Bryn. If they can so easily frame him as the problem to the Kingdom, they will do much worse with surviving kin," he explained calmly. "I am not going to be responsible for putting anyone's life at risk prematurely." He turned to go inside but paused, "We need to regroup and inform the others about the events this week. We will leave fifty percent of the supplies here and discuss possibly returning to the Inn once safety concerns are addressed. But that is not our priority. We leave in an hour." He went back inside and left me standing there. I let my arms fall to my sides. I hadn't even thought about leaving the Inn indefinitely. I knew we would have to flee for Frith, but leaving my home only just hit me. Jerrik walked up to me and put a hand on my shoulder.

"We'll come back. We just need to get out of the Kingdom's eye for a while. I'm sure they are keeping an eye out for you, even if Erikka lied." I moved away from him, heading inside to grab my travel pack. *See, even they think it's your fault. They have to stop all of the Ravens' raids because of you.*

*You are useless.*

*They don't trust you to run the Inn like Bryn.*

*It should've been you.*

*They could've kept saving people if you were the one who died.*

I slammed the door to Bryn's room and began throwing all the random items I had around the room in my bag. My chest was tight, and my head was pounding, causing me to lose focus on trying to calm myself. I looked over to the small side table and noticed the crumpled-up piece of parchment from the night before, and everything quieted.

I don't have time to be upset. This is bigger than me.

I walked over and picked up the paper, smoothing it out with my hands. I took a breath before folding it neatly this time and placing it in a smaller bag in my travel pack. I made the bed for the last time and pulled the curtains closed, stepping out and closing the door behind me. I held the back door open for the elders to haul out the last few crates, and the next thing I knew, we were leaving. I sat in the back of a cart with Brax, feet dangling off the end, as I watched the small town of Lykke disappear through the thickening trees of Willingman Wood.

# Five

We arrived in Frith an hour or two before nightfall. The guards at the city gates waved us through, and its wooden doors creaked as they closed behind us. We stopped outside the Elders' main house. My throat constricted with dread at Ylva 's inevitable devastation when she learns of Bryn's execution. *I can't do this.*

*You deserve to watch their pain. You let it happen.*

I shook my head, lifted myself off the back of the cart, and tried to calm Brax. He was excited to play with Frannigan, the orphanage's dog, who was running circles around us. Once he was down, they pranced off toward the barn together. I watched them while those who had been traveling dismounted from their horses, unarmed themselves, and grabbed their travel packs to take inside. Ragnhild eyed me and walked over.

"We will be holding a city-wide meeting tomorrow morning to announce the news to the Frithians. The other elders are waiting inside. We will be telling them now." I nodded and threw my bag over my shoulder, following closely behind him as he opened the front door. My breathing quickened while my rapidly beating heart echoed in my ears, blocking any other noise from getting past the barrier it created. Askel and Liv, who were in the kitchen preparing a meal, paused to greet us, placing down their utensils after seeing the looks on our faces.

The pounding of my blood through my veins was all I could hear, and it was deafening. I stared determinedly ahead, avoiding the person who had just descended the stairs while they paused, scanning the faces in the room.

*Don't look…*

*Look at her!*

*No! Don't look!*

*Look at her!*

I looked up slowly, and as soon as our eyes met, she knew. The house and everyone in it stilled. No one dared to speak. It was as if everyone held their breath in anticipation of her reaction, knowing just how badly it would break her. And then a soul-crushing wail erupted from her, sending her to her knees.

*You did this!*

*You've ruined everything!*

*Breathe.*

Ragnhild rushed over, as did Jerrik, to assist her down the stairs, but she no longer had the strength to hold herself up. Ragnhild held her as she wept and screamed out in anguish on the floor just before me. Askel had slammed a fist through a cabinet, and Liv let silent tears fall down her face.

*Look at what you did. This could have been avoided, but you let him die alone.*

*I should've died with him. I don't deserve to be here...*

*You should've died, too! Useless!*

It felt as if my chest would cave in on itself any second, and my head began to spin. The screaming sobs from Ylva were the only thing I could hear. I felt hands grab my shoulders and usher me through the house into a vacant room on the first floor. When the door closed, I fell to my hands and knees and drew in desperate breaths I didn't realize I had deprived myself of. Sindre was next to me in an instant.

"Veronica, are you alright?" he questioned, immediately crouching next to me in concern.

My hands were in my hair, tugging at the roots. I had no tears left, yet my thoughts still consumed me.

*I shouldn't be here.*

*I should've stopped Calder.*

*I'm useless to them.*

*I've only brought on more pain by standing idle.*

I curled down to the floor, pressing my forehead on the wooden surface. I couldn't breathe, couldn't see, couldn't move. My world was collapsing in on itself—on me. I could hear Sindre's anxious voice, muffled and coming from somewhere far off. I felt his hands close around mine, patiently prying my fingers from clenching and pulling my hair. Once he freed my hands, he pulled me into his chest. He hummed a slow and methodical folk tune he used to sing to me when our blanket forts weren't enough to chase the nightmares away, waiting for my body to relax enough to unravel in its own time, never forcing me out of where I needed to be in the moment. He wrapped his arms tightly around me and rocked with me. He said nothing, expected nothing. At some point, the warmth of his body broke through my icy shield of panic, and I melted into him, drawing slow, shuddering breaths but finally able to breathe.

We stayed on the floor like this for some time. I felt Sindre stir slightly, and I sat up, moving off him, staring blankly out the window at the dusky sky. He pulled his legs out from around me and knelt beside me. "I'm going to move Bryn 's belongings inside so they aren't left out all night. ... I will come right back." I failed to acknowledge him quickly enough, so he stood and placed a comforting pat on my head before leaving the room.

*I should've fought for him.*

*He fought for me so many times, an endless amount.*

*I put him in this situation, and he died.*

I stood and walked over to the window, pushing the shutters to the sides completely and pulling myself through. I walked quickly over to the rows of wheat just outside the main house, hoping nobody had seen me. I heard a playful bark and froze, quickly dropping to the ground to acknowledge Brax.

"Brax ..." I patted his head and pulled him in for a kiss. *Maybe for the last time.* "Ligdu!" He lay down and whimpered. "Stattu!" I heard him whimper again as I turned and walked through the wheat field, pulling my hood up as I walked out of the opposite end and into the city of Frith. I kept walking east, toward Mount

Eir. There is a rumor of a Nokken stalking the waters where The Seven Sisters Falls empties into. *You are of no use to anyone anyway.*

*This will make their lives easier.*

I walked until dusk turned to night, until my feet felt the soft cushion of the forest floor beneath them instead of the gravelly dirt roads the settlement offered. I walked without dodging the thorn-filled bushes that pulled at my tunic and pants, despite the sounds of creatures lurking beyond the shadows of the trees. I walked despite hearing a familiar, distant voice yelling at me to turn around and come home. I walked … until my legs screamed in pain and exhaustion, until I came upon the bank of Lake Lagom, where I dropped to my knees and stared up at the Seven Sisters Falls just on the other side of the body of water.

*THIS!*

*This is what you deserve!*

I pushed myself up from the ground, my knees wobbling from the quick demand of strength, and stumbled over to the water. I walked in until my shins were wet and paused. I took my weapons belt off and threw it onto the shoreline, along with the daggers at my ankle and thigh. *You deserve this.*

*You are useless in this fight without him anyway.*

*They will be glad not to have to be cautious around you.*

*They won't have to worry about setting you off.*

*They won't have to clean up the mess you make of every situation.*

I walked in further, up to my thighs, and paused again. I felt the water begin to weigh down my cloak. I waited … and waited … until I saw movement under the water near the center of the lake. A twig snapped behind me, and I turned to see if anyone had followed me. When I turned back to the water, I gasped.

Sindre was standing in the lake, waist-deep, a few feet in front of me. His God-like body had beads of water glistening over every inch of his rich, russet skin. In my confusion, I couldn't stop my eyes from looking past his muscular chest, down to his perfectly formed abdomen, and lingering where the water line stopped at the center of the deep V between his hips. He held out a hand to me, and I took it without question. My head felt foggy, heavy even. Something was pulling me to him. As I got closer, he began to back away, leading me further and further and deeper into the lake. The water had passed my stomach when its chill sent a shiver up my spine. I noticed Sindre's usual golden hair was dull, more of a muted brown than gold, and his eyes—they weren't the same beautiful brown but, instead, more of a mossy green.

A flicker of red light flashed above us, and I looked up the cliffside where the Seven Sisters began and noticed a man standing at the top. I moved over to the side to get a better look, but Sindre's fingers caught my chin, guiding my eyes back to his. He grabbed the back of my arm, pulling me closer, his full lips mere inches from mine. He continued walking us backward, the water now nearing my chin. I tried to kick my feet to stay afloat, but Sindre's grip tightened around my arms, holding me down, his fingers pinching into my skin. I tried to speak, but his fingers on my chin were now around my throat, and at the exact moment I moved my hand up to his, he shoved me down under the water.

I felt us moving deeper and deeper with each second that passed. The pinching in my arm turned into a ripping sensation, and the pressure on my neck continued to increase. I opened my eyes to try to see anything, but it was pitch black, the soft light of the moon barely floating down to reach us in between ripples of waves. I tried to kick him but only met a solid mass of a body where I had expected to find legs. I strained my eyes through the growing pressure behind them and was met with a pair of glowing, sickly yellow eyes with the same mossy green irises. *NO!*

*No! I don't want this!* I had let my thoughts get the best of me, and now I have most definitely fucked myself! I could feel my consciousness faltering the further down the Nokken swam. My lungs burned from the lack of air, from fighting all my impulses to try to breathe with every ounce of energy I had left.

*What did I do?*

*No one is going to find me here. ... No ...*

Just as I let go and opened my mouth to breathe, my vision began to fail, but I saw a flame burst through the water. A shrieking cry came from the Nokken as it released its grip on me, slicing my skin with its slimy talons before swimming away. Then there was nothing. I was floating—weightless. I watched a scarlet red flame draw nearer and nearer as my consciousness faded into the background.

# Six

Suddenly, I was forced through a heavy wall of water that shone as bright as starlight and found myself flying above an endless black sea. It was just out of reach, but it seemed as if I could lower my hand down and run my fingers through the dark waters. I looked in the direction I was flying towards and saw an enormous floating castle far in the distance. If it looked that large from here, I could only imagine how immense it was up close.

Within an instant, my body was brutally brought to a halt.

I looked around and saw nothing for miles beside the castle beyond. The wind was whipping at my face, causing my hair to fly around and block parts of my vision, but through the whipping strands of hair, I noticed a woman floating out in front of me.

*"I just found you! Come back to me!"* a familiar voice reverberated around me.

I couldn't tell if it came from the sky or the sea. I looked back at the woman and tilted my head, contemplating her. She mirrored me, doing the same. She was about my height, a bit paler, with significantly longer hair—blonde hair that fell straight past her waist, nearing the backs of her knees. She wore a black dress that wrapped around her chest and fell freely past her feet, dipping into the water beneath us. It was almost as if she wore the sea itself. I found sadness in her bright, golden eyes. Eyes that were shining, ... *illuminated* in the shadowy air. My hand flew to my chest as I felt a massive pounding sensation against it.

"*Come on!*" the voice commanded again, sending a rumbling through the sky and a massive upsurge of waves through the ocean. I looked back at the woman, and she was holding her hand out to me. I reached for it but was suddenly ripped back in the direction I had come from. The woman quickly faded out of view as I felt heavy water poured over me again, and all went dark.

# Seven

I lurched forward and spewed what seemed like endless amounts of water from my mouth and nose. I felt a hand on my back push me onto my side and heard that same voice from my vision behind me. "There we go," they exhaled in relief, and I heard them slump onto the ground next to me.

I was still catching my breath when I heard barking nearby. *Brax.* ... I had no energy to push myself up or even feel any apprehension about the person next to me. I tried to peer through my curtain of wet hair but could only make out the ends of scarlet red curls and a shirtless abdomen before they stood, bringing my attention to their bare feet.

"If you EVER try to off yourself again, ... I will bring you back from Hel just to kill you myself." Their voice was smooth and filled with irritated confidence. The barking got closer, accompanied by the pounding of hooves on dirt. My rescuer stepped forward and disappeared in a swirl of wind that picked up and resettled a few bright scarlet red leaves in their wake. My thoughts barely followed the stranger's sudden disappearance. *Did they just vanish into thin air?* Another wave of water lurched out of my stomach—*or my lungs*—and I fought to relax the tense muscles around my abdomen when a group of branches broke ahead of me.

Brax shot through the tree line and ran straight to me, continuing to bark to alert whoever had traveled with him that he had found his human. Next, a pair of horses burst through the trees and stopped at the bank of the lake as one of the riders jumped from their horse onto the wet ground and ran towards me.

"Gods damn it!" Sindre yelled to himself as he grabbed my shoulders from behind, carefully turning me around. When I looked up at him, panic seized me, and I screamed and hit him in the chest repeatedly.

"No! Get off me! NO! Not again! No!" I was sobbing now, pleading for the Nokken to let me live.

"Hey! Hey! It's me! Veronica!" He shouted, fighting my hands and finally grabbing my wrists to hold them still. "Veronica! It's me, Sindre!" I opened my eyes and assessed him quickly. His hair was golden, bright, and warm, in the same way his brown eyes were. He was fully clothed and armed to the teeth with weapons. My eyes found his, and heartbreak spread across his face as he canvassed me. "Syl! She's hurt!" he called over his shoulder. I looked at our hands and noticed the blood covering them.

Sylve came running from behind him and knelt down next to my shoulder the Nokken had clawed. I watched her in silent shock as her hands hovered over my bleeding arm and healed the wounds instantly. She eyed my throat, and Sindre loosened his grip enough for me to raise my hand and touch it. Warm blood graced my fingers, but the loose flaps of shredded skin made me realize that there was a potential I could be bleeding out. She moved her hands toward my neck, and I flinched away.

"I'll be careful. I won't hurt you," she promised softly. She re-positioned herself behind me and gently laid her hands on either side of my neck. I felt the warmth of her magic caress my skin as it healed me. Once she removed her hands, I flipped onto my hands and knees and began vomiting up the residual water I had consumed near the bottom of the lake. Sylve grabbed my hair and held it out of my face, rubbing my back reassuringly. She suddenly rose and began cursing as she marched towards the body of water not far off from where we were. I looked up quickly enough to see the Nokken in its true form—skin like slimy algae, hair like dying seaweed, its bile-colored eyes shining as it raised itself above the water. It only emerged enough to show its wicked smile of razor sharp, talon-like teeth. Sylve chucked a bit of iron, making direct contact with its head, causing it to hiss and submerge itself back into the depths of the lake. "GET OUT OF HERE, YOU FUCKING BASTARD!" She continued picking up rocks along the shoreline and throwing them into the water long after it had disappeared. Brax joined her, running up and down the bank, barking. The iron pieces will ward off the Nokken for now. The rock-throwing, however, seemed to be a way for her to loosen some frustration after seeing the creature's intent to kill me.

Sindre helped me sit up, and we watched her continue to curse until she suddenly stopped and eyed me. *Uh oh.* She marched over and dropped to her knees before me, grabbing the sides of my face with her hands. Tears were already streaming down her face.

"DID YOU COME HERE INTENTIONALLY?" she choked through a sob. I didn't say anything. ... I just watched her tears fall while she tried to read my thoughts. "Did you *intend* to kill yourself?" she asked in a whisper, dropping her face closer to mine. Tears welled in my eyes, and Sindre sat back in a state of shock, piecing the scene together only after Sylve voiced her concerned accusations.

"It's my— it's my fault. ... I let him die," I stuttered back. Her eyes widened at the same time mine did at the realization of the words. "I LET HIM DIE!" I cried out as my heart cracked open. All my emotions rushed past the floodgates at once, and I fell apart.

"I KILLED HIM! I STOOD BY AND DID NOTHING! NOTHING! I SHOULD'VE DIED FOR HIM! I SHOULD'VE TRIED TO STOP IT! BUT I'M A COWARD AND STOOD THERE AND LET HIM DIE! HE WAS OUR LEADER! MY AFI! MY LIGHT IN ALL OF THIS DARKNESS! HE STARTED THE RAVENS, KEPT THE RAVENS RUNNING, SAVED THOUSANDS OF PEOPLE, AND *I* LET HIM DIE. WHAT USE AM *I* TO ALL OF THIS? ... TO ALL OF THESE PEOPLE, IF I COULDN'T KEEP HIM HERE, COULDN'T KEEP HIM ALIVE? HE HADN'T KNOWN A LIFE WITH NO WORRY! I COULDN'T GIVE HIM THAT WHILE HE

WAS HERE AND NOW HE'S GONE! HOW DO I LOOK ALL OF THESE PEOPLE IN THE EYES AND *LIE* TO THEM? LIE TO THEM AND TELL THEM IT WILL ALL BE OKAY WHEN *I'M* NOT OKAY? HOW CAN I LOOK AT ANYONE ANYMORE AND NOT SEE THE HURT *I'VE* CAUSED? THE SUFFERING *I'M* CAUSING? I CAN'T DO THIS. I CAN'T DO THIS WITHOUT HIM! I DON'T KNOW WHAT TO DO NOW. WHAT DO I DO?! WHAT AM I SUPPOSED TO DO?! " I was distraught, yelling but not at either of the twins. I'd lost the control I was so desperately clinging to. I was screaming into my palms, then up into the sky—until I couldn't speak anymore. The heaving sobs took hold of my body, and I could only grasp at my chest, grasp at the pain that was not in any physical form, hoping that maybe, any second, it would form into something tangible so I could detach it from me and throw it away. Sylve pulled me to her and did not let go. I clung to her as if she was the only thing keeping me alive.

"You are *not* alone!" she cried and hugged me tighter. "We were there too, V. ... So was Ragnhild and Thora and Bergunn. ... We were all there with you. ... We were there too. ..." Her voice trailed off as we began to cry on each other's shoulders. I felt Sindre put his arms around us. I felt the weight of his tears as they fell into my hair. We stayed like this for several minutes, offering each other safety in our embrace.

A few hours passed, and I found myself lying on the ground with my head in Sindre's lap, still trying to stifle lingering sobs and regulate my breathing. Sylve had collected some firewood and lit a fire in front of us. She laid her head across my stomach and grabbed hold of my hand. We stayed there and mourned freely for hours. Sylve had fallen asleep, and Sindre was soothingly stroking my hair out of my face when he finally broke the silence.

"Were you here to— ... Did you mean to?" he asked quietly. I adjusted myself carefully so I could look at him and not wake Sylve. The anguish twisting his facial features brought tears to my eyes that I didn't know I had left in me. I couldn't answer him. I felt ashamed of the reality of my actions. My tears fell from the corners of my eyes, and he looked away from me, his lip quivering as he did. "V ... I—I ..." His shoulders sagged as he searched for his words. "Why didn't you talk to me? Why— ... I am right here. I have always been right here for you, V," he whispered with an air of defeat.

"I'm sorry," I whimpered under my breath. He just shook his head. "I couldn't. ... I thought I had to be strong. All I could hear was Bryn telling me to keep a handle on my emotions. Be calm. Make the right decisions. Don't let your impulses take over. ... I had a moment of weakness when I went after Erikka, and then Jerrik's shop happened. ... I knew I had to reign all of my emotions back in. I had to reign all of *myself* back in and keep her under control. I *had* to. I *have* to. ..."

"You *are* strong, Veronica, stronger than most of us, and it's *not* because you've suppressed your emotions or feelings. And you are not *weak* because you were at the end of your rope. ... I had a feeling something was going to happen when I left. I knew I shouldn't have left you. ... I - I found Brax and ..." A tear fell down his face. I reached up and made him look at me.

"It's not your fault. ... I—I ... I feel like I lost control of everything. He was the only family I had and all of a sudden he was gone. ... My job at Kron Castle is gone. ... Erikka's betrayal made the void from Bryn's absence feel twice as wide. ... My love for her was gone, and nothing but hate and heartbreak filled that space where my love for her should have been." He reached over for my hand and held it in his lap, running his thumb along the back of it. Tears burned my eyes as all of my thoughts came rushing out of me as a heartbroken confession. "It felt as if a hand gripped my heart, squeezed it, and never gave me a moment of relief. ... The pain was— ... *is* so intense, so strong. ... It taunts me at every turn. It grows with every step I try to take forward and only gets heavier as I look at everyone I have ever known and see the pain and grief they are feeling. ... All I could think of was that *I* caused their pain, just as I've caused yours ... and Sylve's." I looked down at Sylve as she slept, her hand in a death grip around mine, even while she was unconscious. "And then Jerrik's shop burned down, Elias was hurt, Brax almost died, and I thought I had lost more people close to me in such a short time. Even knowing everyone made it out ... I knew this had to be tied to me somehow—another warning for us, ... for the rebellion, and I felt so guilty. This isn't your fault. It's like you said; I guess I was at the end of my rope," I admitted quietly.

"Yet," he closed his eyes, "I knew ... I should have taken you away from everything sooner. I should have taken you somewhere safe so you could talk or scream or fight, ... but—" I squeezed his hand, and he opened his eyes.

"Don't. Don't blame yourself. I wasn't forced here by you or by Sylve or Jerrik or anyone else. I'm ashamed of what could've happened. ... But I also need you to understand that you *can't* blame yourself, please. I—I didn't know what else to do, ... what else *can* I do? All I know is that I blame myself for Bryn's death and the fact that everything I lived my life for just turned to ash in front of me. ... I'm still not sure what I can do with him gone. ... I don't know how—I feel like I don't know how to breathe anymore, and it hurts to try to figure it out on my own."

"We are here for you. All of us. We all need to take it one breath at a time, one step, one move. We are here to mourn with you, but we are also here to fight with you. ... Brynjar meant a lot to all of us, and we all feel like we failed him." He rested his head back on the tree he was leaning against. His thumb resumed its rhythmic movement along the back of my hand. "I need you to come home. No matter what, promise me—no, *swear* to me, you won't do something like this again." I turned my head away from him and watched our hands. I let go of his to wiggle my fingers around and grab his pinky with mine, bringing it to my mouth to lay a kiss on it.

"I swear."

He brought our intertwined fingers up to his lips and kissed them as well before setting our hands back down in his lap. "I love you, V."

"I love you too."

I'm not sure when sleep enveloped us, but we were all awoken by Brax barking and chasing after some smaller elk that had traveled to the lake for some water. Sindre got up quickly and chased after him, leaving Sylve and me to extinguish the fire and gather our belongings together. The sun was rising ahead of us, and radiant color beamed into the sky—almost as if the sun was giving the night a little push to rest for the day. The bright yellow and soft pink hues bounced off the mist the wind carried from the Seven Sisters Falls. It was so much more magnificent up close. I have only admired it from afar, one massive expanse of a waterfall split into seven separate falls over the cliffside. Sindre brought Brax back, and Sylve threw my weapons belt over Arvak's back before she mounted up. I headed over to her, but Sindre caught my arm.

"Ride with me," he suggested. He still had a deepened, sad look in his eyes but seemed calmer than last night. Seeing the hurt I've caused my friends linger and affect them through the night, past the quiet moments we spent talking through our thoughts and emotions the night before, even following them into a new day, opened a space for guilt to settle and secure itself to my shoulders. I nodded and walked over to Alsvid. Sindre bent and offered his clasped hands to launch me up over Alsvid's side before he mounted up behind me. I went to grab the reins, but Sindre snaked them out of my hands. "Just relax."

I didn't fight him on it. Despite getting a few hours of sleep, we were all on alert throughout the night. In addition, my entire body ached and groaned from my long walk, fighting off the Nokken and nearly drowning, so I could only imagine my ineffectiveness if I needed to steer Alsvid from any potential danger. Sylve clicked Arvak forward and ordered Brax to follow alongside her, which he did, and we trailed behind them. What seemed to have been a quick trek to Lake Lagom was actually an hour or two ride back to the outskirts of Frith.

Once we reached the center of the growing town, we came upon the Elders holding the town meeting they mentioned yesterday to inform the Frithians of Bryn 's passing. We kept to the edge of the gathering so as not to interrupt, but it was to no avail. I sat up straighter and noticed Ragnhild watching us intently. Sindre nodded, and Ragnhild mirrored him. He put his arm over his chest and bowed deeply. I was about to do the same, but one by one, the Frithians turned to us, placing their closed fists over their hearts, bowing deeply. This act of kindness resurfaced all of my emotions, which caught in my throat. I swung my leg over Alsvid's head and slid to the ground. I was in the middle of placing my hand over my chest to return the greeting when a woman ran towards me, pushing through the crowd. Kalyani slammed into me, wrapping her arms tightly around my neck.

"Thank the Allfather!" she cried. I wrapped my arms around her in response. "I am so sorry." She pulled away from me, tears running down her face. She placed her closed fist over her heart and bowed. "By the Gods, I have so sworn. By my honor, I have so sworn."

I gaped and looked up at Sylve, who just smiled. I turned back to Kalyani, who proudly wore a Raven-embroidered corset around her waist. My lips quivered, and I offered out my arm to her.

"I will fight with you. You have inspired not only me but my boys as well to fight for what we want, to forge our own fates. And for that, I am forever grateful for you," she announced proudly.

I blew out a ragged breath and looked her straight in the eyes, not only being honest with myself but with her as well. She deserves to know that the person she is pledging to fight alongside is a coward. "I'm scared," I admitted quietly with another exhale. She pulled me into her and wrapped her free arm around me, rubbing her hand up and down my back reassuringly in a way I could only assume a mother does.

"The fear doesn't outweigh the reward," she reminded gently. "I will be beside you, as will they." She motioned to the twins, and I took a deep breath. I nodded a *thank you* to her, afraid that if I spoke, I would burst into tears again.

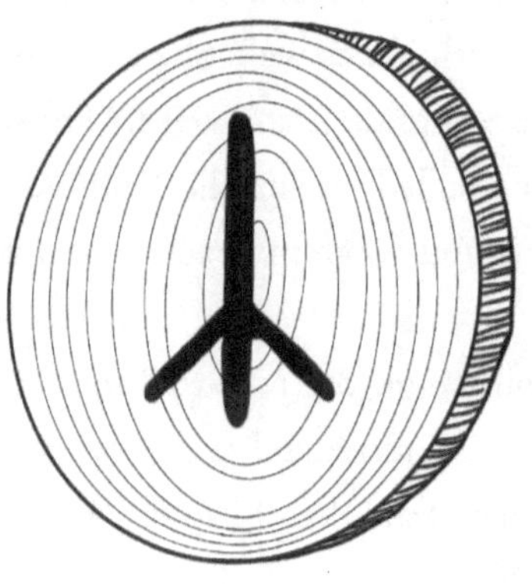

# Eight

I kept myself busy the next day by watching Kalyani's boys at the Elders' home while she helped Sylve and Elias take Bryn's donated supplies and clothing to Frith's orphanage. I was bringing them mugs of water when Raoul spoke.

"Mom told us about Brynjar going to Valhalla." This caught me by surprise, and I looked up at him as I placed their drinks in front of them. Hemming grabbed his quickly and took a gulp. "I'm really sorry he had to go. He was super nice to us!"

I cleared my throat. "Thank you. He *was* super nice, wasn't he?" I smiled, my eyes welling with tears. I blinked them back the best I could.

"He was funny too! At the last place we stayed, when he came to our room to say goodnight, he would be silly and push his nose up and stick his tongue out." He laughed and looked over to his brother, who was mimicking Bryn's silly face. Raoul laughed even more, and Hemming smiled proudly. I chuckled to myself, looking down at the plate of food I hadn't touched, and lost myself in thought for a moment.

I had nearly forgotten that Bryn said goodnight to me in the same way when I was their age. While I was living in the castle for the first few years after he brought me to Sol, he would always, every night without fail, sneak into the room Erikka and I shared and say goodnight. It didn't matter if we had been asleep for hours or were still awake when we shouldn't have been. Once he was released from his duties, I was his top priority. He would bribe Petra—I'm not sure with *what*—to let him past the heavily guarded door and wake me up to spend a few moments together while he told me another tale of fighting monsters and saving people who needed it most. Afterward, he would kiss me goodnight and tuck me back in before slipping quietly out of the room, but never without offering his silly face and stuck-out tongue. Tears welled up and pushed past the failing barrier as the fond memories played through my mind. I wiped them away quickly, smiling softly to reassure the boys.

Hemming had gotten up from his seat and walked over to me, climbing into my lap and resting his head on my shoulder. Raoul didn't speak, but with the emotion on his face from seeing his brother's gesture, I knew this was a big deal. Kalyani hasn't shared much about how the boys were treated in Skirra, but from what we know and what she has mentioned before, I don't blame him for being cautious with each new person he meets. If all he knows are two possibilities—get struck or be ripped from your family in an instant—I could never blame him for keeping quiet and hoping to remain unseen.

With a heavy heart, I wrapped my arms around him and rested my head on his. We remained this way until Raoul finished his meal, and everyone returned, walking through the front door.

I glanced over the top of Hemming's head, and my eyes met Kalyani's, who seemed to be pleasantly surprised to find her youngest son feeling safe with more people. I looked down and realized he had closed his eyes and dozed off, completely undisturbed by the increase in volume as everyone continued their conversations. I shrugged at her, and she smiled, picking up Raoul in one easy swoop as he ran over to greet her. Jerrik and Elias took a seat across from me while Ragnhild sat at the end of the table in his usual spot, and the twins went to wash up after a long day of preparing training regimes.

"Is it okay if I put this one to bed and clean up?" Kalyani asked, placing a hand on my shoulder.

"Of course! Take your time. He's not going anywhere," I offered, patting her hand reassuringly.

"Thank you! Say goodnight to Veronica," she ushered Raoul, who waved at me and laid his head on his mom's shoulder before ascending the stairs. I turned back toward the group at the table.

"So," I started, "have you sold your soul to come to Frith?" I raised my eyebrows at Elias, hoping to quickly keep the conversation about anything other than Bryn. "You are the only outsider that has ever been invited to this city." I didn't know the details yet as to how they convinced the Elders to allow him here. But I knew I could find out later, and I didn't have the energy to question it now.

"I mean, yeah. Pretty much." He smiled as he responded light-heartedly.

"Don't you have family or friends in Exris? Aren't they going to wonder where you have gone?"

"My family are huge followers of the Crown, while I am a bit more … skeptical. I won't miss them too much, especially knowing what I do now. What they have done to you …" He looked over to Jerrik. "What they tried to do to you, too. I might have said something that would have set them off to report me to the Royal Guard anyway."

"They are THAT loyal to the Crown?" I asked, more confused than surprised. I never understood the citizens of Sol who were more like fanatics, as opposed to those who demanded fair treatment from the Royal Family.

He shrugged. "It has been a touchy subject for a few years now." He laughed it off. "Other than that, I usually keep to myself, except when I join Jerrik 's hunting expeditions. Now the only person I care about is here, so …" He avoided Jerrik's sultry gaze and looked around the room. "I mean, I've come to care for all of you that I've met thus far. I just …"

"Oh, I know what you mean," Jerrik interrupted, eyeing Elias's mouth when he turned around again. I cleared my throat and shot a look toward Jerrik.

"Could I ask what the agreement's terms were? I have a curious mind, and I also want to be upfront about my need to know these things," I laughed, readjusting Hemming in my lap so he could be more comfortable.

"Oh, yeah. I have to stay here."

"Indefinitely?" I asked, meeting his gaze.

"Indefinitely," he confirmed, turning to Ragnhild for support. I followed suit and gave him a questioning look.

"He will be sworn in as a Frithian this week, meaning he can't return to Sol for any reason. At least not until we find a resolution for this Skirra mess; then, we might revisit the issue." He took a sip from his mug and eyed me. I eyed him back, still confused. I turned to look to Bryn for some clarification, only to find his chair empty.

*Fuck.*

"I would say it gets easier, but then I would be lying," Ragnhild said from the other end of the table. I nodded and laid my head against Hemming's, rocking him gently from side to side.

"So, Elias, what are you going to tell your family? Aren't they going to be worried when you don't ever show up again?" I asked quietly. He shrugged.

"We can cross that bridge when we get there. Maybe I can send them a letter about running off for adventure and finding love." A smile played at the corner of his mouth, and I swore I saw Jerrik's face redden, but he cleared his throat and grabbed both of their mugs to refill with wine. Elias winked at me, and I smiled.

"I also want to add that Elias has already been associated with us and was targeted in Jerrik's shop fire fiasco, whatever that whole deal was. Whoever was in the shop and spoke with Elias could very well have been the only witness to the attack. They could have gone back to their commanding officer, informing them of who should have died or, at least, wounded and seeking treatment. Keeping Elias out of Sol might give those people the satisfaction of impacting the potential rebellion that Calder wants to prevent," Ragnhild explained. "Whether that is *for* or *against*, I'm unsure." My head was spinning with this overload of information. I hadn't even put much thought into anything that had transpired since the Kingdom meeting.

"Wait a minute. If they are watching for Elias to surface, along with Jerrik and me, why are we *here*? In Frith?" My breathing quickened as my thoughts raced through a hundred different scenarios. "Won't that kickstart a search for us? They might start snooping around where they shouldn't! Especially if they question the Lykke residents. What if they torture them for information? We can't put them at risk like that!" I voiced, keeping my eyes on Ragnhild, trying to read past his contemplative expression.

"I hadn't considered that possibility. Even if it is extreme in nature, … there is a high probability that it could happen, I guess." He ran his hand down the back of his head. "We will hold a meeting with the Elders in the morning. We need to work through a plan as soon as possible, … but you, *young lady*, you need rest. You've had a hel of a past few days." He put his hand on my arm and nodded. "You will be in the meeting tomorrow?"

I looked up at him. "Me?"

"Yes. It would be mandatory, but if it is too much right now, we can always fill you in." I turned my head in confusion, not understanding why he would invite me to sit in on the Elder Council's meeting. He smiled sadly at me. "You are next of kin. You've inherited his chair in the Raven Council," he explained. My face fell. I looked over at Jerrik, who nodded supportively. My mind went blank. "But again, if it's too soon, you are not being forced to attend. However, that will forfeit your vote on how we proceed." I shook my head to get my brain to turn back on. He stood to walk away, but I reached out and grabbed his arm.

"Wait," I eyed Jerrik and Elias before looking at Ragnhild. "I need to speak with you. Privately." He nodded, and I readjusted Hemming in my arms as I stood, laying him over my shoulder so I could give my arm a break. I nodded down the hallway, signaling him to follow me when Jerrik stopped me.

"Do you want me to take him?" he offered.

"That's alright. I don't want to wake him up and give him a scare. If Kalyani comes looking for him, tell her I'll be down the hall," I explained.

I led Ragnhild to the room Sindre had shoved me into yesterday. When I opened the door, my bag was still strewn across the floor, and the window was left open. Ragnhild stepped around me to close it while I shut the door. I reached down to grab my bag, throwing it on the bed so I could rummage through it. Once I found the folded parchment, I handed it to him. He eyed me curiously.

"I found this in Bryn's room the night we returned to the Inn," I explained quietly as I grabbed a pillow from the bed and threw it toward the crack under the door.

He walked over to light the oil lamp so he could read the note, then looked up at me slowly. "Where exactly did you find this?"

"Crumpled up under his bed."

He clicked his tongue and crossed his arms over his chest, losing himself in his thoughts. "I will address this with the Elders tomorrow, but I will need the main house cleared out completely." I nodded, and he held up a finger, hushing me. There was a light knock on the door. I turned to open it, finding Kalyani standing there in fresh clothes and her dark, wet hair pulled off to the side.

"Thank you so much! I'm sorry I took so long," she apologized, holding her arms out for her son. I shifted Hemming gently, waking him just enough to transfer him to his mother.

"Don't apologize! We were bonding." I laughed with a playful wink.

"I'm excited to see how much his confidence and trust has grown. Thank you again. Goodnight. Goodnight, Ragnhild," she called through the door.

"Goodnight, dear," he responded as she walked back down the hallway toward the stairs. "Should I expect you in the morning?" he asked, turning his attention back to me. I hesitated, caught off guard by how quickly he was able to shift topics.

"Uh—I ..." Just then, I noticed Sindre turning down the hallway towards us, and an idea came to me. "Can I have Sindre and Sylve there?" I asked, shifting my attention back to Ragnhild. He narrowed his eyes.

"Why?"

"Well, they need to be informed about our decisions in the future as well. They bring more ideas to the table, and they think of other things I don't consider. We—... uh, work better when we can bounce ideas off each other's words," I suggested, poking Sindre in the ribs as he came to stand beside me. "Right?"

"Right," he added, rubbing where I had just assaulted him. Ragnhild looked between us and then locked eyes with me.

"We don't usually allow non-council members to sit in on meetings. The only reason you three were in on the last one was because there was an urgent motion to assemble, and Brynjar included you in his announcement," he explained. I could feel Sindre's stare burning into the side of my face.

"I understand, but they are the only two who have been informed ... about our *cause*." I shot my eyes down at his hand, which still held Bryn's note. He clenched it tighter and stepped out of my room, passing by us, and headed down the hall.

"The Nyhus siblings may be present during the meeting, but only if *you* attend. Like the last meeting with Brynjar, they get no votes toward anything we may discuss, but any knowledge and opinions they bring will be heard."

"Thank you." I nodded, and he returned the gesture before leaving us. I turned back to Sindre, whose eyes were filled with questions.

"What did I agree with?"

"Nothing important. I was trying to get you and Sylve into the Elders' meeting in the morning. I hope you don't mind." I motioned him inside the room and closed the door.

"Is everything alright?" he asked, holding onto my elbow when I tried to walk past him. I couldn't look at him and wasn't sure why.

"I'm okay, just a tad bit overwhelmed." I smiled and stepped away from him, moving out of his reach to make sure the window was locked. There was a scratch at the door, and Sindre walked over to open it, letting Brax into the room. He jumped onto the bed, walked over to the edge, and stared at me whining.

"Shh. I'm fine, buddy." I walked over and wrapped my arms around his furry neck, giving him a loving squeeze before letting go. He followed up with some reprimanding barks and howls but ended up curling himself into a ball on top of my pillows. I rolled my eyes at his dramatic display.

"Brax seems to always know when you're lying, ... especially when it comes to how you're truly feeling," Sindre added under his breath. I turned to look him up and down before rolling my eyes again, grabbing my bag, and putting it on top of the small dresser near the door.

"Will you be there?" I asked softly, turning to look at him but avoiding his eyes. There is a new tightness in my chest when I look at him. I *know* he is Sindre and not the Nokken, but its ability to take on his likeness was unsettling. He stepped closer to me, his eyes searching for mine, gauging my reaction.

"What's wrong? Talk to me." I swallowed hard and held my breath. *I can do this.* I had to push this reaction aside because I would die before I EVER told him the Nokken seduced me using HIS form. I would *never* escape the teasing, and frankly, I don't have the capacity to handle it right now. So, I looked up at him, right into his soft brown eyes, and let his calm and comforting presence wash over me. I looked him over and noted that everything about him was warm. His eyes, the way his skin glowed, and even his golden hair were warm-and inviting. The polar opposite of the Nokken's portrayal of him, which was so cold, empty, and unsettling. I will have to hold onto his warmth, and maybe that will be my escape from the Nokken's residual grasp.

"It's been a crazy few days. That's all," I answered, my half-hearted smile fading just as quickly as I attempted to put it on.  "Don't worry too much about me. I don't want to take away from your own feelings."

He nodded. "Let's make a deal then." He began to pace the small area in front of the bed. I raised an eyebrow at the theatrics. "I'll attend the council meeting tomorrow with you if ... you allow me to stay with you tonight."

I cocked my head in confusion. "What— Why do you want to stay *here*?" He didn't answer immediately. Instead, he turned his body slightly and looked back at the window before returning his eyes to mine. "Sindre, I'm not a child. I told you I'm okay now."

"No, you're not a child, but you are not *fine*. You are hurting deeply, and I ... " He looked up at the ceiling, placing his hands on his hips and letting out a long sigh. "Just for this one night, please. It would help me sleep." Feeling exposed, I hugged myself. He has always been able to read me like a book without a cover. I let my thoughts wander for an answer, and it became apparent that he knew me better than I knew myself. *Having company sounds nice.*

"Okay. You have a deal." I stuck my hand out, and he stared at it for an awkwardly long moment. Eventually, he grasped it and pulled me into him, wrapping his arms around me tightly.

"Thank you," he whispered into my hair. I returned his embrace and breathed in the mixed scents of the surrounding woods that clung to Sindre's clothing, letting the earthy musk ground me for the night.

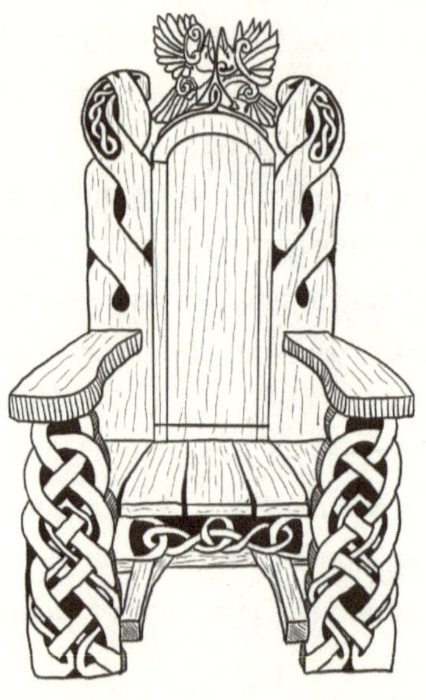

# Nine

Sylve and I followed behind Sindre as we entered the main area of the house. We just finished ensuring everyone taking refuge here had left so we could hold the meeting without fear of listening ears. We walked into the dining space, and the Elders were pulling curtains over the windows and locking the doors before gathering around the giant oak table. Everyone seemed revved up and ready to jump into action—everyone except for Ylva. Her hollowed face was long and drawn, and her eyes watched me as I moved to stand next to Bryn's chair at the head of the table. At the other end, Ragnhild motioned for all the Elders to take their seats, which they did, leaving me standing awkwardly next to the twins.

Ragnhild motioned to me and nodded toward the chair. I looked over, noticing the raven engraved into the back and the worn ends of the armrests that I'm sure lasted through countless heated conversations. My stomach turned. They expect me to take *his* seat and fill *his* role? As if I am even capable of living up to the type of person he had been or bringing as much knowledge and civility to the table as he could. My throat tightened the longer I stood there, and the more my thoughts crashed around inside my head. Sindre cleared his throat, stepped around me, picked up the chair, and walked with it to the other side of the room, placing it along the wall. He nodded at me as he returned, and Sylve put her hand in mine, giving me a reassuring squeeze before guiding me to stand at the head of the table.

Ragnhild nodded, and we mirrored him. "I call this meeting into motion," he stated plainly. "The Nyhus family is here to offer guidance, knowledge, and counsel but will not receive the opportunity to vote in any matter of discussion. Do you agree to this?" He motioned to the twins, and they both nodded. "Alright. Before we begin, we offer our deepest condolences, Veronica. Brynjar has left an immeasurable impact on all our lives *and* this city. And if you need anything, and we mean anything, we are all here to support you." I looked around at each of the Elders, who all nodded and placed their hands over their chests, offering a half bow. All of them except Ylva, who continued to sit quietly with silent tears streaming down her face.

"Thank you." My voice cracked as I spoke, so I cleared my throat and bowed in return.

"Before we update the three of you on the time we spent with the Frithians, I need to bring something extremely upsetting to the table." He reached into the pocket on the end of his tunic and pulled out the crumpled piece of parchment I gave him yesterday, passing it to Thora on his left, whose face fell after she read it. Ragnhild held up a finger to his lips, signaling for the message not to be read out loud. Thora then passed it to Liv, who passed it across the table to Bergunn, then Askel, and then finally Ylva, who clenched her jaw and crumpled the parchment into her fist.

"One of our own?" Askel snarled through gritted teeth. The energy in the room had shifted to become painfully tense and lethal. Whoever the traitor is has hell coming for them. Ragnhild raised his hand to gather everyone's attention.

"I don't think we should discuss it right now. Brynjar made it a point to find a way to get this …" he paused, contemplating his words, "*gift* … to us. We must be attentive to this issue and keep our eyes and ears open. We have no other information at this time." He held out his hand for the note, and Ylva slapped the ball of paper in his hand. "I will keep this particular *gift* in my possession, and if at any point you need to study it, just ask. But we need to keep track of it, so it stays with me." They all nodded as he put the parchment back into his pocket. "The original reason we were called today was because Veronica brought up a very possible scenario that could take place in Lykke and impact Frith's concealment."

"Well, it seems there already is that risk," Bergunn interrupted.

"This is the one we can talk about at the moment. That is why we will focus on what I will explain to you."

Bergunn raised his mug and eyebrows before taking a swig.

"Actually, Veronica, would you like to explain?" I was caught off-guard, and all my thoughts disappeared. Blood rushed to my face, and my throat tightened, completely hindering my ability to speak. Sindre stepped in front of me, blocking me from expectant eyes.

"Just breathe," he instructed softly, putting his hands on my shoulders. "You can do this. We are right here with you." I looked over at Sylve, who still held my hand and smiled supportively.

"If you can get us started, we will help move it along. Then it won't be nothin' but a thing," she assured, squeezing my hand.

I nodded, and Sindre stepped aside. I looked up at Ragnhild apologetically, but all he did was nod. I took a deep breath and cleared my throat.

"I am concerned for the citizens of Lykke. We can assume that Jerrik, Elias, and myself will be watched closely after this week's events and our disappearance ... might—uhm ..." My mind blanked as all thoughts disappeared from existence, leaving me unable to finish.

"The Crown could start questioning and harassing the people in Lykke if they are not around to be monitored," Sylve finished confidently, squeezing my hand. I nodded at her, thanking her silently.

"And with what they did to Bryn, we shouldn't expect anyone outside of the Ravens to keep our missions a secret if they are resorting to torture," Sindre added, keeping his expression calm but contemplative as if he was just realizing what his words meant.

"Have you not told them yet?" Thora questioned Ragnhild, a hint of a smile tugged at  her lips.

"No, I hadn't had the chance until now. I wanted to address their concerns first." He inclined his head toward Thora, and she picked her mug up and drank. He stood slowly, bracing himself on the table until he was completely upright. "We will come back to your concern in a moment. The Frithians have come to a rather unanimous decision regarding the conflict in Sol." My eyes widened in anticipation. It must have slipped my mind with everything else going on. Ragnhild beckoned to Askel, who stood and turned to face the three of us.

"The Frithians have decided to fight against the threat of Skirrian rule," he stated proudly, placing a closed fist over his chest. I might have stopped breathing then because my lungs began to burn. "It was leaning toward non-involvement at first, but ... when we announced the nature of Brynjar's passing, every single citizen jumped on board." I was overcome with emotion as I felt Sindre squeeze my shoulder, a gesture of silent support. My knees buckled, and I fell to the floor. Tears streamed down my cheeks. Stoically, Ylva rose from her place at the table and slowly lowered herself in front of me, laying her hands on my shoulders and giving them a tight squeeze. My eyes met hers, and the tattooed lines extending out from the corner of her eyes added a fierceness to the fire that I saw in them.

"He will not die in vain," was all she said, her eyes fixed tightly on mine, determined despite the tears that left them. I nodded, and she pulled me into her, but for the first time since I had known Ylva, the warmth was missing from her embrace. Bergunn cleared his throat to gain our attention, and she helped me to my feet before taking her seat.

"How does this tie into our concern with the citizens in Lykke?" Sylve questioned as I wiped my face. Liv turned to answer next.

"Most of our attention will be on preparing for the rebellion in Frith—helping train those who want to fight, using weapons and combat, and making travel preparations. There will be much to do: creating a system for new warriors to follow, establishing leading commanders, teaching them strategy, and keeping everyone informed on *what* needs to be done, *how*, and *when*. This will take a lot of time—and a lot of help." Her face was focused as she spoke, a hint of annoyance as she glanced at Thora, who had gotten up to refill her mug with wine for the third time since the meeting had started. "We will need all hands on deck to create an effective band of warriors that work well together in a very short amount of time. So, sending any of you back to Lykke will affect our ability to do that."

"Not only that, but we have lost all access to the castle. We are going to be planning and building blindly unless the Allfather sends a breeze of information our way," Bergunn added while casually re-braiding his beard.

"Frith is at risk as long as Jerrik, Elias, and I are not in Lykke." I wiped the remaining tears from my cheeks and readjusted my stance. "I'm sure there are already masked warriors monitoring the town, keeping their eyes and ears open for us. We have to go back."

"Why? So you can make another attempt at the Royal Family?" Thora sneered as she walked past me with her freshly refilled mug. She plopped into her seat, spilling some of the liquid onto the table, keeping her eyes on me. "Or, what else? Hmm, let me think. Oh, we can send her back to Lykke so she can stumble upon another Nokken?" I felt my anger peak past whatever chamber it was hidden in, boiling into a burning sensation in my chest. Askel slammed his hand down onto the table, earning an unamused eye roll from Thora.

"That's enough! You know we would all do the same in her position. Shit, I'm surprised she even bothered with the Princess and didn't go straight for the bastard himself!" His poor attempt to lift the focus off of me flopped when Liv cut in.

"She IS a risk! Despite how we may or may not have handled ourselves in her position, we *can't* trust her. Especially with having this incident happen within the past *two* days," Liv broke in, towering over Askel who remained seated.

"We will keep her in check," Sindre added confidently, puffing out his chest ever so slightly. The Elders looked at him like he had just declared his undying support for the Crown.

"You two won't be going back to Lykke. We need you here to help train the Frithians," Ragnhild explained, motioning for Liv to sit back in her chair.

"What?" Sylve questioned, looking over towards me.

"You two are the most gifted warriors in all of Sol. Why would we send you away? Sylve, look at how quickly Kalyani became *efficient* with the bow. You have a gift of teaching and training new warriors, helping them to understand the basic principles and put them into practice. And you, Sindre, the same with combat. We cannot spare either of you for guard duty in Lykke," Ragnhild said.

"And the new one, Elias? He cannot go back either. With Bryn's warning, he poses too big of a risk outside of Frith. We can't allow it," Bergunn added calmly toward Ragnhild, who was contemplating his suggestion.

"Jerrik is more than capable of keeping an eye on me if that is an honest concern." I sent a sideways glance toward Thora and Liv. "If anyone comes looking for Elias? He is dead—he succumbed to an infection from his injuries. At least until the *gift* has been found." I looked around the table, and they all sat quietly, then almost simultaneously turned to face Ragnhild, who stood slowly.

"Motion to vote," he announced clearly, and the other Elders stood. Ragnhild nodded at the twins, and they took a few steps back away from me. I looked back at Sindre, whose body seemed tense, and his jaw was clenched. "In support of sending Jerrik and Veronica back to Lykke for the time being." He remained standing and raised his hand. Askel followed suit, as did Bergunn. Thora and Liv kept their hands down and took their seats. I looked over to Ylva, who looked up at me slowly.

"I'm sorry. ... I don't think it's worth the risk," she spoke quietly before taking her seat. It was an even vote. Three to three. I looked back at the twins, and they were both pleading with their eyes. *Don't go back.* But I had to. I can't endanger the innocent people in Lykke. That's not what Bryn would have wanted to happen in the wake of his death. So, I raised my hand.

"The majority has voted in favor. It is settled. In regards to Bryn's departing *gift*," Ragnhild pulled out the crumbled piece of parchment and wiggled it between his fingers before returning it to a hidden pocket over his chest. "We will begin keeping records of each Raven and their scheduled posts to see if we can make any headway toward our culprit." He looked around at each Council Member, and they responded with a nod. "This meeting has come to a close." The Elders all stood, and Askel and Bergunn shook my hand and welcomed me to the Council despite the circumstances. Meanwhile, Thora and Liv both left the house to get started on sanctioning the warriors into groups. Ylva came over to me, her face drawn.

"I hope you understand my vote, dear. I— I— Sol is not a safe place to be right now and ..." I grabbed her hands with mine and squeezed them.

"I understand," I assured her softly.

"Please stay vigilant, dear." Her hand softly stroked the side of my face. "Come back home." I nodded, and she smiled half-heartedly before clearing the table and helping Bergunn clean the dishes. When I turned around, the twins were gone, but Ragnhild was there, holding out his arms for an embrace.

"You did well today." I nodded, unsure of the right words to say. "Sending you away from the safety of Frith is a difficult decision for us to make. We do not take this lightly, and we all hope you can fully comprehend the severity of this decision."

I cocked my head to the side. "If you don't think it's a good idea for me to go, then why did you vote yes?"

"There are many moving parts, and your presence in the Kingdom is needed. Keep your cool when you go back. Stay at the Inn. *Don't* leave Lykke. Train only at night and keep the doors and windows locked. Do you understand?" His face hardened, losing all traces of humor.

"Yes, sir."

He nodded and stepped around me, pausing briefly. "I will inform Jerrik of our decision. You will need to leave in a few hours and be back in Lykke before dusk." I nodded, and he disappeared.

As soon as he was gone, I felt Sindre and Sylve's presence re-entering the room, their stares burning into my back.

"Why?" Sylve asked quietly. I turned around to face them both as she seemed to sit in defeat at the table. "Why would you vote to go to Lykke without us?"

"I have to be at the Inn. What other option is there?" I threw my hands up in the air.

"We could have continued working through a solution," Sindre cut in, his jaw taut.

"Maybe we could have switched between the two of us each week or something along those lines," Sylve added.

"They made it clear. You both are needed HERE. They don't need me. They don't need Jer. The citizens in Lykke aren't safe unless we are there."

"Yeah, yeah, we know there is a potential that they MIGHT be in danger. The reality is, that's only a speculation, Veronica! And you are NOT safe in Lykke. Gods, Calder targeted YOUR family because of the sway the Leif name holds over the Kingdom. YOU are the only one left! YOU hold the last bit of influence over the people, and he knows that. YOU ARE WALKING INTO A GOD DAMN TRAP V!" Sindre was yelling by the time he had finished, and when he finally took a breath, he realized he had lost it for a moment. Sylve only looked at her brother sadly as he pulled his hands down his face and stormed out the back door. I remained standing there, overtaken by his outburst.

"Sylve, I— ... We have to make sacrifices."

She stood and walked over to me, stopping just out of reach. "Is this the right sacrifice to be making?"

A pause.

She shook her head at my lack of response and walked out of the room.

*Is this the right thing to do?* It has to be. I won't let innocent people be tortured because of my absence. ... I must go back.

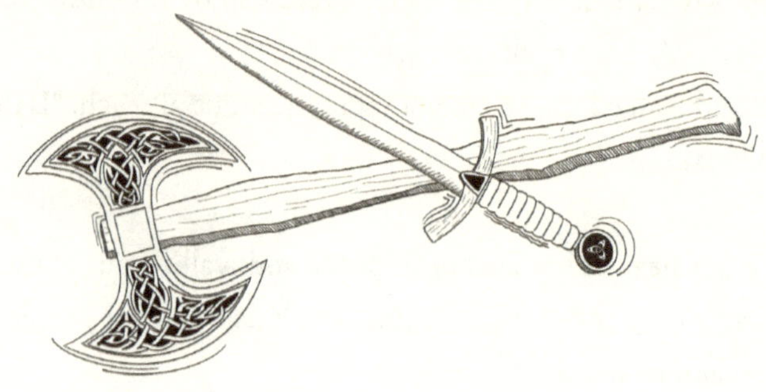

# Ten

When Jerrik got to the main house, he secured Arvak to the wagon we would take back to Lykke. The twins, Ragnhild, Askel, Ylva, and Liv, had come out to send us off and give instructions for the coming weeks.

"Keep an eye out for any guards lurking through the town. They won't be in uniform but will be watching and listening," Liv informed grimly as she threw a bag full of weapons into the back of the wagon. "Keep one in every room where you can quickly reach for it."

I nodded and looked over at Jerrik, who eyed the bag filled with different knives and axes as if they were completely foreign objects. He loves his bow, and I'm sure he would rather carry a spare arrow instead of using an axe in battle. He also prefers a good wrestling match over actually killing people, which might be another reason for his reservation with the plethora weapons we had been given.

"*Don't* leave Lykke, either," Askel commanded, his deep voice stern. "The further away you place yourself from us, the higher the risk of something happening and lessening our chances of being able to respond quickly enough." He walked over to embrace us. "We will send a small crew of Ravens in a few weeks to check in and give updated instructions." We nodded wordlessly again at our orders, the moment becoming more and more real as our departure neared. Ragnhild stepped slightly ahead of Askel and Liv, placing his fist over his chest.

"Stay strong. We will get a plan to you soon."

"By the Gods, I have so sworn," I recited mindlessly, mirroring his gesture.

"By my honor, I have so sworn," the three Elders responded, bowed slightly, and then returned to the house. Both Sindre and Sylve were extremely tense, but I offered an arm out for a warrior's embrace, not wanting to leave things on a bad note with them. Sylve rolled her eyes and pulled me in for her warmest of embraces despite the annoyance that coursed through her. Jerrik stepped around us and grabbed Sindre in one of his giant bear hugs.

"Please, Veronica," Sylve whispered, "follow their orders and *stay* at the Inn." She pulled away from me and jumped into Jerrik's arms, leaving me to Sindre, who looked so stiff he had to be uncomfortable. My throat constricted after feeling his irritation throughout the muscles in his arms as he wrapped them around me. He didn't say anything as he had already voiced his concerns this morning. When we released each other, he grabbed the side of my neck firmly, forcing me to look up at him.

"Come home," he tried for a commanding tone, but I caught a hint of helplessness in his voice, turning his words into a pleading farewell.

Since I'm useless with a bow, I'm left to lead the wagon. I took my place at the reins while Jerrik armed himself with his bow and sat next to me. The twins stood stoically as we rode toward the large wooden gate, the lingering tension leaving a heavy weight on my chest the entire journey back to Lykke.

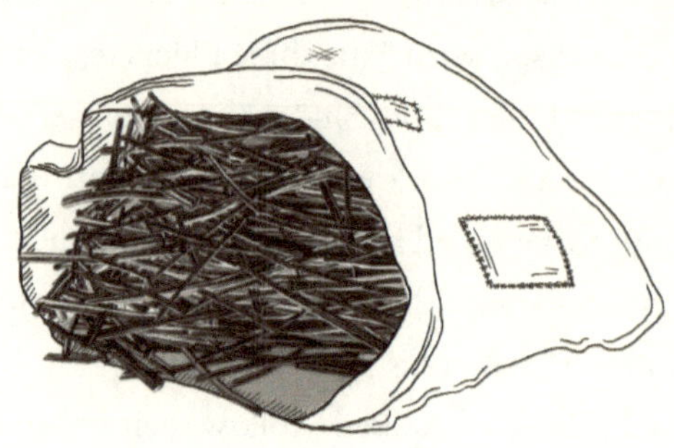

# Eleven

A week had dragged by—a week of aimlessly walking through the Inn during the day, checking and rechecking every hour that the weapons Liv had gifted us remained in place; a week spent sleeping on the small couch in the common area because I panicked the first night in Bryn's room. As soon as I stepped foot inside and laid eyes on his bed, my thoughts spiraled, drowning out any sense of reality. Jerrik found me after some time and had to help loosen the grip I had on my hair and led me outside to get some fresh air. Once we finished spending some time lying in the grass out front, we went back in, and I soon realized I couldn't go upstairs either. The loneliness the empty Inn had in place of its usual welcoming embrace was crushing.

Jerrik worked tirelessly every day to craft as many pieces of fighting armor as he could for the many people in Frith who would need protective gear. Meanwhile, I overloaded my days with mindless tasks, hoping to keep any thoughts about Bryn or the state of the Inn subdued until nighttime came so I could train in the barn.

I peeked past the shutters on the front windows, scanning the few citizens either going for a stroll or working around the pier across from the Inn. Anger began to shove its way to the top of the box I've locked my emotions in, and to smother it, I slammed the shutters shut.

"I think it's time you took a break, and actually let me teach you to use these weapons properly," I suggested to Jerrik, leaning over the back of the couch.

"Uhhhhh, I'll get to it later. I still have a lot of work to do." He waved his hand in the air and continued working.

"Jerrik ..."

"Veronica."

"Jerrik, you've been pushing me off all week!" I urged, annoyed at his constant procrastination. He paused what he was doing and looked at me.

"I will get to it soon. I've got to determine how to piece these together. The tool I need is somewhere in the rubble of my shop in Exris, so it's taking longer."

"I understand that, but you must learn how to wield a weapon other than your bow."

"I," he emphasized, putting his fingers to his chest, "don't have to do any-thing." He smiled sarcastically and returned to his work. I sighed in annoyance and made my way to the back door.

"Well, I'm going to start early. I'll be in the barn." He waved me off without a word, and I rolled my eyes. When I stepped outside, I grabbed a knife from its holster at my lower back and spun it into the air, catching and tossing it repeatedly as I walked over to the barn. The sun was just setting. I didn't linger on the lifeless colors painted across the horizon.

When I walked into the opening of the wooden building, I threw my knife at the practice dummy I had moved into the center of the walkway, sticking it directly in the middle of its makeshift forehead. I ripped the knife out and began to land a barrage of blows, masterfully dodging the wooden arms that spun around the body each time I hit them, just as I had been doing all week. The same routine, the same mind-numbing steps. *Just follow orders and wait.*

*Do nothing and wait.*

Sweat was dripping from my nose when I heard a footstep behind me. I whirled around and threw my knife near the person standing in a hooded cloak. It lodged into the wall next to their head, cutting a rope that triggered a mechanism I had set up in case something like this happened. The hooded person looked up as the hayloft fell open, and an open bag of grain rained down in front of them. I used this opportunity to pull myself up onto the front wall of the horse stalls and run along it towards the intruder grabbing onto a support beam and swinging off my perch, sending my feet through the dusty air and into their chest, which forced an audible grunt from them as they hit the ground.

I landed and rolled to my knee, pulling the sister swords from my waist, and lunged toward the stranger. They rolled out of the path and scrambled to their feet, ripping the hood from their head.

"Veronica! It's me!" Mazen shouted, putting an arm out to deter my attack. I turned my head to the side, scowling at him with disgust.

"Well ..." I twirled my swords in a circular motion and took a step toward him. "Now I'll know who I'm killing." His eyes widened, and he quickly scanned his surroundings, but I wasn't going to play with him. He dies now. I lunged at him, bringing one sword down and swiping the other near his waist as he dodged the first.

"Veronica! Hold on!" he begged, barely dodging my second attack. He kept looking around, and that's when I noticed he wasn't pulling his weapons out. I swung again, and he grabbed my wrist, pulling me toward him, locking his arm up with mine, and grabbing my incoming strike with his other hand. He held our arms above our heads in the small space between us. "I need to talk to you! Please, I'm here as an ally," he insisted through gritted teeth, continuing to fight against me.

"Fuck you!" I spat and swiped his leg out from under him with mine, sending him to the ground. I crossed the swords above my head and plunged them down, but he reached for a small board nearby and used it to thwart my attack again, causing my blades to lodge into it.

"What's going on out here?" Jerrik bellowed from behind us. I turned to find him standing just outside the barn with his bow, an arrow notched. Finding us in our current standstill, Jerrik drew his arrow, forcing Mazen to pull the board toward himself, throwing me off balance. He then pushed himself up, twisted to the side, and wrapped his legs around one of mine. As I fell to the ground beside him, I let go of my swords, allowing Mazen to abandon the board and wrap his arm around my neck, locking me in place as a shield between him and Jerrik.

"I'm friendly!" he grunted, holding his free hand up while using his other to pull me back onto him. Jerrik locked eyes with me. I felt Mazen tuck his head down directly behind mine, removing any clear shot Jerrik could've had. *He could have killed me earlier.* I didn't hear him coming until it would've been too late.

*He could kill me now, but he isn't.*

I shook my head at Jerrik, and he lowered his bow. Mazen released his hold on me, spilling me onto the floor beside him. He perched on his elbows and watched me push myself onto my hands and knees. Jerrik helped me up, ignoring Mazen, who remained on the floor. After I stood and began to work my swords out of the wooden board, Mazen stood and remained silent, watching. I only retrieved one sword when I turned to him, annoyed.

"What are you doing here, Mazen? Do you also have a death wish?" He turned his head before neutralizing his expression, nodding toward the house.

"No," Jerrik snapped from behind me. I pulled out the second sword, sheathed both, and walked over to grab my knife from the wall.

"What do you need to talk about?" I questioned, closing off his exit on the other end of the barn, trapping him between Jerrik and me. He put his hands up, turning to face me.

"Things that might get me killed if I speak freely outside," he admitted, waving at the space around him. I glanced at Jerrik, who nodded and turned to go inside so he could hide his supplies. I crossed my arms over my chest and watched Mazen, resisting the incessant urge to send my fist through his face.

We stood in silence until Jerrik returned a few minutes later and led us inside. As we passed through the kitchen and entered the main room, Jerrik turned sharply, almost causing Mazen to run into his chest.

"You have sixty seconds to offer a good reason to remain in this house, or you get the boot." He glared down at him, and Mazen took half a step back and cleared his throat, turning to me.

"I have information on the person who reported your Afi to the King." Shock washed over me, and silence fell between us.

"Well then, ... take a seat," Jerrik offered quietly, his demeanor flipping completely. Mazen followed Jerrik and sat across from him in one of the chairs. Jerrik waved me over to sit beside him, but I couldn't move. He stood and was next to me in an instant. "Are you okay?" I looked around the room and ended up finding Mazen 's saddened eyes.

"I know you probably won't believe me, ... but I am truly sorry about what happened," Mazen stated softly. I shook my head and walked over to sit on the couch, Jerrik following suit and placing a supportive hand on my back.

"I believe you. I just wasn't expecting this," I admitted under my breath. He nodded in acknowledgment and took in a breath of his own.

"A few days before I saw your grandfather being ... escorted to the throne room, I was at the library pretty late one night. As I left, I passed a person in a hooded cloak speaking to Ulrik at the front doors. I couldn't see the person's appearance because they wore a face covering, but I heard a very deep, rough voice, and they were about the same size and stature as Ulrik. Every time I saw this individual again, they were similarly attired, so unfortunately, I have nothing else to offer." My thoughts were spinning, trying to connect this information to make any sense of it.

"I'll get some drinks," Jerrik announced and pointed at Mazen, who raised his hand, declining the offer.

"I don't understand," I shook my head as I spoke. "What did this person say? What could warrant Calder ordering the guards to take Bryn in the first place?" I asked.

"I don't know. I couldn't hear the conversation. I only realized that the reason your Afi was brought there was because of this person. And, when Bryn showed up at a meeting I had to sit in, he was there as well."

"What?" My eyes shot up to his. Jerrik walked back in and handed me a mug as he took his seat. "You sat in on a meeting? What kind of meeting? With Bryn?!" Mazen paled and shifted uncomfortably in the chair. "What—what happened in this *meeting*? What did they ask him?!" My voice rose significantly as my questions remained unanswered.

Jerrik cleared his throat. "Veronica," he said, and I looked over at him. "Are you sure you want to go down this path?"

I tilted my head in confusion. "What do you mean? Of course, I want to know what happened to him. All of it! I *need* to know," I turned to Mazen. "Please."

The muscle in his jaw twitched and he nodded. "The King asked the same set of questions."

"Wait, *why* were you in this meeting?" I interrupted.

"Erikka's presence was requested the morning before the Kingdom *performance*." He dropped his head and leaned over on his elbows.

"Erikka ... knew?" I'm not sure why I was surprised. I already labeled her as much of a traitor to me as Calder, but maybe there was a part of me hoping it wasn't true. He nodded, and my throat tightened.

"Can I have something made clear?" Jerrik added. "Was this a meeting or an interrogation?" I didn't need to look up to know the answer to that question, and it seemed Mazen didn't need to answer it for Jerrik to understand either because I saw him tighten the grip on his mug out of the corner of my eye.

"Did they beat him?" I asked despite having seen the answer with my own eyes. I wanted confirmation.

"Yes."

"Who?"

"Calder. Ulrik. A few different guards held him."

"Did *you* ever hold him?" Jerrik asked sharply.

"No, but I watched and did nothing," he reiterated, clenching his fists over his knees. "I'm sorry for that." I looked up at the ceiling, trying to breathe past the tightness that consumed my neck and chest and threatened to twist my stomach.

"What were their questions?" I asked quickly. He cleared his throat and ran a hand up the back of his neck.

"Umm, ... are you planning on rebelling against the Crown? How many people have you gathered to fight with you? Who knows about the King's plans for the Kingdom? The questions were in reference to an impending revolution." My brows furrowed as I chewed on his words.

"What did Brynjar say?" Jerrik cut in.

"Nothing. ... He never answered. Not a single question." Mazen shook his head. I already know what happens when you don't answer Calder's questions when he wants you to. Not answering them at all ... for days? I shook the thought from my mind.

"You said, 'In reference to a revolution,' what else would they have questioned him for?"

"They weren't really questions. ... They would ask him things to try to aggravate him. An attempt to, I think, bait him into offering information he didn't want to."

"Like what?" I asked plainly, not expecting Mazen to readjust himself uncomfortably in his chair. I looked at Jerrik and then back to him. "What? Why did you do that? What did they ask him?" I urged further, glaring at him to answer me.

"He—King Calder asked him if— ... if you ever told him." A moment of silence passed, and I looked at Jerrik to find the same confused look I felt was plastered on my own face.

"What does that mean? If she told him what?" Jerrik asked, placing his empty mug on the table.

"I'm not sure it would be appreciated if I said it openly." Mazen looked at me cautiously, and I cocked my head.

"I'm not sure what you're referencing," I admitted, shaking my head. He pursed his lips into a tight line and closed his eyes.

"If you told Brynjar that King Calder would beat you in your meetings with him," he stated in defeat.

"No," I breathed out, my voice barely a whisper. The mug I held slipped from my grasp and fell to the floor, spilling red liquid at my feet. At the same moment, my stomach lurched into my throat, and I covered my mouth as I ran for the bathroom before retching into the bucket.

*Calder told him*—the one thing I vowed to take to my grave, to spare Bryn's heart from knowing of the pain he couldn't protect me from. But he died ... *knowing*. My thoughts slammed the memory of him hauled into the arena to the forefront of my mind. The apologetic look he gave me. ... It wasn't because he knew he was going to die. Somewhere past the ringing, I could hear Jerrik yelling at Mazen about something I couldn't decipher.

A knock at the door a few moments later brought me back to Midgard, and I realized I had curled myself into a ball on the bathroom floor. I pulled myself up the counter and dunked my hands into the bucket of water, rinsing out my mouth before splashing water over my face and neck to ground myself. When I finally opened the door, I was surprised to find Mazen, not Jerrik.

"He is out back getting some air," he explained quietly, reading my reaction. I nodded and walked past him to the kitchen, grabbing a clean mug, filling it to the brim with mead, and chugging it in one go. Mazen cleared his throat, forcing me to turn around. "Do you want to get some air? I can walk with you if you would like?" I nodded mindlessly, and he walked out the back door, announcing our departure to Jerrik, who stormed back into the house. Jerrik walked over to me as I finished downing my second mug and put his hand on my shoulder.

"Are you okay to go? Do you want me to go with you? Do you trust him?" he asked, looking over his shoulder at Mazen, who didn't flinch at the insinuation.

"Yeah, I'll be fine." I put down my mug, and Jerrik grabbed the back of my head, gently kissing my forehead.

"Be safe. Don't let anything happen to her," he sneered in Mazen's direction, who half bowed in response. We walked out the back door and around the Inn to the road. The moon was nothing but a sliver in the black sky with millions of stars around to keep her company. I went to walk down the road, but I quickly noticed Mazen wasn't following me. Instead, he was walking toward the pier. I stopped and waited for him to say something, but he never did. He just shoved his hands into his pockets and walked silently. I changed course and followed his lead. When we reached the end of the dock, he had already sat and dangled his legs over the water. I remained standing for a few moments, contemplating the small reflection of moonlight on the water and the sound of the calm waves washing up underneath the wooden structure we stood on. Mazen patted the open spot near my feet, and I complied, taking a seat beside him. I took a deep breath to try and calm the emotions surging against the backs of my eyelids.

"No," Mazen began, "let it out if you need to." I looked over at him, but he was already scooting back, facing the opposite direction, and moving to sit directly behind me, pressing his back into mine. He didn't say anything more as we sat there back-to-back. I hadn't realized tears were sliding down my cheeks until one slid down my neck and pooled between my breasts. I laid my head back against his and opened myself completely to the dark blanket of the night sky. I let it soak up all of my sorrow, all of my heartbreak. If only so I could fall into a weightless sleep and return to the life I had a few weeks ago.

*I don't want to be here.*

# Twelve

I awoke in the morning on the couch at the Inn. How I got there, I have no idea. When I rubbed the sleep from my eyes, I could barely make out a figure on the chair across from me. I had to wipe my eyes again to fully remove my drunken sleep and saw that Mazen had pushed two chairs together to sleep on last night. He had a blanket thrown over his shoulders, with one arm over the top of it and a dagger clenched in his fist.

I flung my blanket off just as Jerrik walked in from the kitchen. I nodded at him, igniting a pounding headache, and released a deep groan. He bumped the chair Mazen was sleeping in with his hip as he passed, startling him awake.

"Good morning, you two. If I may make a request, can we refrain from falling asleep outside of this house in the future? Carrying you both in was not the highlight of my night," Jerrik snickered as he sat next to me. I looked over to Mazen, who was putting his knife away.

"You didn't wake up, Mazen? I don't recall you drinking enough, or at all for that matter, to warrant such a deep sleep," I jested. He looked at us through sleepy eyes and disheveled hair, embarrassed. Seeing him like this was foreign to me, without his usual tidy orderliness. I liked it. He was subtly handsome in the bright morning light, wearing wrinkled and loose clothes. I felt my cheeks warm, so I looked away toward Jerrik, who also seemed to be enjoying the view.

"Travel days hit me hard, but never *that* hard. I'm sorry for the inconvenience," he offered Jerrik.

"Oh," Jerrik cleared his throat, "it really wasn't a problem. I was just giving you two some trouble," he laughed softly. I looked around the room and realized Jerrik's things must still be hidden, sending guilt washing over me. He has been crafting and working on armor every minute of sunlight since we've been here. So, Mazen 's presence definitely puts a kink in his schedule, and that's something Jerrik doesn't normally appreciate.

"Mazen, when are you heading back?" I asked plainly. Jerrik elbowed me in response. "Ow!" I rubbed my arm, shooting him a nasty glare.

"I should be leaving soon. I need to stop in Exris to visit my mother." He ran a hand through his hair. "And with how hard I slept last night, I need to get back tonight since I have a shift two days from now." I nodded as I stood and walked into the bathroom to freshen up.

I dunked my hands into the fresh bucket of water as I stared at myself in the mirror. My eyes were swollen, a reminder that last night was not a nightmare. I splashed water over the raw skin around them and held it there, relishing in the cool, calming sensation that radiated over me, settling my mind. I walked over to the kitchen to find something to eat, and Jerrik followed me.

"Hey, can we talk about last night?" he asked quietly.

"No," I answered while grabbing a piece of jerky and ripping a chunk off with my teeth." I also need you to keep that information to yourself and *never* speak of it. Do you understand?" I stepped up to him, toe to toe, leaning over the curve of his belly. "I don't care that we are friends; if anyone finds out from you, I *will* kill you." I pointed the jerky up at his face, and he mimed a locking motion over his pursed lips. "Good," I nodded and grabbed another piece of jerky before walking into the family room. I paused and looked around, reaching underneath the table to check if an axe was still hidden there. I froze when Mazen came out of the bathroom. *Gods, I'm losing my mind.* It's the same routine. The same mindless routine I've been forced to repeat since we've been here. I regret not bringing Brax with us. If I had, I at least could have spent my time training with him instead of walking around aimlessly to kill time until the sun went down. Jerrik walked in behind me a moment later, and an idea popped into my mind. "Hey, Jer," I announced innocently.

"Yes?" he responded cautiously, turning slowly to face me.

"We should go to Exris with Mazen; he would be a relatively safe travel buddy, and we can also look for the tool you need while we are there," I suggested, glancing over to Mazen, who thought nothing of my request. However, Jerrik was trying his best to maintain his innocent yet contemplative composure even though I could tell he wanted to throttle me. Did I corner him? Yes. Yes, I did, but I need to get the fuck out of this house, or I might go insane.

"Well, we really need to stay at the house, don't we? We still have more of Bryn's things to pack away," he offered sweetly through a clenched jaw.

"We have been packing his belongings all week. A quick trip to Exris won't hurt. We can get some drinks at the tavern and relax a bit. We have been working non-stop. *Especially* you!" I emphasized, walking over to give him a shoulder massage. "I'll pay for drinks too! Since the shop hasn't rebuilt yet." He turned to look at me and scowled. I smiled brightly in return.

"What happened to your shop?" Mazen questioned.

"You don't know?" Jerrik asked.

"No."

"His shop burnt down," I explained briefly.

"Yeah, it *burnt* down," Jerrik scoffed. I pinched the back of his arm to remind him to keep our conspiracies between us, but Mazen noticed and gave me a puzzled look.

I shrugged it off and cleared my throat. "Anyways! Jerrik, you need that one tool you mentioned the other day. So, we can get it. I need a change of scenery. Please," I begged him, clasping my hands together.

"Veronica."

"I wouldn't mind some travel companions," Mazen added quickly, looking around the room when we both turned to look at him. I grabbed Jerrik's arm and spun him around to face me.

"Please, Jer," I begged. His stare was blazing.

"Veronica, you *know* this isn't a good idea. It's actually a very dumb thing to do. We were told—" I squeezed his arm tight to stop him from finishing his sentence, then feigned innocence, pleading with my eyes like a child who wanted five more minutes to play outside.

"Just for the day. Just *one* day! We can keep everything brief. ..." I made one final attempt to seal the deal by plastering a pleading look on my face. His shoulders dropped in defeat.

"Fine. One day only! And you are paying for ALL of my drinks," he admitted, shaking my hand off his arm. "Pack now. We must leave soon to make it back tonight." He walked outside to ready the wagon and Arvak.

Meanwhile, I was having a private celebratory dance in the main room. Mazen's laughter reminded me that I wanted to thank him. I turned to face him, and his face fell in concern.

"I've been meaning to thank you." He instinctively began to brush off my words, but I held out my hand to stop him. "I'm serious. You had no reason to risk coming all the way here to speak to me. I'm not sure why you even made the trip, but I feel no malicious intent on your part, and I wanted to tell you that it means a lot."

"I ... We ..." He reached out and pulled me in for a hug, catching me so off guard that I froze, standing straight as a board as he wrapped his arms around me. "Something is going on at the castle, and I can't figure out what," he whispered.

"But it feels off–much more so than usual." He released me and stepped back before continuing, "you deserve to know, and I had a feeling you would be looking for this person anyway. Thought it might help." I cocked my head, but he shook his as Jerrik peeked his head into the room.

"Let's get going, you two! We've got to make this quick!" He eyed me specifically before heading out the back door. I looked back at Mazen, but he passed me to pick up his belongings on the floor.

"Oh no, you don't," I threatened under my breath. "I need you to explain what you meant." He looked up as he folded his change of clothes and shoved them into his travel bag.

"I can't."

"You will." I stepped in his path when he tried to walk around me.

"If I break my bond of silence, then you need to tell me something."

"Anything," I insisted, crossing my arms over my chest. He paused and looked up at me, contemplating.

"What do you know about *why* your grandfather was going to start a rebellion?" he asked cautiously. My heart sank, and I pursed my lips, disappointed that Mazen could still be looking for information for the Crown. Whether that is solely Erikka's or Calder's, I wasn't in a position to risk it.

"He wasn't. That's the tragedy of it all," I answered as I turned on my heel to head outside. It wasn't really a lie. I'd forced the idea on the old man. And now he was gone.

Mazen grabbed me by my wrist, stopping me. "I know this question seems a likely one from a Royal Guard, and you probably think I'm trying to get information from you so that I can run back to the King with it. But I swear on my life that is not who I am, nor are those my intentions," he declared quietly.

I did not look back at him as I spoke. "Tell me what your concerns are within the castle walls." A pause. I pulled my arm out from his grasp and walked into the kitchen, the sound of his boots on the wooden floor following close behind.

"The King has brought up Skirra only once, and it seemed he had not intended for Erikka and me to be in the room when he did. More masked warriors with unknown identities are showing up. I've braved asking around to see if anyone knows what the King has planned, but no one knows anything." I turned slowly to find his face drawn out in concern, tacking a pinch of guilt on top of the weight of disappointment I felt earlier. How could I put Mazen and Calder in the same category? I've known Mazen for five years, and never once has he been blindly complicit. Despite his usually quiet persona, he would always ask questions. Well, one at a time. With maybe a max of one occurrence a week.

"He plans to merge the two Kingdoms," I revealed under my breath. His eyes widened in disbelief. "Do with that what you will. But I will kill you, slowly, if it comes back to me." I grabbed my travel bag hanging on the wall and walked to the back door. "Don't make me regret trusting you."

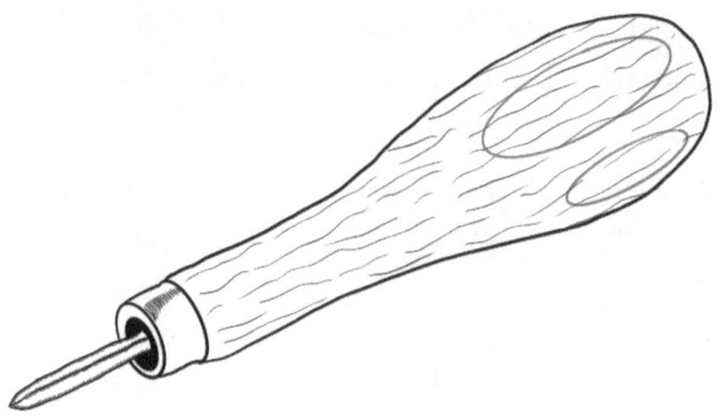

# Thirteen

We parted ways with Mazen once we entered Exris and continued towards the heart of the trades town. Jerrik ushered Arvak forward in a trot, catching me off balance in the wagon and sending my hands flying to catch myself on the edge.

"Hey!" I scolded.

"Don't *think* I don't know what you did," he mumbled in annoyance.

"Whatever do you mean, friend?" I asked innocently, only to be met with a furious glare.

"I'm honestly impressed. Using a card from *my* deck— flawlessly, might I add." He laughed to himself as he shook his head. With an exaggerated flourish of my hand, I swept my arm out to the side and offered a half bow to conclude my performance. "Little shit."

"I love you too, Jer." I smiled. I scooted over to sit behind him on the wagon floor and watched the dirt rise and settle in our wake until the hustle and bustle of townspeople surrounded us. I eventually moved next to him as he steered us down the street toward the remnants of his shop, eyeing the pile of charred wood. I placed a hand on Jerrik 's shoulder to brace him as he pulled us to a stop in front of what was once his livelihood.

He took in a long breath. "Alright, we are looking for a diamond tip awl blade with a birch handle," he stated confidently, turning around, only to find me thoroughly confused. His features sagged while he thought of an easier explanation of what we were hunting for. "A very small needle with a wooden handle, but the needle has a four-pointed tip instead of one larger one." I nodded and hopped out of the wagon. We both walked up to the pile of rubble that had awkwardly fallen on top of itself. "So, it will probably be completely black from the ash. ... Gods, help us," he observed, taking the first step into the mess, sending a small puff of soot into the air.

We spent about an hour lugging lumber beams and stone siding off the top of one pile and onto another to scour the bottom of the wreckage. Covered top to bottom with soot and dirt and coughing from our constant inhalation of both, we had nearly given up our search until I kicked a small pile of rubble on the floor in frustration.

"Ow!" I flinched and bent over to pull out a tool from my boot. I wiped the dirt off with my pant leg and inspected its tip, which I'm confident had left a lovely hole in my toe. I gasped with relief. "Jerrik! I found it!" I exclaimed loudly, making my way over the pile of debris as quickly as I could. However, I got my foot stuck and fell face-first on the ground, sending a massive cloud of ash into my face and initiating another coughing fit, but this did not deter me. I shook my foot free and continued toward the front of the shop, falling into Jerrik, who was waiting there, bracing himself.

"Odin bless you, child," he mumbled, rolling his eyes at the trail of the ash cloud I left in my wake. I handed the tool to him, and he sighed in relief, eliciting a similar reaction from me. "This is it. Thank the Gods." He turned to walk back to the wagon, but I cleared my throat, catching his attention.

"Would you mind giving me a hand?" I asked sheepishly, standing in the center of what once was his shop. He laughed to himself and came back, waiting for me to grab his arm before throwing me over his shoulders like a lamb. After he navigated through the obstacle course, he placed my feet down on the edge of the wagon. "Thank you."

He nodded and packed his precious tool into his travel bag. "Alright. I think we definitely deserve some drinks."

"Agreed!" I cheered.

"I heard they are twice as effective when someone else pays for them," he joked, elbowing me in the arm. "I'm excited to experience this tale!" He laughed as he jumped up onto the box seat. My mood dampened ever so slightly, but he deserved way more than a few drinks. I smiled to myself and let him relish in this small victory.

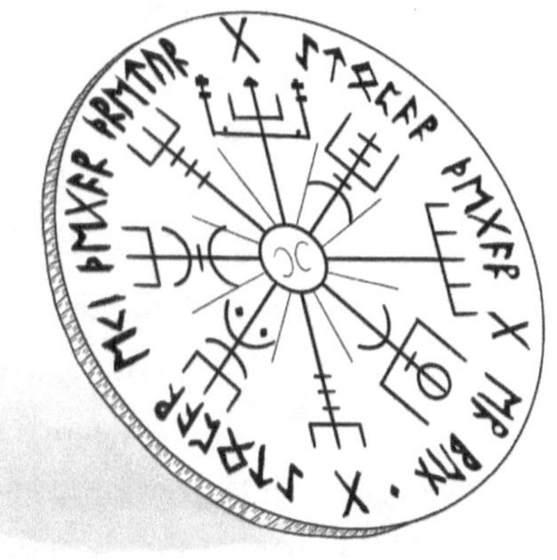

# Fourteen

Jerrik handed me the least dirty rag he could find from his pack and motioned for me to wipe my face. One swipe and only a small area of the cloth was left unsoiled. As we neared the entrance to The Dark Sun, he pushed me off to the side near a well opening, pulling up a pail and throwing water over his face and hands, motioning to me to follow suit. After drying my face, we walked into the tavern, stopping before Ragnar's table to remove our weapons and hang them on the wall next to him.

Reality hit me as a hushed silence fell over the tavern. Ragnar's usual irritated glare softened as he nodded solemnly at me. My chest constricted from the pressure of hundreds of eyes on me, all with varying emotions behind them. Some were as I expected—sad, full of pity, and even uncomfortable stares. Meanwhile others were filled with smug satisfaction, disgust, contempt, and indifference. I felt anger pump through my veins when a sweet voice called out across the tavern.

"What are all of you heathens staring at? Mind your own business!" Rune made her way over to greet us while waving her hands in the air and shooing her patrons to continue with whatever they had been doing. Her intense blue eyes shot daggers at those who scowled in our direction until they found us and softened. She opened her arms wide and gave Jerrik a tight hug. "I heard about your shop. Is that lad Elias okay?" she asked.

"He umm … actually, he passed from an infection from his wounds. …" Jerrik answered solemnly, letting his shoulders sag. *Great job Jer!*

"Oh, … I am so sorry." Rune offered, rubbing his arm supportively.

"Thank you," Jerrik nodded, placing a hand on his chest.

Rune looked at me with the same soft, apologetic look that held enough weight to bring tears to my eyes. She opened her arms, and I stepped into them. Despite my filthy ensemble, she hugged me tightly and whispered. "My heart breaks for you." I nodded silently into her white, coily hair before she pulled away and jutted her chin toward the bar as she walked in the opposite direction. "I'll be there in a minute."

Jerrik and I both sat at one end of the long wooden counter, and I felt the heat of the stares along my spine. I clenched my fists at the reality that not *everyone* knew Bryn, and even fewer understood his true character. Now, I guess people will always think of him as a traitor to the Kingdom and view me as one too. They have no idea, and it makes me want to scream.

Jerrik cleared his throat and grabbed my attention. "Don't let it get to you." He nudged my shoulder with his, and all I could do was shake my head. Rune reappeared with a sealed envelope, and slid it across the bar towards me. The same symbol my grandmother had carved into Bryn's wooden chest was drawn on its back.

"Brynjar gave this to me years ago." She smiled fondly at the memory. "He had given it to me when I took my first steps toward building this tavern. He helped me establish my groundwork here in Exris. … Always kind, always helpful," she paused momentarily, contemplating her next words. "And oddly, he was always very realistic." I snorted at the truth in her statement. She turned, grabbed a couple of mugs for us, and filled each with care. "I asked how I could repay him for all his help and support. I wanted to show I appreciated him and his time, but he just handed me this sealed envelope." She tapped it with her finger. It was clearly filled with coins, but it didn't seem like much. I looked back up at her, and she nodded towards it again, so I broke the seal and opened it, surprised to find a handful of the Royal Currency inside. Each coin was worth at least five times the regular currency in Sol. It is mainly used between the Royal Family and the appointed Jarls of the area for ease of larger payments, trading high amounts of goods, or paying out collected taxes. The King used to pay his Chieftain with the Royal Currency but stopped shortly after Brynjar retired. It was never explained as to why.

"He said at some point he would need to rent a room here and he had wanted me to hold on to this until then. I thought it was odd, but I obliged and have had it ever since." She raised her mug toward the folded parchment before taking a drink. "I want you to know this is here, and if you ever need a place to stay, I will keep a room for you. You are always welcome."

"Thank you, Rune. ... I don't know what to say." I cleared the emotion from my throat and placed a hand on hers. "Thank you." She smiled sadly before turning to look over at Jerrik.

"And whenever you are ready to rebuild, Jerrik, I will be right there with you," she boasted proudly.

"I sure hope so!" He laughed. "I don't know anyone else who can help me with all the heavy lifting." He lifted his mug toward her, and she laughed, holding up her toned ebony arms and taking turns kissing each of her biceps. A burly man with a missing forearm approached us and slammed his mug on the counter. I looked up at him cautiously but was met with sorrowful eyes and a half smile.

"He was a good man," he declared earnestly. The man hoisted his mug in the air and turned to face the rest of the tavern. "Tonight, we drink in honor of Brynjar!" Cheers erupted as most of the patrons held up their mugs in unison, and the man turned back to me. I raised my own and clinked it with his before taking a swig.

"Veronica," Jerrik leaned over and whispered in my ear. "Remember, we need to head back soon."

"Don't worry." I patted his forearm. "We will be out of here in no time," I assured, raising my glass towards him and drinking deeply.

This marked the beginning of a night spent celebrating the life of a man who made an immeasurable impact on people's lives. There were countless stories shared of times before the war and how he helped people before Sol was formed. He seemed to have always been a generous person who cared for other people. I can only aspire to love others the way he did.

A drinking contest ensued after the sharing of each story, gradually throwing most of the patrons into a drunken frenzy of emotions, including myself and Jerrik. Hours passed, and at some point, I found myself comforting a man twice the size of Jerrik in my arms as he shared his own interaction with Bryn—a short story about his wagon wheel falling off on his way to the castle and Bryn stopping to help him re-secure it.

"He helped put it back on. Just like that!" he sobbed.

"Just like that?" I whimpered out my question.

"Yes! Just like that!" he cried. He covered his face with his hands to conceal his tears as I rested my head on top of his, letting my own fall down my cheeks. We stayed like this for a few moments, letting our breathing even out and the murmur of the tavern calm us. I don't know how much time passed, but I felt someone shaking my shoulder, forcing my eyes open. I looked up at Rune, who was pushing the man I had last spoken with off my lap.

"Can you scoot out from under him?" she groaned under the weight of his torso. I nodded and tried to move away, only to have the side of my face introduced to the hard floor. "Odin, help me," I heard Rune remark from behind. I felt her firm hands grasp my arms and peel me off the floor, sending my head whirling around the room. "Looks like this might be a good time to cash in Brynjar's favor," she laughed to herself while I attempted to figure out what was happening and how long I had been out.

"Whe— where is Je— Jerrik?"

"I've already helped him up to a room."

"But— We need to go ... back to Lykke," I slurred slowly, unsure if my thoughts were being spoken aloud.

"You know, Jerrik said the same thing." She lugged one of my arms across her shoulders and braced her other arm around my waist. I'm not sure why she held on to me so tight. I swear, I'm able to walk just fine—minus the headache. "You two are more alike than you think. Despite butting heads all the time."

She smirked as I tripped over the first step of many. I pulled my arm back and insisted on climbing the stairs on my own. However, only a few steps up, and I felt hands pushing up against my back, keeping me straight. "Your room is over there." She pointed to the other side of the tavern, across the opening to the first floor below. My eyes followed the balcony around the perimeter and back to Rune. She laughed at the look on my face and held out her arms. I didn't fight her this time and fell into her, letting her support me as we made our way around the tavern.

We made our last turn around the corner, and I looked up to count the doors until I reached my assigned room, but my eyes snapped over to the woman passing by. I locked onto her bright green eyes as she neared. She had a curious expression, and the smirk on her lips awakened the butterflies in my stomach; a sense of familiarity overcame me. She wore black leggings and a silken green tunic that paled in comparison to her eyes. Her scarlet red hair was braided along one side of her head while the other flowed freely in wavy curls down her back. I stopped walking as she passed, catching Rune off guard. He chided me as I watched her walk away.

"Come on now! You can make friends tomorrow." Rune moved me along and opened the door to my room, helping me to the small hay bed. I fell face-first into the pillow and exhaled a breath of relief. "I'll see you in the morning," she stated as she headed out the door.

"Thank you, Rune!" I yelled after her—or at least I thought I did. My words must have been muffled from my pillow because I heard her laugh before closing the door behind her.

# Fifteen

I woke up the next day with a headache so cruel I wouldn't wish it upon my enemy. Well, ... maybe I would. *Oh yeah, I definitely would.* A groan slipped past my lips as I heaved myself off the bed and over to the window, pushing the wooden shutter open to peer outside, only to instantly regret it. I closed the shutters and turned to the bathroom, yearning to rinse cold water over my face. My stomach flipped at the cool shock against my skin, forcing me to grip the edge of the counter and clench my jaw shut. Gods, I hope Rune has something for this, or I'll be fucked for the rest of the day.

I decided to head downstairs to find Jerrik. I can already feel his annoyance, and I am not even sure he is awake. The thought of going back to the Inn made my throat tighten. When I opened the door, the faint smell of food wafted through the air, teasing my stomach somewhere in the realm between nausea and hunger. I peeked over the balcony and immediately spotted Jerrik at a table in the center of the room with his back to me. *Here we go.* I took a deep breath for confidence and made my way around. Only then did he see me and wave.

"Good morning," I moaned as I took my seat.

"Morning?" He laughed. "How about afternoon?"

"You're joking." I looked around, but the tavern was always darker inside than outside. With the few windows accessible to the main area, it's impossible to tell. "I'm sorry." I rubbed my hands down my face.

"Ah, no worries. I only woke up an hour ago and started working on my own headache," he admitted. "I think we needed a night like that anyway. It was getting stuffy at the Inn." I nodded, pushing my thoughts off the impending journey back. A small cup with steaming liquid was placed before me, and a hand brushed across my back. I turned to watch Rune gracefully maneuver herself through the tables, dropping off drinks and food every so often. When she looked back at me, I mouthed a dramatic *thank you*, and she winked before carrying on.

"She is amazing," I marveled as I wrapped myself around the small cup, letting the steam warm my face.

"Indeed, she is," he agreed, pausing before continuing, "but we need to head back today."

I looked up at him with a pout on my face. "Do we?" I questioned quietly. His face dropped in response. "I meant what I said before we left," I admitted before taking a sip and letting the warm herbal concoction settle my stomach and mind.

"I know you did, but this *situation* is hard for everyone. We all have to make our sacrifices."

"Can't I just stay a few days? I can start a few bar fights! That could be how I keep up with training," I offered enthusiastically, putting in a little more energy in an attempt to convince my friend to directly disobey our orders. *Selfish? Yes. Yes, it is.* But I know it's just wasted energy at this point because I know he isn't okay with the idea, nor can I *actually* stay here safely. *I wish it could be so easy.* He shook his head and stood.

"I am going to get Arvak from the barn and get the wagon set up. By the time I'm finished, your headache should be bearable, and then we *must* leave."

I slumped back onto the table and circled the cup's rim with my finger, nodding at his plan. A few minutes passed before the pounding in my head dulled to a more manageable level. As I raised my eyes to lazily scan the room, my gaze caught on the woman from the night before.

She sat relaxed in her seat, an arm slung over the back of the chair, her tunic opened to a deep V, baring nearly the entirety of her chest, with her cleavage peeking out from under the fabric. She had her legs spread apart, one bent in front of her and the other stretched to the side. Her stare was unrelenting as if beckoning me over to her, which she was doing successfully because my curiosity got the best of me once again. I stood, grabbed my cup, and walked over to her, setting it down on her table and taking a seat across from her. She had that same smirk from last night playing at the corner of her mouth.

"Do I know you?" I asked.

"Do you?" she echoed wryly. Her voice was rough but sensual in nature. I gaped but couldn't form words after her response caught me off guard.

"I— Uh, I don't think so." I frowned as I pinched the bridge of my nose, massaging it. "But you seem familiar."

"So, you *don't* remember me?"

"Remember you from where?"

"Just ... in general." She gestured her hand across the air. I noted a scar on her palm and when she laid her hand on the table, there was another on the back of her hand. Runes.

"I remember you now," I mumbled under my breath. I pointed at her scars, which she glanced at before tilting her head at me. "You were at the funeral, weren't you?"

"Was I?" she asked.

Annoyance pushed at the back of my throat. "Yes, you were. I remember seeing the scars on your hands. You had given me a relic of sorts."

She raised her head in thought. "Ah, yes. You're welcome, by the way." She nodded towards me.

"Uhmm—" I bit my bottom lip to hold my tongue. "I'm sorry, I don't know what I expected from this conversation. I'm going to leave now." I stood, grabbed my empty cup, and turned to go to the bar.

"Leaving so soon? We were just getting acquainted," she purred from across the table.

"I've suddenly become uninterested," I offered a tight-lipped smile and walked away. When I reached the bar, Rune grabbed my cup in stride, cleaned it, and placed it back under the counter.

"Is she everything you dreamed of last night?" she jabbed, turning around to get her next order ready.

"You dreamt of me last night?" a voice asked from the seat next to me. I jumped violently. Rune was also startled and turned slowly to face us, offering her best smile while I looked around, trying to figure out how she got over here so quickly. "I'm flattered, honestly." She held a scarred hand to her chest, drawing my attention to another scarred rune hiding underneath her tunic.

"No. I didn't. She was—"

"Would you like me to get you anything?" Rune cut in quickly.

The woman's attention shifted as she answered. "I'd like a room for a few nights," she said, her green eyes piercing as she focused on me once more.

"Of course! Let me see where I can put you." Rune smiled and shot me a look. "I'll be right back." I held my breath for a second, burning my gaze into the back of Rune's head, hoping I could influence her to come back with my thoughts.

"What is your name?" she asked. I turned to face her slowly.

"Veronica."

"Hmmm."

*That's it? A 'hmm'?* "What's your name?" I forced myself to ask in return, hoping to see a shred of humility, a fraction of a redeeming quality, anything.

"Loki," she answered confidently, her posture remaining aloof. My mind blanked on the coincidence. She had to be joking.

"Like ... the God?"

"Exactly," she smiled slyly. I used every ounce of the already minuscule amount of self-control I had to stop from rolling my eyes. *Odin, help me.*

"Fitting." I smiled.

"Thank you."

I looked around the tavern for any sign of Rune, but she hadn't returned. I tried my best to continue the conversation.

"So, Loki ..." She leaned against the bar, closing the distance between us. I leaned back instinctively. "Where are you from? What's brought you to town?"

"Nosy, are we?"

"Just ... trying to get acquainted," I retorted. She nodded and leaned back casually, placing her foot on top of the chair and resting her elbow on her knee.

"I'm a traveler now due to circumstances I may or may not have created for myself. I have no home, per se. And I'm here because I'm..." She paused thoughtfully. "I'm trying to find someone."

"Who?" I asked.

She held my gaze for a few moments before answering. "Someone I knew a long time ago," she paused. "In another lifetime, it seems." Her eyes studied me carefully, and I cocked my head to the side, intrigued.

"It was *that* long ago? You don't seem older than thirty," I said and laughed.

"Oh, I feel *infinitely* older than I look. Time must pass differently for me." She chuckled to herself, confusing me more. I shook my head and decided to keep moving past the non-answers until someone came to get me; whether it be Rune or Jerrik, I don't have a preference.

"So, is this person family? A partner? A friend?" I pushed, leaning in to convince her my interest level was higher than I made it sound. She responded with a breathtaking crooked smile that had me sitting straighter in my seat, my stomach fluttering.

"By the end of everything, ... all three? Something I had never had before, something I took for granted," she admitted sadly before switching on her playfulness. "That's why *you* interest me."

"Wha— Me?" I asked halfheartedly, still trying to shake the giddiness in my abdomen. She didn't answer. Instead, she held my gaze, and I felt a shiver dance down my spine; a faint memory teased the back of my brain—the familiar hair, egotistical posture, and deep V tunic. I was grasping at it, but the memory refused to form fully. Then Rune returned, sending whatever remnants of a memory I had away on the breeze she created as she passed by.

"How are we doing over here?" she asked kindly. "Drinks?" When we didn't answer, she clasped her hands together. "Drinks it is!" Loki reached into her pants pockets and placed a handful of gold coins on the counter as payment. Rune's jaw dropped at the pile before she swept it off the counter and into the small satchel at her side. "Lots of drinks, got it!"

"How do you have money like that if you are a traveler?" I blurted out, realizing just how rude it was after I voiced my curiosity. My cheeks burned, and I lowered my gaze. "Sorry." Her finger caressed my chin and gently tilted it, bringing my eyes up to meet hers.

"Don't be. Don't *ever* apologize to me," she demanded softly. My face twisted in confusion, and I pulled away from her touch.

"That is an unusual thing to tell someone *not* to do." I laughed awkwardly, taking a few chugs from the mug Rune had placed in front of us earlier. Despite my attempt to lighten the mood, Loki's face remained serious.

"I don't deserve it," she responded plainly. I was going to interject when Jerrik walked up.

"Alright. I've got everything put together. You ready to go?" he asked, not realizing I was speaking to someone. I looked between the two and stood.

"It's been ... interesting," I offered to Loki, who lazily looked at my friend, analyzing him. I waved to Rune as she hurried back to us behind the bar.

"Wait! Wait!" She glanced between Loki and me before locking eyes with Jerrik. "Can't you guys stay a few nights?" she pleaded.

"I can't. Unfortunately, all of my supplies are at the Inn, and I really need to get back to crafting." His stare was unyielding. He pursed his lips together, signaling that the discussion was over. "I've got to earn coin to rebuild somehow."

I shrugged at Rune. "We can visit in a few days," I teased, glancing over at Jerrik, who crossed his arms across his chest. "Maybe ..." I ventured. He lowered his head, dismissing any possibility of us returning. "Probably not ..." I added, the words tasting bitter on my tongue. A look of disappointment flashed across Rune's face. Loki stood and reached out to Jerrik in greeting, and I tensed for some reason.

"We haven't been introduced. My name is Loki." She smiled that breathtaking, crooked smile, causing my face to warm once more. She glanced over at me and then focused on Jerrik, who took her hand and shook it sternly.

"If you are going to try to convince me to stay, don't waste your breath. We have to leave."

"Oh, I bet I could," she countered. "You see, I have a special skill set that I was born with." She looked around and quieted her voice, "but that is beside the point. To my understanding, the things that require your presence in Lykke don't require *her* presence. Or am I wrong?" She turned to me, but I clenched my jaw shut. I refused to get in the middle of this.

"Her *safety* is my concern. I can't leave her here." He crossed his arms over his chest again.

"I'll keep an eye on her! She will be safe at the tavern!" Rune added excitedly.

"Hardly," Jerrik retorted. "You've got," he lowered his voice, "Royal Guards in and out of here all day and night. I know you understand the risk." He directed his gaze toward Rune. She lowered her head in thought. Loki held Jerrik's shoulder as if they had been good friends all their lives. Jerrik stared at her hand uncomfortably.

"Well, we can easily handle a few of these ... guards," Loki stated boisterously. She looked into Jerrik's eyes, and I could have sworn Jerrik's eyes glazed over, but it happened so fast that I shrugged it off.

"You know," Jerrik paused, trailing off in thought. "I think you're right. You guys can handle it for a few days. Right?" He turned to me when he asked, and I shook my head, confused, mouth gaping, at a loss for words.

"Of course!" Rune chimed in happily. "I'll make sure Veronica gets training in too! She can put some of these brutes back in place for me this week." I looked at Jerrik incredulously.

"Jer, are you sure you're alright with this?" I asked cautiously.

"Yes. I've got too much work to do to keep an eye on you anyway," he admitted blankly.

"You aren't my bodyguard. I can watch myself and have been doing just fine all last week," I added.

"Right! Right! Well, I must be going. I'll be back to get you in a few days," he announced before turning around and walking out of the tavern. Guilt washed over me, and I debated walking after him to make sure he was okay, as it felt like he had abruptly disconnected from the conversation, but Loki grabbed my arm.

"He will be fine," she assured, sitting back down at the bar and picking up her mug. I shook my head and went to walk after him, but she grabbed my arm again. "Sit down," she demanded. I tore my arm from her grasp and glared.

"Touch me again, and we will have a problem," I warned before running out of the tavern. The brightness of the afternoon sun was shocking for a few moments. I had to cup my hands over my eyes to help me focus on locating Jerrik. I called out his name a few times but never got a response. I ran over to the side of the tavern where the horses were kept and saw him pulling the wagon toward me. I waved at him, but he didn't acknowledge me. I stepped out into his path.

"Jerrik! Hold on!" I yelled at him, but he continued pushing forward as if he didn't hear or apparently even see me because I had to step out of the way or risk being run over by my own horse. *What the hell was that?* I watched him ride away, down the street, and out of sight before returning inside.

"Well, was he actually okay with it?" Rune inquired, pushing my mug toward me with a slender finger.

"I don't think so. He would've run me over with the wagon had I not stepped out of the way. He acted as if he didn't hear me yelling for him," I responded sourly, grabbing the mug and taking a few chugs.

"All is well. You've got what you wanted, and that was more time here, wasn't it?" Loki asked.

"Not exactly. All I wanted was more time away from the Inn," I turned to her and smiled sharply. "But I will take what I can get." She raised her mug toward me in response.

"To time away from the Inn then."

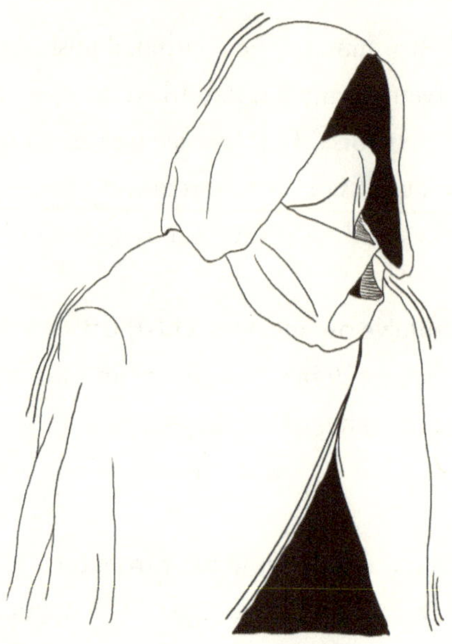

# Sixteen

Loki disappeared not too long after Jerrik had left for Lykke, mentioning she was retiring to her room for the night. I'm not sure why someone would go through all the trouble with a stranger and then leave, but to each their own. However, she was gracious enough to tell Rune she would cover the expense of whatever I drank for the night, so I was not about to waste the opportunity the Gods had blessed me with.

I only had about five drinks when anger started rising in my chest. I was stuck chewing on the way Jerrik had left earlier. *Why did he act that way? I was ready to leave with him. It's not like I was begging and throwing a fit to stay.*

"Veronica!" Rune called from a group of people near the center of the tavern. Two men seemed to be arguing about something, with Rune standing in between, trying to get them to snap out of it. "I don't feel like doing this at the moment! Do you mind?" she asked before stomping on one of the men's toes, following it up with a sucker punch to the gut. The man groaned in pain and found his seat with his comrades. However, the other man kept at it. She nodded at him and walked towards me at the bar. "He needs to be put out," she stated with a smile and a wink.

"You think I will go out *that* easy? Who do you think *you* are?" he taunted, throwing his arms out to his sides.

He wasn't much taller than me, but he had a solid build. His arms, legs, and abdomen were all round, but you could tell the man could pack a punch. I downed the rest of my drink and then turned to Rune.

"I'll see what I can do." I dipped my chin in acknowledgment before turning to face my opponent.

"Magnus! I told you the next time is the last time! You fucked around, so it's time to go," she ordered firmly. I looked back at her to find that she had jumped onto the bar and sat lazily with a drink in her hand, raising it towards him. "I will thoroughly enjoy watching someone hand it to you," she added with a smile. The man growled confidently at his new challenge.

"We'll see," he laughed, stalking toward me slowly. "You think *you're* going to kick *me* out of here?" He eyed me up and down, bringing his fists up in preparation for the fight to begin.

"No." A burp escaped me, and I brought a hand to my mouth. "Oooh! Excuse me! But no, … you are going to *want* to run out of here," I challenged grinning.

Magnus laughed at me, then moved to grab one of my outstretched hands, which I swiftly swatted away before following up with a proper slap across his face. I kept my expression neutral the best I could because I knew the shock on his would make me laugh. Instead, I shrugged in response to his look of bewilderment. He positioned his fists between us, and instead of waiting for him to move this time, I latched onto one of them. Stepping quickly towards him, I ducked under his arm and twisted it tightly behind his back. He groaned at the pressure in his shoulder, and just before he sent his free arm back at me, I kicked him, sending him stumbling to the floor. When he turned around to face me, his face was red with embarrassment.

"What the hell are you doing?!" he yelled. "Fight me!"

"I would love to, but that would require your participation," I countered.

He scrambled back to his feet. "Rune! THIS is how you do things now?" he questioned, annoyed. "You hire some pathetic help who can't even fight?"

"I think she's doing a great job." Rune smiled at me and raised her mug again.

"Hey!" I called out. "Eyes on me." I closed the distance between us and sent a fist toward his face, which he blocked, but I followed with a punch to the stomach. He groaned in pain and decided to try his best to send a barrage of blows in my direction. I weaved around each of his attacks, bored with the simplicity of his tactics. I decided to spice things up a bit, and when he charged at me, I flipped backward, kicking him in the jaw as I did. He stumbled, dazed, but so did I from the headrush.

Once the room stopped spinning, I charged him, using his shoulders to vault into the air and wrapping my legs around his neck before flinging my body towards the ground. I caught myself on my elbows and contracted my abdomen to pull him to the ground, his head making first contact. That move resulted in an empathetic groan from the audience. Meanwhile, my stomach was having trouble catching up with my movements, so I cupped my mouth, unsure if I could trust myself.

I stood over Magnus, who seemed unable to move, before walking back to Rune. She handed me a fresh mug of mead as Magnus groaned on the floor. He attempted to pick himself up but ultimately decided to lie where he was. I raised my mug toward him and turned around to take my seat.

"Ragnar," Rune called out into the tavern. He appeared from the crowd and nodded his acknowledgment before picking up the man and heaving him out of the tavern. She turned to walk around the bar, patting my back. "That was fun. Don't you think?" she asked cheerfully.

"Maybe next time we can pick someone who can fight. That would be *more* fun," I laughed. "If I can dodge every punch DRUNK they shouldn't be allowed into the tavern in the first place."

"Well, you've got time to irritate the right person here." She winked at me before walking off, leaving me to the thoughts I wanted to avoid. So that's what I did.

I soon noticed a presence beside me at the bar, and when I turned my head to look at whoever sat way too close to me, I saw a man in a black cloak with his hood pulled over his head. I leaned forward to get a good look at his face.

"Tormod?" I questioned aloud. "What are *you* doing here?" I felt my face contort in confusion.

"I'm just checking on you, … making sure you are doing what you are supposed to be doing," he answered flatly. His grating voice frayed any remaining nerves that survived the fight.

I waved my hand at him. "Yeah, yeah, I just needed a break from the Inn. I'll be back in Lykke soon." I grabbed my mug violently and took a swig.

He nodded at me. "So, you *do* recall what your orders were?" His usual annoying grin was plastered on his face.

"Yes. Yes, stay in Lykke, *don't leave.* I got it," I answered under my breath.

"Hey! Don't be mad at me. I'm just here to make sure nobody has to get hurt. … No one else has to get hurt, right?" he asked, leaning into me.

I shoved my elbow into him to move him out of my personal space, his question lingering on my mind. *What type of an asshole question is that?* "Get off my case! I'm just waiting for Jerrik to come take me back home."

As he threw his hands up in surrender, his cloak slid down his forearms, revealing inflamed, irritated skin that seemed raw and possibly shaped like the bottom half of a sun. Before I could get a better look, he lowered his hands, quickly covering it. "Alright, … I'm glad I can report back that all is going well. Messages seemed to have been received."

"Why don't you tell Ragnhild to send someone I *like* the next time he wants to check in. Someone who I'd want to drink with. Sylve or Sindre is preferred," I barked at him as he turned his back to me. There was an uncomfortably long pause, and I was about to ask him what was wrong when he resumed walking and left the tavern. *That was weird.*

# Seventeen

The next few days seemed to morph together. Loki had yet to show herself at the tavern since the day Jerrik left. I drank enough for my thoughts to quiet but would be met with them as soon as I opened my eyes in the morning. My solution to this was to take hits while I was helping Rune break up bar fights; that way, I would wake up to my body aching instead. It worked beautifully, and days passed without a thought about the world outside of The Dark Sun Tavern … until this morning.

My body felt as if it had melted into the bed. Each limb I tried to move felt heavier than the next. My arms were splayed above my head, and they caught when I tried to pull them down to my sides. ... My stomach dropped, and my eyes snapped open, realizing that my wrists had been tied together around the wooden headboard. *What the fuck?* I don't remember taking anyone to bed with me last night.

"I didn't realize you were such a heavy sleeper," a scratchy voice sounded from a darkened corner of the room, causing my body to go rigid.

"Last night must not have been too much fun if I have already forgotten about it," I teased. He didn't respond right away. I heard him huffed a dry laugh, but it soon went quiet again. The shutters were closed tight, so seeing whoever was in the room with me past my sleepy vision was nearly impossible.

"There has been so much chitter-chatter about you in that damn castle ... I would have thought restraining you would have been much more difficult." I tried flinging my legs off the side of the bed to face the man, but my ankle caught. *Fuck.* I was completely restrained, and now I barely have the linen covering me. I flipped onto my stomach, twisting my arms above me and attempting to pull myself up toward the headboard. I could only move forward a few inches until the rope around my ankle went taut. "Turns out I just had to wait until you were asleep," the voice now sounded from a different location, as if the intruder had stood. I turned my head to try to look at him, but he was in a blind spot. I tried to flip back over to fend off a potential attack with my one free leg, but he grabbed onto my ankle. "Don't move," he ordered sternly. A cold shiver prickled across my skin at the abrupt contact. No matter how loud the voice in my head was screaming at me to fight back, I didn't—*I couldn't.* I couldn't even move my head to the side to see who he was. I was frozen in place, a fox in a snare, waiting for the hunter to decide my fate.

"Who are you?" I asked coldly. "Are you one of the King's snakes? Here to kill me for him, like the little puppet you are?" Another shiver ran down my back as he softened his hard grasp around my ankle and ran his fingertips lightly up the back of my calf.

"I am no one's puppet," he stated sourly.

"You are doing a great job at convincing me," I scoffed.

He laughed and continued to trail his finger up along the back of my leg as he neared the head of my bed. "You have a very interesting personality," he noted. My face twisted in confusion. "I am here on my own agenda, darling. I've got my own objectives to see through and I need clarification on a few ... details."

"So, what are we doing here?" I asked, irritation clawing at the barrier of fear that kept it at bay. He trailed his finger past the linen that covered my behind and onto the exposed skin of my back.

"I don't think you realize how *insignificant* your life really is. ... So, I'm going to show you in an attempt to spare you later," he whispered softly into my ear as he worked his hand into my hair and grasped the back of my head. "This is what I will do to you," he stated before a violent cold sensation wrapped itself around my head, squeezing tightly. The discomfort wasn't what brought tears to my eyes. It was the vision I saw—or at least quick glimpses of one. A rock— no, a boulder; blood stained the ground around it. What looked like intestines were strewn over the rock formation, and two small dead bodies beside it. I heard an intense hissing, and my sight began to falter, shifting back and forth between the horrific scene and my hands that were secured to the bed. A snake, larger than any I'd seen before, curled itself around the giant boulder and opened its mouth wide, fangs gleaming and dripping with venom. I pulled in a small breath that seemed too big for my chest.

"And this ... is how you will feel." The tightness around my head spread quickly over my entire body, sending a violent wave of nausea and fear to my stomach. My throat tightened instantly, and an existential dread settled into every fiber of my being. Silent tears began to roll down my cheeks, one after the other. I felt him push down onto the back of my head, forcing my head into the pillow beneath me. I tried to resist but found no strength or ability to control my body. He pushed harder and held me down until my body thrashed against him, desperate for air. "Let this be a warning to you, mortal. Stay away from the fire-headed Loki, or I'll kill you in the most unpleasant way," he warned. I felt a quick breeze on my back, and at the same time, the pressure on the back of my head disappeared. Immediately, my door slammed open as I was gasping in ragged breaths while trying to console myself after my emotions had been so severely manipulated.

"What's going on in here?" Loki demanded while she strode towards me, looking me over. "Did you have some fun last night?" she asked playfully, shifting away from the concern I had detected in her question moments earlier.

"Get these OFF OF ME!" I yelled, tears still streaming down my face.

"I mean, I could just continue on with the fun," she teased.

"NOW!" I screamed. Puzzled, she wordlessly pulled out a knife from a hidden place and cut the rope that held my arms so I could pull my wrists free. I sat up immediately, pulling the linen to my chest and hurrying to untie the rope at my ankles. The longer I stayed in bed, the more intense the urge to crawl out of my skin became. Once free, I stumbled over to the bathroom and vomited into a wooden bucket, expelling the lingering terror from my gut.

"Ah, so it was *too* much fun, huh?" I could hear Loki ask from the doorway, her laugh severing the final thread that kept my frazzled nerves intact. I rinsed my mouth with the water in a spare bucket and shoved past her to get to my clothes, which were strewn all over the floor. I let the linen drop as I bent over, picked up my tunic, and threw it over my head, jumping into my pants as I hobbled out the door without acknowledging her. I was walking so fast that Loki had to nearly jog to keep up with me as I stormed downstairs and looked for Rune, who I spotted coming out from a back room.

"Rune!" I called out as steadily as I could, which must have failed because her face fell with concern immediately.

"What's wrong?" she asked, setting a platter full of food down at a table. She nodded toward the patrons who ordered it, and they gave a thumbs up, releasing her to come over to me.

"I need a new room or new locks, whichever I can get my hands on first," I spewed frantically, noticing how out of breath I was from the delayed adrenaline rush I was experiencing.

"What happened?" she asked, placing her hands on my shoulders and looking me over before stepping behind the bar to pour me a small cup of water.

"Someone broke into my room and was in there with me this morning," I explained quietly. I noticed Loki had followed and remained beside me, silent, as Rune leaned over the bar. "Someone you didn't intentionally bring with you last night?"

"No. They made it clear they could've killed me, then went into astonishing detail of how they would do just that while I lay there tied to the bed." I chugged all the water before rubbing my face with both hands.

"Oh, I'm so sorry." Her eyes widened with surprise. "I don't have any empty rooms." I lowered my head and took a calming breath. "I can run to the blacksmith's, but I can't guarantee a new lock by tonight," she offered wearily.

"She can take my room," Loki cut in. I turned to look at her.

"Are you sure?" Rune asked.

"Yes. We can swap rooms for the night," she stated, switching to a more playful tone in the next moment. "Or we can share? I can keep a closer eye on you that way." She smirked.

"As much as I appreciate the sentiment, you don't need to be keeping an eye on me," I retorted. "Actually, ... can I speak with you?" I asked, standing to walk toward the front door. She raised her eyebrows at me, then at Rune before following me outside. Once I passed the threshold, I took three more steps and turned on my heels to face her, causing her to skid to a stop directly in front of me. I stabbed my finger into the center of her chest. "You and me? Are not a thing, and this needs to be the last time we speak." She looked at me, curiously tilting her head before pinching my finger between her own and tossing it off to the side.

"Well, that was a sudden change of mood," she pouted, brushing out the wrinkles in her tunic. "I don't quite understand why you're insinuating that I am bothering you—or have been—especially since you are the one who came onto me first."

"You came to me at the funeral," I contested.

"An entire Kingdom seemed to be present. What makes *me* so special?" She leaned towards me with a raised eyebrow.

"Wha— " Dumbfounded, I gaped as I tried to think of a response. "The point is," I lowered my voice, "you've got weird people coming after *you*. Apparently, so do I. So, I think it would be wisest not to get involved in each other's shit," I suggested, crossing my arms over my chest.

She eyed me up and down, her face turning serious. "Who was in your room this morning?" I looked around and shook my head. I know better than to speak so freely. I heard her growl in annoyance as she grabbed my arm and pulled me along the side of the tavern until we reached the horses, stopping between a random pair. "WHO was in your room this morning?"

"I don't know! I wasn't able to look at them." I bristled, pulling my arm free from her grasp.

"What does that mean? That room is uncomfortably small, with nowhere for someone to possibly hide. How did you not see them?"

"I— I don't know. I couldn't look at them. I tried, but I physically couldn't." I let my mind wander back to the feeling of not being in control of my body. "It doesn't matter! What matters is that this person made it clear what will happen to *me* if I continue to spend time around *you*. I don't have time to spare on something so meaningless that comes with such a ridiculous price."

"Yet you have enough time to drink all day and night to avoid whatever people are coming after *you*?" she countered calmly. When I didn't respond, her eyes gleamed with a sultry look. "I think," she continued as she stepped closer to me, forcing me to step backward until I made contact with the exterior tavern wall; she placed a hand next to my head, and my stomach tightened in sweet anticipation as my brain screamed at me to not let anything happen, "until our mysterious hate clubs make any substantial move against either one of us, we should squeeze in as much time together as we want." The corner of her mouth turned up. My stomach clenched tighter as she lowered her head towards me.

"I ... think almost suffocating me to death is a pretty substantial move against someone." She froze, and I watched her smile melt away.

"They touched you?" she asked dryly.

"Well, I wouldn't describe it as a touch," I recalled. She pushed off the wall and turned her back to me, heading toward the road at the front of the tavern. I heaved myself off the wall and followed her.

"Hey! Where are you going?" I called. She stopped to face me once she was in the middle of the street.

"I've got something to look into." She smiled mischievously. "Don't miss me, Angel." A horse-drawn wagon cut between us, and when it passed, she disappeared. I turned in small frantic circles, looking for her bright scarlet hair but she was nowhere to be found. I walked back into the tavern and found an open seat at the bar as Rune hurried over.

"What was all that about?" she asked curiously.

"There *has* been a red-haired woman here the past few days, right?" I asked, confusion clouding my thoughts.

Rune turned her head to the side. "Yes?" she answered hesitantly. "Weren't you just speaking with her?"

"Yes. I just— I need a drink," I admitted, shaking my head.

"Alright," she announced as she placed a fresh mug in front of me. "I'm working on finding a new lock before nightfall."

"No worries, Rune. I will bar the door tonight, so don't rush on my behalf."
She nodded and got back to running the tavern, leaving me alone for the
remainder of the day, only filling my mug once I had emptied it.

# Eighteen

Between drinks I found myself dancing along with the crowd to the music the tavern musicians played. My head was spinning faster than I could keep up with when I bumped into another woman and spilled her drink all over myself. I stood in shock and looked up embarrassed.

"I'm— I'm soooooo sorry." I held out my arms out to the side, realizing that the entire front of my tunic and pants were soaked.

She glared at me before pointing a finger at me. "You owe me another one!" she demanded.

"Of course! Of course! Uhhhmm, ... just one second." I held out a hand and stepped away, catching Rune just as she hopped behind the bar.

"Rune, I need to borrow a change of clothes. Please ..." I drawled drunkenly, spreading my arms like wings to show the mess I had on me.

"What did you do?" She laughed.

"I was spinning too fast and knocked over a woman's drink." She turned her head at me and smiled sheepishly.

"I think I have an old pair you can have. Come here." She waved at one of her tavern workers to take over and offered me her hand. I took it, and she led me down a hallway towards a door that must be the entrance to her private quarters. "Come on." She led me into a large, cozy room with a grand four-poster hay bed off to the side.

"This is niiiiiiiiiceeeee," I admired, slowly walking over to the inviting bed.

"Oh, no, you don't." She grabbed my arm, led me to a plush couch, and sat me down. "Take your clothes off and stay there," she ordered as she walked down another short hallway. *I wonder at the size of this room.* I took my clothes off and laid them over the arm of the couch just as she returned with a fresh tunic and skirt. "Now, I don't think I have a shirt that would fit you, but we can keep the tunic open in the front and use this corset to keep it in place, and this is a wrap-around skirt, so it should work." She held the clothes in her arms, and I stumbled over to take them and fell into her arms. "You know what." She held out her hand to stop me. "Just stand there. I'll get you fixed up."

She motioned for me to bend over so she could throw the tunic over my head, which I did, and just as she said, it was a tight fit. She kept the front open, and my breasts filled it to the fullest extent. She wrapped the skirt around my waist and tucked the end of the tunic into it. When she stepped back to retrieve the corset she picked out for me, I swayed my hips back and forth, admiring the graceful flow of the fabric. The skirt was asymmetrical, showing off my thick, strong legs that I am proud of—well, leg.

"Okay, turn around and stop moving." Rune laughed while pulling the corset tight around my waist, securing my top in place.

"You are a genius." I smiled while cupping and un-cupping my breasts. "They don't feel like they are going anywhere!" She laughed at me again and turned me around to inspect her work.

"I know." she admitted proudly, "AND they look fucking amazing. You're welcome." She smiled triumphantly and took my arm, leading me out of the room and back into the bar. I paid Rune for a fresh drink and brought it over to the woman whose drink I had spilled a few minutes earlier. She looked over me with overwhelming disapproval and snatched it out of my hands.

"Could you have taken any longer?" she sneered. I twisted my face in annoyance and shrugged.

"I mean, I could have spit in it, BUT you're welcome," I retorted before turning to walk away.

"What did you say, Veslingr?" she spat from behind me.

I stopped and turned to face her with my jaw clenched. "Oh, did I say could have? I meant I did, Dunga!" I retorted, rolling up a sleeve and stepping towards the woman. She was handing her drink to a friend, readying herself to fight a battle I knew she wouldn't be able to finish despite my drunkenness. I pulled my fist back in anticipation of clocking her in the face when someone grabbed my arm from behind me. I whipped my head around to find Loki staring down at me with a wicked grin before looking at the woman.

"Excuse my friend," she cooed at the woman, eyes glowing brilliantly under the shadow she created between us. "You wouldn't want to start something you couldn't finish." The woman's face contorted uncomfortably at her words. It seemed as if she debated making a move but yielded under Loki's commanding aura. She nodded and turned back to her group of friends, signaling Loki to lead me away from them and toward the center of the tavern. I scowled at the woman, but a sudden yank on my arm jerked my entire body forward.

"What the hel are you doing?" I asked, annoyed that I couldn't make the woman take back what she called me.

"I wanted your time," she purred, securing me to her chest and pulling me along as she danced.

"I told you we need to leave each other alone." I closed my eyes to lessen the effect of spinning.

"Only due to someone's life being at risk, and I found a solution," she grinned. "So, feel free to enjoy me." My stomach clenched at her words before my lewd thoughts followed. I stole a glance at her mouth, and she didn't shy from noticing. "I won't stop you, Angel." She halted our dance and raised an interested eyebrow, taking my hand and walking backward until she reached a booth table along the wall, away from most of the crowd.

"What— " I couldn't conjure more words because every corner of my brain was enthralled with lustful ideas.

"Just in case you are shy in front of a crowd." She beckoned as she sat casually at the booth, leaning back confidently and laying her arms along the back of it. "Away from prying eyes, … I'm here for your enjoyment," her voice called to me, summoning a longing hidden deep inside me, and lured it to the surface. I took a slow step toward her, ready to surrender.

I came to stand before her and lifted the front of my skirt to the top of my thigh, placing a hand on the back of the wooden seat behind her head, and slid my shin over her leg, following up with my other one to straddle her. She lowered an arm and ran her fingers softly up the outside of my thigh, teasing the prickled skin hidden under my skirt. I pushed into her touch, feeling a sense of familiarity there, a safeness.

"I want you to tell me what you want," she purred into the base of my throat, her soft lips brushing against my skin.

"Kiss me," I ordered breathlessly, offering my neck to her. The pressure she applied started off gentle, switching from one collar bone to the other, slowly working her way up toward the underside of my jaw. Each kiss sent a shock wave of heat to my face and an ache between my legs. She began pulling tiny areas of skin between her lips, sucking on it until it edged the scale of pain, drawing a breathless moan from my lips. I could feel the stares, and when I quickly scanned the room, the confirmation of an audience only increased my arousal. One of Loki's hands worked its way up underneath my skirt, grabbing onto my ass and urging me toward her, while the other wrapped around my waist and held on to my back.

"Gods, I want to take you right now. In front of all these people," she whispered into my ear. I ran my hands on either side of her neck and pulled myself over her, looking down into her eyes.

"And what if you did?" I teased, smiling seductively as our lips skimmed past each other.

"I don't think you'd be welcomed back," she warned, her voice coaxing me toward her like a lamb to slaughter. I brushed past her lips, leaving her reaching for that connection. I kissed along her ear, trailing down the side of her neck. That's when I felt a different texture on her skin. I kissed it again, then pulled back, holding her hair out of the way so I could see what it was, and froze. She had a scar on her neck, *a rune*, almost like a brand. The drunken ecstasy disappeared instantly, and I became all too aware of the tension in Loki's shoulders and the sudden lack of lust in the way she held me.

*It isn't just a coincidence that I've seen this same scar before.* My mind was racing faster than I could keep up. I sat up straight, removed her hand from under my skirt, and analyzed it, flipping it over to the palm and back again to note the scars on either side, *runes.* My breath trembled at the terrifying realization of who this was. She had the same scar on her neck as the man who attacked Calder at the castle—the magic wielder who was able to manipulate a tree and disappear into thin air. If they could do that, they could disguise themselves into a less recognizable form. She held onto my hand to steady the trembling I hadn't noticed, lifting my gaze to meet theirs. The look in their eyes was calm but knowing, as if they knew I had made a connection. I let out a ragged breath.

"Who are you?" I asked with my next exhale.

She smiled slyly. "I've already told you, … I'm Loki."

"LEIF!" Sindre's voice boomed throughout the tavern. I whipped my head in his direction just as he passed the weapons check, shoving Ragnar out of his way and locking eyes on me. I began to feel very small but relieved he showed up when he did. He stormed over to us with a rage brewing in his eyes. "We are leaving," he growled through a clenched jaw. "Now." Loki just about threw me off to the side and stood up, blocking Sindre from reaching me.

"I don't think she *wants* to leave," she stated, stepping in his path again when he tried to step around her. Sindre paused and took in a breath, his nostrils flaring in agitation. When he opened his eyes, he peered over Loki's shoulder at me.

"I think she knows that she *needs* to," he retorted, his calm facade wavering. Loki had put a hand on Sindre's shoulder as if she was going to push him back. Instead, she held it there.

"You should turn around and go," she spoke softly to him. Sindre slowly turned his head to stare at the hand on his shoulder before looking up at her, his brown eyes burning with irritation.

"You," he placed a hand on her shoulder, grasping it firmly and guiding her out of his way, "should stay out of my way," he said with a sarcastic smile. My eyes widened as I noticed Loki's demeanor changed from calm to murderous, but as I stood, she laughed to herself and took a moment to contemplate Sindre.

"*Interesting,*" she acknowledged, looking him up and down.

"I want to leave," I cut in before things escalated. "Let's leave." I grabbed onto Sindre's wrist as I passed between him and Loki. I didn't look back despite feeling Loki's green eyes watch me as we walked away. Fortunately, we passed Rune as we left, and I told her I would return her clothes the next time I visited. Once we stepped outside, Sindre stopped.

"What the hel are you doing?" he asked sternly. I turned to face him slowly, ready to get an earful but he only crossed his arms over his chest and waited for an answer.

"I was going stir crazy at the Inn. I needed a change of scenery," I explained a bit sheepishly.

"You were given orders," he noted between clenched teeth, "very important and direct orders." He walked past me toward the horse ties, and I followed.

"I needed a break, Sindre. Besides, I am more than capable of taking care of myself," I countered. He turned sharply to face me, his brown eyes flashing dangerously, catching me off guard.

"This isn't about *you*, Veronica!" The harsh way he spat his words caused me to flinch. "Your orders were not given to you because our issues are centered around you! They were given to you because there is a much bigger problem at hand, and *your* fucking decisions can impact multiple aspects of *our* problem." He clenched his jaw shut and shook his head, mounting onto the back of Alsvid and offering me a hand.

I hesitated to grab it. "I don't understand why you are so upset. Tormod was just here checking in on me. He didn't seem upset at all, pleased actually!" I said, throwing my arms out in confusion.

"Tormod?" he questioned sharply, his face contorting in confusion. "The Elders did not tell me they sent him." His focus veered off course momentarily but quickly realigned with me. "Regardless, I can't be here for you how I want to be, Veronica. I need to be able to trust you explicitly. We all do, ... but we can't." He motioned with his hand for me to take it, and I did, hiking up the end of my skirt over my thigh so I could swing my leg up and over Alsvid 's back, settling in behind Sindre.

"I'm sorry," I offered quietly, scooting closer and wrapping my arms around his waist.

"Prove it," he urged bitterly, urging Alsvid forward toward the edge of town.

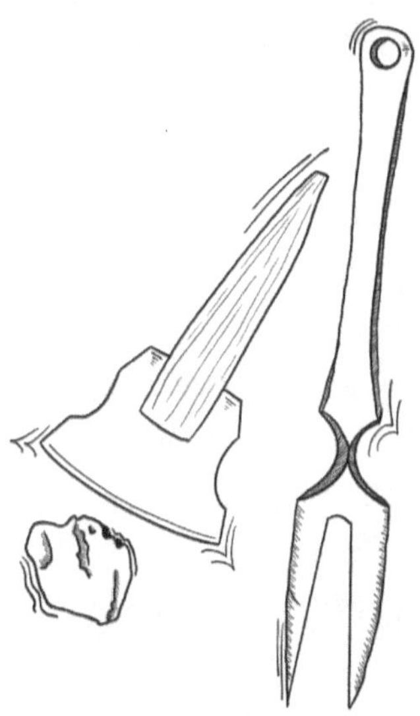

# Nineteen

Sindre continued past the Inn and rode straight to the barn behind the house, stopping outside the entrance to let me get off. He grasped my forearm while I swung my leg over Alsvid to slide off and gently lowered me to the ground. He then dismounted and grabbed my elbow, stopping me when I turned to head to the house.

"I want to warn you, … Jerrik is a little bit out of it," he spoke softly, his tone shifting to concern from the harsher one I received earlier. "When we showed up this morning, he was acting weird. It was as if he was frozen in some sort of trance. … Once we woke him, he started panicking. He was extremely disoriented and said he doesn't remember anything from the past few days." He shook his head again and dropped my arm, walking Alsvid to her stall adjacent to her sister's.

I left Sindre to finish with the horses and hurried into the house, my concern for Jerrik rising with each passing second. I walked through the back door, nearly blazing through the kitchen and into the main sitting area, only to find Jerrik sitting on the couch, surrounded by all his crafting gear and supplies. His folded hands were pressed under his chin, and his blank gaze was focused on the fire in the hearth.

"Jerrik?" I said cautiously. His eyes locked onto mine instantly, tears welling up and brimming in his eyes. He stood slowly, wobbling as he came to his feet. I hurried over to catch him and hold him steady.

"Veronica?" His voice sounded dry and parched as if he desperately needed a drink of water. "What the hel happened?" He wrapped his arms around me tightly, letting his tears fall, our embrace allowing relief to replace his fear. "I don't remember anything, V!" He pushed me away from him and held me at arm's length, a wild look on his face. "I swear! I did not intend to leave you. I don't even know how I got here! Are you okay? What happened to me? What happened to *you?*"

"Woah! Woah!" I urged him to sit down and took the spot next to him, taking his hands in mine and holding them tightly. "I'm fine, Jerrik! It's okay. I have been at The Dark Sun for the past few days. Nothing happened." I offered him a faint smile, and he seemed to relax slightly. "But as far as what happened to *you,* ... I have no idea."

"I only remember speaking to you and Rune at the bar." he said, staring down at the floor. I heard the back door click shut, and Sindre stepped into the sitting room. "Then all of a sudden, Sindre was shaking me, and I was here!" He turned to Sindre and me with an apologetic look on his face. "I am so sorry, Veronica! I have no idea what came over me. I swear, Sindre, I was not planning on leaving her in Exris! I swear I planned on taking her back with me even if she fought!"

Sindre crossed the room and sat opposite of us in a chair that looked much too small for him. He gave a quick, dismissive wave of his hand. "We are all here now, and we are all okay. I don't want you to keep worrying about it, Jerrik."

"Gods," Jerrik paused, dropping his head into his hands. "Anything could have happened."

"But nothing happened, Jer. This isn't your fault." I rubbed his back trying to reassure him.

"No, it isn't your fault, but I'm almost positive it is *yours*, Veronica," Sindre cut in. I snapped my eyes up at him, eyebrows pinched in the middle.

"How is this *my* fault?"

"How is it not? Jerrik is found here, WHERE YOU BOTH *should* be, and I find you, hours away, at the tavern with your tongue down a stranger's throat. If you were enjoying yourself when we found him the way we did, you had to play a part in this. I *know* he wouldn't have left you there." Sindre leaned forward and pressed his elbows onto his knees, his eyes smoldering with irritation.

"I had no part in what happened to Jerrik! He left the tavern so suddenly that by the time I caught up to him, he was already in the wagon and leaving town! I had no idea he was even unwell. He was fine when we last spoke. ..." My words trailed off as I contemplated my memories of that moment—Jerrik's glazed look that flashed across his eyes and disappeared once he turned away from me.

"Did you try to stop him? Call for him? Anything?" Sindre interrogated, annoyance trailing the end of his words.

"Stop him?" I scoffed. "I stood directly in his path, yelling at him! And if I hadn't moved, he would have run my ass over. I'm sorry I didn't let *that* happen." I quickly turned to Jerrik, tone softening. "I'll be honest, I thought that was weird at the time. You acted as if you didn't even hear me," I turned back to meet Sindre's angry eyes. "But I was then stuck in Exris with no safe way back, so I made the most of it."

"*You* had orders to follow," Sindre reiterated sternly. "You shouldn't have been in Exris in the first place." I opened my mouth to retort but was cut off by an angelic voice from upstairs, and my chest loosened as I heaved a sigh of relief.

"Sindre," Sylve spoke calmly as she descended the stairs, "that's enough." I stood from my seat next to Jerrik and nearly ran to meet Sylve, wrapping my arms tightly around her.

"Sylve. Thank the Gods you're here," I mumbled into her chest. I heard her suppress a laugh and clear her throat.

"Well, I wasn't about to let *him* come visit by himself. That hardly seems fair." She smiled at me and released her embrace, opting to link her arm with mine as she walked to stand in front of Sindre and Jerrik.

"This is serious, Syl." Sindre nearly exhaled his entire statement in defeat, watching helplessly as the mood shifted with her presence.

"Yes, I understand. But we aren't here to fill Brynjar's role," she reminded him. Her words caused the breath to catch in my chest. She squeezed my hand in hers at the slight increase in tension. Sindre nodded in agreement and sat back in his chair, crossing his feet on the small table in front of him. "The reality is, something happened to Jerrik that we cannot explain at the moment. I am suspicious that other magic wielders within the Kingdom are hiding their abilities. We should probably look into why this one chose to use their powers on Jerrik," she nodded toward Jer, who mirrored her gesture, seeming more at ease with the idea that leaving me at the Inn wasn't entirely his fault.

"Weeeell," I drew out the word and paused when everyone's eyes focused on me simultaneously. I cleared my throat to find my confidence and continued, "Sindre had shown up at the tavern at the perfect moment because I had an epiphany of sorts." This forced Sindre to lean forward again, in interest instead of frustration. "The woman I was with," I looked over at Sindre, who paused to think back to that moment, then nodded, "I'm ninety-nine percent positive she is the person who broke into the castle a few weeks ago."

"Are you sure?" Sindre asked, a fire igniting behind his eyes.

"I've noted similar scarring on both of them. When I was as close to them as I was at the tavern, I uncovered the same scar on their neck. The same one I noted on the attacker during the breach."

"You do understand how that makes *this* entire situation that much more frustrating, right?" Sindre asked through a tight jaw. Sylve held out a hand to calm her brother. "Right?!" he repeated towards his sister.

"Yes," she agreed, dropping my arm from hers and motioning to the couch with her hand, taking the seat in the open chair next to Sindre's. "We are going to need a hel of a lot more information than that, V. What was this person doing with you? Wanting from you? Did they ever try to hurt you?"

"Were they using magic on you, too? Do you even remember your time at The Dark Sun?" Sindre asked. I held up my hands to pause the questioning.

"Wow, that is a lot to reflect on. Let me start by letting all of you know I may or may not still be a bit drunk." Sindre's expression fell with boredom at my revelation. "But I will try my best to share what I know. I DO remember my entire time at the tavern. Well, to a certain extent," I admitted sheepishly and continued, "although I can say that I am certain I wasn't under any other influences but my mugs." Jerrik let out a small *hmph*, a breathy chuckle escaping him before looking up at everyone.

"You guys *did* miss a great celebration." He smiled but quickly sobered when he was met with Sindre's unamused stare. I thought back to the person who had broken into my room and the feeling of someone else's influence over my body and emotions, and my stomach turned. That was the only time I was possibly being influenced by magic.

"What?" Sylve cut in, pulling me from my thoughts.

"What?" I echoed.

"What were you thinking about?"

"Someone else had shown up at the tavern this week. I think they are a magic wielder as well. I was remembering what it felt like when they used their abilities to influence me to feel something specific."

"Feel what? Were they hurting you?" Sindre questioned.

"Somehow this person—again, I have to guess because I have never experienced anything like this—but I think they were able to manipulate my emotions. Don't ask for specifics; I don't know how and there is no need to share when and where this happened," I added quickly.

"Why was this person with you in the first place?" Sylve pressed, her eyebrows pinched with concern.

I let out a sigh of annoyance. "Look, I didn't think much of it then. It seemed stupid that I had found myself in the middle of something I had no idea existed or why, but I was warned, in a slightly aggressive way, to stay away from Loki."

"The redhead's name is Loki?" Sindre asked.

"Yes, and trust me, the name suits them." I rolled my eyes.

"I'm confused," Sylve stated, her face twisting awkwardly.

"Oh, I am just as confused as you are. Loki found me immediately after, and I said we needed to go our separate ways. Ultimately, Loki disappeared for a few days, only to show up again today."

"So, this Loki person must have done something to me then, which is how we ended up in this situation. Loki is the only other potentially confirmed magic wielder I have been in contact with," Jerrik added confidently, rubbing a hand down his tired face.

"That seems most likely," Sylve pondered out loud. "Did this Loki ever let on to why they had taken an interest in you? Besides the obvious." She winked at me, and I shooed it away with a hand.

"No." I smothered a laugh. "Literally, no. They said I reminded them of some person they were looking for, blah blah blah. I interested them, blah blah—very surface level. I didn't pick up on anything more. I didn't even think twice about it. I just left it at that and tried to avoid them. I only made the connection that they were the same person who attacked the King when Sindre walked through the door."

"It didn't look like you were avoiding them," Sindre jabbed, standing to go into the kitchen. I made a swipe at his leg, but he avoided it gracefully. I caught Sylve's insinuating stare.

"Hey! It was a moment of drunken weakness," I offered, raising my hands in surrender. "You'd understand if you saw them." She shook her head at me while holding back a smile. Sindre walked back into the room, drink in hand, stopping to stand between Sylve and me.

"So, we have accomplished nothing with this conversation," he stated.

"Well, we now know there are at least two other magic wielders in Sol," Sylve countered.

"And this Loki person is the same person who attacked the castle, and they continue to show up at random times," I added.

"What do you mean? You've seen them more than once?" Sylve asked.

"Well, they attended Bryn's funeral. They were in their female form, I guess, and gifted Bryn an amulet of some kind. I didn't pay too much attention to it. I was more drawn to the scars on their hands. They look like brands in the shape of runes. That's how I connected them as the same person at the tavern." We all sat for a few minutes and silently contemplated this relatively useless information. I was becoming more curious about the twins' thoughts. *Why have they become so interested in finding other potential magic wielders?*

"Well, why don't we shift gears," Sindre suggested, rolling the tension out of his neck. "We need to update you two on what we've been doing. We have only been permitted a day to pass on information, check in, and then return." I leaned forward, eager for the conversation to move on to something else.

"As far as the training goes, about seventy-five percent of the Frithians who can physically contribute are picking up on combat quickly and efficiently. However, I'm only confident with about half of our participants with weapons," Sylve explained.

"That's amazing, isn't it? How many people are you training?" I asked.

"A couple hundred."

"Oh." I hadn't realized the number of people the twins would be responsible for. I know the Elders and other Ravens were there to help, but I'm sure they have been overworked. I looked between them, just now noticing the tiredness that weighed down their features.

"Wow, guys. I wish we could offer to help." Jerrik added.

"Well, you could've helped by staying put. Following orders?" Sindre jabbed.

"Sindre," Sylve spoke sternly, "why don't you take Jerrik to help finish unloading the wagon from our journey and fill him in? I'll explain things to V." Sindre stared at her cautiously but ultimately obliged, leaving us alone. I sighed, feeling the room lighten as Sindre took his heavier aura with him.

"Geez, he can be such a hard ass sometimes." I joked, turning to find Sylve's face drawn and worried.

"Veronica, Brynjar is dead," she announced softly. My back went rigid at the harsh reminder.

"I'm aware," I spat, the corners of my mouth turning down.

"I know you know. But I don't think you *realize* what that means," she said, her eyes softened as she looked at me, melting the icy wall that protected my emotions. "He isn't here to reprimand you anymore when you make a dumb decision. He won't be here to pick you up when you falter and help guide you down your path." I sat there and felt her words slash through my brain and connect with the rational part of me that usually stays out of reach. My shoulders sagged, bearing the weight of the reality I've been avoiding for weeks. "V, … no one here will be able to fill that role going forward. And quite honestly, … we don't have the luxury to try to *be* that for you either." She came to sit next to me, throwing an arm around my shoulder and squeezing me to her.

"I'm sorry," I offered numbly. "I don't know why I do the things I do. I just— … I was losing my mind here."

"I know you know better. I also know that you are an adult and more than capable of making decisions that are best for you when necessary. To add on to that, you are a kick-ass warrior who is well-equipped to handle herself." She removed her arm from my shoulder and opted to bump hers into mine. "We all need a reality check sometimes, even if it might be difficult to accept."

"I'm sorry for the worry."

"Well, ... keep this between us." She leaned in and lowered her voice. My mood improved instantly at the hint of mischief that danced off her tongue. "I don't think your impromptu trip to Exris was wasted time. The rebellion needs to find a way to get intel from the castle, whether the Elders agree or not. Our efforts in Frith are useless if we have no idea what Calder is planning. If we wait much longer, we might be too late."

"What does that have to do with my tendency to avoid my problems with mead?" I half-heartedly teased.

"You've discovered *two* other magic wielders in the Kingdom. One of whom seems to enjoy *your* company. Maybe we can go back and find them, talk to them a bit, and see if they would be willing to explain how their magic works." Her eyes lit up as she continued to materialize a plan in her head. My jaw dropped in disbelief.

"One, what the fuck was the wake-up call for if you are planning to have me go back to Exris and disobey orders again? Two, I'm not sure I'm even following how learning the way *their* magic works will get *us* intel from the castle?" I moved away to create space between us on the couch.

"One, you needed it. Regardless of whether you stayed put or not, I was still going to propose this plan of sorts to you. Two, you said the intruder disappeared into thin air at the castle, right?"

"Yes?"

"Well, they must have gone somewhere. Maybe if *I* could learn how to do that, move from one place to another with my magic, ... maybe I can get into the castle and listen in on things." She faltered for half a second, but I noted it. Her lack of confidence in her ability hadn't improved since she last attempted to play around with it.

"Although I am more than eager to go undercover with you, there is no way that Sindre will be up for that. Don't you need to head back to Frith tomorrow anyway? We don't have the time, nor can I guarantee that these magic wielders would show again *or* be friendly."

"I've already got a plan for that. I'll take care of it," she stated surely.

I contemplated her words. "Is the Elder Council debating sending a mole?"

"The votes, apparently, are evenly dispersed. Without you there to vote on the matter, it remains at a standstill. Neither side is budging."

"If someone knew I voted in favor of a mole being sent into the castle, ... then the plan would be put into action, right?" I asked with a crooked smile.

"I would have to agree with you, Council Member Leif," she said, smiling slyly in return. I stood, walked through the kitchen, and peeked out the back door. Jerrik and Sindre were busy loading boxes full of crafted armor from Jerrick's two weeks of intense labor. I closed the door quietly and returned to the sitting room.

"What were you planning?" I asked, eager for us to adventure on our own like we did when we were younger. We were all teenagers when the twins and their father decided to settle down in Lykke. We would create elaborate plans on how to bust the fighting rings during our training, which at the time were undiscovered and left unpunished. Somehow, Bryn would approve our excuse to leave the Inn late at night, and we would be out for hours, hunting and asking questions. We had even traveled as far as Exris to find answers that would point us to the rings. Eventually, we discovered we could infiltrate the fighting clubs if we signed up as fighters. I guess the Kingdom can thank Sylve and me for the extra coin they now collect due to our particular interest in sleuthing. And to think, we were only doing that for fun.

"I first need to send Jerrik back in my place. I think I can persuade Sindre to budge, so leave that to me, and DON'T open your mouth when it comes time for me to beg. You do that, and he'll catch on." She placed her thumb on her chin, thinking. "We need to lure those magic wielders to you somehow."

"Okay, you can scratch that from the agenda."

She looked at me, confused. "You were just supportive of it a minute ago!"

"Not that part. I only trust *you* and *your* magic. These other two people are unpredictable ... and powerful. We can't trust they won't kill us. But the plan I will suggest might be *significantly* more dangerous."

# Twenty

Sindre concocted a stew of sorts out of the remaining supply of food. Luckily, the twins brought more to eat with them on their trek back. We ate in silence and were about halfway through our meals before Sylve spoke.

"Jerrik, how are you feeling now that you've gotten some food in you?" she asked sweetly.

"You know, I hadn't realized how hungry I was until Sindre started cooking." He slurped the rest of his bowl and stood to get another helping. I followed after him shortly.

"If you can't remember anything since the last time you saw Veronica, it might be safe to say you also haven't eaten anything since then. You might not have been hydrating either." She pushed her bowl off to the side and crossed her arms over her chest, looking after him with concern.

"If he hadn't been drinking for that long, he would be dead," Sindre cut in, eying his sister over the top of his bowl as he drank the remainder of his stew.

"He might as well have been," she scoffed, gesturing her head in Jerrik's direction as he sat. "Look at how sunken his face is. He's severely dehydrated. You can't deny that." Sindre looked over at his friend and nodded in agreement. She turned to face him, placing a hand on his forearm. "Are you sure you are feeling okay? You look awful."

"The headache I've had since I came to has been intense, but I should snap back to normal in a few days," he reassured her by squeezing her hand. She turned to Sindre and looked at him through her big brown eyes, putting on the face that got her her way nearly every time she made it. I noticed Sindre slightly tense at the sight of it. *Great, ... he is going to be on alert now.*

*He knows what she is doing.*

*He's got to.*

"I think he might benefit from some time in Frith," she stated quietly, letting the unspoken bond between them carry on a conversation without us.

"Why?" Sindre asked.

"You know, I'm right here," Jerrik added before blowing away the heat on his spoonful of stew.

"I'm sorry," Sylve added, squeezing his arm. "I think you should go to Frith. Almost a week with potentially no food or water? You need to rest properly and regain your strength without being on alert every hour of the day." She looked over at me. "Also, I know Veronica is difficult to keep entertained. I can take this next shift," she suggested, placing a closed fist confidently on the table as if only the strongest of people could take on such a task.

"I'm not difficult," I mumbled under my breath and was met with three pairs of rolling eyes. I shook my head and buried my annoyance with my next bite of food, remembering Sylve's warning to keep quiet or risk wrecking her plan.

"No," Sindre said firmly, setting his bowl on the table.

"Reason?" Sylve retorted.

"You two are trouble together. No way. I can stay here."

"The only reason sending Jerrik to Frith works is because he should be able to cover *my* side of training this upcoming week—bow work, long-range shots. Since it's non-combative, he can rest and instruct. I mean, I did learn everything about the bow from *you*." She motioned toward Jerrik, who gave a sarcastic half-bow.

"You can cover for me then," he threw back, holding his hand out for everyone's empty bowls. I placed mine on top without making eye contact and nodded my thanks. I'm a terrible liar, and if Sindre looks too long, he will read me like a book.

"The Elder Council won't be happy with second best," she responded cooly, leaning back in her chair. "Jerrik is THE best archer—*especially* long range. But I come second best in hand-to-hand in every style. We've tested it, remember?" She raised an inquiring eyebrow toward her brother, whose back was to us, as he cleaned the dishes and put them away quietly. We sat in a growing silence that had me fidgeting in my seat uncomfortably. I moved forward, sitting on the edge, when I caught a death glare from Syl that sent my back pressing into the wood behind me.

She let a few more minutes pass by, eventually clearing her throat once Sindre sat at the table across from her. He looked over at me and caught my eyes. *I have to stay strong here, keep it innocent but not too innocent to be suspicious.* My eyes began to burn. ... *Was I not blinking?*

Jerrik cleared his throat across from me on the other side of the quaint table. "You know, I wouldn't mind a change of things. I don't want this to come across as selfish, but if I can lower the risk of whatever happened to me this week, I'd jump on it." He shrugged his shoulders. "Maybe your *abilities* can combat that type of attack if these people were to show up again," he added. Sindre and I snapped our eyes to Sylve, who became a bit sheepish.

"Uh, I may have kick-started his healing when you went to find Veronica," she admitted softly.

"Syl," Sindre spoke with irritation.

"What? Do you blame me? You saw him when we found him. He is our friend, and I couldn't let him work that out alone. I had to help," she defended her actions, crossing her arms over her chest.

"And I appreciate it dearly," Jerrik added, placing a large hand on Sindre's equally large shoulder. "I don't think I'd be able to form cohesive sentences if she hadn't."

"Keep that information between the four of us," Sindre ordered, turning his head to speak to Jerrik directly. "We haven't told the Elders yet. Only a handful of the Ravens know, and they promised to let us speak to the Council on our own. Don't speak to ANYONE about her abilities. Do you understand?"

"I swear," Jerrik reiterated, holding a fist over his heart.

"Thank you," Sylve added, mirroring Jerrik's gesture. A few moments of silence followed.

"Ok," Sindre stated.

"Ok?" Sylve repeated.

"Jerrik can go to Frith if he thinks it would benefit him. You'd have to stay here with Veronica. At least until the Council decides it's been long enough, and she no longer needs to show her face in Sol. Which, by the way things sounded before we left, might be another week." The twins looked at Jerrik for a response while he looked up at me.

"I wouldn't offend you if I admitted to preferring a break, right?" he laughed lightly as he asked.

"I mean, ... maybe a little offense." I side-eyed him and eventually shook my head. "No, I can understand how you're feeling. An attack like that feels extremely invasive. I would go to Frith, too, if I had the option," I admitted, offering a pitiful smile.

"It's settled then," Sylve declared, placing her hands on the table. "In the morning, Jerrik will take my position and travel back with Sindre." She nodded toward Sindre and Jerrik, and they both nodded in agreement before rising from their seats.

"Also," Sindre added, "I will ask the Council if they sent Tormod to check in with you."

"Tormod was here?" Sylve asked, turning to me.

"He found me at The Dark Sun not too long ago," I answered. *I couldn't remember the timeline of the past few hours, let alone days. Everything seemed to have blurred together while I was staying at the Tavern.*

"Did they mention anything to you?" Sindre asked Syl. She shook her head. "Weird. I will follow up with them then," he said as he turned away from us.

Sylve turned to me and offered her hand. "Off to bed?" She winked at me as she asked, a hidden celebration of victory.

"Please," I answered under my breath, taking her hand and working overtime to not let too big of a smile plaster itself on my face.

# Twenty-One

Sindre and I were loading up Jerrik's boxes of leather work in the early morning light, hidden behind the shadow the Inn cast across the back gardens. A fine mist floated just above the ground up to our waists, swirling in hypnotizing movements when we walked through it. I stopped to notice the sunrise around the house's edge, just past the pier. The sky was a deep ruby red that faded into pinker shades as it rose into the sky. Bryn loved sunrises. I bit my lip, ripped my eyes away from the beauty the sun goddess gifted us today and returned to work. *He would have especially loved this sunrise.* I thought to myself how he would have stopped us from working and brought us out front so we could appreciate it. Tears stung my eyes when Sindre shoved the last box into my arms, which I caught with a grunt.

"You alright? Can't believe it's our final box or what?" he joked, his cheeky smile dimming when I struggled to snap back with a snarky comment. "I can load it," he reassured, holding his arms out to take the box from me. "What are you thinking about?" he asked.

I moved out of his path, wanting to finish the task on my own. "I'm alright," I said, letting a light-hearted chuckle slip through as I fanned the potential tears away. "Just thinking of Bryn," I admitted.

"Ah," I heard Sindre say from behind me. When I turned around, my face met the warmth of his chest, taking in his woodsy scent. His arms fell gracefully around my shoulders as he hugged me to him. I wrapped my arms around his waist, accepting the tender moment with an open mind, knowing he wanted to be there for me when he could. "You know," he started softly, placing his chin on top of my head. "Bryn told me once that the sunsets reminded him of his daughter, but sunrises reminded him of you. ... Now, I can't speak to what that might have meant to him *personally*, but I can agree." He pulled me away from him and placed a comforting hand on my head. "The sun rises, even on the darkest days and darkest nights. She will push past the stars and break through the clouds to offer her light to the world. You are a sunrise, Veronica. You will persevere, ... just as you always have." He moved his hand to the back of my head and pulled me toward him once more, placing a delicate kiss on the top of my forehead and hugging me before breaking away, leaving his words to resonate with me. A few minutes passed, and I had readied Alsvid at the front of the cart and taken my seat on the back of it when Sindre, Sylve, and Jerrik finally emerged from the Inn.

"Well, damn. It took you long enough," I joked.

"Aye! Get your ass off of my cart, you twit," Jerrik yelled after me, pulling his bow over his shoulder and letting it rest across his back. I jumped up with a laugh and held my arms out to catch the embrace of his big bear-like arms. "Don't give her a hard time," he whispered into my ear while, at the same time, pinched the back of my arm.

"Ow!" I jumped back and rubbed the spot he attacked. "I don't give Sylve hard times," I retorted. "Just you two." I smiled heinously and received two dramatic eye rolls from them.

"You guys travel safely," Sylve stated as they both loaded up into the cart. Sindre looked back at us through narrowed eyes.

"Stay OUT of trouble," he ordered. Sylve and I exchanged an innocent glance before looking back at him.

"We always do," she cooed, her sweet response accompanied by a bright smile. Sindre shook his head as he ushered Alsvid forward.

"I'll be back in ONE week!" he called back from down the road as we waved him goodbye. Finally out of sight, Sylve turned to me with a giddy expression, her body nearly vibrating with anticipation.

"It's time to get ready."

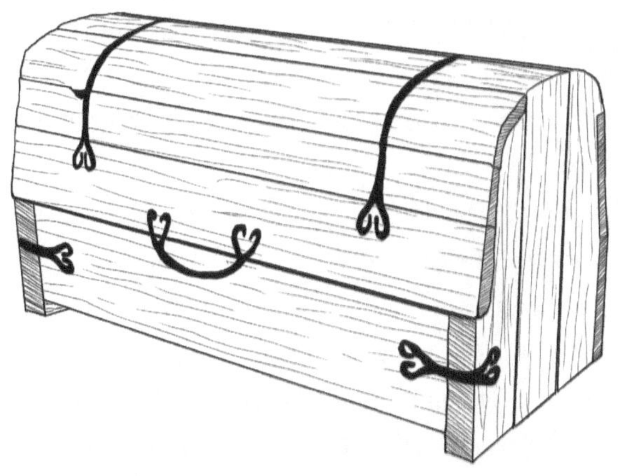

# Twenty-Two

I couldn't recall my nightmare exactly, but it consisted of an overwhelming feeling of death and destruction. When the harsh morning light abruptly clawed at my eyes, I peeled back an eyelid to watch Sylve fling open every shutter on the Inn's first floor. The same ones I had kept closed since Bryn's passing. I turned over to shove my face onto the couch when I noticed Sylve facing me.

"Good morning, Sunshine!" her voice chimed across the room, forcing me to pull my pillow over the top of my head. "We've got a lot of traveling to accomplish today, V. I hope you aren't going to force me to get you off that couch," she cautioned sweetly. I contemplated if I should get myself up for the day or take the risk that she wouldn't follow through on the said threat. Apparently, she was ready to go immediately because I wasn't graced with any time to make a decision. I suddenly felt her grasp under my bicep and leg, deadlifting me off the couch and holding me suspended in the air. I flailed in protest, preparing to break my fall in case she decided to drop me.

"Really, Syl?" I groaned..

"If we are going to be disobeying orders, we at least will be doing so in a timely manner," she stated matter-of-factly before dropping me onto the floor, stepping over me to grab a pile of fresh clothes, and tossing them onto the couch next to me. "We've got to get to Sol's town by the end of the day. We can stay at my father's house for the night and have an entire day tomorrow to get what we need and leave."

"I think I could've had another five minutes, don't you?" I asked while leveraging my torso off the ground with my elbows.

"Love you!" her voice rang out as she walked into the kitchen. "Breakfast in five, then we leave." I rolled my eyes, got off the floor, changed, and managed a few bites of food before being dragged out of the Inn.

I helped her get Arvak attached to the cart, and we loaded in, staying light on supplies. We brought a few smaller knives originally gifted to Jerrik and me, along with a pack of food that would last maybe a day and a half. When I asked why we couldn't pack more, she explained that if we packed extra food, that would give us extra energy to mess around and not return when we needed to. I sighed and pushed her out of the way to steer Arvak on our journey.

"This would be a great time to explain the rest of your plan for us in detail," she quipped, elbowing me and bringing my attention back to Midgard.

"Right, okay. Try to keep up," I smirked as I ran through the details of the plan I proposed last night. We need to scrap the idea of finding Loki and the other magic wielder we don't know and focus instead on contacting someone we *do* know—someone who also knows a significant amount of information about magic in general.

I explained more about Mazen to Sylve and how he had begun to help me understand a basic level of magic and its users right after the attack on the King. If we could find Mazen—and may the Allfather help us so he is off-duty when we get there—he could show us around the library and point out the books he referenced when he was learning magic. If we read the books with the least amount of information, we can borrow the ones we need to delve into and take them back to Lykke at the end of the day. Then, we can spend the rest of the week studying and possibly have Sylve practice honing *her* magic.

"So tomorrow we arrive at the castle and, what? The first thing to do is find Mazen? We could go straight to his quarters and check his room," she suggested.

"I most likely won't be able to go anywhere near the warriors' private quarters in the castle itself. The library is at least its own entity, separate from the castle itself. I have less chance of being spotted if I only show myself there," I added.

"Are you banned from the castle?" she asked, surprised.

"Not formally."

"Ah." She nodded. "You've finally realized how big of a risk this is? I didn't even have to tell you?" she asked, a sarcastic smile lighting up her eyes.

"Aren't you proud?" I laughed. "You bring out the better person in me." I bumped her with my elbow, and she laughed.

"I'm so proud of you!" She hugged my shoulders and squeezed tight. "So, how do we expect to contact Mazen if we can't go to his room?"

"I …can't go to his quarters. I was hoping you would be willing to do that part alone."

"Oh. Where will you be?" she asked cautiously, not wanting to express her concern about splitting up so close to our biggest threat.

"I'll be in the library, waiting. You can even walk with me there and then track backward to find Mazen. That way, I can get a head start on finding material, just in case he isn't available, and we are left to figure it out on our own." She shook her head, as if contemplating all our options.

"For the sake of time management, that will have to work. I can drop you off at the library and circle back for your friend." We both nodded in agreement. "I'll need directions on how to get there—a specific path to take that could get me in and out with the least number of eyes recognizing me," she added.

"I can draw one up at your father's house tonight," I offered. "Do you think he will be home? I haven't seen him in ages."

"He has been on an expedition for some time now. It is possible." She stared off into the sky, recalling the timeline of her father's trips. Mr. Nyhus has always been a traveler, which is how they originally came upon Lykke and the Kingdom of Sol. He had plans to travel the lands and see all he could see to find something that had been lost to him long ago. ... At least, that is a huge part of his spiel before he leaves for each expedition.

The twins were just ten years old when they and their father traveled into Lykke, meeting Bryn almost immediately. Mr. Gudmund Nyhus quickly fell in love with the Kingdom and planned to settle down. The twins opted to work with Bryn after overhearing him explain the Ravens to Gudmund one night, which Bryn would never do with a stranger. However, Mr. Nyhus had happened to be on a late-night stroll when the Ravens were returning from a raid. If I remember correctly, he was sworn to secrecy that night, but the twins' interest was piqued, and they became persistent in beginning their training.

Around the time the twins turned sixteen, Gudmund had become restless and could no longer ignore his passion for exploring. He asked the twins if they wanted to travel with him again or stay in Lykke, and they chose to stay. He decided to keep the home that he built in Sol's town and use that when he visited between his trips, spending most of the year traveling and only settling back in during the winter months when the weather made expeditions difficult. The twins bought their own home in Lykke to stay closer to the Ravens and, coincidentally, as far away from the Crown as possible. Mr. Nyhus has always been wary of the King and the idea of one man ruling over hundreds of people, a perspective that clearly rubbed off on his children. That also might be part of the reason why he was always traveling. Besides being an adventurer at heart, he didn't see the need for someone to dictate any aspect of his life— a sentiment I deeply respect—bringing my attention back to why we were headed to the Nyhus residence in the first place.

"You know, Syl. ..." She turned her attention to me. "If he is home, this might be the only time to tell him about what is happening," I suggested quietly.

"I was just thinking about that," she admitted, propping her foot up on the bench where we sat, resting her elbow on top of her knee and her head in her hand. "He is going to try to convince us to leave with him," she added to no one in particular.

"He doesn't know about Bryn, does he?" I asked, almost hopeful to not have to revisit the fresh wound I was struggling to keep from bleeding.

"No," she answered under her breath.

"That is going to make it worse, ... isn't it?"

"Yes."

Silence fell between us.

"You don't have to stay," I offered softly.

She snapped her head over to me so fast I thought she had broken her neck. "Don't say that, Veronica!"

"I'm just saying!" I put my hands up in defense. "You guys can leave before things get ugly. You never know what the outcome may be. If there is a chance you can maintain your family, ... I would understand."

"YOU are also my family. Jerrik! Ragnhild! Ylva! The rest of the Elders! The Ravens! The children at the orphanage! They are all my family," she paused and took in a breath. "I am deeply offended that you would think I would pick up and *run*." She shook her head vehemently.

"I know you wouldn't!" I placed a hand on hers. "I'm sorry. I— I didn't mean it like that." I was on the edge of falling into a crevice of loneliness before she made her declaration, a reminder that even though my blood family is gone, my found family is still very much alive, and this fight we are preparing for is bigger than any single one of us. "I'm sorry," I repeated, pulling my hand away from hers and returning it to the reins. "That was stupid of me to say."

"Yes, it was," she huffed, rolling the tension out of her neck. "The discussion with my father, whether it happens tonight or not, will be difficult. At the end of the day, he knows it is *my* decision, and it is *Sindre's* decision separately, on what path we choose for our *own* destinies." I nodded in agreement.

A few moments of silence passed before I spoke. "Well, I do ask the Gods for your father to be home this visit. It has been a while since I've seen him," I added slyly. Sylve turned to face me slowly, her eyes narrowing as she shrewdly calculated whether to ask for clarification or throttle me before I could say more.

"Leave him alone!" she stated incredulously. "The man is constantly on the move and comes home to rest and doesn't need to fend himself off against you!" She laughed but had a slightly uncomfortable look on her face.

"Okay! Okay! But I'm just saying, if he makes a move in my direction, I won't stop him," I stated before bursting out in a laughing fit at Sylve's look of complete shock and utter disgust at my revelation. Her face turned red, and she hid her face with her hands, groaning audibly.

"I hate it here."

"What! Why?" I joked. "I have the most beautiful group of friends on Midgard. I can't help that their parents are twice, if not three times as beautiful. I can't. That would be dishonest of me." I laughed.

"I'd rather you be with Sindre than my father."

"I'll take either ... or both." I laughed bracing for a solid punch to my shoulder. "Gods, help me."

# Twenty-Three

We arrived in the small town just outside the castle walls a little past sundown. I begged Sylve to let us make a quick pit stop at The Dark Sun in Exris so that I could return the clothes Rune loaned me. But alas, the visit wasn't fast because she offered us a drink and a plate of food, and neither of us could resist. *How rude would that have been if we did?*

Sylve guided me towards her father's home, a long house that was nearly identical in shape to an overturned longship. I can count on one hand how many times I've visited this house. Until Bryn retired, I spent most of my time at the castle with Erikka. Then, once I moved out, I stayed at the Inn, training, and training, and more training.

As we pulled the wagon to a stop out front, we noticed a warm light coming from inside the window furthest from us. I heard Sylve gasp in excitement and then leap from the back of the wagon, sprinting to the front door and nearly knocking it down with how hard she pounded her fist on it. I grabbed our two small bags from the back and was making my way to her home when the door flung open.

Mr. Nyhus stood in the doorway in all his mighty glory—his long locs, graying at the roots, were tied back and much longer than Sindre's. His russet brown skin refused to crease, regardless that he was within five years of Bryn's age. Even with a round belly you can see that Gudmud passed along his stature to Sindre—his broad chest and thick arms creating a towering silhouette, yet he exuded the most welcoming aura despite his size. It was clear that he was caught off guard as multiple emotions flickered across his face within seconds—irritation was first, then confusion, a little shock, more irritation, then excitement once his daughter jumped into his arms.

"You're home!" Sylve cheered over her father's shoulder.

"I am," he laughed wholeheartedly, wrapping his arms tight around her and slightly lifting her off the ground. "And you are home too! What a coincidence this is."

"When did you get back?" she asked, planting her feet back onto the floor.

"A few days ago. I've been getting everything caught up here. I was planning a trip to Lykke once I've taken care of some errands, but I'll accept a surprise visit anytime." He smiled, patting her head lovingly. "Is your brother here with you?" he asked, looking out to find me standing awkwardly between the wagon and the front door.

"No, but Veronica is," she answered, waving me in. As I neared the entrance, Gudmund's curious stare grew into a heart-stopping smile. He has Sylve's big, bright brown eyes but Sindre's wide nose. His hair had grown significantly longer than I'd ever seen—nearly past his waist. His beard was also peppering, the only true indication of his age, with two short braids twisted into it on either side of his chin.

"Veronica Leif!" he announced formally, opening his arms wide. "It is so good to see you." His hug was honest and inviting—not as warm as his children's, but you could melt into his arms just the same.

"Mr. Nyhus. I can say the same. You look amazing! You haven't aged a day." I offered my most earnest smile as I pulled away from him. He smiled widely at my statement, causing the corners of his eyes to crinkle sweetly. Sylve must have caught me drooling because she bumped into my shoulder as she passed to grab the bags from my hands.

"Thank you. It has been a while since the last time I've seen you, hasn't it?" He brought his finger and thumb to his chin, contemplating my appearance. "You've changed, ... but what is it?"

"Well, ... I—"

"No, no! Let me figure it out," he cut in, focusing on my face. I could feel my cheeks burning when he finally clicked his tongue against the roof of his mouth. "You've got a new scar!" he pointed out confidently. "I like it! It suits you."

"It gives character," we said in unison, paused, then burst into a shared laugh.

"I'm glad you get me." I winked, and his heavy hand patted my shoulder.

"So, what brings you girls to town?" he asked, walking over to Sylve and throwing an arm over her shoulder lovingly.

"Not anything particularly good, but I'm glad you're here. Gives us one positive thing to come out of our trip." She smiled weakly, and Gudmund noticed immediately.

"What's going on?" He looked between Sylve and me, turning to face us.

"Have you spoken to anyone since you've been here?" I asked, pained.

"Just in passing and at the supply stands. Why?"

"A lot has happened, ... and a lot is changing as we speak," Sylve stated quietly. "We need to talk."

Sylve sat everyone down at their dining table. Despite my greatest effort to avoid being included in the conversation, I was ultimately ushered into the seat beside her father, with Sylve on the other side of him at the head of the table. At least two hours passed with the amount of information Sylve dumped onto her father. She started with the breach at the castle, then the summons to the Kingdom meeting, conveniently withholding the fact that she has magical abilities. She eventually explained Bryn's death—murder, as Sylve described it. I felt Gudmund's hand slide over onto my forearm, but I refused to look at either of them. I kept my gaze and mind as far from this conversation as possible, despite the threat of tears pushing past my eyelids remaining present throughout the entire conversation.

She continued explaining our meetings with the Elders, leaving out the discussion she had been sworn to secrecy during her attendance. She also skipped our experience at the lake. She went straight from the funeral to the meeting, where it was decided to send Jerrik and me back to Lykke. She explained the threats we are facing with the King and the fact that we no longer have insiders with the Crown, so knowing what Calder might feel towards me being in the area was now *impossible* to determine. Finally, it came time to tell him about Calder's plans. She briefly touched on it when explaining Bryn's death, but he had more questions.

I excused myself while she elaborated on what the political games mean for us and Frith, what that means for everyone in the Kingdom, ... and what it could mean for them as a family. I stayed vigilant as I slipped out of a side door and onto their porch, keeping my small knife at the ready as I stood along the wall, letting the crisp night air brush along my face. I closed my eyes for what felt like half a second when Sylve poked her head out.

"My father wants to speak with you. Is that okay?" she asked. "You don't have to if you don't want to hear it right now. He will understand." I knew she was referencing the pity and sympathy conversation.

"It's alright. He's late to the party. I know he means well." I smiled as I walked over to her. I quieted my voice so only she could hear as I passed. "Besides, alone time with the *man*? How could I refuse?" I chuckled at her eye roll and tongue click of disgust.

She pushed me down the hall and back into the main room. "He is in the sitting area. I'm going to go make sure our room is ready so we can get some sleep." *Our* room because we usually opt to sleep together any chance we can. We can call it a routine of sorts. Since we were young, a sense of comfort has always settled over us when we do, and we can also expect a good night's sleep.

I walked around the couch Mr. Nyhus was sitting on and took a seat opposite him, offering a half-hearted smile in preparation for what was going to come.

"I'm so sorry about Brynjar," he offered sadly, lifting a heavy hand and placing it on his chest as if the news caused him physical pain. "He was an extraordinary man."

"Thank you," I responded quietly, noticing how low my head hung down as I leaned on my elbows over my knees. His hand caught my knee and shook it lightly.

"How are you doing?"

I gazed at him, my vision blurring through my already damp eyelashes, making it impossible to lie to him. "I'm taking it in waves. Some days are worse than others," I replied, shocked since it felt like this was the first time I had been honest with myself in weeks. Relief spilled over my shoulders, and the lifting weight kept me talking. "I struggle with the reality of it, the permanence. I still blame myself. ... Every step I take feels unstable, like, at any moment, the next step will be too high or too low, and I will fall again. I'll fall and break all of the pieces of me I've been trying to fit back together around the hole that's been left in me when he died."

"Ah." He nodded in understanding. "I know that feeling well. When I lost— ... When my wife disappeared, I felt very similar feelings, a lot of confusion. The iron grip on your heart each time you were reminded of them would constrict and hinder its ability to beat properly. All you can do is ride the waves sometimes. Just float if that is all you can handle." He offered a gentle smile in place of the slight frown he let creep onto his face. "I pray the Gods help guide you through this difficult time. Maybe Loki could bring you some laughter," he joked, but my back went rigid. I attempted to relax as soon as I felt myself tense, but he had eyes like a hawk. "Is everything alright?"

"Yeah! Sorry. I'm just on edge." I feigned a laugh. "I can't help but wish the Gods would do more than send a laugh my way. Maybe they could stop the madmen that continue to threaten innocent people's lives?"

"That would be ideal, wouldn't it?" He smiled sadly, letting silence fall between us. "Veronica, ... my kids mean the world to me."

"With how much they mean to me, I can only imagine how much they mean to you." I smiled softly, and he mirrored it affectionately.

"A parent's worrying will never cease. Not even as we pass onto the next life will our concern for our children diminish." I nodded in understanding. "I know Sylve and Sindre have created unbreakable bonds with not only those in the organization but with you. Something as strong as that bond needs to be cherished, replenished, and never taken for granted." He rubbed the back of his neck, and I became wary of where he might take the conversation. He let out a sigh before continuing, "Of course, I want to know they are safe, ... or to believe they are, and knowing that they are going to be *choosing* to put themselves directly in the path of a very real problem. ..."

"I'm not sure anything I say will ease your nerves, Gudmund," I stated quietly.

"Promise me you will fight for them the way they will fight for you." He looked straight into my eyes, past them even. It felt as if he looked deeper, finding the version of me I was hiding deep down inside and pulling her to the surface, ensuring she understood his seriousness.

"Of course I will," I stated confidently, placing a closed fist over my chest. "I would give my life for them."

"Good, ... because they will do the same for you."

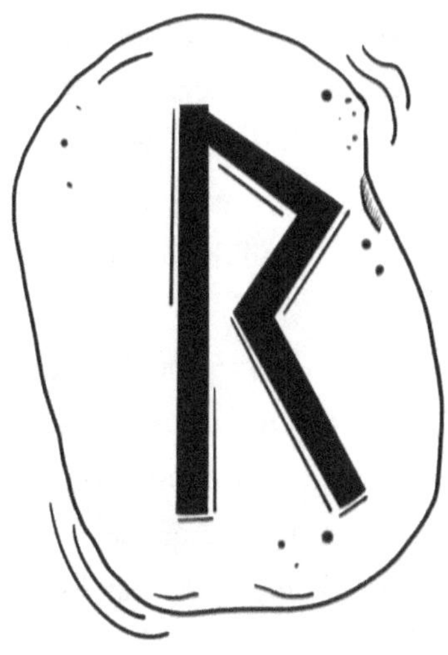

# Twenty-Four

The next morning, it was I who had the honor of waking Sylve up. My nerves kept me tossing throughout the night, and even though my eyes were shut, I did not rest for longer than a few minutes at a time—*so much for a good night's sleep.* Sylve got up quickly, and we took a few minutes to eat the food Gudmund prepared for us.

"Are we going to travel by foot to the castle?" I asked after stuffing a spoonful of eggs into my mouth.

"What? No," Sylve responded, confused by my question. "Why would we do that?"

"I don't want Arvak to alert anyone to our presence as soon as we arrive. Especially since she will be tied to a post near the library. I'm afraid someone will recognize her."

"Hmm."

"You two can take my horse for the day," Gudmund added. "I won't be ready to leave for a few days, so I won't need him."

"Thank you." Sylve stood with her cleared plate and placed a hand on her father's shoulder, leaning over to kiss his cheek. "We will be back by sundown."

He nodded and wiped his hands with a towel before placing his plate on the counter. "I'll go ready him." He smiled at his daughter lovingly. "No cart, right?"

"No," she responded as she cleaned their plates. I waited to do my own plate once she had finished.

"Did the conversation go better than you expected last night?" I asked.

"I mean, ... sort of. He was taken aback at the severity of the issue and was disturbed about Brynjar's passing." She paused to tuck her hair behind her ear, contemplating if she wanted to put it up or leave it down. "He had a moment of realization last night that we would more than likely be separating our family and officially embarking down our own paths."

I nodded in understanding. "Do you feel okay? After you guys talked?"

She shrugged. "We're good. I love him dearly." She smiled, laughing to herself. "He can be overbearing."

"He mentioned he was leaving at the end of the week. Any specific plans?"

"Oh, he told me this would be the time to trek the expedition of his lifetime." She threw her arms out to her sides and spun in a dramatic circle, laughing as she did.

"To find—" I started to finish her sentence.

"The most precious thing that has been lost to him for some time!" We finished our sentences in unison.

"So, this is it? That time has finally come for him?" I asked, bringing a more serious tone to the conversation.

"Yeah," she responded solemnly. "I know he always says that he is looking for that *oh-so-precious thing*—whatever it may be. But this time, ... he mentioned that this is an expedition he doesn't expect to return from." My eyes snapped up to hers, watching as they built up with tears. "So, either we go with him or stay here. ... A final goodbye either way." I walked over and wrapped my arms around her tightly. I held her for a few moments as she gathered herself.

"I'm so sorry, Syl."

She wiped a tear from her cheek. "He wants to tell Sindre and say his goodbyes since he doesn't foresee Sindre being eager to join him on his journey. ... He plans to meet us in Lykke in a few days. I'm hoping Sindre will show up with news around the same time."

"Did he mention where he was going?"

"He has a general idea. He spoke to some people on his past trips to gather information on a land northeast of Osera. He mentioned that a group of travelers have been trying to pass the Skadi mountains to see for themselves but have been unsuccessful thus far. He thinks he can help them trek towards where the Skadi and Sylph mountains meet. He's hopeful there will be a passable area there."

"And then what? What do they do if they *can* pass?" I asked, my eyebrows pinching together.

She shrugged her shoulders. "They will travel unknown lands or waters looking for whatever he lost I guess."

Gudmund walked in with a smile on his face. "Alright, he's ready when you two are."

"Are you ready?" Sylve asked, switching her mood seamlessly.

"Ready as I'll ever be."

We all walked out together, and Sylve gave her father another big hug before mounting the horse. He opened his arms towards me, and I embraced him without hesitation, peering around him to wiggle a playful eyebrow at Sylve, who gagged mockingly in response. She held out her hand for me, and I hoisted myself up behind her.

"Thank you, Mr. Nyhus," I offered as Sylve turned us around in a circle.

"Anything for you girls! Be safe." He waved as he turned to head back into the house, and Sylve motioned us forward.

# Twenty-Five

As the drawbridge and outer castle walls came into view, I drew the hood of my cloak over my head, letting it fall past my eyes. Sylve's was halfway up, resting lightly on top of her head. We thought if we pulled off a scene of a *sleeping riding partner*, then no one would question my choice of winter cloak or who was hiding under their hood on such a beautiful early summer morning.

I felt the pounding in my chest intensify as we rode over the drawbridge. I'm sure the sound of each hoofbeat along the wooden surface beneath us seemed much louder to me than anyone else. I kept my forehead pressed into the center of Sylve's back and my body as relaxed as possible, with my arms wrapped limply around her waist as we passed the guards stationed at the castle entrance. I didn't dare breathe until Sylve moved forward to stretch her back, signaling that we were in the clear. I feigned a waking stretch and rubbed my hands down my face to continue covering my identity while I peeked through my fingers at who may be around. I didn't recognize anyone, but I noticed a significant presence of guards.

"What the *hel* is going on here?" Sylve whispered over her shoulder. She was referring to the shocking number of masked warriors stationed throughout the small town surrounding the castle itself.

"Something isn't right," I noted, keeping my head down. "Get me to the library. Finding Mazen needs to become a priority." She nodded and ushered her father's horse to quicken his pace as we passed the main entrance to Kron's castle. The massive iron doors were closed with double the number of guards standing before them. *Something had to have happened.* Erikka came to the forefront of my mind, and I soon found myself irritated for instinctively worrying about her.

*She killed him.*

*She let him die.*

I dismounted once we came to a stop outside the library. It is a large stone two- or three-story building with intricate stained-glass windows on either side of its main wooden doors. I noted a smaller set of doors on the side that seemed to be the entrance people used instead of laboring to open the more significant option. Its exterior resembled the castle's design but on a smaller scale. I'm embarrassed to admit I have never been inside until now, so I'm hoping I can navigate the shelves by myself.

"Where are the directions?" Sylve interrupted my thoughts with her question.

"Right." I sorted through the small satchel around my waist until I felt the coarse piece of parchment with written instructions for Sylve. "Here," I stated as I placed it into her hand. "You'll find the entrance down there; take a left once you reach the corner, and there will be a short hallway on the right. That's the door you can enter; the instructions begin once you are inside *that* door." I directed her attention past the library, toward the farthest side of the castle from where we stood. She nodded in understanding, stuffing the parchment into her weapons belt. She began to walk away, but I caught her wrist. "There is a lot more activity here than usual. My directions were based on the least guarded entrance, but I can't guarantee that there is no guard there today."

"I thought as much." She smiled. "I'll handle things the best I can." She looked towards the library and glanced around at the people walking, shopping, or working before speaking again. "Are you sure he can be trusted?"

"I think …" I looked toward the sky, silently praying the Gods don't disappoint me. "Yes."

"Okay." She placed a hand on the smaller sword she secured around her waist. "If he gives me the sense that he isn't, he dies today."

"I've already mentioned that possibility to him before." I winked at her, and she nodded.

"Get to studying," she ordered lightheartedly, leaving me in front of the library. I turned and walked over to the side door entrance, squeezing in past a few patrons who were leaving, keeping my head down. Once inside, I brushed off the hood of my cloak, keeping it on top of my head so I could take in the vastness of the library before me.

My heart dropped to the pit of my stomach at how impossible this task had become. The library was indeed three stories tall, with a grand spiral staircase at its center reaching up to the higher floors. On the first floor alone, there were hundreds of shelves holding thousands of books.

"What. The. Fuck," I whispered to myself as I went searching for some sort of directory. *There had to be one, … right?*

I began walking past the shelves, glancing down the aisles as I did, looking for someone who looked like they worked there. I almost returned to where I started when I heard a soft voice call out to me.

"You look like you are lost." A quiet laugh. I turned around and was met with a striking young woman with bronzed skin. The top half of her dark hair was pulled up into a voluminous bun while the rest of her brushed-out curls fell over her shoulders. She had perfectly sculpted, thick eyebrows that squared out just above her dark brown eyes, a red bindi placed neatly between them. She held a small stack of books in her arms.

"Is it that obvious?" I asked, embarrassed.

"Ahhh, a little," she said and smiled sweetly. "Maybe I can help you." She stepped towards me.

"Yes? Possibly? Could you show me, um—" I couldn't figure out how to word my question. Although it doesn't seem like she recognized me from anywhere, I don't want to raise any red flags if someone was listening and overheard our conversation. "Are there any books about the Gods?" I knew I sounded stupid, but small talk isn't my cup of tea.

She nodded confidently as if I had asked for the most read subject in the building. "Of course, follow me. They are located on the second floor." She smiled and led the way up the grand staircase. She stopped at the landing and held out her hand, motioning to an aisle. "From here, all the way to the wall, you can find plenty of books about the Gods." I noted at least ten shelves from where we stood to the wall she was pointing at." If you want more of a *recreational* read, these first three aisles will house those stories. In the next three, you can find speculative theories around the possibilities of the existence of *other* Gods. Then, the final three will be full of informational history about *our* Gods." She nodded and smiled. Meanwhile, it took a few seconds to realize I was gaping, stricken with disbelief at the selection before me.

"Uhm, thank— thanks. That is very helpful." I stammered, offering a sheepish smile. She nodded again before returning to the first floor. I braced myself for the insurmountable task before me and walked to the last aisle along the wall. *When you don't know where to start, just pick somewhere random and get to work.* I ran my finger along the spines of the books, briefly reading the titles as I casually walked along the bookshelf.

*Who are the Gods?*

*Gods and Their Stories.*

*Mjolnir: What makes it heavy?*

*Freya: Goddess of Love and War*

*Odin, The Allfather*

*Ragnarok: The End of the Cosmos*

*The God's Prophecies*

*Loki: God of Mischief and Chaos*

My finger hovered over that book longer than the others. I was about to pull it off the shelf when my eyes caught another further down. The words on the spine reflected the light from the window with its gold foiling.

*Gods, Magic, and Monsters*

That is where I can start. I noted where the Loki book was on the shelf so I could come back and get it later. I grabbed the other book and skimmed the first few pages, looking for the contents page.

*Page 45: Magic, And How the Gods Used it.*

I flipped through the pages and began reading the first few paragraphs, barely beginning to grasp that the Gods had specific abilities they were born with when the hair on my arms stood straight up, chasing the goosebumps down my spine.

*Someone is watching.* I turned to walk out from the back of the aisle I had tucked myself into when I heard his voice—Vali.

"Fancy meeting *you* here." He was adorned in his silver wolf mask and leaning against the shelf in front of me, blocking my path. How he appeared without me hearing him is beyond me, but here we are, and my instincts are screaming at me to un-corner myself. I attempted to ignore him completely, but he moved in front of me again.

"Not feeling up to a chat?" he asked innocently.

"No." I tried once more to step past him, and this time he closed the distance between us, forcing me to hold the open book to my chest to avoid touching him. He glanced down and raised an interested eyebrow.

"Interested in the Gods?"

"No."

"I would hope not," he said in a low voice. He smiled, but his eyes threatened.

"Do you need something from me?"

"Oh, no, no, no. Not at the moment. But if you are interested in learning more about the Gods, I could be useful to you." He plucked the book from my hands and skimmed the pages before snapping it shut with one hand.

"What do *you* know about the Gods?" I spat, turning to feign interest in looking for a new book to replace the one he had snatched from me. "And why would I bother listening to you when I'm more than capable of reading it myself?"

"Well," he chuckled under his breath. "Let's just say I've had plenty of spare time to learn all there is to know about the Gods." I hadn't realized how far down the aisle I had walked until I hit the back two walls. Vali cornered me, placing one large hand on the shelf beside me and the other mirroring the gesture on the opposite side. I turned to face him, refusing to let him see my fear. Yet, I had a strong feeling he could sense it as his silver eyes began to glow as he towered over me. "And to answer your second question, ... I don't think you have time to waste *reading* hundreds of books to obtain the information you're looking for." My face froze at his statement, and he lit up in response. My eyes shot down the aisle, calculating some form of escape that wouldn't draw too much attention. Vali laughed softly. "I won't bite." His smile was wicked. "Yet."

"I don't *need* your help," I stated confidently, opting to slip underneath his arm, taking the book from his hand as I did. "Thanks anyway."

"Alright. Maybe you don't care much about the Gods. I am just as versed in the field of *magic* ... and *monsters*." I turned quickly and shoved the book into his stomach, catching him off guard; a look of disbelief lingered in his eyes for half a second.

"Are you *insane?*" I asked under my breath. "You should know better than to talk about that so freely." I glanced around, unease growing under my skin.

"Isn't that what you were reading about?" he asked curiously, wiggling the book in his hand. Embarrassment came over me, warming the skin on my face. He clicked his tongue at me repeatedly. "I'm curious about your need to know ..." He glanced around, mocking me. "About magic," he whispered.

"I don't need to know about *anything*." I turned my attention back to the bookshelves and continued reading the spines—well, pretending to since I couldn't focus with his stare sending icy needles into my skin.

"Well," he huffed as he walked past me, placing the book back into its slot and grazing his arm against mine. When he pulled away, a familiar twist of nausea hit my stomach, and my head went foggy. "Don't fight me," he whispered. I turned to face him. The voice in my head was screaming in defiance, but my body disregarded my mind and kept me close to him.

"What are you doing?" I asked quietly. I recognized this feeling. It was the same feeling that came over me the morning someone had broken into my room at the tavern. My body wasn't mine. My actions weren't mine. I was surprised I was able to form my own words. With his arm lounging nonchalantly across the bookshelf, he slid closer to me until our faces were mere inches apart. I thought my skin would burst into flames from the disgust that was working tirelessly to rip me away from him. He lazily twirled a strand of my hair around his finger.

"Using magic," he whispered into my ear. The flames that had built up within me extinguished. "Do you want to know how? I could explain to you how it works. I could *show* you endless ways to use just *this* specific skill. ... Who knows? You might enjoy it." My breathing shallowed at the helplessness that consumed me. I had no idea how long it would take Sylve to find Mazen. *What if she doesn't?*

*What if she spends all day looking for him because we changed plans?* My thoughts teetered on the edge of control, ripping through my head with all the possible things that could happen within the next few moments.

*Breathe.*

I focused on silencing my inner chaos and decided the safest thing to do was play along. Any other option would garner too much attention. I needed information anyway, and if a magic wielder could inform me, I could save time on reading a couple of hundred books in a week.

"Okay," I stated. "You may have piqued my interest. But I must ask you something." My brows furrowed in confusion.

"Yes?" he asked eagerly, leaning his head closer to mine.

"Why are you so intent on helping me?" This caught him off guard. He pulled away to look at me curiously.

"That might be the only question I can't answer at this moment." He continued running his fingers through my hair.

"Why?"

"I still have my own learning to do. I must be certain you are who I think you are." My face twisted with a mixture of disgust and confusion. The fact that this man, whom I didn't know, admitted to studying me made me even more uncomfortable.

"Who do you *think* I am?" I asked cautiously.

"I'm unsure if I should say."

"What's the harm? I'm confident I can confirm any beliefs or doubts you may have," I retorted sarcastically. He chewed on his thoughts for a moment, which surprised me. I didn't think it would be that easy to persuade him.

"Sigyn," he responded plainly, scrutinizing my reaction. I paused, not knowing how to react, as the name did not ring a bell.

"Who?"

"The Goddess of Fidelity and Victory? Sigyn." He raised an inquisitive eyebrow. I tried desperately to keep a straight face, but I could not hold back my barking laugh for very long. I covered my mouth with my hand when someone walked past the opening of the aisle where we stood and flashed me a dirty look.

I cleared my throat before responding. "I'm sorry, but no." I looked into the wolf mask with a childish look on my face. "I can confirm one hundred percent that I am no Goddess of anything." He turned his head and stepped even closer to me, gazing into my eyes as if searching for something.

"Are you sure?" A charming grin adorned his mouth.

"Just to humor you, I will say ninety-nine percent sure." I smiled sweetly. He responded with a quiet *hmm* before moving his arm off the shelf and grabbing hold of my waist.

"Walk with me," he ordered. The same queasy feeling overcame my stomach and muddled my brain when I tried to fight him. I had no choice but to obey his demand even though I wanted to rip his arm off.

He led me up and down each aisle. "Ask me what you want to know. I'll see if I can give you what you want. ...''

Without much thought, I asked the first question on my mind. "How?"

"How what?"

"Forgive my preference to remain cryptic despite it not being *obvious* to you why I need to be."

"Right. Because *magic*," he whispered, earning an eye roll from me. "It is a form of manipulation. I can perform this through touch, others may be able to manipulate through creating images, and some can do both."

"Who has the ability to do this? Anyone?"

"Not just anyone. You have to be born with the ability to ... perform." He winked at me, but I ignored him, directing my eyes to the books we were passing. "For the record, not everyone has the ability either."

"No?" I turned back to him.

"A person, or other, would have to be born with an innate set of abilities they can grow into and utilize. Now, don't ask what other ones there are because there are too many to name." I pondered his words—*an infinite number of potential magical abilities.* Helping Sylve navigate hers might prove to be more difficult than I thought.

"Where do they come from? These abilities? How is it decided who gets what?" I asked.

"An easy yet complicated thing to explain, I'm afraid." He let go of my waist and stood before me, leaning along the bookshelf once more. "The way my mother taught me about my own abilities all fell back to the creation of the cosmos. Do you know how the Nine Realms came to be?"

"I know how they ended," I stated.

"You do?" he inquired excitedly.

"Unless my instructor fabricated the idea of Ragnarok," I retorted cautiously.

"No. That was a fulfilled prophecy." He scratched the edge of his mask near his temple. "A brief history lesson then." He smiled. "Ymir, a magical giant, was slain by Odin and cut into nine parts, creating the Nine Realms: Alfheim - home to the Light Elves; Vanaheim - home to the Vanir Gods; Jotunheim - home of the Giants; Niflheim - world of Ice, Fog, and Mist; Helheim - home of Hel and the *Dishonorable* Dead; Nidavellir - home of the Dwarves; Muspelheim - home of the Fire Giants and Demons; Asgard - home of the Aesir Gods; and Midgard - home of Humans. They ALL formed *around* Yggdrasill, the World Tree, with Midgard at its center." By the time he finished listing the Nine Realms, I had already forgotten where the story had started.

"So, just to clarify, ... a big magical giant dies and creates the Nine Realms, which are homes to a multitude of creatures and beings?"

"Yes, simply put."

"And how does this tie into magic distribution?" I asked skeptically.

"It *is* the magic distribution." He lowered his head and looked at me from under his lashes. He noted my lack of understanding and continued. "Let's envision a web." He held out his hand, fingers splayed and motioned to it with his other. "Web," he stated. I nodded in annoyed understanding, and he continued. "Now, let's pretend my fingertips represent the Nine Realms. Ignore the fact that I don't have nine and use your imagination." He pointed at the palm of his hand. "Web, Yggdrasil. Fingers, Realms." He lifted an eyebrow at me, questioning my ability to follow along.

"Surprisingly, I'm following quite easily," I responded sarcastically.

"Each Realm has its own set of abilities in its own section of the *web*, right? But the *web* itself is one entity. So, power and abilities can mesh and interlace with each other in some areas, increasing the diversity of magic. A never-ending cycle, if you think about it." He contemplated his words but shook his head, keeping his thoughts in line. "With a web, there is always a center, which in our case is *technically* Yggdrasil, but Midgard inside of that."

"So, humans don't have access to the magical web?"

"Up until Ragnarok, no."

"What happened after Ragnarok?"

"The Nine Realms were destroyed." He closed his fist, displaying the destruction of the realms.

"But ... not all nine. Midgard is still here," I crossed my arms over my chest.

"Well, all of the Realms are here as well. At least, what is left of them." He unfurled his fingers and closed his fist again. To me, it looks as if the nine realms all collapsed into Midgard, but I needed clarification.

"What do you mean, *here*? On Midgard?"

"Presumably." He remained vague. There is no way he, or anyone, could know definitively.

"Okay then, is Midgard now your theoretical 'web'?"

"No. The web is just a way to grasp the intricacy of how magic is dispelled."

"But you said that Midgard now has access to magic, post-Ragnarok?"

"No, I didn't," he said as he turned his head.

"It was implied. How else would humans be able to wield magic?"

"They can't," he stated assuredly, almost confused by my words.

Ice ran cold through my veins.

"What do you mean?" I asked cautiously.

"Well, I guess that isn't entirely true." He looked off to the side. "The Gods, Odin specifically, blessed Midgardians with Seidr when Ragnarok began—a subset of magic that offers the use of certain abilities, among other things, to help prepare Midgard for the merging of the Nine Realms, I would assume."

"What kind of abilities?"

"Prophecy, mediumship, enhanced healing capabilities towards others' ailments and wounds," Vali muttered, looking around where we stood. "I think there might be the occasional Midgardian blessed with increased strength and longevity of life. Some might be blessed more than others, but most don't receive anything at all. A prominent figure who is *chosen* to harness *all* of these abilities, who I've actually seen with my own eyes recently, is The Volva. Do you know about her?" he asked.

"Yes. She is a high priestess who is capable of communicating with the gods to tell prophecies. Or so I'm told," I answered confidently.

He nodded with approval. "Very good. See, you know more about human magic than you think you do." He smiled sarcastically, and I peeled my eyes away from his.

The only thing that aligns with Sylve so far is the healing aspect. *Maybe he doesn't remember all of them. Or perhaps he is bullshitting me entirely, and all of this is a lie.*

"What else did Odin bless Midgard with, besides these abilities?"

"Safety, for the most part, from complete eradication from existence." He smirked at the idea. This confused me, but he continued nonetheless. "An advancement of society."

"What does that mean?"

"He gave the re-birthers the knowledge of how to build an advanced society. This is why you have running water, intricate buildings, the ability to farm, yield crops, and hunt to provide food in large numbers."

"Okay. … Who are the *'re-birthers'*?"

"The Midgardians who survived Ragnarok," he stated matter-of-factly. "The ones who were left to re-birth or recreate life here on Midgard. Survivors from other Realms integrated into Midgard once their home-realms were destroyed."

My mind stuttered at connecting everything I knew with the new information he was telling me. The legends of the light and dark elves, the ones I've seen before and fought off, are not only true but explain *why* and *how* they are here in the first place. The legends of the trolls and giants and dwarves must be real, too. *They are also here on Midgard.* I suddenly felt a hel of a lot smaller standing here, knowing that such creatures walk the same ground I do, and relatively undetected. … *How is that possible?* Vali grazed my elbow with his fingers before I realized what he was doing, and the nausea returned, less intense than the first time but still detectable. "Take my arm and walk with me." He held out his arm, and I interlaced mine with his at his request, resuming our weaving through the same handful of aisles. "Anything else I could assist with?" he asked, holding his hand to his chest.

"Yes, … is there any way to determine what abilities are attributed to humans versus non-humans?"

"Well, I've already told you the abilities humans were given."

"What about the rest of them?"

"What did you call us? ... *Non-human?* That's it! The *non-humans* have them." He laughed to himself, but my face fell. I would've stopped walking if I could, but my body wasn't under my control. He guided us down the last aisle, the one I had walked down initially, and I heard Sylve call out my name from behind me. She was out of view when I turned to look for her. "Before I go, ... I wanted to reiterate something that I feel like you might have forgotten." He stepped in front of me abruptly, roughly grabbing my chin with his thumb.

"Veronica!" Sylve called out to me again with a hushed tone. She sounded closer now as if she was about to turn the corner to where we stood. Vali tipped my head back and moved his head closer to mine, grabbing my attention for the final time.

"Keep ... away ... from Loki," he threatened; my eyes widened in time with his grin, while the same terror I felt at the Dark Sun raced through my body. "And you might want to wrap things up here. The King is about to be informed of your proximity to the Crown." Within half a second, Vali disappeared from in front of me. Nothing but an empty aisle of full bookshelves was before me.

*Non-human. What is he if he is non-human?* Vali is the man who threatened me at the tavern. Not only did he manipulate my emotions and my body, but also my mind. He sent images into my head so I could see and *feel* them. *Non-Human.* He is warning me about Loki. Loki is the name of a God, but ... could they be? The one I've spent time with ... is an actual *God.* Sylve grabbed my arm and turned me around to face her, tearing me away from my thoughts. I'll have to push my potential findings to the side. Mazen stood just behind Sylve with a bewildered look on his face.

"Haven't you found anything?" she asked, looking between my empty arms and the full aisle behind me.

"I ... Uh—"

"What are you doing here, Veronica?" Mazen asked quietly once he'd pushed past Sylve.

"Studying," I answered, keeping my eyes locked with Sylve, trying to convey that I've learned something important despite being empty-handed.

"Are you okay?" she cut in.

"No," I responded, turning to Mazen. "What the fuck is going on?" I whispered to him. He motioned for us to walk down the aisle, tucking us away from prying eyes and ears.

"Nothing good, knowing what I know," he whispered as he glanced around us, shifting his weight from one foot to the other nervously. "I think they ...," he motioned around his eyes with his fingers, referencing the masked warriors throughout the Kingdom, "are Skirrians," he spoke so quietly under his breath that I barely heard him. "And the King has everyone's eye out for you."

"Has she been formally banned from the city?" Sylve asked.

"No, but that doesn't mean she is welcome. I've been listening; if he finds you here, you won't leave," he warned, raking his hand through his hair. "Sylve filled me in on what you need to know." He removed a bag he had secured around his chest from over the top of his head, opened it, and walked down the aisle, grabbing books as he went and placing them in the bag. "I can't tell you what I know, but these should be the most helpful." I noticed the Loki book was still on the shelf, so I grabbed it and tucked it under my arm.

"Mazen," I said his name quietly to get his attention. He finished grabbing the books and closed the bag, handing it to me. "Come with us."

He shook his head slowly. "I can't. ... Erikka—," he sighed, rolling his neck. My jaw tightened. "Things are complicated, even more so over these past couple of weeks. I can't leave her here. ... I'm the only original guard of hers left. The others have all been replaced."

I took my concern for her safety and shoved it deep into my personal pit of hel, locking it away. "I understand," I said and nodded my acknowledgment.

"How much time do we have?" Sylve asked. Mazen looked between us, understanding that she wasn't asking about our escape window. He looked conflicted, the muscles in his jaw flexing.

He began to shake his head. "Not long," he spoke under his breath, his eyes alerting us to the severity he couldn't articulate.

"Okay. Let's go." Sylve turned and led us down the aisle toward the stairs but stopped just before taking the first step down. "Shit." She turned back to us and pushed me away from the stairs. I glanced over the railing and saw a group of masked warriors speaking with the nice woman from earlier, who pointed them in my direction. One of them was wearing a hooded cloak, and once they reached for the railing, I saw a brand of the Kingdom's insignia on their forearm. It stirred up a blurry memory, one that hovered just out of reach.

I turned away from the stairs. "Fuck him," I muttered under my breath.

"Who?" Sylve asked.

"Vali," I pushed between clenched teeth.

"Who?" Mazen and Sylve asked in unison.

"I'll explain later, we've got to find a way out, and it won't be from downstairs." I turned to Mazen. "You know this place better than anyone. Have any helpful ideas?"

He motioned for us to follow him as he climbed the next set of stairs leading to the top floor. When we reached landing, he made a sharp turn toward the back of the building. "There is a window in this back corner that I like to open to sit and read. I've never scaled the side of the building, so you'll be the first to do *that*." We followed him past rows of shelving until we neared the window. I tightened the strap to the bag of books across my chest while he unlatched the window and pushed it out and up. Both he and Sylve stuck their heads out to assess our situation.

"Lucky for us, we can shimmy down the roof's peak to get us just past the second floor," Sylve noted.

"There is a stained-glass window on the first floor, but if you can't avoid it, you shouldn't draw too much attention," he instructed, then ducked back inside.

"Thank you," she said as she bent down and slipped through the window, lowering herself to the roofline below. Once she had cleared the window space, Mazen waved me over. He offered a hand to help lower me down since I lacked the inches that Sylve could use to her advantage. Once my feet touched the roof, he tucked his head back inside.

"Mazen!" I called for him in a hushed tone. He stuck his head over the side of the building. "We have a horse tied out front of the library."

"If you can get out of the castle walls without him, I will bring him past the bridge and meet you near the center of Sol's Town." I nodded, and he disappeared once more.

"Wait! Mazen!" I called again, and his head popped out, but this time, irritation and anxiousness were written across his face. "Thank you."

"You're welcome. Now get out of here!" he demanded, closing the window.

I took a breath and began my descent from the roof. By the time I had reached the edge that dropped me off between the first two floors, Sylve had made it to the ground. I looked around to see the steps she took but everything seemed just out of reach for me. I looked at Sylve for some guidance.

"Lower yourself down past the edge of the roof. There is another smaller jut-out just below you to land on. Then lower yourself to the ground." I nodded at her instructions. I would do anything she said without question; even though I couldn't see the roof she said was beneath me, I knew it was there. When I let go of the roof and dropped, my feet found the ground. I landed semi-gracefully next to her, and we both turned toward the castle.

"Do you think we should try the town?" I questioned, wondering if going toward the castle would be the best idea.

"You saw how many guards were crawling all over the place this morning. Now that they know you are in the area, they've probably been sent *away* from the castle."

"Making it the smarter move to work around it than through a shit ton of guards. Got it! I'm caught up now." We both pulled the hood of our cloaks over our heads and quickened our pace as we crossed the road between the library and the castle, sticking to the outer wall I had instructed her to follow earlier. We had both dressed the part to avoid being noticed if something like this were to happen—black floor-length dresses with black cloaks to match any of the warriors on duty.

We turned the corner that led us to the back side of the castle and nearly ran into a door that opened just as we approached it. A woman in a hooded cloak stepped out and stopped in surprise. When she looked up at us, my legs went numb, and my anger boiled. Instinctively, I reached for the short sword at my side, but Sylve's hand caught my wrist.

"Veronica," Erikka whispered my name as if she were seeing a ghost.

"Don't make this difficult, please. We are just trying to leave, Your Majesty," Sylve spoke softly and offered a tight curtsy. Although she seemed more than polite, I knew how quickly she could turn that off if she needed to.

"You both are extremely lucky that *I* found you first!" she exclaimed, sounding as if she was reprimanding us. Sylve and I looked at each other. "Follow me, and I can get you out of here." She pulled a key from the sleeve of her shirt. I noticed that she wasn't wearing her kingfisher peony pendant or crown and was in a maid's dress. She reopened the door she had just come through and slipped inside. I caught the door just before it closed and hesitated. *This could be a trap.*

"This could be a trap," Sylve whispered, echoing my thoughts and tugging gently on the back of my cloak. "We can't trust her."

"I was just thinking the same thing."

"Close the door. We can walk along the backside of the castle ourselves." She analyzed the direction we were heading. Erikka returned to the door, opening it enough to stand directly in front of me. The scent of lilac wafted past my nose, bringing back memories I didn't need clouding my head. She looked between Sylve and me.

"I know you don't trust me, rightfully so. But please, just for a few minutes, pretend," Erikka begged softly, pleading with her melancholy blue eyes. Sylve suddenly pushed my back, sending me straight into Erikka and down a few steps I didn't know were there, closing the door softly behind her.

"It looks like we don't have another option with the group of guards making their way along this face of the castle," she said under her breath. I had grabbed Erikka to catch myself from falling and only now realized I was still holding her elbows as she held mine. I let go and set myself straight, pulling away from her touch. Erikka cleared her throat and started down the stairs.

"Hold on," I called out, bringing Erikka to a halt. "Where are you taking us?" I asked sourly.

"I'm going to lead you down into the dungeons and out the other side near a hole in the curtain wall," she explained, attempting to wave us down the darkened stairwell.

"That's not suspicious now, is it?" I asked sarcastically, standing my ground as Sylve held her ear to the door. Erikka stopped and turned back to me, climbed the few steps of stairs between us, and dropped to her knees.

"Please, Veronica. Please come with me. He *can't* find you here. ... I'm begging you to give me an ounce of trust. One last time." I felt my mouth open, but no words came out. When I turned to look at Sylve, her eyes were wide as she looked at the Princess of Sol on her knees in front of us.

"Fine," Sylve cut in. "No funny shit, Your Majesty." Sylve's final attempt to remain diplomatic wasn't her best attempt, but it would do.

We followed her down the stairs. It was almost too dark to see despite the staggered oil lamps every couple of feet. After a few minutes, the ground flattened out, and iron bars and metal shackles were squared off and hanging from the walls and ceiling. The smell of rust filled the air and the sudden temperature change sent a small shiver along my back.

Erikka placed a finger against her lips—a signal for us to remain silent as we passed occupied cells. We turned a corner to exit the dungeon and were walking down a slim stone hallway when I had a realization.

"Where is your guard?" I asked cautiously. Sylve slowed down half a pace in front of me at my question, coming to the same potentially dangerous realization.

"The castle went on lockdown, so she is currently stationed outside my private quarters. She doesn't even know I'm gone," she explained quickly.

"How did you get out without her noticing?" I questioned, curious to hear her answer.

"I've got my secrets," she stated plainly.

"Yeah, clearly," I spat. She stopped for a moment and threw a glare—one only I knew was pretentious—in my direction. Sylve tensed, but I stood my ground and stared right back.

"When your life isn't your own, you've got to have one thing to yourself," Erikka explained before she turned and continued walking until we met another flight of stairs that took us back to ground level. As we neared the wooden door, she pulled out the key from earlier and unlocked it, opening it just enough for her to check the surroundings and exit. "Straight ahead, there is a slim break in the wall. I pull the vines over it to keep it unnoticed. Just push them out of the way, and you should be able to squeeze through," she instructed plainly, keeping an eye at the top of the wall for guards.

"Thanks for your mercy, Princess." Sylve curtsied to her once more and cut across the small gap between the castle and the wall, pushing past the vines and disappearing into the void Erikka had promised would be there. I nodded my thanks and went to follow Sylve but was caught by the wrist.

"Veronica," she whispered lightly. I looked over my shoulder at her without feeling, without emotion, waiting for her to say something, but she didn't. Instead, her sad gaze met the floor, and she released me from her grasp. I turned and hurried to the wall, pushing past the greenery and slipping through the tight space, having to stop to readjust the bag of books that kept getting caught in the awkward space. Once I slipped out the other end, I found Sylve sitting against the wall waiting for me.

"Well, that was a wild ride," she breathed out. I nodded and quickly wiped away an involuntary tear that had broken past my walls. "Hey, ... are you okay?"

"I'm fine." I offered her my hand and leveraged myself to help her stand. "Let's go find your father's horse." I winked, and she rolled her eyes. We walked for about a half-hour into Sol's town before we spotted Mazen near a vegetable cart. I whistled between my fingers and caught his attention.

"I was beginning to get worried," he admitted, rubbing the back of his neck.

"It looks like it," I joked, eyeing the crate of cabbage he had just purchased.

"Well, I had to do something with my time." He laughed, handing the reins over to Sylve.

"Thank you," she said softly, causing Mazen to blush.

"You are welcome." He bowed slightly and stepped out of our way as we mounted up. "Don't come back," he ordered quietly. I looked at him curiously. "You know what I mean," he reiterated.

"I know, I know. That just sounded *rude* coming from you, and it threw me for a second." I winked at him, and he waved me off. "Stay safe," I called out.

"You, too!" He waved.

"Why didn't you tell him about Erikka?" Sylve asked as she led us toward her father's home. I let out a deep sigh before answering.

"Because ... she needs to have one thing," I admitted, laying my head gently against Sylve's back in mental and emotional exhaustion.

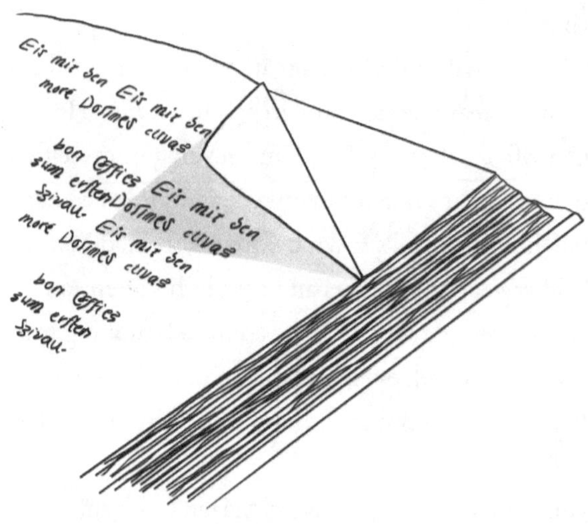

# Twenty-Six

We left early the following day to head to the Inn after coming to terms with the amount of literature we needed to consume by the end of the week. Sylve warned her father about the increased threat within the castle walls and urged him to spend the rest of his time preparing for his expedition at her and Sindre's home in Lykke if he could. He promised her he would and planned to stop by on his way through town.

I insisted on leading our journey back home so Sylve could get in a few hours of reading. My brain wasn't quiet enough to focus on such a task, and on top of that, I was hopeful Sylve would find the information explaining where her abilities came from before I had to explain what I had learned in the past twenty-four hours. I had handed her "Gods, Magic and Monsters" a few hours ago, and she was enveloped within its words until we arrived at our destination.

"Find anything … good? Helpful? Enlightening?" I asked while I held out my hand to assist her as she jumped onto the ground.

"I'm not sure," she admitted, grabbing her bag from the back and slinging it over her shoulder. I tilted my head in response. "It's done a great job explaining Gods and their magical abilities but not so much on humans."

My stomach tightened nervously as we walked through the back door. I turned to lock it. We both quickly walked through the house to make sure no one had broken in before I retrieved the books from my bag and stacked them on the table.

I placed my hands on my hips and faced Sylve, who had already grabbed a blanket and wrapped herself in it, taking her spot on the couch. "Do you remember Vali? Or at least ... the fact that I mentioned someone by that name yesterday on our way out of the library?" I questioned.

"Yeah, what was that about? Does he work there?"

"No. He showed up in one of those masks around the time I was banned from underground fighting." My smile faded at the painful memory—my concern for worrying Bryn, our argument the night I got home, our talk on the lawn while we watched the sunrise, ... and his shared concern for Calder's reaction to my bruised face.

She looked at me through thoughtful eyes, connecting the dots. "A Skirrian?"

"I assume."

"What about him?" she asked curiously, removing her thumb from between the book's pages and closing it completely.

"He found me at the library shortly after I got there, and within a few minutes, I realized he was the other magic wielder I had encountered at The Dark Sun."

"How do you know? If he wears a mask at the castle—"

"He used his magic on me. He called it a manipulation type of magic, and I recognized how it made me feel at the tavern. It's hard to explain."

"You don't need to. ... What was he doing with you? Did he try to hurt you?" she asked, concern growing in her voice. I decided to keep his odd interest in me supposedly being some Goddess to myself.

"No. He found me, and it started as just pestering, but he noticed the book I was reading and then insisted on sharing his knowledge on the subject matter." I rolled my eyes and shook my head, sitting in the chair across from her. She tilted her head with curiosity. "If what he said was true, then I've learned something I must share with you."

"Okay?" Sylve drawled, her eyebrows furrowing with worry.

"He started off by explaining magic as an entire entity. Where it comes from, how abilities are distributed, and a general idea of magic types."

"The book I was reading on the way back touched on that and attributed certain abilities to things in specific Realms and whatnot."

"Oh, good. So, I don't have to revisit that?" I laughed.

"No." She chuckled in response. "I think I grasped that pretty easily."

"Alright. Well, ... I asked what kind of abilities *humans* have or were gifted with, however he worded it. ..." I leaned forward onto my knees and looked at her before continuing. "He mentioned abilities that heal, prophecy, medium-ship ..." I let the air still between us, waiting for her to say something.

"And?" she asked nervously. I shook my head slowly in response. "What other abilities are there?"

"He said, besides those and *maybe* enhanced strength and longer lives, ... humans can't wield magic." We stared at each other for a moment, and I noticed the rise and fall of her chest quicken.

"Then what about his manipulation magic?" she asked in a whisper.

"I don't know. ..."

"What about—" She held her hands out, a faint light building in her palms before she clenched her fists, the faint swirling of magic under her skin fading as quickly as it appeared.

I stood and walked over to her, laying a supportive arm around her shoulders as I sat beside her. "We will figure it out, Syl," I reassured quietly. "Nothing changes. Nothing. I'm here with you." I shook her lightly, angling my head to catch her concerned eyes. "We will figure it out," I soothed softly. "Our answers are going to be in these books somewhere, okay? If we find anything, crease the corner of the pages. We can group review those at the end of the day, try and piece together what we can." She nodded blankly, and my heart sank in my chest. I can't imagine what she is feeling at this moment. I don't want her to feel alone. If only Sindre were here or her father. "When did your father say he would be in town?" I asked as I got up from the couch.

"Uh—He … uh ... he said later this evening," she stammered.

"Maybe we can ask *him* about it? Maybe he knows something that he hasn't shared with you guys?" I suggested softly.

"I—He ..." She chewed on her lip for a second. "It couldn't hurt. The worst outcome is he might think I'm insane."

"Hey, at least he will think we both have lost it and not just you."

"Right," she responded numbly. Her mind was far from here, and I wasn't sure how to get her back.

"What do you need right now? How can I help you?" I asked quietly, placing a supportive hand on her knee.

She looked up at me slowly, lost in her own head. "Can you just sit with me?" she responded slowly.

"Of course." I offered her a sad smile and shifted through the books on the table until I found *Loki, God of Mischief and Chaos.* I then laid back on the couch, giving her the space she wanted while remaining present for support whenever she needed it.

A few hours passed, and Sylve had since sprawled out over my lap while we both dove into our books. She finished the one she started on the way back to Lykke and moved on to another, *The Life of the Gods,* while I was only halfway through mine. However, I was soaking up all the words on the pages, fear settling in the forefront of my mind for what I had come to accept as the truth.

According to the text, Loki was, or is, a major God most noticeably recognized as the cause of Ragnarok. He is the son of Farbauti—a Jotunn and Laufey—a Goddess, with two siblings, Helblindi and Byleistr; blood brothers with the Allfather, Odin; married thrice: once to Glut, then to Angrboda, and finally ... Sigyn. He has six children: three with the giantess Angrboda, whom I had known about through my teachings at Kron castle—Hel, the Goddess of Death; Fenrir, the Giant Wolf; then Jormungandr, the World Serpent. He birthed the eight-legged horse Sleipnir. The book also mentions Loki had two children with Sigyn—twin boys Narfi and ... Vali?

I paused and laid the book flat on Sylve's back, trying to connect this to what I'd experienced, but it didn't make any sense. Vali doesn't seem to admire Loki when he speaks of him, but the text says that Loki had a son named Vali? *Is it just a coincidence?* I thought about what Vali said. He thought that I was Sigyn, or at least trying to decide for himself if that was who I might be. As absurd as that sounds, I guess it would make sense for him to search for his mother. But why would he *threaten* his own mother to stay *away* from her husband? I rubbed my hand down my face and groaned, forgetting Sylve was in my lap.

"What's got your brain aching?" she asked, keeping her eyes on her book.

"I don't think I could explain my confusion if I tried. The Gods' family trees are so fucking confusing," I moaned before picking my book off her back.

"You're telling me. The way the magic is split into such fine categories has my brain fried. On one page, it will say, '*Gods are born into specific roles that come with certain abilities to aid them in performing these roles,*' but on the next page, it will tell me that the Aesir Gods learned how to wield magic in different ways than the Vanir Gods, and the Aesir Gods were shunned for it. Oh, my Gods, nothing is making any fucking sense." She shook her head as she turned the page and continued on.

As I dove back into my reading, I came upon the story of Loki and Sigyn. I couldn't help but let my nosiness kick into overdrive, wanting to learn how their marriage came to be. My stomach was in knots as I read. I felt as if I was peeking behind a curtain into someone else's life, as if Loki would burst into the room at any moment, and embarrassment would flood through me as if I had been caught reading someone's private journal entries.

The book says that Sigyn was betrothed to someone else when she first met Loki, and although they had gotten along, the Goddess was set on marrying the God Theoric. Loki had him murdered and then cast an illusion on himself to pass as Theoric until after the wedding ceremony was complete. Only then did he reveal his true form, angering the Gods with such a dirty trick. ... *So this Goddess, Sigyn, didn't even INTEND to marry Loki in the first place? Sick.*

Despite my disgust with the situation, I carried on, learning that marriage was the Gods' most absolute binding law, and nothing, not even Odin's willingness, could break the bond once it had been made. Odin himself offered Sigyn the chance to look for a way out of the agreement, but she ... declined. She declined his offer and instead devoted herself to a marriage she had been tricked into.

I shook my head and closed the book, frustration building in my chest for unknown reasons. I tapped Sylve on the back so I could get up, and I went to the kitchen for a drink.

"Do you want one?" I called back to the main sitting room.

"Please!" she responded.

When I returned, Sylve had her hand outstretched so I could place a mug in it before I sat down. I had only taken a few sips of wine to refocus when Sylve nearly choked on her drink.

"Are you alright?" I asked, watching her wipe the remnants of her drink off her chin and place the mug on the table in front of us.

"Holy hel, Veronica," she stated in disbelief, looking between me and the pages she held.

"What?" I asked, concern weighing my words.

"It says here that …, 'Gods could and would form relationships with creatures from other Realms, making their offspring Half-Gods and granting them partial magical abilities. These offspring would be called minor Deities ... or Demi-Gods'," she read aloud.

"And?" I asked cautiously.

She looked up at me, fear of herself held in her eyes. "These offspring ... would usually inherit an offensive and defensive set of magical abilities from their Godly parent, or *parents* if both wield magic."

"Okay. So, … your mother. Do you remember her?" She shook her head absently. "Not at all?"

"It's always just been Sindre and our father. I—I don't remember her," she admitted. Her eyebrows met in deep thought, as she rubbed her forehead in frustration.

"Okay. Has the book said anything about what *type* of abilities these minor deities had?"

"It hasn't specified anything. But it confirmed what you said earlier about humans and their abilities. They are extremely limited and have never ONCE been described as magical." She flipped through the pages of the book, stopping to glance over one every now and then before closing it and tossing it into the finished book pile.

"Well, your father might know -"

"Why wouldn't he have told us if he knew?" she snapped, throwing her hands in the air. "Why would he keep such a secret from us? What did he expect to happen to us?"

"Hey!" I interrupted, dropping to my knees in front of her and taking her flailing hands in mine. "Hey, we won't know until we ask him. Okay?" I ran my thumbs on the backs of her hands reassuringly. "What we *do* know is that you are a magical being, as odd as that sounds. We've seen it. Your magic is beautiful; you have so much potential to expand on, and you can do amazing things with these gifts. And regardless of what exactly you might be, ... human or Demi-God? Deity ...? You are still my best friend, and I will be right by your side throughout this entire ordeal." I squeezed her hands and noticed her eyes were welling with tears. My words were met with silence. "Tell me what you are thinking about," I demanded softly.

"I'm scared, V," she admitted. "Never EVER would a possibility like this cross my mind. What the *fuck* do we do?" She removed her hands from mine and stood to pace the room. "What about Sindre? He won't believe me when I tell him. He— We are twins, V. We are one and the same. That means he must have some abilities, too, right?"

"It's possible, but we can talk about that later, once we are back in Frith with Sindre," I advised quietly. "We really should prioritize speaking with your father tonight, if possible. Get that out of the way so we can have a better idea of what to do going forward."

"You're right," she declared, placing her hands on her waist. "I'll confront my father and find out the truth, and I can inform Sindre once we get back." She nodded at me, turned, and walked into the kitchen. I moved to take a spot on the couch as she walked back in with a plate full of dried meats and two potatoes. "We need more energy to get us through these books this week," she declared and laughed. "It seems as if it is going to take a harder toll on us than intended." I snatched a piece of jerky from the table, ripped off a chunk, and chewed it until it settled into my cheek.

"You are damn right about that!" I agreed and moved the Loki book over to the finished pile, grabbing a new one and settling in next to Sylve for our next reading binge.

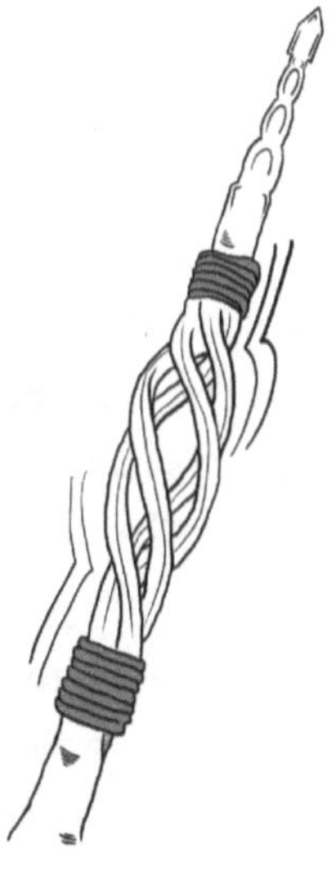

# Twenty-Seven

A few hours passed when a knock at the door nearly made Sylve and me jump out of our skin. I insisted Sylve stay seated as I grabbed my knife, tucked it into the back of my pants, and hurried over to the door. I mindlessly opened it, expecting to find Gudmund, but instead was met with a stranger and their entourage. However, even though the woman standing there was someone I had not met, I knew who she was by her presence alone.

Standing in the middle of four individuals, their hoods fully drawn over their heads—male or female, I couldn't tell from the identical shapeless forest-green cloaks—was a young-looking woman with pale white skin and long blonde hair that fell past her waist. She was adorned with woven jewelry and a few belts, with varying-sized satchels secured to them. She wore a blood-red dress with long white sleeves under a thick woven cloak. Atop her head, she had a headdress made from antlers with an assortment of raven feathers and woodland foliage woven within and around each point. But the most recognizable accessory was the staff that she held in her hand, which was heavily adorned with numerous rings and bracelets. Towering over her, the staff was made from solid iron with a distaff near the top, a small replica of a house sitting just above that, and bronze detailing swirled around its entirety. Anyone would know who this woman was with a simple glance—*The Volva.*

"Sylve," I cautioned over my shoulder. I could hear her throw off the blanket as she hurried over to the door, her hand on the weapon at her leg.

"Oh!" She moved her hand away from the hilt of her weapon, wiping both hands on the front of her pants. "We're so sorry. Uh— We weren't expecting—"

"I was called here, not summoned," The Volva interjected smoothly, bowing her head forward slightly.

It's customary that you allow The Volva into your home if she were to show up, offer her the head of the table, and treat her as you would a Royal. So, I moved to the side, as did Sylve, "We don't have a table here," I admitted, and we motioned her in.

"One is not needed." She waved her tattooed hand toward the sitting room, and the four hooded disciples moved in unison. They pushed the couch out of the way and put a single chair near the center of the room in front of the hearth. Once they had finished redecorating, they turned to me and Sylve, placed a hand on our shoulders, and guided us to the floor in front of the chair. Only after we were sitting uncomfortably on our knees did The Volva move from the door to sit down, pounding her staff heavily on the ground—I'm assuming—to initiate her ritual. A heavy silence fell over the room as a member of her entourage pulled out a narrow strip of black cloth and stood behind The Volva, placing the fabric over her eyes and securing it behind her head. Sylve and I shared a confused glance between each other.

"May I ask *why* you are here tonight?" I cut in, noticing The Volva going rigid before relaxing. She pointed her finger at me and firmly held the staff in her other hand.

"I've been called to *you,*" she droned mindlessly. It seemed like she wasn't entirely with us in the room, as if when the cloth was placed over her eyes, she was transported somewhere. I noticed that two of her disciples began to play the drums, which again seemed to appear out of nowhere. The beat was painfully slow in the beginning but gradually quickened as the Priestess began to recite some incantation I couldn't understand. "You are lost, child?" she asked into the air between us.

"Um ... Not necessarily?" I responded sheepishly.

"Then, you know your fate?"

"Does anyone?" I jested.

A small smile played at the corner of her lips, but it suddenly turned into a scowl. She sat straighter in her seat, nearly hanging onto her staff for support as she held out the palm of her hand to me.

"This reading has been called to me by the Gods, and as their loyal servant, I will do everything in my power to honor them and continue to use the gifts they blessed me with. To deny this calling, this reading, would be equivalent to denying the Gods themselves. Do you accept this?" she asked. I rolled my eyes and shook my head, turning to find Sylve tight-lipped and urging me toward The Volva with her head, a scolding look in her eyes.

I let out a sigh before placing my hand in hers half-heartedly. "Yes, I accept your reading," I conceded. In less than a second, she clutched my hand in a death grip, holding my wrist at a painful angle.

"You are in pain. Mourning. Death is a catalyst for what awaits you," she spoke. I looked over at Sylve, who seemed entranced by the whole experience, unlike myself. The deep beating of the drums steadied and fell into a hypnotic rhythm, aiding in my ability to relax despite the discomfort in my hand. "I see a second life—a choice— No, choices. You were gifted the freedom to choose without interference. Memories will not hinder you here." She turned her head to the side, toward her staff. "I see Ravens. They are also a gift for you to use as needed in this new life. A gift from ... the *Gods*," she rasped, her last word breathless. "The *Allfather* bestowed them to *you* as a gift," she reiterated.

I looked at Sylve again for reassurance, but she wasn't paying me any mind. *What the fuck is this woman talking about?* Gifts from Gods and second lives and Ravens. *Wait ... Is she talking about the Raven from the castle?* She said *they* were a gift, but I've only seen one.

"The throne is yours to take," she continued monotonously, getting ready to say her next piece without a second thought.

"What?" I interrupted, and she went rigid again as if I had halted the blood flow in her body.

"The throne is yours to take," she repeated solemnly.

"What throne?"

"I do not know any more than what the spirits across the Realms tell me."

"Wha—?"

"Shh!" Sylve shushed me and punched my arm. "She can't elaborate, V. We can think about it later, now hush." The Volva nodded her appreciation towards Sylve before regripping my hand. She cocked her head to the side and then snapped her head in my direction; an eerie feeling settled over me as she looked at me from behind the cloth.

"Are you a fellow witch?" she asked, surprised.

"N— No?" I answered, my eyebrows furrowed in confusion.

"You are not practicing?" she repeated. "Working with Deities?" I felt Sylve's eyes snap to mine, which I slowly turned to meet. The look on her face was closer to excitement than confusion, but I felt The Volva wasn't referring to my friendship with Sylve.

"No. I am not versed in witchcraft," I reiterated quietly.

"Do *not* lie to me," she snapped, her sharp nails digging into the back of my hand. I tried to jerk away, but her grip did not yield.

"I wouldn't!" I hissed back.

"I can sense a Deity attached to your spirit—*intertwined*. You are lying."

"I have no clue what you are talking about." I used my other hand to rip hers off mine, rubbing my hand once it was free. "I'm not working with any Deities. I don't even know how someone does that in the first place. I have more important things to be doing than playing pretend with the Gods," I spat. She gripped her staff tighter, and the whites of her knuckles shone against the candlelight that was illuminating the room.

"I'm curious," she remarked as stood slowly, holding her palm out in front of her. One of her assistants went to her, emptying the contents of a small satchel into it. "What kind of power does one have to intertwine a Deity with their *spirit,* their *soul,* and not even realize it has happened?" She abruptly hurled the contents she held into my face, taking me by surprise. The smell of lavender hit my nose as I quickly wiped the herbs from my face and fell back on my ass. She raised her staff and struck the ground hard, sending out a deep ring of vibrations. The hearth behind her chair caught fire, and the room fell silent. The

Volva turned her head to the side, noticing the energy that had entered the room before turning back to me, the cloth still covering her eyes. She held out her hands again, and another person emptied the contents of a different satchel into her palm.

"Don't you—" This time, I was met with rosemary to the face, the smell hitting me just as roughly as the lavender. I scrambled to my feet to defend myself from more herbal attacks but was swiftly restrained by two of the four followers in the room and forced back onto my knees. "What the fuck is going on?!" I groaned under the pressure of their grip. Their strength took me by surprise; their shapeless outlines led me to believe they wouldn't be much of a match. Sylve started toward me but was soon grabbed by the other two and pinned to the floor. The flame in the hearth grew significantly in response to the herbs being thrown at me. "What kind of magic does *that*? What are you doing?" I asked The Volva directly, nervous about disrespecting her further but unsure of my safety.

"That is not *me*, child." Again, she held out her hand, and it was filled promptly. Whatever contents she held were immediately thrown into my face while she pounded her staff onto the floor. My rage grew with the flame that awakened behind her. The fire had grown so full and fast that flames licked at the edge of the opening, risking escape from its confinement. "Protective, it seems, of you. This Deity—who is it?" she asked me sternly.

"I don't know what you are talking about!" I screamed in response.

"I will find out for myself if you continue to deceive me and refuse to answer." She held out her hand again; it was filled, then thrown into my face once more. The staff pounded onto the floor. I struggled against the grip of the two people who held me.

"I'm telling the truth!" I yelled, letting my rage carry me forward, nearly breaking free from my hold and coming face to face with my accuser. I knew she couldn't see me, but I could feel her burning glare through the blindfold.

"Fine." She reached around my waist and took the knife I had stashed in my waistband earlier. She felt it in her hands, sensed its weight, then pointed it in my direction. The flames roared higher, crawling up the wall and threatening to burn the interior of the Inn, stealing my attention from the blade that pressed into my neck just below my chin. My concern shifted from my well-being to the imminent threat of the out-of-control blaze. "Then I think we can work together to find an answer on who this is."

Sylve started to fight against the people who held her down, getting to one knee before she yelled out in distress. "Stop this! This is madness!"

"As is the way with *Gods*," she stated confidently just before she dragged the tip of the knife across my throat, splitting my skin open enough for blood to spill onto the floor.

The fire exploded up the wall. A wave of warm air blasted across the room, and I swore I heard Sylve scream my name, but my mind kicked into survival mode. I fell to my knees and pulled my hands up to my neck, running my fingers along the cut to assess the damage. I breathed in, and a slight sense of relief settled over me. I turned to look at Sylve, but she wasn't beside me. Instead, she was now lying on the floor against the wall due to the blast that followed the heat wave. The Priestess and her entourage were also scattered around the room, but it was The Volva who was splayed out face down beside me on the floor. An imperious yet familiar voice sounded from the hearth.

"*The Way of the Gods?*" I looked up at the flame now fanning out across the ceiling and watched in disbelief and terror as a man emerged from its center. No, not a man. A God—Loki.

Loki emerged from the flames as if they were forming him with each step he took further from the hearth. His broad chest was bare and smooth, with the exception of a scarred rune on the left side of his chest, similar to the ones on his hands and neck. He had horns like a chamois, protruding from his head just past his hairline, stretching at least a foot or two above him. His scarlet hair was set ablaze. Despite stepping away from the fire looming behind him, two fiery strands spiraled around his horns like vines. His green eyes were incandescent, not only with rage but with light. I was frozen to the floor where I had fallen onto my knees and let my hands fall limply in my lap, watching silently as he walked over to me. His thumb lightly grasped my chin, lifting my eyes to meet his. He barely tilted his head to examine the wound on my neck, and his jaw tightened in annoyance.

"No. ... The Gods are set in their ways, actually." His hand drifted away, his fingers gently swiping up blood, and slowly walked over to The Volva, who remained on her hands and knees, paralyzed in fear.

Loki moved like a feline, taking each step carefully as he stalked towards the Volva, dropping to one knee and lifting his hand to gently grasp the cloth that still covered her eyes. He singed it with the tips of his fingers, letting a small flame catch and gradually burn the fabric until it disappeared. Terror instantly washed over her face.

"But *madness*? That's *my* specialty," his words turned sinister, and a wicked grin split across his face, sending a shiver across my skin.

I snuck a peek at Sylve. She had regained consciousness and silently looked on in horror at what was playing out before her.

"We both know there are other ways you could have figured out who I was. Am I wrong?" he asked greedily. The Volva's skin turned a sickly shade of gray. She remained frozen on her hands and knees before the God of Mischief and Chaos. He turned his head, waiting for a response.

"N—n—no. You—you are correct," she stuttered, eyes bulging in fear.

"I know," he responded and stood swiftly, grabbing The Volva under her arm and lifting her to stand next to him. Her knees wobbled, and he grabbed her by both shoulders, keeping her standing for a moment. "Stand in confidence before the consequences of your actions, my dear." His smile was so deadly, so predatory, that it would instinctively overwhelm anyone with the urge to flee. "No one likes a back peddler." Loki turned and walked across the room, picking up the staff lying on the floor, and returned to the Priestess, offering it to her. "Here, would this help?" he asked sarcastically.

"N—no. I—I—I can't." Her arms and legs trembled as he held it out for her to take.

"You will," he demanded coolly. She obliged, reaching for it and immediately leaning against it for support. "That's better. Don't you feel more *connected* to the Gods this way? You can *hear* our calls and our wishes, right?" She nodded silently. "Just like you should have listened to *my* call, right? My wish for you to *stop* harassing her. ..." He turned his head to look at me, his eyes softening before hardening his glare as he looked back into the eyes of my offender.

"I—I—"

"You ignored me?! Even as you held this ... staff?" He motioned down its length with his hand mockingly. "Even with my very obvious warnings?" He indicated toward the fire blazing along the walls and ceiling behind her. She remained still, tears brimming over the edge of her eyes.

"I—I apologize. I— Please forgive me—" Just as she started to kneel, his hand caught her by the throat, and she dropped her staff, sending it clattering to the floor as her hands grasped onto his for air.

"Let me remind you, … or rather, let me ask you. I want to see what you *know*. Who gave you your gifts?" he asked calmly. His hold remained firm around her neck.

"The Gods," her answer came between labored breaths.

"And what am I?"

"God of ... Mischief."

"I am." He smiled proudly, lifting her off the ground and carrying her back toward the chair, now off-centered to the hearth. "So, I guess first and foremost, you're welcome." He nearly slammed her down into the chair before he continued speaking. "Then, just so everyone here knows, I can easily rip these abilities from your being and let *the Way of the Gods* choose the next Volva. … Leaving you …," he remarked, examining her from head to toe as she sat in the chair shaking, tears streaming down her cheeks, "quite dead." He smiled viciously at her tears.

"I— I understand. I will— will abide by the will of the Gods," she sputtered between sobs.

"Good." He turned to look at me again, analyzing my hands that still clutched my bleeding throat, and the calmness that enveloped him a moment before disappeared. "Now, for your punishment!" He slammed his hands down on top of hers, locking them onto the arms of the chair. The Volva's eyes widened as she tried to pull herself away from him. "Don't EVER lay a hand, knife, or otherwise, on things that belong to ME." His hands erupted into flames, starting at his elbows, wrapping down to encase hers. Her screams of pain were deafening.

Within the same second, Sylve leaped from where she was and attempted to close the distance between her and Loki to attack. But he knew. He raised a hand in the air, pulling flames from the ceiling into his palm, and brought a stream of fire down on Sylve. A pleading cry left my lips as I watched her brace for impact. She used her magic to form a translucent shield along her forearm, blocking the attack from above, looking just as stunned as Loki did. This interaction gave me enough time to revive myself and push forward.

I turned and grabbed an axe from under an overturned table and lunged for the open space between Loki's legs, hooking the axe around his ankle and rolling between them, pulling as hard as I could. I righted myself and came to stand between him and The Volva. Once he hit the ground, the attack on Sylve stopped, giving me an opening to pull the young woman from her seat and throw her across the room into Sylve's awaiting arms. The Volva's entourage had already made a run for it.

"Get her out of here!" I yelled above the increased roaring of the flames. Sylve nodded and pushed the hysterical woman out the front door. I tried to run after them, but a wall of fire pushed the door shut behind them, trapping me inside. I stopped mid-run and turned to face him, drawing both my swords. Loki slowly pushed himself to his feet, his demeanor teetering on the edge of rage and amusement.

"I come to your defense, and that's how you *repay* me?" he asked, eyes glittering with anger.

"I don't recall praying for the Gods' help," I retorted, twirling my knives in my hands.

"I don't think you would have the vocal cords to do so had I decided to let her slit your throat," he replied, drawing the flames from around him down his forearms once more until they formed into short swords in his hands and solidified into steel. My mouth gaped at the display of magical ability. "Easily impressed?" he asked confidently, a smirk growing along his lips.

"No, ... and I think your idea of a slit throat might be different than the reality of one." I motioned at the wound across my neck. He raised an eyebrow but didn't respond. "What? Easily silenced?" I jabbed.

He cackled at my words. "That requires a needle and thread," he responded, stepping toward me. I positioned my arms to defend myself but snapped my head toward the window when I heard a loud crash, spotting Sylve just past the half-burnt shutters on the back of Arvak. I turned back to find an arrow had gone through the window and impaled Loki in his chest, near his shoulder.

"Veronica! Come ON!" Sylve yelled from outside. Her attack had forced Loki to withdraw his flames so I could make a break for the door. I swung it open and ran towards her, holstering my swords mid-sprint. Once I was close enough, Sylve ushered Arvak in my direction, reaching out for me and hoisting me up while in motion so I could swing my leg over and catch my seat behind her.

Flames erupted through the Inn, and half the house burst into flames as Sylve turned to ride away. I looked back as my home got further and further away, shattering my heart into a million tiny pieces. We rode quickly down the path, and I was caught off guard when we passed Sylve's house.

"What are you doing?" I yelled over the wind that swept past our ears. The air cooled my exposed wound, forcing me to cover my throat.

"We are going to Frith!"

"What? Why? What about your father?" I was met with silence. "Sylve! We still need to speak with him!" I tugged her arm to remind her what we still needed to accomplish here.

"We can't!" she responded sternly.

"We have to! Syl, stop!"

"No, Veronica! It isn't safe here! I refuse to bring whatever just happened anywhere near my father. We will figure it out on our own," she said. It seemed she was trying to reassure herself more than me before pushing Arvak towards Willingman Woods.

"We aren't prepared for this trek! Especially not at night!" I pleaded. My need to stay in Lykke was painful. *I'm not ready to let go of everything yet.* The Inn is all I have left.

"We will be fine. We are more than capable," she reasoned, but the tightness in my chest was suffocating.

"Syl, I can't breathe," I nearly whimpered my words. She looked at me over her shoulder. She knew it wasn't because of the still-bleeding injury.

"Let me get us somewhere safe," she insisted, her doe-like eyes begging me to keep it together for a few more moments. I nodded and tucked my head into her back, pulling in stuttering breaths as she steered us past the tree line and into the woods.

# Twenty-Eight

Sylve finally pulled off into a small break in the trees. A few slivers of moonlight shone through the tops of the tree line, allowing us to see each other but not much else. This journey through dark elf territory would be dangerous without a torch or any other form of light. This disadvantage could be deadly. Arvak hadn't even come to a complete stop when I launched myself off her back, falling to my hands and knees in the lingering mist hovering on the forest floor.

I didn't even bother trying to withhold the tears pouring from my eyes. The Inn, … Bryn, … all gone. Everything is currently being destroyed, and I could do nothing to stop it. *Once again, I couldn't stop it.*

*Useless!*

"Veronica, … I'm so sorry," Sylve offered as she dismounted and held onto Arvak's reins, keeping her attention on our surroundings. I couldn't respond between my aching cries and ragged breaths. I didn't want to hear her. Hearing her would only solidify what just happened. My heart couldn't take it. "V, we can't stay here long," she warned under her breath. She stood next to me, placing an arm around my shoulder, and forced me to stand straight so she could access the frayed skin around the front of my neck. A light appeared from Sylve's hand and disappeared just as quickly. The breeze no longer stung my throat.

"I COULDN'T STOP IT! AGAIN!" I screamed into my hands, squeezing myself down into a tight ball, hoping I could stop my emotions from exploding.

"I know. I know! I hate to say this, but I need you to do this later. This really isn't a safe place to lose it right now. I'm so sorry," she coaxed sweetly as she handed me a hard truth. I sat back on my heels and suddenly lost my vision, grasping onto Sylve to keep me upright. When my vision returned, I was watching the Inn burn from the sky.

"VERONICA! Hey!" I could hear her screaming at me. I could feel her shaking my shoulders but couldn't see her. I was circling the fire, watching as the townspeople gathered to fill buckets to extinguish the flames. It already looked as if the severity of the incident was under control. "VERONICA!" I thought I squeezed her shoulders but was unsure, although I felt it was safe to assume by the way she slightly relaxed. *Would she hear me if I spoke?*

"The Ravens," I noted breathlessly.

"What? What Ravens?" she asked.

"The Volva, she mentioned that Ravens were gifted to me," I explained as I continued to watch the Inn's flames come to a smolder. "This has happened before. I can see what the Raven sees," I trailed off as my view switched, it seems, to a completely different Raven.

"Wha— What are you seeing?"

"I just saw the Inn. ... The townspeople are working to put out the fire," I whimpered in semi-relief.

I felt her pull me in for a hug, the warmth of her chest meeting mine. "Are you okay otherwise? Your eyes ... are like pools of ... liquid smoke? It's the craziest shit I've ever seen," she admitted cautiously.

"I'm okay. You could feel me squeezing you?" I asked as a new vision came into view.

"Yes."

"Okay." *So I can still control my body and speak normally. I just lose my sight. That's not terrible.*

The Raven from which I was now seeing through was flying towards a tree line. A quick look around the area confirmed it was coming from Lykke and heading towards Willingman Woods. There was a blurb of red just below the Raven, who dove down towards it, sweeping in front before perching on a tree. Once it was settled, it looked down, and there was Loki, looking up at it, … studying it.

"It's Loki," my voice trembled with rage as I said his name.

"You are seeing him?" Sylve asked, rubbing her hand down my arm.

"Yes, he is at the edge of the woods," I responded, irritation growing in my words. I could hear him as he spoke to the Raven in the tree.

"Are you Huginn or Muninn?" he asked the bird, who only responded with an ear-piercing shriek. He covered his ears from the sound and then stood up straight. "Huginn, got it." Loki stepped toward the tree line, but the Raven dove at him, scratched at the skin on Loki's back and perched again in a nearby tree.

"Look, you nosy little bastard, I'm not above setting you on fire," he threatened. The raven turned its head, and Loki stilled, standing straighter. "No way," he said breathlessly, stepping closer and turning his head. I could feel his eyes meet mine as if he could look past the Raven's and see me sitting up in the tree watching him. "Come to me, angel. I know you can see me." The blood in my veins boiled at the nonchalance in his voice and the total disregard for the destruction he had left behind.

"Veronica, what are you seeing?" Sylve cut in, breaking the buildup of anger.

"He wants me to come to him."

"Loki? Is speaking to you?"

"Yes." The bird shrieked again, and my vision went dark, my sight returning to that of a concerned Sylve in front of me. I gasped slightly as I felt my consciousness return to my physical body. I pulsed my hands open and shut.

"Are you back?" she asked, waving a hand in front of my eyes.

"Yes," I answered, jumping to my feet and walking over to Arvak. I grabbed an axe from the holster near the front of her saddle.

"What are you doing?" Sylve jumped up to follow me.

"I'm going to fucking kill him," I seethed through a tight jaw. I turned to walk through the woods toward the section the Ravens had shown me.

"Whoa!" She grabbed my wrist and turned me to face her. "Besides the fact that you *can't* kill him ... because, as you know, he's a *God*. You can't walk through these woods like that. Are you insane?"

"You won't stop me, Syl. I need to confront him. I need answers. I want him to pay for what he has done to my life! You heard the Priestess; she said death was a catalyst for everything that's been happening. What if *he* was the rat that told Calder about the rebellion? What if *he* got Bryn killed? He just blew up the Inn! That's my final straw! Done! So, you can either come with me or head to Frith. But either way, I'm going back there," I stated, my confidence unwavering. I hadn't felt this much anger, let alone any emotion, for a few weeks now. I didn't allow myself to. But I was at a tipping point. Sylve stood there and weighed the two options I gave her. A quick check of our surroundings and she turned back to Arvak, mounting up with ease.

"I'll take you to him, but if there is any sign of trouble, WE leave. Do you understand?" I nodded in response and mounted up behind her, pointing her in the direction near the edge of the woods.

Once we arrived, I pulled on her shirt, asking her to stop. She abided, and we both dismounted.

"Stay back in the tree line for as long as possible," I whispered. "He doesn't seem to want to hurt me, so I'd rather you wait until I might need help. That way, I don't put you in danger if I don't have to." She nodded in understanding.

"Don't do anything stupid, V. This isn't someone you can take on. Especially by yourself."

"I'll do the best I can," I reassured her before turning, axe in hand, weaving in and out of the trees, making my way towards the edge of the woods.

As the trees thinned, I noticed his scarlet red hair a few feet away. I was impressed with the accuracy of the Raven's guidance. I didn't even need to think about where we were going; it felt almost instinctual.

"I'm half surprised you came," Loki cooed from the clearing. I was put off by his ability to see or sense me since I couldn't see him fully from where I stalked through the trees. "I only am surprised because I seem unable to *entice* you to do things in my favor." My back stiffened at his words. *He's tried to force me to do what he wants.* I stepped out from behind the trees, axe held out at my side, ensuring he could see it. He only glanced at it and then back at me, a silly smirk on his face as if he was holding back a laugh.

"Entice me? You mean manipulate me?" I asked sourly.

"Yes, exactly." He leaned against a tree as I strode further into the opening, positioning him between me and Sylve, who was hiding somewhere in the trees behind him. When he turned toward me, I noticed a trail of blood from the wound left by Sylve's arrow on his bare torso. He noted that I was looking at it and rolled his neck in annoyance. "A decent shot. Would've killed a man if I had been one." He touched the edge of his wound with his finger.

"A great shot. Actually, a superb shot since she could hit a God without hardly trying," I replied, smirking.

"Right." He smiled, going quiet and silently watching me as we faced each other. "Are you going to attack me?" he asked, amused.

"Thinking about it." He scoffed. "I *should* kill you," I stated confidently.

"I'd *love* to see you try." He grinned wickedly. There was no hesitation when I pulled back my axe and threw it directly at him. The blade of the axe struck true, lodging into the tree next to his head. He looked between me and the weapon beside him with raised eyebrows. "Was that an *intentional* miss?" He asked, his eyes ablaze with excitement. I gaped, my mouth opening and closing repeatedly, not knowing how to answer since it would imply that I either didn't *want* to hit him or I was unable to. *Bastard.*

"What do you want with me?" I asked bluntly.

"What else would I want with my wife? To live happily ever after," he answered sarcastically, folding his hands to his chest mockingly.

"I am NOT your wife," I retorted sternly.

"I am led to believe differently."

"I don't give a fuck what you believe. I am not your wife. I am not anyone's wife. I don't even know you nor how in the living hel a *God* has ended up choosing me to be some plaything."

"You say God with so much disdain. Is there a particular reason?" he inquired, pushing himself off the tree. I noticed his slender abdomen contracting to bring his body upright. I shook my head to keep my thoughts on the threat at hand and not on the Godly body in front of me.

"Besides the overall shit that humanity has become without interference?"

"We cannot control mankind, nor can we control any other creature or being," he retorted plainly.

"Well, maybe the fact that I've had *two* potential Gods fucking with my life for the past few months? That might put a bad taste in one's mouth."

"I thought I put a rather delightful taste in your mouth." He winked in my direction, and my thoughts immediately returned to our interaction at The Dark Sun Tavern. I clenched my jaw at the memory.

"Right, ... a deception. One of many, I assume," I spat.

"I was not being deceptive with you. You asked who I was, and I told you." He stepped toward me, but I stood my ground, not wanting to show fear by keeping a safe distance between us. "You even asked for clarification, and I confirmed your question."

"Why would I think that some random person named Loki might actually mean the literal God?" I asked, placing my hand on the hilt of my sword. He eyed my movement and put his hands up in surrender but continued to walk toward me.

"Well, the possibility might be pretty low." He looked off to the side in contemplation, then back at me, his green eyes attempting to melt the hardness around me. A crooked smile split across his face that made my stomach twist in knots. "You could have asked for proof." He held his hand in the air, conjuring a flame in his palm and letting it dance along and in between his fingers. As I watched his display of magic, my rage resurfaced. I pulled my sword, swiped at him, and pointed it at his chest, demanding him to keep his distance.

"I want you all to leave me alone," I warned.

"All who, angel?" he asked, dropping his hands to his sides and smothering the flames. "I and the woman at the tavern are the same being." I noted the identical scars on his hands, confirming what he said was truthful.

"I already figured that. You are also the same man who attacked the castle," I stated boldly.

"Indeed. However, I want it to be known that had your king not threatened your life, I would have never had to show myself." I took that bit of information and stored it in my head, waiting for a better time to dissect it.

"I wasn't referencing all of your forms," I reiterated. "Your son has been pestering me just as much as you have. And whatever fucked up family dynamic that exists, I want to be kept out of it." I demanded, watching as his face turned from playful to irritated.

"My *son*?" he asked, offended.

"Yes. Vali, your son," I said. His eyes began to glow angrily as he took slow steps toward me, pushing into the sword I held to his chest. I did not yield until crimson blood began to drip from where the tip of my weapon had broken past his skin.

"*My* son, whom you speak of, has been DEAD for a very long time," he explained, forcing doubt to settle in my mind. I thought back to the text I read. *Maybe the author had gotten something wrong.* "Vali is here?"

"Unless all magical beings are deceptive, that is what he calls himself. He seemed more than educated on Gods, magic, and the Cosmos. So, who else would he be?" I asked skeptically.

"A cruel coincidence, it seems, that my son's murderer shares his name. Isn't it?" he sneered, his eyes blazing. "Even more of a coincidence that he is still living after Ragnarok … and is here now." My head was spinning with the information I was receiving. "What has he wanted with you?"

"I could ask you the same question. I thought it was weird that a son wouldn't want his mother to rekindle with her husband."

"So, you know you are Sigyn?" he asked, his eyebrows flying up his forehead.

"I am not this *Sigyn* you two keep referring to! And no! I only knew about this person because I forced him to tell me why he was bothering me, which seems to be a theme around here." I raised my sword once more and took another step back so that I wasn't impaling someone who wasn't attacking me.

"I can confirm that you *are* Sigyn. How this has come to be, I'm not certain. But I know it to be true." He held out his hand and twirled his finger in the air between us as if playing with an invisible string.

"You are insane," I huffed in disbelief.

"I don't think so," he countered, summoning a flame in his hand, and lunged for my arm with striking speed. I attempted to pull myself away from him, but he was much faster and stronger. My mouth was open, but no sound came out as we both stared down at his hand, which was tightly wrapped around my forearm, both engulfed in flames. But my forearm wasn't burning, nor did I feel any of the heat that should be there.

"What are you doing?" I asked sternly, dropping my sword from the hand he held and catching it with my free hand, twisting the blade down so that I could send its hilt into his nose and pull my arm free from his grasp. His head barely jerked back from the blow. I had at least expected him to stumble and wipe away any snot I had knocked loose.

"It seems that I am not insane and that my magic does not— well, it cannot—affect you."

"Why?"

"That must have something to do with the Norns. We will have to ask them about that later." He flashed his crooked smile at me again, his eyes lighting up with hunger ... and lust?

"We nothing. This is it for me. I'm done playing along with delusional Gods."

"I would be more cautious speaking ill of the Gods in front of anyone other than me. I don't intend to hurt you. However, others won't hesitate once they've taken offense," he warned, walking toward me again.

"Stop!" Sylve yelled from the tree line behind him, her hands glowing with magic, ready to attack. *If she even knew how to do that.* Loki turned to face her slowly, allowing me to take a few steps out of his reach so I could make my way toward the trees.

"I'm okay," I reiterated, putting a hand up to show the arm he had just held. "No need for more magic."

"Oh, she can't help *that.*"

My head snapped towards him. "What does that mean?" I asked cautiously.

"Magic will activate in the presence of mortal danger. It's a survival instinct," he explained, igniting a flame in his palm and tossing it from one hand to the other. I stepped between the two of them, continuing to back toward Sylve.

His eyebrow shot up. "Do you think you are just going to leave?" he asked in amusement, a menacing smile tugging at the side of his mouth.

"I am. I told you I don't want any part of this."

"Well, whether or not you WANT to be a part of this, you are. You are the reason it exists." He began walking forward, closing the distance between us. I heard a twig snap behind me, meaning Sylve had made her move toward us.

"Oh no, I'm not finished," Loki stated, kindling a small flame in his palm and throwing it in her direction.

"No!" I yelled, lunging for his arm with my sword, but I was too late. I looked back at Sylve to find her trapped inside a ball of fire, the light under her skin glowing and swirling erratically, trying to find a way to save her, but without the knowledge, she couldn't fight back.

Enraged, I swung my weapon at his throat, which he dodged masterfully, stepping back with grace. I did not let up. I continued to go on the attack, swiping at his abdomen, then his neck and leg, but with each attack, he danced just out of range. I was growing agitated at the lack of ground made in this altercation, and fatigue began to creep into my muscles. Suddenly, he disappeared from in front of me. I heard him speak from where Sylve was still trapped, now fallen onto her hands and knees inside his dome of fire.

"Ah, ah. I would hold off on wasting any more of her time," he warned casually. "I have spent thousands of years in holes that led deep into Midgard's core. Caves where *I* found it difficult to breathe and even more difficult to create a flame to keep me warm or bring light to the dark cavernous walls around me. Within my years of captivity, I have come to learn that the flames I can conjure only seem to burn their strongest when I've got direct access to *fresh* air—air that blows the leaves from the tops of the trees to the ground below. The further I was forced underground, the thicker the air became, and the more my fire wavered in strength before ultimately being smothered out completely. So now, I have learned I can decide *where* I source my flame from." He gestured his arm toward Sylve, "The longer she stays in *there*, the less air she has to breathe." I was shaking with anger, clenching my jaw so hard I thought my teeth were bound to crack. But I conceded reluctantly dropping my weapons to the ground beside me. "The right choice, angel," he drawled. He smiled slyly, then disappeared again, leaving Sylve entrapped. I felt his presence directly behind me; his breath brushed my ear.

"Why?" I was seething, but all I could think about was how much time Sylve had remaining before she would pass out. *I need to do what he says. Comply now, fight later.*

"See, you may not remember me, but I, … remember you." He lightly ran his fingertips over the top of my shoulder and down my arm, sending invisible lightning across my skin. "You might have *forgotten* everything we had, everything we were," he murmured as his fingers lightly grabbed my hand before stepping around to stand in front of me, his body uncomfortably close to mine. He lifted my hand up to his chest over his heart, placing it over the scar. Being this close, I can see now that it was the Algiz rune, a protection symbol. His skin was smooth beneath my touch; even his uneven scar felt soft despite its discoloration. He whispered his next words onto the top of my head as if reassuring me. "If there was anything left for me to lose, I'd give it up for you. Nothing matters more to me than this." He squeezed my hand, which he still held to his chest.

"You don't even know me," I breathed. I glanced over to Sylve, who was now lying on the ground, not moving. My heart leaped into my throat, and I pulled my hand away from his touch. "Keep dreaming," I spat.

He grabbed my chin with his fingers, angling his face down, his lips nearly in contact with mine. "I will," he whispered before disappearing. I sucked in a breath and immediately ran over to Sylve, her fiery enclosure dissipating with the breeze.

"Sylve!" I called out, sliding onto my knees beside her and turning her over, checking to see if she was breathing. I brought my face down to her mouth, feeling her faint breath against my cheek, and relaxed slightly, opting to look around to check our surroundings. Loki was gone, as were the Ravens. I whistled for Arvak, who emerged from a thicket a little way down, whistling again to call her over to where we were. "Sylve," I whispered, grabbing her face between my hands. "Shit!"

I stood and went over to Arvak, checking the few packs that were already strapped to the saddle for any water, only to find empty waterskins. If only I knew where the nearest water source was, then maybe I could run and fill this for her. I gasped quietly, an insane idea coming to mind. One that would possibly solidify everything that I had been denying all night. *I could use the Ravens, but how do I even do that? Do I just ... ask?* I looked down at Sylve, who remained unconscious, and dread took root in the pit of my stomach. *I have to try. I have to help her.*

"Ravens?" I said out loud. "Ravens, can you help me?" I have never felt more stupid in my entire existence. *Maybe I have to call them by name?* What did Loki say when he noticed one? Uh - Hugo? Hewjin? *Gods damn it!*

My thoughts went back to The Volva speaking about the Ravens. She had said they were a gift from the Allfather, Odin. I know he had two Ravens, but what were their names? I scratched my head for a moment, and then it came to me—Huginn and Muninn!

"Huginn? Muninn? Can you help me?" I called out into the darkness beyond me. After a few moments of nothing happening, the tightness in my chest clutched at my throat. I'm wasting time here when Syl needs help, and I'm unable to help her. A rustling near the tops of the trees made me jump, and when I looked up, there they were. Each raven had one black eye and one milky white eye, staring down at me with their heads cocked, ... *waiting for instruction?*

"I— Uhm, I need to find water," I pleaded with the birds. They took off into the darkness, camouflaging with the black sky above them. Then, my sight went dark, causing me to stumble forward and grasp onto Arvak's saddle for support. *This will take a while to get used to.*

I watched through the Ravens' eyes as they soared over the tops of blurred trees, diving down into the leaves and branches until they perched on one just above a small running creek. It had to be nearly two hundred or so meters from where we currently were. The Raven squawked, and my sight went dark once more, returning my vision to my own eyes. I shook off the heavy feeling in my head and bent down to lift Sylve up over my shoulder. There is no way I could safely get all the way to this creek while leaving her here; even if I left Arvak with her and went on foot, it wasn't worth it.

I carefully pulled her up and caught her under the shoulder, moving her onto Arvak's back, closer to the front of the saddle. Once I threw her arms over the mare's back and trusted that she wouldn't fall, I hurried to the other side and pulled her up and over. The ride won't be comfortable for her laying on her stomach like that, but it is the best I could do. Carefully, I positioned myself behind Sylve, adjusting her to lay on my legs rather than the packs there, and urged Arvak forward in the direction of the small creek.

I was on guard as best as I could, but still unable to shoot an arrow if I needed to protect us from an ambush. Once I heard the quiet trickle of the stream, I had

Arvak quicken her pace, weaving in and out of trees until we came upon our scarce water source. I dismounted smoothly and carefully pulled Sylve off Arvak, nearly dragging her to lie next to the small stream of water. I went back over to the packs and rummaged through them until I found some general healing components and grabbed the waterskin, returning to fill it promptly. I ripped off the sleeve of my shirt at the elbow, letting it soak up some water, and placed it over her forehead. I could tell that her body immediately seemed to relax at the coolness, and she stirred.

"Sylve," I whispered. "Sylve, can you hear me?" I continued to mix some of the healing components on a flat rock, grinding them up using another stone, hoping that this concoction might help her.

"Mmmm?" she moaned from next to me, and when I turned, she was trying to sit up.

"Whoa! Hold on. Let me help you." I eased her back down with little resistance. I scraped the ground herbs into the waterskin, shaking it vigorously before placing it in her hand. Carefully, I helped her lift her head so she could take a few sips at a time. "Are you okay?" I asked quietly. She nodded silently in response, letting her head rest on my lap. I looked up at the sliver of night sky visible through the treetops and thanked whatever Gods that had helped—all of them except Loki. I felt a warm tear stream down my cheek and down onto my neck, but I let it be. Sylve will understand.

"Bastard," she breathed out weakly.

"Indeed," I reassured, stroking her hair away from her face. We stayed like this for a while. Syl took more sips of water until she could eventually sit up on her own, opting to lean against a tree so I could stand and keep watch over the small area we occupied. Once she became aware and regained her energy, I walked over and kneeled in front of her. "I am so sorry, Syl." She began to object, but I held up my hand. "He could've killed you, over some delusional Godly— ... I don't even know what to call it. I'm so sorry to have gotten you caught in the middle of this," I offered, grabbing her hand earnestly.

"It isn't your fault. You didn't know this thing existed. ... I'm with you," she reassured and squeezed my hand. "Thank you for helping me." I shook my head at the absurdity of her sentiment. "It is the least you could do after all. Dragging me into your *Gods'* drama." She cracked a cheeky grin and I gaped in shock.

*There it was.* We both laughed for a second before hearing something move in the woods around us. Sylve tried to stand, but I motioned for her to stay down.

"I've got this," I whispered.

"Hey!" she yelled under her breath, pulling on the edge of my pants. I turned and she motioned toward Arvak. "The bow." I turned to look at her, an incredulous look on my face.

"The bow!?"

"You've got it. You've been practicing, right?"

A moment of silence.

"Right. ..." I turned and grabbed the bow off the side of the saddle, slinging the quiver over my shoulder, taking an arrow and notching it. I breathed in steadily, listening to the sounds of the night. A loud rustling came from behind us, and I turned in its direction; pulling the arrow back. Then I heard the sound near Sylve, and followed its movement with the bow. Sylve ducked out of the path of my arrow.

The creature that hid in the dark began to circle us even faster, rustling through the treetops, then a splash in the creek, and back to the treetops again. *It's playing with us.* Then we heard another noise—deep thudding steps on dirt echoed off the trees, disorienting me and eventually growing louder than the sounds of our current threat.

That's when I saw it—a dark elf, its narrow slit for a nose, razor-sharp teeth set in a too-wide smile, its near-death, pale skin. It turned its head at us, and I raised the bow, pulling back the arrow, waiting for it to move. The thudding of the next unseen attacker was getting so close it sounded as if they would find us in a few seconds. I had to make sure I eliminated this elf if we had any hope of avoiding the next one. I took another breath and watched as the creature stepped closer. I released the arrow, but instead of soaring to my desired target, it caught on the string and bounced off, falling to the ground between my feet.

"Fuck."

It smiled, teeth bared, and catapulted toward us. I pulled my swords out and ran at it, planning to lure it away from Sylve, but an arrow whizzed past my head and struck home in the center of the elf's face, the impact of the arrow sending it tumbling backward. I froze and looked at Sylve, who had stood and leaned against the tree. She was shaking her head at me, indicating that she wasn't the one who shot the arrow. I peered past Arvak and noticed a glint of gold. Sylve noticed it at the same time and breathed out a sigh of relief, sliding back down the tree until her butt met the ground.

"Sindre?" I called out into the trees, the tightness in my chest easing as he appeared between them, leading Alsvid by his side. He slung his bow over his back and hurried over to Sylve.

"Are you okay?" he pestered, checking her over. She swatted his hands away in annoyance.

"I'm fine! Gods! I'm okay," she reassured. "What the hell are you doing here?" she questioned in complete shock.

"I felt you'd used a huge amount of power. It almost knocked me on my ass. It scared the fuck out of me!" He rubbed his hand across his chest, reliving the experience. "I knew something was wrong, so I left immediately."

"Well, … we are both okay. Mostly," I offered, shrugging my shoulders in defeat. The events of the night have taken a toll on me and have officially made its way to my body. He looked at me with an expression I couldn't quite place.

"It's time to get out of here. We can talk about what happened later," Sylve ordered from the ground, holding out a hand for Sindre to help her to her feet.

"We are closer to Lykke; we will go back to the Inn and head for Frith in the morning," Sindre suggested. He paused when he noticed Sylve sneak a glance in my direction. I felt my mouth turn down involuntarily. "What?" he asked.

"The Inn is gone," I revealed solemnly. "It's been … burnt down." I saw my words slice through him, and an instant look of loss and grief struck his face. I bit down on my lip to keep it from quivering. I turned and grabbed the arrow from the ground that had failed to help us earlier, strapping the quiver and bow to Arvak's saddle.

"We can go to our house for the night," he suggested. He looked as if he were going to come to my side but stopped himself, turning back to help Sylve mount up onto Alsvid.

"That is a good idea. Father is there, and … he needs to speak with you. So, I guess this all works out," Sylve stated, her energy depleting significantly after pulling herself atop her horse.

"What happened?" Sindre asked, looking between the two of us in disbelief.

"Later," I said, smiling half-heartedly and mounting up onto Arvak. He raised an eyebrow at me, silently asking if I wanted a riding partner. I shook my head. "She is very weak. She will need help." He nodded and hurried over to his sister, taking his place behind her and leading us out of Willingman Woods.

# Twenty-Nine

Sindre knocked on the door to his home while I helped Sylve stand just behind him. When their father answered, his face paled, and he ushered us in promptly. I led Sylve to sit on the small couch in the center of the room, but she waved at me to let her be.

"What happened to you two? And when did *you* get here, son?" Gudmund asked, walking over to embrace Sindre in a bear hug. The two men held onto each other for a heartfelt moment. I'm sure their time spent apart was now hitting them. We waited to speak until after they had separated and refocused.

"We need to revisit our conversation from yesterday, Father. Speak with Sindre about your next expedition, then I've got more questions," she ordered softly, patting the spot next to her for me to sit. I held up a finger and hurried over to their kitchen, grabbing some water for the both of us and opting to cuddle next to her while Sindre and his father stepped outside to speak.

A few moments later, a hand on my shoulder woke me from a deep sleep. *I didn't even realize I had drifted off.* I turned to find Sylve just as confused as I was. I looked up at Sindre, who was staring down at me with a disheartening look. "Are you okay?" His voice was soft and warm. It could have lulled me back to sleep if I closed my eyes.

"I'm okay," I smiled half-heartedly. "I'm just exhausted. Are *you* okay? I know how hard that conversation had to be." He nodded and walked around the couch, asking me to make room for him by tapping my leg gently. I scooted closer to Sylve, who sat up before leaning back into me. Once Sindre took his seat, I laid back on him. He wrapped an arm around my shoulder and let my head rest on his bicep, his fingers slowly caressing down the outside of my arm.

"That was ... unexpected," he admitted quietly. "But also, I guess I should have known. I've just been so preoccupied with the training that I didn't even have time to think about it." He let out a long sigh and let his head fall back.

"I know exactly how you feel," Sylve reassured, reaching back blindly to grab her brother's. Sindre moved to reach for her. "What did you decide?" she asked.

"I'm sure the same as you, Syl." He laughed quietly. I could feel his laughter vibrate through his chest, sending a relaxing sensation through my own.

"Good," she said. We lay quietly for a few moments. "I'm sorry," Sylve stated out of nowhere.

"For what?" Sindre asked, continuing to run his fingers along my arm.

"I'm going to change everything."

"Sounds dramatic, but I'll support it," he responded nonchalantly. Sylve sat up and leaned against the opposite end of the couch, staring at him intently as if they were having a conversation I couldn't hear. I turned my head to look at Sindre, and his brows were furrowed together as he watched her.

I sat up suddenly and looked between them. "What the fuck. ... Ar— Are you two talking right now?" I interjected, redirecting their focus to me.

"It's uh— ..."

"Twin thing," Sylve finished, shrugging her shoulders nonchalantly. I shook my head in disbelief.

"Is it?" I reiterated with wide eyes.

She paused for a moment and looked away. "I— I don't know," she responded. Gudmund had walked back into the house from outside. His eyes were red and irritated as if he had been crying.

"Father," Sylve called softly. He sat down in front of us on the short table in front of the couch. "*What* was our mother?" she asked bluntly. He sat up straighter, staring off into his memory.

"She was a wonderful woman—smart, beautiful, mesmerizing." His eyes glazed over with the sweet thoughts of his love.

"That's not what I asked," Sylve broke in, pulling him from his reflective state. "*What* was she?" she repeated. This time, he understood her question, looking between his two children.

"An enchanting mystery," he answered lovingly. Sylve held her hand out, conjuring a small sphere of wispy light in the center of her palm. Gudmund's eyes widened bigger than I had ever seen anyone's before. He lunged for her hand, closing it inside his.

"*What* was she?" she repeated, and he looked up at her with worried tears in his eyes.

"I did not expect this outcome." He looked between his children with a mixture of love, adoration, and fear. "How long have you been able to do this?"

"A few months. Unless you are some magical creature who has been able to hide it from us so effectively, we would appreciate knowing *what* we are. Where *this* came from." She looked at Sindre, who was analyzing his father's reaction.

"I don't know. … Your mother was the magical being. These gifts did not come from me, unfortunately." He smiled sweetly at the light Sylve let reappear in her palm before he closed his hand over hers once more, putting out her magic. "She never told me what she was. … I don't think I ever cared to ask. I fell so madly in love with her within only a few shared moments that it didn't matter to me. Her magic was a huge part of her essence, her mystery, her being, … and I accepted it for what it was." He smiled sadly at the twins, an apology written in his eyes. "I hadn't thought about the possibility of her abilities being passed to you. I don't know why I never considered it. It just hadn't mattered to me for so long with your mother that I wouldn't have cared either way."

"What happened to her?" Sindre cut in. "Where did she go? She bore your children, then what?"

Gudmond's head and shoulders dropped. "We all lived together for a few years. Around the time you guys turned three, she told me she had to leave. Her people were summoning her for a cause she had to prepare for."

"She left?" Sylve asked breathlessly.

"She had to. ... I couldn't stop her. Trust me, I tried. But with an instant flash of light, ... she disappeared," he admitted.

"Why don't *we* remember her?" Sindre asked.

"I always wondered if you kids had any memories of her. ... A tragedy, it turns out, that you don't. Maybe you were too young when it happened. She loved you both dearly, more than anything. It broke her heart when she realized she had to leave you behind." Gudmund knelt before Sindre and Sylve. "I'm so sorry I never told you." Sylve threw her arms around her father's shoulders, and Sindre grabbed his hand.

"We don't blame you," Sindre admitted. "Would it have been helpful to know? I'm sure it would've, ... but you had your reasons, and we've turned out alright." He smiled softly, and his father nodded in reassurance.

After a few silent moments, I spoke up. "I hate to interrupt this touching moment, uh, ... but could I ask for some clarification?" Sylve released her father and pushed herself back up onto the couch. He shook his head. "When Sylve asked *what* she was, I'm wondering, was she a ... *creature*? Or more human?" He turned his head at my question.

"She was definitely human presenting, just a magical being inside that."

"Possibly a ... God?" I pushed.

His stare went blank. "I— She— I guess. Is it possible? She never said anything. I feel a God would announce their status, no?" he stammered.

"Depends on the God, it seems," I retorted, unamused, earning an arched eyebrow from Gudmund. A silence fell over the room, so I stood. "I feel like you all might have more to speak about tonight. I am going to wash up and try to get some sleep before tomorrow. I will request a meeting with the Elders, and I hope you both will join me, if possible. If not, no worries." I smiled at the twins, and they both nodded. Sylve stood and hugged me, murmuring her thanks in my ear for aiding her tonight. I kissed her cheek and stepped out of the room, waving them all goodnight.

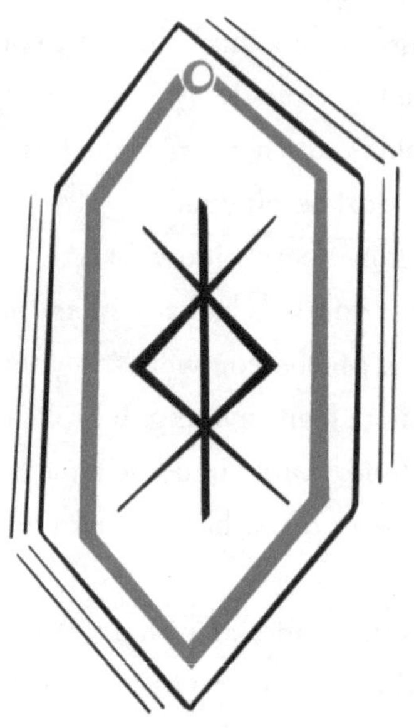

# Thirty

We waited until the sun was near midday before beginning our trek to Frith, lessening our chance of running into any creatures that lived in the woods. Sindre went to check out the Inn, or what was left of it. I refused his invitation to join him. That would be another heartache I couldn't handle right now. I even avoided him when he returned because I didn't want to see the outcome on his face.

I sat back in silence to allow the twins as much time as we could afford to say their final goodbyes to their father. I fumbled over my words, which were riddled with apologies when it came time to hint at our need to hurry to Frith. Once we departed, we pushed the horses as hard as we could until we arrived at the wooden gate, waving at the door master to let us in. The creaking of the iron wheels and the wood under distress made my stomach turn. Tightness began to spread across my chest, like the start of a flame on a string, and it traveled up my neck. Suddenly, the slow pace at which the gates opened annoyed me more than anything, and I spurred Arvak forward and through the growing crack between them before they had the chance to fully extend.

We rode to the main house and pulled our horses over to a hitching rail. The sun was setting in the distance just above Mount Eir. The light bouncing off the clouds in the sky made it seem as if an entire other Realm was near collision with ours. *Funny that it also felt that way.* I dismounted from behind Sylve and hurried inside, looking for Ragnhild.

"Veronica! Welcome back!" Kalyani's voice rang out from the kitchen. She hurried over to me for a warrior's embrace, and I was delightfully surprised by the gesture. "Where is Sylve?" she asked curiously.

"It's good to see you," I responded warmly. "She is tying Arvak outside and should be in shortly. Do you know where Ragnhild is? Or any of the Elders, for that matter?" She peered around me toward the door before answering.

"They are all in town right now. Finishing up training for the day."

"Oka—"

"Veronica?!" Raoul called from the top of the stairs before I could question Kalyani for more information. I stepped around the wall to peek about the corner, catching a surprised Raoul halfway down. A huge smile cracked across his face. He leaped down the stairs, and I scrambled to catch him.

"Gods, Raoul! What is wrong with you?" I laughed, hugging him tightly.

"You've been gone for so long! I've learned how to use a knife!" he informed me excitedly, wiggling out of my arms and pulling his knife from a holster around his waist.

"Raoul!" Kalyani reprimanded. "No playing with weapons. You promised!"

"I was just showing Veronica," he pleaded, sheathing it back in its place.

"Training yards ONLY," she demanded. Her attention was stolen by Sylve and Sindre walking through the door behind me. She breathed a sigh of relief before hurrying over to Sylve and hugging her instead of offering the warrior's embrace I had received a few moments prior. "Are you alright? Sindre rushed out of here, saying something had happened. ..."

"Yes. I'm just fine," Sylve smiled and bent down to pick Raoul up in a hug, who literally fell from her arms over to Sindre's shoulders. "How has everything been around here?"

"A lot of hard work. But it's getting easier, more routine," she answered wearily. Sylve put a supportive hand on her shoulder, and Kalyani nodded.

"Where is everybody?" Sindre asked while simultaneously roughhousing with the child who was climbing all over him.

"Training in town. I was going to call a meeting. Care to join me?" I offered.

"Yeah, as long as I can bring this bale of hay," he joked, pointing at Raoul on his shoulders and looking toward Kalyani for permission.

"Of course," she laughed.

"Hey! I'm not a bale of hay!" Raoul contested.

"Oh, I think something may be trapped in my hay. I should probably shake it out, huh?" he asked me, his eyebrows moving up and down comically, and I nodded in amusement. I suppressed a laugh as I opened the front door and let Sindre leave first, the sound of giggles wafting back as he shook Raoul upside down by his ankles. Despite bringing news of a looming battle to Frith, Raoul's laughter brought a smile to both Sindre's lips and mine.

While we walked through town towards the training areas, which Sindre mentioned they moved since the space was too small now, he quizzed Raoul on all the weaponry information he had taught him these past few weeks. As we neared the training grounds, I slowed my pace, staying just outside the arena and stopping completely to lean up against the small fence that outlined the grounds.

Thora noticed me first and whistled over to Ragnhild, who looked surprised to see me. I nodded in the direction of the house, and he raised his eyebrows, pointing down to the ground, a silent gesture to ask if I needed to speak to them right this minute. I nodded again, and he whispered to Thora, who left promptly, presumably to carry out his instructions.

"I'll race you back," I challenged Raoul, getting a head start toward the house.

"Hey! That's cheating!" I heard him contest from behind me.

"No worries! I'll stop her," Sindre growled. "Let's go!" I grinned as I heard Raoul's laughter close behind, anticipation grasping at my limbs as Sindre remained silent. It wasn't until he was a few steps behind me that I heard him snarl a warning, causing Raoul to laugh maniacally again. A hand caught my wrist, nearly causing me to trip, but Sindre's arm wrapped around my waist, picking me up so that I wouldn't fall. "Run, Raoul!" he yelled out to the child, whose sounds of joy continued to emanate as he ran ahead of us.

"I was not cheating," I murmured, crossing my arms across my chest while he kept me suspended in the air.

"Oh, you *definitely* cheated." He smirked, putting me down on the ground, and turned me to face him. His eyes wandered over the details of my face before he pushed a strand of hair behind my ear. "I'm worried about you," he admitted. My heart skipped a beat, and I felt my face warm at the sincerity of his words.

"I'm okay," I smiled. "Don't worry about me right now. We have a huge task ahead of us."

"And what if this Loki decides to show up in the middle of it? Tries to hurt you or … take you?" he asked.

"What if he does?" I retorted softly, locking my eyes on his. Sindre's gaze switched from tender to cold in an instant.

"I'll kill him." His jaw tightened.

"Then, there isn't anything to worry about." I played with the edge of the 'V' in his tunic, letting my fingers trace the visible lines of the tattoo on his chest.

"It's not that simple," he objected under his breath.

"It needs to be. At least for now, … it needs to be."

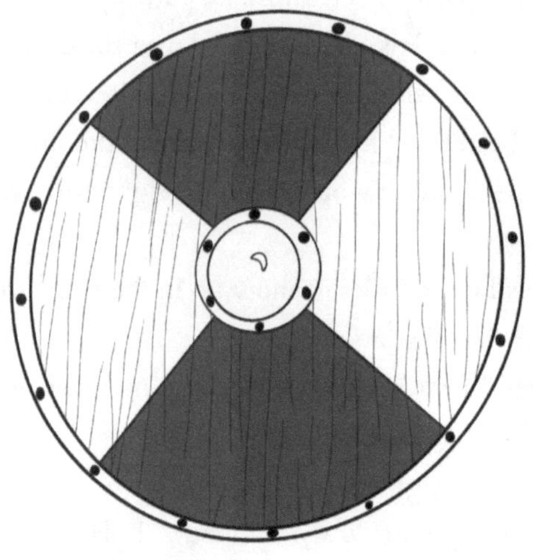

# Thirty-One

S indre and I caught our breaths and relocated the horses to the barn. We then entered the house, finding most of the Elders dusting the dirt off of themselves after abruptly ending their training sessions in preparation for a meeting. Sylve held Hemming in her arms and followed Kalyani, who led Raoul out the front door behind us, giving us the privacy the Council requires. I noticed Ylva wasn't here yet as Ragnhild walked over to greet us.

"Welcome back," he said. "Although it was unexpected. We were preparing Sindre to retrieve you in a few days," he noted. I noticed the signs of exhaustion on his face—the lines of weariness etched on his forehead—more prominent since Bryn's passing.

"Things have changed. I've found information I would appreciate being able to share as soon as we can get started," I responded, my stomach twisting with anticipation of their reaction.

"Will the twins be joining us?" he asked. I looked at him slyly.

"If you would allow it, I would appreciate their presence."

He nodded and whistled loudly for everyone to take their seats, causing Sindre and I to flinch being in such close range.

"Where is Ylva?" I asked quietly, pulling Ragnhild closer as we approached the large wooden table.

"She has been unavailable lately," he admitted sadly. "I've sent Thora to find her and bring her here."

As if on cue, Thora and Ylva burst through the front door, Sylve reentering behind them. Thora held a firm grip around Ylva's elbow, which Ylva promptly ripped away as soon as she stepped inside.

"I'm plenty able," Ylva spat as Thora passed by, rolling her eyes. "Why the hel are we having another meeting? It's not like anything has cha—" Her eyes connected with mine, and her words disappeared. A look of relief replaced the anger. "Come here, child. My Gods!" We met each other halfway, and she threw her arms tightly around me. I could feel her frame had shrunk since the last time I was in Frith. It made my chest hurt, knowing she was still grieving just as hard as I was.

"Thank you for coming," I whispered into her ear. "I've missed you."

"If I knew you had returned, I wouldn't have fought." She smiled at me. "Is everything alright?"

"Oh, absolutely not." I laughed awkwardly. "Can we convene?" I asked across the room, surprising not only myself but Sindre and Sylve with my sudden increase in confidence.

"Take your places," Ragnhild demanded. He waved his hand at the table, ushering everyone to their chairs. "Meeting is in session; the Nyhus twins are here for counsel and will not receive a vote on anything we discuss." Everyone nodded and took their seats—everyone except me. Bryn's chair was back in its place at the other end of the table, with Odin's Ravens etched into the top of the headrest and the worn-down rounded handles on the arms. *There is so much to live up to in this seat.* Sindre went to move it out of the way, but I stopped him, my chest strangled with emotion.

"It's okay," I breathed out, stepping in front of Bryn's chair and taking my seat. I met the eyes of each Elder - Thora, Liv, Bergunn, Askel, Ylva, ... Ragnhild. Each of them showed me, in one way or another, respect for embracing the role and responsibility that came with Bryn's seat as a Raven's Council Member. *It's time to step up. It's time to fight for what we believe in.*

"A few days ago, I was informed that the Council had come to a standstill regarding sending someone to the castle for information."

"Oh, here we go," Askel spoke, rubbing his hands together greedily, amped up with excitement.

"What did you do, girl?" Thora hissed, less than pleased.

"I simply voted in favor. Then I went *myself* and found the information we needed." A chattering murmur arose across the room, some bickering on the dumb decision and how risky it was, while others praised me for actually trying to find out something. "Listen!" I slammed my fist down on the table, catching everyone off guard. "We have run out of time. These masked warriors are supposedly *confirmed* Skirrians, and their presence has increased tenfold since the last time I was there. An inside source told me that they are replacing many of the original Royal personnel with these warriors, and *nobody* knows who they are or where they are coming from. My source has watched a ship leave every night from Port Sisu. I assume that is how they are bringing in these people. Every night, they are dropping off more." I sat back in my seat and crossed my arms, chewing on my lip, the realization of what that meant hitting me now.

"It seems like Calder has already begun merging the two kingdoms," Bergunn stated, running his hand through his hair.

"But it isn't a merging. Is it?" Liv questioned. "They aren't moving *civilians* here, just militant warriors."

"Well, that tells us everything we need to know about his true intentions," Askel commented.

"We've already known his intentions. Well before this cluster fuck," Ylva retorted, twirling one of her knives with its tip on the wooden table. "We need to move NOW!" Ylva stood, stabbing it down. "Right now," she repeated. "Get ahead of them moving more Skirrians in."

"They are already here, ... in large numbers, at that. We won't be stopping anything," Thora countered, earning a burning glare from Ylva.

"I don't feel like everyone is ready for a move yet," Bergunn cut in. "We still have groups of people who can't handle certain weapons."

"We can't wait until *everyone* masters the art of war. We should be able to trust those of us who have already experienced war to guide these new warriors with confidence," Askel countered.

"We do need to act now," I reiterated, rising to my feet. "Maybe not *right* now, but within the next few days. ... It's time."

Ragnhild gazed up at me with the same silent thought that he usually does, letting this information stew in his brain for a moment. "I fear you are right. ... It is time." He looked around the table, everyone nodding as their eyes met his. "I progress this session to a vote. We take the night to speak to the people of Frith and let them know the time has come. Let everyone spend this night with their families. Then, tomorrow morning, we will have everyone and everything packed up and ready to leave by midday. We will stay at the Inn in waves, moving half of a group simultaneously. Stop one, Lykke. Stop two, Exris. In two days' time, we will be at the gates of Sol's castle. We will fight for the freedoms we have fought for once already. All in favor, ... please stand." All the Elders stood at once, each holding a fist over their hearts. I was already standing, but I slowly brought my fist to my chest, nodding as I did.

"For freedom. ... For Bryn," I paused, biting my lip to keep it from quivering. "By the Gods, I have so sworn."

"By my honor, I have so sworn," the Elders recited in unison, seemingly dismissing themselves from the meeting.

"Oh, one more thing," I called out, hoping I didn't have to explain myself. Everyone paused and faced me. "The Inn has been burned down. We will have to find alternative housing." I was met with incredulous, confused, and heartbroken eyes. "Don't ask. If anything, just know we really don't have much time."

Ylva walked over to me, tears brimming in her eyes, and grabbed my arms. "For Bryn," she repeated, her voice cracking with emotion. I pulled her in for another hug, and we held each other for a moment. She has always been the closest thing to a mother figure to me. I will always appreciate how she loved Bryn and was always there for him when he needed someone. I will forever be indebted to her. "He would be so proud of you," she stated softly, calling my own tears to the edge of my eyes.

"Thank you," I breathed out, letting her pass by me to begin informing the Frithians. The remaining Elders followed with warrior embraces as they left the house with a hel of a lot of work ahead of them. I turned to follow Bergunn out of the door, but Ragnhild stopped me.

"We've got this tonight. Why don't you guys get some rest? We can handle it," he offered politely.

"No, I really want to help. There is so much to do—"

"Veronica," he stated calmly. "Rest." He squeezed my shoulder and left me standing in the house with Sindre and Sylve.

"You didn't even need us that time," Sindre joked, punching me in the arm.

"You did great, V," Sylve cut in, rubbing the spot on my arm that had just taken the blow from her brother.

"I thought I was going to vomit," I admitted plainly, staring blankly after Ragnhild, lost in thought. Sindre and Sylve's laughter at my mindless comment returned me to Midgard.

"I hope you would've done it, at least, toward Sindre's side," she joked. I shook my head, barely registering the conversation.

"In two days. … TWO days, … we risk everything." I shook my head in disbelief as fear of the unknown settled in. *Would I see them again?*

*What if one of us dies?*

*What do we do then?*

*What if we all die?*

*What if we are unsuccessful, and they send us to Skirra?*

*What if they have more warriors than we do?*

*What if our tiny Frithian army isn't enough? Isn't ready?*

"I know that look," Sindre interrupted, walking over and pulling me into his chest, the smell of cedar and leather filling my nose. "We will cross those bridges when we get there. Just breathe for now."

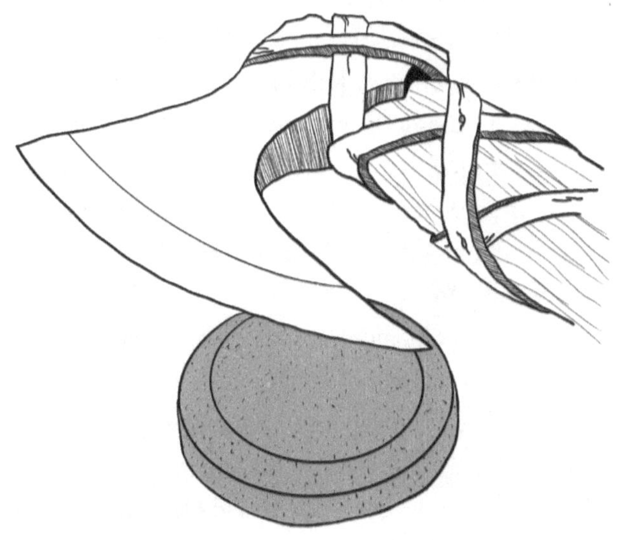

# Thirty-Two

I secured a sharpening stone between my knees, picked up an axe from my assortment of personal weapons beside me, and carefully ran its blade across the stone diagonally. The crisp night air rejuvenated my lungs with each slow breath I took. Once my axe was sharpened to my liking, I placed it back on the ground and picked up one of my sister swords, analyzing it under the light of the night sky, which had found a new life tonight. Diluted blues, purples, and greens danced across the dark expanse above Frith, leading one's eyes to the crest of Mount Eir on the far side of town—a breathtaking sight, a teasing scene, really. Being able to behold such beauty and peace on the cusp of its potential demise twists your heart in inexplicable ways. I noticed Brax's tail wag slowly at my feet when my visitor finally spoke.

"Care for some company?" Jerrik asked from somewhere behind me. I heard more than just his footsteps as twigs snapped and the grass shuffled from multiple places around him.

"Depends." I laughed, shaking my head. "Who makes up your entourage?" I turned around on the fallen tree I was using as a bench and let the heat of the fire warm my backside. Jerrik was accompanied by my favorite people—Sindre, Sylve, and our newer friends, Elias, Kalyani, and her boys. I smiled at them as they greeted Brax before taking their places around the crackling flames. Jerrik and Elias sat across from me, Kalyani and Sylve next to them, while her boys each chose a lap to sit on. Sindre sat next to me and passed me a mug of mead. I grabbed it greedily and mouthed a *thank you*. "Since you brought me a mug, I'll welcome the company."

"We appreciate your acceptance," Sylve jested, putting her hands near the fire to warm them. We sat quietly in each other's presence, allowing ourselves to feel the calm before the storm. I looked around at all of them. Elias laid his head on Jerrik's shoulder, his blonde hair cascading down his chest and onto Jer's arm, tickling the hairs on his forearm. Sylve held Hemming tightly on her lap, listening intently to the story Kalyani had just begun to tell her boys. She pulled the bottom of her head wrap over her face, leaving only her eyes showing, before jumping at Raoul, who sat between them, sending the two boys into hysterical laughter. Syl's eyes were warm and tender as she laughed with the small family. They might have been glowing more than her hair was in the presence of the flames beside her.

I turned to look at Sindre and caught him watching me. I screwed my face up in a silly manner, and he shook his head at me, returning his gaze to the warm fire before his solid hand patted my knee. "What are you thinking about?" he asked quietly to avoid disturbing the other conversations.

I sighed to myself. "I hope we can get back to this," I admitted, looking around at everyone again. "I don't think I've accepted our fate yet." I offered a half-hearted smile and looked over at him, his deep brown eyes searching for more past the color in mine.

"It's hard to accept something that technically hasn't happened yet," he nodded. "I feel the same."

"It's all happened so fast, hasn't it? Am I the only one who feels that way?" I laughed to myself, feeling like I may have lost it.

"No. ... No. We all feel that way." He nodded toward the group, and when I looked at them, they had lost interest in their conversations and were nodding along with him.

"It's been one thing after another," Jerrik chimed in, grabbing Elias's hand.

"Have either of you decided to fight?" I asked Elias and Kalyani, who nodded at Elias, signaling him to speak first.

"I won't be fighting," he smiled sheepishly. "I've been slow to progress in any of the training I have tried to dabble in. I'll be better utilized in town for less warrior-centered roles like healing and helping care for the children in the orphanage." He ran his hands through his hair nervously.

"It's as noble and necessary a task as any," I encouraged, offering him a smile. "Thank you for wanting to help at all. Not many would have been so willing to trust us blindly and make a stand against the Crown." He nodded and smiled as Jerrik squeezed his hand. I looked over to Kalyani, whose eyes lit up instantly. "And you?"

She nodded furiously in response. "I am fighting," she stated confidently. I looked at her boys, and she turned to Raoul, petting his head lovingly. "I've talked to them about it." Her voice softened, filled with love and heartache.

"Yeah, Mom is going to fight to keep the bad people away. They won't hurt us as long as she goes to fight," he said proudly, keeping his hands on his hips.

I nodded in response. "We will be there to help her," I promised discreetly.

"All of the Ravens will be there! The protectors!" he yelled, pumping his fist in the air.

"They will stay at the orphanage until our return," Kalyani added, looking up at me quickly through her long eyelashes, the crackling fire reflected the *if* in her eyes that she didn't need to say aloud. "Hemming has grown fond of Dagna and Torsten, so ... they should be okay." She sounded as if she was trying to convince herself more than anything as she pulled Raoul's head in and kissed his forehead, prompting him to throw his arm around his mother for an embrace.

"We will get you home," I promised, watching the tears in Kalyani's eyes well up.

"They are worth fighting for. I am not afraid," she announced confidently, looking up at Sylve. "May I tell them?" she asked. Sylve nodded and readjusted Hemming in her lap. "I've asked Sylve if she would be willing to ... take over

... if anything were to happen, and she accepted." She reached out and grabbed Sylve's hand. "I am forever grateful."

"We will get you home," Sylve insisted, hugging Hemming again. The group quieted, a more solemn mood settling around us. After a few minutes, Jerrik and Elias turned in for the night first, then Kalyani and the boys. Sylve left with her to help with Hemming since he had fallen asleep in her arms. Sindre intended to go with them, but I placed a hand on his leg, requesting that he sit down again. Once they were far enough away, I moved closer to him, hoping to keep our conversation as quiet as possible.

"I've been so out of touch with everything. I had a question pop up earlier but wasn't sure who all knows about it." He nodded and put his arm around my shoulders, pulling me closer. I scoffed. "Is this necessary?"

"I'm unsure," he whispered into my hair. "This sounded top secret." I could feel him smile against my head just before I elbowed his side, drawing forth a taut laugh.

"Has anyone gotten anywhere with the ... rat?" I asked under my breath. He responded with a thoughtful '*hmm*' as he rubbed his chin.

"All I know is the Elders planned on keeping a record of every Raven showing up for daily duties. They noted a few missing but kept their findings among themselves." It was my turn to offer a speculative *hmmm* and rub my chin, to which Sindre elbowed my side teasingly.

"It worries me that we haven't found this person yet. It will put every move we make at risk going forward."

"That will have to be discussed with the Elders. They've kept whatever findings they uncovered to themselves."

"Mazen had come to the Inn a few days after we got there." He turned his head slowly to look at me. I refused to make eye contact and continued to explain what happened. "Don't worry, I was originally planning on killing him, but he refused to fight." I saw Sindre shake his head from the corner of my eye. "I believe he can be trusted. He helped Syl and me escape the guards at the cas—" I slapped my hand over my mouth after I realized I hadn't told him about our excursion to Sol's town.

"You know, ... I caught that at the meeting, and I forgot to bring it up." He leaned back on the log we sat on, resting back on his hands. I slowly looked over at him, keeping my hand on my mouth. He shook his head while his eyes were gazing up at the sky. "Gods help me," he begged openly. I spotted the thick lines of his chest tattoo poking out from the opening of his shirt, the light of the fire illuminating his russet brown skin and golden hair that fell over his shoulders.

"Sorry," I offered quickly. "It was something I had to do, … and Sylve refused to let me do it alone."

"Thank the Gods for that," he laughed, rolling his head towards me. I smiled sarcastically before grabbing a smaller blade from my weapons pile and began sharpening it.

"ANYWAY, I trust Mazen. When he came to the Inn, he was coming to tell me what he knew about a person who arrived at the castle the night before Bryn was brought there."

"Oh?"

"He only gave me a general physical description and said the person was wearing a cloak that kept them covered. He also mentioned he assumed this person was a male because of the deeper voice and square stature. But he knew that alone couldn't solidify his hunch."

"So, … not very helpful?" he asked curiously. I let my mind wander a bit; the description of this dark cloak stuck out to me tonight. … But why?

I gasped when it clicked. "Holy Hels! It's Tormod." I looked at Sindre, my eyes wide with realization.

"The rat?" he asked.

"I think it might be. Did you ask the Elders if they sent him to check on me in Exris?"

"I did. They said they didn't but wouldn't elaborate on who they had been keeping tabs on, so I'm unsure if that is connected with their findings or not," he replied calmly.

"At The Dark Sun, he was wearing a black cloak with the hood up. … He made a remark that he was checking in on me to make sure I was doing what I was supposed to so that no one else had to get hurt. … I thought he was talking about, … Gods, he was getting intel for Calder. He was threatening to hurt one of us." My eyes darted from point to point, following my thoughts as I moved from one piece of this puzzle to the next.

"Wow," Sindre breathed out beside me, leaning back in disbelief.

"Oh my gods, … I was so drunk. I could have compromised everything! I wasn't even THINKING about the rat." My heart was racing, and my erratic breathing was tethering on the edge.

"Okay, okay. Breathe." Sindre moved from beside me and dropped to his knees in front of me, placing his hands on both my legs. "Talk to Ragnhild tomorrow. For now, that is all you can do. You don't need to overthink anything because it is time for us to mobilize. If it is true that Tormod has been the rat this whole time, we will find him at that castle in two days, and he will pay for what he has done to us … and to Bryn."

I nodded slowly, bringing down my heightened sense of urgency to a more manageable level.

"Was there anything else that Mazen told you?" he asked calmly.

"Well, he also enlightened me on Bryn's treatment. … Things they questioned him about. All of that good stuff." I smiled at him weakly, and he nodded in understanding.

"I'm sorry."

"This is the sole reason my heart holds any excitement for what is to come. Driving my weapon through Calder's chest will bring me closure," I stated confidently, clenching my fists around the handle of my knife.

"Will it?" Sindre asked, gazing down at the weapon in my hand.

"If it doesn't bring closure, then it will break me. … I will never allow my family or friends to be used as pawns again," I vowed, fixing Sindre with a determined stare until he met my gaze. "Never. Again."

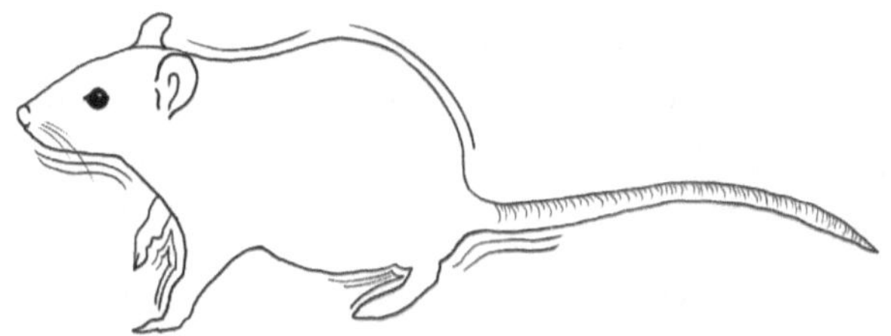

# Thirty-Three

I couldn't sleep much during the night and ended up finding Sylve's room to bunk with her until the morning. If Sylve knew I had woken up as early as I did, she might die from shock. She still might once she sees my belongings packed and waiting in the cart we are taking to Lykke today.

After I loaded my things, I found Ragnhild tending to the horses in the barn and hurried over to him before he busied himself with another task.

"Good morning!" I called out, waving to make sure he saw me.

"What— I'm quite surprised you are awake so early, Veronica." He laughed, nodding a greeting at me.

"Couldn't sleep much," I admitted, closing the distance between us and accompanying him into the large wooden structure. An array of whinnying and snorts hailed us as their breakfast provider neared. Arvak was closest to the entrance, so I snatched an apple from Ragnhild's basket and offered it to her, stroking her nose lovingly.

"That's a normal reaction," he assured, placing the basket on the floor out of the horses' reach before filling the wooden pails with grains. I turned from Arvak, took a bucket, and began filling it myself, thinking I should keep my head busy if I wanted it to stay quiet.

"Would you tell me if it wasn't?" I quizzed, arching an eyebrow skeptically.

"Of course," he answered confidently. I nodded to myself silently, letting him get his work done without being too much of a distraction. It wasn't until I noticed my leg bouncing that I cleared my throat, finally pulling his attention from his errands. "Yes?"

"I think I know who the rat is," I stated plainly, glancing outside the double barn doors beside us.

"You do?" He jumped slightly at the thought and felt through his utility belts until he found a piece of parchment. "We've been keeping records of the Raven's attendance over the past couple of weeks. These three have been absent from their stations. Could it be any one of them?" He held out the parchment for me to take.

*Siv Hjorth*

*Tormod Helvig*

*Kirk Borg*

I felt the utter shock spread across my face while Ragnhild continued tending to the horses. I opened my mouth to speak but found myself at a loss for words. *It is him. I could've ruined everything. What if I have and I don't remember?*

"We can't confirm that any of these people have done anything wrong," he reassured. "But we all were just as shocked as you considering the possibility."

"Tormod."

"That's who you think it is?" he asked, stopping what he was doing to turn his full attention to me.

"I know it is. He was in Exris at a tavern where I was staying a week ago. … He was trying to collect intel for Calder, but I didn't realize it at the time. … I had thought you sent him, but Sindre told me you didn't."

"He has been missing for some time now," Ranghild pondered. "When Sindre informed me of him showing up in Exris, we immediately put him on the list, and he never showed up again. We were all hoping it wasn't true." My thoughts flashed back to when Tormod was sitting beside me at the bar and noticing the half-sun mark on his forearm. Then, the memory of a hooded warrior in the library with the kingdom's insignia burned into the same spot on their arm followed.

"If my memory and assumptions serve me correctly, then he has been branded with the kingdom's insignia," I added quietly.

"Well, … I guess we will be seeing him soon then, won't we?" He shook his head in disappointment.

"What about these other names? Siv?" I asked, confused.

"Siv has only recently missed her post. She returned last night. Thora has been keeping an eye on her. We haven't seen Kirk in a few weeks either."

"She is close to Tormod. … Is it possible she's feeding him information?"

"The threat is there, but Siv has been relentlessly training and rallying all the new warriors for weeks in preparation for this fight. It wouldn't make sense if she was, … but it is possible," he answered solemnly as he turned back to feed the horses.

"Who is Kirk?" I asked.

"He's been stationed mainly at the gate, a younger fellow." I nodded and took a calming breath.

"So, he could also be a rat? Someone who just up and left with Tormod and could be at the castle?"

"Another possibility, but not something we need to spend more time mulling over. We will soon face our betrayers; if they have fled to Kron's castle, there is nothing more we can do."

"Do you have Bryn's note?" I asked suddenly.

"Not on me. It's in my room." He wiped his hands on the end of his tunic. "I can go get it."

"I would appreciate that. I will finish up for you." He nodded and walked out of the barn. I remember Bryn's message being worded oddly, and I wanted to give it a second glance. While waiting for him to return, I finished packing grain into large sacks for our travels ahead. I had just begun loading them into one of the wagons outside the stables when Ragnhild returned with Bryn's note in hand. "Thank you," I offered as I reached for the parchment. He placed his hands on his hips and analyzed the work I finished in the short time he was gone.

"Well, thank you for the help and for the information regarding our traitor. I will make sure Thora keeps an even closer eye and maybe even an ear on Siv. We will keep a lookout for Kirk as well," he stated. He picked up the final grain bags and lugged them into the back of the wagon. "I'm going to head inside. Askel almost has breakfast ready. Get a plate when you are done."

He patted my shoulder and turned to walk away, leaving me alone. I hopped up onto the end of the wagon and opened Bryn's note again, emotion catching in my throat.

RaT aMOng De ravOns

My thoughts remained on the fact that this was the last message Bryn intended to get to us. *To me.* The last thing he wanted to say. *Needed to say.* I wonder how long he knew about this and if he kept it to himself so that whoever he suspected wouldn't know he was on their scent.

I pushed aside my grief and re-read his note again, and again, and again. Then, I held Ragnhild's note next to Bryn's and read them both, my eyes darting between them. After a few minutes, the words started to rearrange themselves on the pages, with some becoming clearer while others faded into the background. It's no accident that Bryn made some of these letters larger than the others. *He knows how to write properly.*

*RTMODO*

I looked back at the list of names and nodded, clarity finally gracing my unsure thoughts.

*TORMOD*

A quick rearranging of the larger letters spelled Tormod's name. Bryn tried to tell me, but I found out too late. I clenched the list of names in my fist and pushed myself off the cart, heading toward the house. I opened the door as calmly as possible and found that everyone was awake and lingering in the kitchen. The smell of roasted pork greeted my senses, initiating an audible grumble in my stomach. And sure enough, Askel came through the back door with an entire roasted pig. Ylva followed behind him with a generous platter of eggs and Bergunn with an even heftier serving of potatoes.

"A hearty meal before we travel south!" Askel announced proudly, dropping the pig onto the large wooden table. Everyone offered their thanks and expressed excitement with a constant murmur of cheers, some 'mmms,' and a few friendly pats on the back. Sylve spotted me as she descended the stairs, sleep still heavy in her eyes.

"Well, I am beyond surprised and impressed with you this morning," she offered with a yawn, coming to stand in front of me. "Not only were you awake earlier than I was, but you also *seem* awake." She laughed to herself, coaxing a grin from the corner of my mouth.

"Gee, thanks." I rolled my eyes and wrapped my arm around her hip, walking us both toward the food being devoured at the table. She stifled another laugh and threw her arm around my shoulder.

"Are you feeling okay?" she asked at a volume meant for me alone. Her tone had switched from playful to concerned.

"Nerves," I admitted. She nodded in understanding.

"I've noticed I tend to oversleep when I'm nervous," she admitted. I shot a look at her, and she glanced at me through the corner of her eyes. "You are not alone in your feelings." She squeezed my shoulder before taking off to catch a plate of food.

Despite my stomach groaning, I couldn't find the motivation to grab my own. Instead, I opted to sit on the stairs and wait for everyone to finish before potentially ruining this moment of camaraderie between all of the Ravens. Someone cleared their throat in front of me. Sindre was standing there with two plates. How I hadn't noticed him is beyond me. I must have really zoned into my own thoughts.

"Ragnhild wants to make sure you eat," he said, sitting beside me. I attempted to scoot over to give him room, but my shoulder met the railing, leaving not nearly enough space to sit comfortably, but did Sindre care? *Of course not.* I shook my head at his massive frame that hunched over his plate of food.

"Would you like me to move?" I asked, my eyebrows raised and a silly smile plastered on my face as I watched him start shoving food into his mouth.

"No, I'm good," he reassured, mouth full. "I slept like shit," he stated between bites. "I'm definitely not looking forward to this first stretch of traveling."

I nodded in agreement. I pulled a piece of meat from my plate and placed it on my tongue, my stomach groaning in satisfaction.

Once everyone finished, I helped Askel clean the plates while the others packed extra food for the road. I peered over my shoulder, seeing who all remained at the house, when Ragnhild placed his hand on my other shoulder.

"Did you find what you were looking for in that letter?" he inquired softly.

"I did. It confirmed that I was right. … It is Tormod," I stated, looking around the room once more. He, too, scanned the room before nodding and then cleared his throat to grab everyone's attention.

"I'm calling a quick meeting with the Council," he announced loudly. "If the rest of you don't mind giving us some privacy."

With that, the few non-council members who joined us for our morning meal said their goodbyes and exited the building. I noticed Sindre and Sylve were heading towards the door, and before I could stop them, Ragnhild spoke up. "Nyhus twins. You may join us if you wish under the same circumstances as our previous meetings." They turned and nodded in understanding, placing a hand over their chest.

The Elders gathered around the table in their designated spots, opting to remain standing as Ragnhild mentioned that the conversation would be brief. They looked at him, waiting for him to begin, but instead, he motioned toward me with his hand, so they turned the rest of their attention to me. I felt Sindre and Sylve's comforting presence on either side of me and took a breath—no *need to drag this out.*

"Tormod. He is the rat," I announced confidently. I felt Thora open her mouth to question my words, but I held out my hand to stop her, pulling the two pieces of parchment from my waist belt, opening them both, and sliding them toward the middle of the table for all to see. As they all leaned over to analyze the two notes, I continued to explain. "Bryn knew how to write properly. We all know that. So, I took the larger letters out of his message and compared them to the list of names you created. … They rearranged to spell Tormod's name perfectly. Not only that, but Tormod came to me while I spent time in Exris. I had assumed that Ragnhild had sent him to check on me and didn't think much of it until it was far too late. From what I can recall, he might've been branded on his arm with the kingdom's insignia as a test of loyalty to the Crown." I waited for someone to chime in. Instead, each one took their time to observe the evidence in front of them. And each one eventually clenched their jaw or fists in acceptance.

"He'd better not show his face before we get to the castle," Liv growled.

"Bastard. ... He worked the most with Brynjar, nearly the closest. How could he do that to him?" Bergunn asked no one in particular.

"I'll kill him," Ylva seethed from beside me, her axe twirling against her fingertip, glinting from the sun shining through the back windows.

"I guess there is nothing left to question here," Askel announced, gripping the back of the chair in front of him.

"Siv and Kirk?" Thora asked, looking between all of us. Silence. "Siv only just returned yesterday. Other than that, I don't know where she was."

"And Kirk?" Ragnhild asked Askel, who shook his head.

"He works and lives just outside the doors to the city. He has been missing his shifts for a few weeks now. I was reassured he had fallen ill, but I never had time to visit," he admitted through a tight jaw.

"Well, we know it's Tormod. Siv has been close to him for years, so all we can do is monitor her. I don't know about Kirk, but if he is another traitor, we will soon find out," I stated.

"We don't have time to investigate the other two. If we come across them, apprehend them for now," Ragnhild ordered. The Elders all nodded in understanding. "You two as well." He motioned toward the twins, and I saw them both nod from the corner of my eyes. *I really doubt there is more than just Tormod. We would've been led on to believe so. Bryn specified RAT in his note. He would've said rats had there been more than one.* I nodded anyway, knowing that anything was possible after Bryn's passing. "Our time has come," he added, craning his neck to look out the window. "The first group is ready and heading to Lykke shortly." He turned around and looked at me, his chest rising, filled with a mixture of air and confidence. "Are we ready?" he asked in my direction but not *at* me. The Council all stood straight and placed their fists over their heart. I hadn't realized it, but I found myself mirroring the gesture in unison with them.

"By the Gods, I have so sworn. By my honor, I have so sworn." We all spoke our vows together, then briefly exchanged a warrior's handshake before concluding the meeting. When I finally got around to Ragnhild, he held onto my arm, keeping me from pulling away.

"We will be half a day behind you." He nodded. "I'm not confident that our small group of warriors here will be enough to fight for this Kingdom, ... but it might be enough to *sway* the Kingdom to fight *with* us." My jaw tightened at his words, realizing he had the same doubts and concerns I'd had since Bryn's death. He looked deeply into my eyes, tightening his grip on my arm. "What the people don't know *can't* hurt them, scare them, or threaten their livelihood. But what they *do* know can cause friction, move mountains, force change." He released his grip and motioned toward the door. We walked out to the barn, passing the relatively large group of warriors, new and established, packed and ready to travel. "I would like for you to take Grani," he stated, coming to a stop in front of Grani's stall, the all-black steed waiting patiently to be taken out.

"Wha— I," I choked on my words. Bryn cherished his horse deeply, hardly ever allowing anyone to ride him out of fear that Grani would attach himself to someone else. A small smile spread across my face as I began to stroke his neck. The mere thought of Grani bonding with another would have Bryn rolling in his grave, and it's primarily the reason why I accepted such a gracious gift. "Thank you," I spoke softly. Ragnhild nodded and unlatched the stable door so I could lead him toward the awaiting warriors.

"You've upgraded as well?" I heard Sylve ask from in front of me. I raised my hand to block the sun and found her atop Arvak, smiling brightly.

I nodded my head confidently. "I would tell you to take care of her, but I know she loves you," I said and smiled.

"Oh yeah. We've had plenty of time to bond." Sylve winked and urged her forward to walk a tight circle.

"She looks good on you," I admitted, turning to lug myself up onto Grani's wide back.

"Veronica," Ragnhild called from behind me. I turned Grani to face him, his arms tucked behind his back. "We will meet in Exris in two days." I nodded, and he put two fingers in his mouth to whistle loudly, signaling for our small fleet of warriors to be ready. Then another whistle sounded near the front of the group, and I spotted Sindre there, explaining the directions to our travelers. I looked around and did a short set of whistles until Brax came running through the crowd.

"Med Mer!" I ordered him, and he fell in beside Grani, ears forward, ready to go. "Good boy."

Another set of sharp whistles made its way toward the back of the group where Sylve and I were stationed, and the mass of warriors began to move forward. We passed through the gates and the small bundle of tree houses that guarded the city. The creaking and settling of the wood behind us sent a chill over my body. We were only a few steps into Willingman Wood when Brax began to whimper; his nose turned to the east, and his ears shot back. I pulled Grani to a stop, grabbing Sylve's attention and causing her to stop as well. I watched as Brax followed his nose a few steps before taking off into the woods.

"Shit!" I cursed under my breath and flung my leg over the top of Grani, dismounting swiftly and running after him.

"Veronica!" Sylve yelled, looking as if she was about to run after me.

"Hold Grani! Brax must have found something!" I reassured. "I'll be right back!" I held out both hands, signaling her to stay, and she nodded, reaching over to grab Grani's reins. I turned and ran in the direction Brax went until I couldn't see Sylve anymore and paused, listening for any indication of where he had run to. My eyes caught something moving across the ground beside me, and when I looked down, I noticed it was a tree limb with red leaves moving out of sight to my right.

Despite my rational self screaming to ignore it, I couldn't. Following Loki's trail only felt right, and sure enough, it led me through a couple more feet of trees to find Brax sitting in front of a decomposing body. The stench struck me a few seconds after I soaked in the sight. I shoved my face into my elbow, peering over the body to see if there was any indication of this person's identity. I noticed ink on the person's skin through a tear in their shirt. I grabbed the nearest stick, pushed the fabric out of the way, and read *Borg. This was Kirk.*

"Med Mer," I called Brax, turning to head back toward Sylve. I noticed a scarlet red leaf near my foot, and when I moved in its direction, it tried to lead me back through the trees. I hurried over and tried to stomp on it, but it disappeared instantly. "I don't need your fucking help," I grumbled through clenched teeth.

Once I cleared the few trees, Sylve spotted me, and I heard a sigh of relief leave her lips.

"What was that about?" she asked, handing me the reins.

"Brax found Kirk," I stated, taking my seat on Grani and urging him forward.

Sylve moved in close beside me. "Dead?"

"Yeah."

"Well, then. Unfortunately for him, we might never know what happened to him," Sylve noted sadly.

I nodded in agreement. "Let's hope he died fighting and is resting in Valhalla," I said tightly, to which she agreed, and we hurried to catch up with the rest of the group.

# Thirty-Four

When we arrived in Lykke, I hurried to the front of our group to let Askel, Ylva, Liv, and Sindre know what I found when we left Frith. They looked at each other before waving forward our entourage. I waited until they passed by to fall in line with Sylve, Jerrik, and a few other Ravens who were escorting people to their sleeping quarters for the night in the houses surrounding the twin's home.

Eventually, we made our way to the Inn, and as it came into view, everything went numb, ... silent. My mind was the quietest it had been in weeks, and my skin failed to register the warmth of the sun. Even the muscles in my back quit aching from the long ride. Everything just ... stopped.

There were piles of debris sectioned into reusable material, stones that could be repurposed, and completely charred wood was left scattered around the house. Small groups of people were working through the mess. It would have normally warmed my heart, but it did no such thing today.

Detached is all I felt at this moment.

"Miss Leif." An elderly man shimmied out of the rubble and headed toward me with a concerned yet cautious look on his face. His eyes scanned over each of the heavily armed Elder Warriors who were waiting for my arrival. The man wiped away the dirt from his face and waved at me. It was Arlan, the man who built Bryn's funeral ship. I pulled Grani to a stop and let him walk to me. "Miss Leif ... I'm— We couldn't stop the flames. We are so sorry." His voice cracked with emotion. The Inn was not only a loss to me but to our community as well. A home to all if one ever found themselves lost.

"You don't need to apologize, Arlan. The fire was not your fault. I'm sorry I have not been here to help you." I looked around at everyone who was still salvaging the bones of the structure. "There's no need for you all to keep doing this," I pushed through sad eyes.

"Yes, we do. We all owe so much to Brynjar. We are honored to help, especially with such a horrible tragedy." He eyed the Elders once more and then looked at Sindre, who smiled at him half-heartedly. "Wha— What is going on?"

I looked toward Askel and Ylva and was met with reassuring nods. *It might be enough to sway the Kingdom to fight with us.* Ragnhild's words echoed in my head, and I now knew what he meant.

"Are there any Kingdom Guards in the area?" I asked.

Arlan eyed me and answered cautiously. "No? Not that I've seen recently. "

I dismounted from Grani and handed the reins to Sindre, walking over to Arlan. I placed an arm around his thin shoulders and guided him back to the remnants of my home. I asked him to gather those who were near so that I could explain what we were doing in Lykke. I shared details about the Raven's and Bryn's legacy with the group. I told them exactly what Calder planned to do. Then I asked if they could offer shelter to the warriors who would be traveling to fight against Skirrian rule if they were unable or unwilling to fight against the Crown's threat.

"Of course," Arlan offered, holding a fist against his chest, surprising me. "We will begin spreading the word of this news, and most of us will be able to quickly ready sleeping accommodations."

"Thank you, we appreciate your help." I offered a half bow with a hand over my chest. Arlan looked past my shoulders and nodded. I turned to see where he was looking towards. The Elders and a few Ravens who were nearby also put their fists over their chests. Arlan beckoned to them.

"Please, follow me. I can take you to a warm bed tonight," Arlan offered as he walked away from us. The Elders led the last three wagons of warriors to where they planned to house them.

"How are we doing?" Sindre asked from behind me. I looked over my shoulder at him.

"*We?* Do *we* share the same feelings?" I asked sarcastically, raising an eyebrow.

"I feel *we* might share a connection here or there." He shrugged. "But my radar is a bit fuzzy at the moment, so I wanted to check in." His eyes were working overtime to pull the truth out of me. He was trying to get my emotions to surface, but they wouldn't. *I wouldn't allow it.* At least not now.

"I'm fine." I smiled, turning back to look around, realizing that everyone had stopped working to pass along the news I had just shared with Arlan.

"V ..." he pleaded softly behind me. Luckily, Sylve and Jerrik walked up, ending our conversation.

"A few of the younger townspeople are asking if they can join us," Jerrik stated in shock. "I don't know why, but I didn't think anyone would want to help us."

I nodded. "Well, it is their home, too. We can definitely use the younger women and men. If we can keep the Elders safe in town, they could help with healing and supply needs." Jerrik nodded and went to turn away, but Sylve paused, pulling Jerrik back.

"Are we sending anyone to sanctuary in Frith?" she asked quietly.

"No," I answered sternly. "We have already compromised Frith's safety enough. The Frithians who have chosen to fight with us have agreed not to tell anyone where Frith is. Its location remains a secret. And, we pray to the Allfather to keep it that way after this is all over."

"Okay," she responded cautiously before walking back down the street with Jerrik. I turned away, hoping to walk away from Sindre while his attention was on a villager who had asked him a question. I nearly made it to the dirt road when Alsvid stepped in front of me, with Sindre sitting atop her, his arms crossed.

"Really?" he asked.

"I'm not in the mood to talk right now," I admitted, annoyance playing at the end of my words.

"Fine. If you are avoiding me, then maybe you could at least take Grani back," he suggested coolly. I looked up at him as he subtly raised his eyebrow.

"Right." I went to reach for the reins Sindre kept on the opposite side of Alsvid when I noticed something move swiftly out of the corner of my eye. I caught a glimpse of a person in a hooded cloak darting behind a house. Without a second thought, I ran after them, leaving Sindre in confusion.

"Hey! V! What are you—?" I didn't hear anything else because blood was rushing through my ears. All I could hear was the thrumming of my pulse and the thought, *'What if it's Tormod?'*

When I reached the edge of the building the person had stepped behind, there was no one there. *They disappeared.* At least, I thought so until I heard a branch snap among the trees further ahead. *They must have made a break for the tree line instead of keeping close to the houses.* I ran into the thicket and zigzagged through the small, wooded area. I was about to stop to listen when I spotted them in front of me. I pushed harder, my feet feeling as if I could jump and take flight; an odd pain in my shoulders surfaced and disappeared as quickly as I noticed it.

"Hey!" I yelled out, knowing damn well that wasn't the smartest thing to do. However, my legs were beginning to burn, and if the prey knew they were being hunted, they were more likely to stumble. "Stop!" I saw them falter for half a second and turn back. I couldn't see their face under the hood before they turned and took off again. I growled in irritation, pulling out the knife from my lower back and launching it mid-stride, successfully lodging the blade in their shoulder—a hit I wouldn't have been confident I'd make if they hadn't allowed me to close the gap a second earlier.

The impact sent them forward, spinning to the ground. As they struggled to their feet, I lunged for them, sending us both rolling into the dirt and brush. I rolled my weight over until I was on top, forcing them onto their back. I then perched myself up onto one foot to stop our momentum. Their hood fell back, and I discovered Siv underneath me, eyes wild with confusion and anger, her face nearly as deep red as her hair.

"What the FUCK, Leif?" she yelled at me.

"What are you *doing*, Siv?" I questioned sternly, rage rippling over my skin from hearing the irritation in her voice. *How dare she get angry with me.*

"None of your goddamn business." She swiped the blade I lodged in her shoulder, using it to slice my exposed calf. Then, she bucked her hips, throwing me off her and creating enough space for her to flip upright. I hissed in pain, clutching my fresh wound with one hand while quickly unclipping the axe off my back with the other before diving after her and hooking her ankle with my weapon. She fell to the ground again but couldn't stand or run this time. I rolled to my feet and stood over her, my boot crushing her ribs, with the edge of my axe against her neck.

"I think it is every bit *my* business," I stated through clenched teeth. Siv's eyes darted to the right as the sounds of rushing footsteps neared.

"Veronica?!" Sindre yelled through the woods.

"Over here!"

Sindre found us first, followed by Jerrik, Sylve, and Ylva. Each of them slowly surrounded us to cut off any escape route.

"What's going on?" Ylva asked cautiously.

"I was just going to ask her that myself." I turned back to Siv, adding pressure to the edge of my axe. "Where were you going? Sneaking away from the crowd? Under the Raven's cloak ..."

"I wasn't! I was wa— walking. I was going for a walk!" she stuttered, wrapping her hands around the foot I leaned onto.

"We don't have time for this shit," Jerrik declared, pulling his bow from around his shoulder and notching an arrow in it, pulling it tight and aiming at Siv. Her eyes widened at the sight of him. If a man that large pulled a weapon at me in a fit of anger, I'd be intimidated as well. "What the FUCK were you doing?!" he demanded an answer.

"Were you going to tell Tormod?" Ylva interrogated, her fingers fluttering to the hilt of her sword. "You were going to tell him, weren't you? Tell him our final plan—"

"What are you talking about?!" she cried wildly, her expression now riddled with confusion. I looked back at Ylva, eyes wide.

"It doesn't matter anymore, Veronica. We are in the middle of our raid. Everyone who doesn't know there has been a rat in the Ravens needs to ...

because once we find him, he's *mine*." She spoke these words with promise before pulling her sword out of its sheath and closing the distance between us. Jerrik looked at me out of the corner of his eye, confused, but remained confident in his stance. I was suddenly thrown off Siv and onto the ground, with Ylva replacing me. She grabbed Siv by the collar and held her short sword just under her chin.

"You have *five* seconds. ... Five. ... Four. ... Thr -"

"I WAS GOING TO LOOK FOR HIM, OKAY?! But I SWEAR I have NO idea what you guys are talking about! He ISN'T a RAT. He told me he had to go to Lykke for something a few weeks back, and he never returned! I thought maybe he had an assignment, but I asked around a few days ago, and nobody heard anything or knew of anyone getting assigned to the town!" she explained quickly, almost tripping over her words as she spoke. "He's NOT a rat! He would never!" she reiterated, distraught, craning her neck away from the blade Ylva was holding against her throat.

"One thing is certain," Ylva growled through gritted teeth. "Tormod has betrayed us all... But right now, I can't decide whether or not to believe *you*."

"NO, he— he wouldn't! He ..." She looked at me, begging me with her eyes to deny what she was being told. I pushed myself off the ground, wiping my hands on my pants, refusing to address her.

"Why were you going to look for him? In the middle of a rebellion, ... why?" Sylve asked calmly, placing a supportive hand on Ylva's shoulder.

"I just wanted to make sure he was okay! He— He ... never disappears like this," she admitted.

"Are you two close?" Jerrik asked, his arrow still drawn taut.

"He is like a brother to me, ... my only family," she stated earnestly. Ylva shoved her to the ground before stepping off her. Relief filled Siv's face as she remained on the ground, in no hurry to get up.

"I don't trust her," Ylva added, sheathing her sword back in its scabbard. "Why would his *sister* not know about his plans *or* not be helping him." She shook her head and turned around to face the group. "Do you think we are stupid, girl?"

"I feel she is being honest," Sylve chimed in. She put her hand on Jerrik's arm and ushered him to lower his weapon. "I have known Siv for a long while."

"We've known Tormod for just as long, Syl," Sindre spoke sternly but calmly.

"Yes, but you know they are two totally different people. Their auras—it's like night and day." Sylve countered.

"Are you seriously going to let her go because you feel their *auras* are different?" Ylva snapped, annoyance flaring her nostrils.

"No. I thought she could be detained and kept with someone on watch for the next two days. That is if you still want to fight for our cause." She turned back to Siv, who propped herself up on her elbows.

"I never faltered from our cause," Siv responded curtly, her expression souring. Sylve reached into a pack that Jerrik was wearing around his shoulders, pulled out a length of rope, and walked over to Siv. She guided her to stand and secured her arms behind her back, taking any weapons strapped on her backside and securing them through her own belt.

"Ylva, you can be her personal babysitter," Sylve suggested, walking Siv over to the Elder Raven and holding out the end of the rope for her. "The Elders could meet about this since a vote would probably be the best way to decide what to do with her. We can't make rash decisions right now. That's not how we do things, and I'd rather not *start* doing things this way when tensions are high." Ylva took the rope without question, now seeming to have better control over her emotions.

"Let's go with that and head back," Sindre added, holding his arms out to usher Jerrik and me through the trees.

Jerrik hurried over to me and bent down to whisper in my ear. "Why did no one tell me there was a rat?" he asked, annoyed.

I looked up at him slowly before rolling my eyes. "We couldn't go around telling people our suspicions, Jer."

"But it's *me* we are talking about. I feel like I should have known! I could've been keeping an eye out, too," he pushed with a hushed tone. I eyed him again and was met with a groan. "You're always keeping me out of the loop with important information."

"Come on! You just brought Elias around. We didn't want you to second guess that or think we were watching him." I was going to wave him off but stopped myself, grabbing his arm for reassurance. "We never suspected him, by the way." He gave me a single *humph* before dropping his questions.

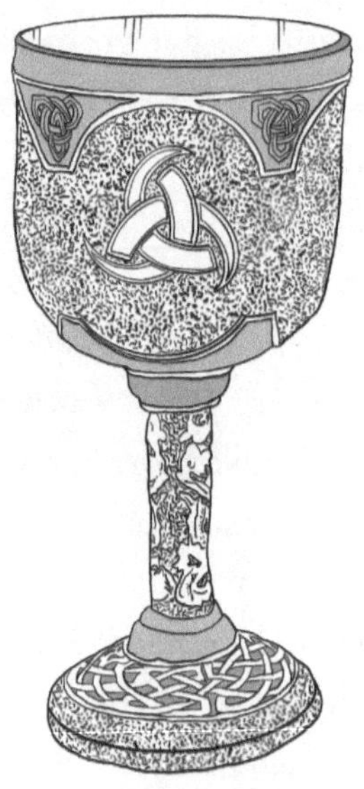

# Thirty-Five

The next morning, we packed up and headed to Exris with more warriors than we had arrived with. Since last night, Ylva basically had Siv leashed to her waist. The Elders all agreed to keep her close and have faith that she was being honest.

We kept the same formation as our trek from Frith to Lykke, except Askel chose to ride with us at the rear of the group. It was almost midday, which meant we should be nearing the edge of the trade's town soon. I looked at Askel, who seemed lost in his own thoughts. His coppery hair was braided tightly down the middle, exposing his neck to showcase his wolf tattoos on either side. He slowed his horse down to a trot, falling back in line with mine, and tore his gaze away from the horizon, arching an eyebrow at me.

"Do you need something?" he asked inquisitively.

"No, no," I answered quickly, shaking my head. "Well, ... I have been wondering how this is going to work." He turned to look at me, puzzled and unsure of my statement. "Exris is a trades town. A very busy one at that. Are we really going to just walk through there, set up shop, and not expect people to fight us? Or ask questions? Or even stumble upon the Kingdom's warriors or patrol guards?"

"If anyone gives us any trouble, we will handle it." He nodded at the three hundred or so warriors ahead of us. "I think we can persuade a handful of patrol guards from their posts." He winked at me, but I couldn't return the playful spirit as the pit in my stomach grew heavier.

"Are we going to tell the people there too?" I asked, adjusting my seat.

"If they will listen."

"And if they don't?"

"Then maybe Ragnhild can convince them once he arrives tomorrow. Until then, we will keep the casualties low."

"So, we are going to *kill* the people we are trying to protect?" I snapped sarcastically, whirling over to meet his gaze.

"If they choose to fight against us, then yes. We will have to."

I scoffed in disbelief. "There is no need to resort to that," I retorted.

"Then I guess you better be pretty damn convincing." He motioned with his chin for us to follow him as the group came to a stop. We rode to the front, where the Elders were waiting for us to join them. A crowd was forming at the town's edge, blocking us from continuing onward. I immediately began scanning the crowd for patrol guards but didn't notice any standing around.

"We need to make our way to The Dark Sun Tavern," Askel announced, his voice clear and confident. "We will make an announcement to the townspeople there." A murmur broke out through our small audience, and a woman stepped out to wave us forward.

As we rode further into Exris, people followed in waves until we reached the front of the tavern. Barely a few moments had passed when Rune stormed out of the tavern, axe in hand.

"What the hel is going on out here? If the lot of you don't clear out from in front of my business, I'll start swi—" Her eyes met mine, then found Jerrik's, then the twins. Confusion registered on her face, and her raised arm slowly fell to her side. I swung my leg over the top of Grani and pushed through the few people between us. Sindre, Sylve, and Jerrik each did the same. The three Elders were more on guard, hands ready on their weapons of choice.

"What is going on out here, Leif?" She eyed the Elders who remained mounted atop their horses behind me, then cautiously scanned the length of the crowded street. "Or better yet, what did you do, Leif?"

"Before we announce it to the town, I need to know where you stand and if you are uncomfortable hosting us for the night. ... If you object, we will make this announcement elsewhere out of respect for your wishes," I offered softly. I could feel the hope in my eyes, the pleading. I don't have another plan if she refuses to support our cause this way. I hadn't considered it a possibility until I realized how large an audience we acquired.

"Okay?"

I moved closer to her, gently holding her elbows and leaning into her ear to speak. "Calder is planning on merging Sol with Skirra and has been working on this for months. There has been an influx of unidentified masked guards at the castle, and an inside source claims they are Skirrians. Each night, they ship in more of them. At some point soon, ... they will start implementing their way of governing." All she did was nod silently. "We are all here to fight this, and another group arrived in Lykke today to fight as well. To fight for *this*." I motioned toward the town, and her eyes followed.

"So, ... you need the tavern?" she asked slowly.

"If you feel inclined to help us this way, we would appreciate it. We only need lodging for tonight. Tomorrow, we head for the castle." She looked at me sadly. I'm not surprised she is hurt by this news. I expect everyone to be. ... All of the people of Sol *should* be.

"I will help. I'll clear the first floor of patrons for the remainder of the night. You can stay there. I don't have enough blankets," she added, tilting her head down the street.

"We have supplies. You don't need to worry about our comfort. We have all been made aware of what to expect." She squeezed my forearm in response. "Thank you." I smiled half-heartedly. I turned back toward Askel, Ylva, and Bergunn and nodded. They mirrored my gesture, and all three turned their horses and began to make an announcement to the townspeople.

"We are a group called Odin's Ravens!" Askel started, his voice projecting as far as he could send it. "And we have been working together since the foundation of Sol to raid the outlying towns within Skirra to save as many souls as we can from their abusive regime." Worried murmurs broke out across the sea of people, all of them looking at each other.

"Since our establishment, we have been working not only under the Skirrian radar but our King's as well. A group of us who fought in the war led these raids, including the late Brynjar Leif," Ylva added strongly. I could feel people's eyes rake over me, but I held my head up high. Regardless of how these people may have twisted views about Bryn, I will always be proud of my name.

"We are here now after a sequence of events that led us to information on the Crown's plans with Sol," Bergunn continued as he adjusted himself in his saddle. The stirrups had been specially customized for his shorter legs. "Calder plans to merge Sol with Skirra," he announced loudly to the crowd, causing an uproar, and a cacophony of jumbled questions were hurled at us. Jerrik pulled out a gjallarhorn and blew into it, quieting everyone and commanding the crowd's attention. Askel looked back and received a nod from Jer, ushering him to continue.

"Within and around the castle are groups of masked warriors that no one knows who they are or where they came from. They have not been permitted to speak to anyone or answer any questions. We believe these are Skirrian warriors whose presence is the initial step of their infiltration of our Kingdom," he explained.

"Each night, a ship filled with these Skirrian warriors make their way through Port Sisu and are received at Kron castle. If we want to save Sol, save our way of life, to save all that we have fought for and against all those years ago, this is the time that we stand up and fight once more," Ylva added proudly.

"We are not asking for more of you to join us," Bergunn clarified. "We only want to explain what is going on, as we ALL have the right to know what our King plans to do with our home—with our lives."

"We want to make something clear," Askel began, turning his horse in a small circle to scan the crowd with his eyes. "If you do not believe what we are telling you today and your loyalty to the Crown influences you to move against us, ... we will not hesitate to cut you down. We will ensure we can successfully take a stand against Kron and the Skirrian warriors that are here." His warning sent chills down my spine. I'm sure the absoluteness in his words made their impact, not only on me but on everyone who could hear him.

"But if you are enlightened to fight, to join us against Skirra, and make it known that the people of Sol DO NOT agree with the King's decisions; if you agree that we WILL NOT stand idly by while he plans to destroy ALL of our lives, then you can seek one of us out, and we will find a group to place you in," Ylva offered.

"In twelve hours, our raid against the Crown will commence," Bergunn declared. "By the Gods, I have so sworn. By my honor, I have so sworn." In unison, all the Raven's Warriors recited their oaths and pounded their fists over their hearts, marking the end of the announcements. The three Elder Ravens each rode along the length of our ranks, shouting orders. As the carts laden with supplies were pulled to the rear of the building, Ravens were assigned to stand watch, and the rest moved swiftly in every direction. Another wave of emotion clenched my stomach at the sight of it, forcing me to dodge into the tavern and run for the first available private bathroom.

After I pulled my emotions together and took a couple of breaths, I left my small sanctuary and stepped into the heart of the tavern. People bustled about, hauling supplies inside and claiming spots along the walls for the night's rest. Rune was breaking a sweat, pouring drinks in every mug she lined up at the bar, free for anyone. Jerrik was beside her, assisting where he could. All these people are preparing to go to battle for Sol. Meanwhile, I'm preparing to kill the King. The thought unsettled me—I'm unsure of why my heart felt this way, but for now, that is how I feel. *My only purpose, my only goal, is to send Calder's head flying from his body.* Whatever consequences may follow, I welcome with open arms.

"Do you want a drink?" Sindre asked from beside me, causing me to jump out of my skin. I placed a heavy hand over my chest, having to calm myself all over again.

"Fuck, Sindre!" I complained. "How are you so damn quiet sometimes?" He stifled a laugh and shook his head, pushing himself up from his relaxed position against the wall. The liquid in the two mugs he held sloshed over the edges. He extended one to me with a raised eyebrow. "Of course." I accepted the cup, cradling it in my hands, hesitant to drink with my unsettled stomach.

"Our message was received well," he stated plainly, walking with me to the bar's counter.

"Yes, it seems that way. We have gained a surprising number of warriors." I nodded toward the line that formed past the front doors of the tavern, leading past Bergunn and Ylva.

"Askel spotted a pair of Royal Guards earlier," Sindre stated abruptly.

I tensed and turned my head towards him. He looked as calm as ever while my stomach clenched in anticipation. "And?" I urged.

"He took Syl and caught up with them before they left Exris and ... sent them with a message." A small smile turned up the corner of his mouth.

My eyebrows arched in response. "What message?"

"Oh, something along the lines of ..." He waved his hand nonchalantly. "The Kingdom of Sol will not sit by and fall back under the Skirrian regime or some similar formal decree."

"Are they not worried about Calder ordering an attack on us here overnight?" I asked.

"The Elders insisted we would know long before they left Sol's town. They have nearly a dozen Ravens stationed near the edge of Exris, all on scheduled rotation for the night until Ragnhild and the rest of us arrive in the afternoon." He shrugged off his explanation and leaned into his mug, emptying it with only a few chugs.

"You're really this calm?" I asked, my eyebrows lifted quizzically.

"For now. I know we are doing the right thing, and even if tomorrow falls to shit, ... we will be fighting with and for honor." He raised his empty mug, clinking it against mine. "Then off to Valhalla." I spat my drink across the counter and looked at him in shock.

"How about we don't say shit like that." Concern draped across my face in response to the sly smile that tugged at his mouth. "I get the sentiment, but if you are so content with death tomorrow, I'd rather you be placed at the back of our formations."

"You know what I meant."

"I don't care! Don't say shit like that! Our intention for tomorrow is to come out alive. Our goal is not death."

"But you know it *is* a possibility?"

"I'm well aware. ..." I was clenching my mug so hard that my knuckles turned white. *Why would he say something so morbid?* We all know what is at risk, but our goal is not to travel to Valhalla tomorrow. It is not to send our fellow Sol warriors to Valhalla either. Our goal is victory. We *must* disarm the Royal Guards and save our killing blows for the masked Skirrian warriors. We can only hope that Sol's guards will hear us out and realize they would be defending the Skirrian regime and not everything they have been trained to fight for and protect. It might be a long shot, but we have to try. "Don't plan on going anywhere but that throne room. We go home together."

He lifted his glass slightly in acknowledgment and placed it back on the wooden counter. Turning to scan the room with his eyes he concluded our conversation.

Brax walked in through the front door with Jerrik, bouncing happily at all the people he would receive food from tonight. I waved him over and whistled for Brax, who turned suddenly and bounded over to me, jumping into my arms for his usual overenthusiastic embrace. When he flopped his head back to give Jerrik his '*I love this so much*' look, something caught his attention, and he got up to walk away from us through the room full of people to sit at someone's feet, tail wagging. I looked around a few people to see who Brax took an interest in, and my heart stopped.

Loki was sitting casually at a table full of our warriors, who didn't seem to mind his presence. He wasn't in any sort of disguise like he had been before. He was in his male form, chest on display through a black tunic. His scarlet red hair sported double braids running along one side of his head while the other half flowed freely in loose waves. He sat up straighter to greet Brax, who was now standing and wiggling his butt excitedly. I don't know how, but one second, I was standing between Jerrik and Sindre at the bar, and the next, I had Loki by the collar of his shirt, my axe wedged into the table beside him. I placed Brax in a '*down*' position in the same instance.

"What the FUCK are you doing here?" I demanded through gritted teeth, remembering that I shouldn't attract more attention to the God I was standing over. A God ... I was threatening with a weapon. *What the hel am I doing?*

"I have joined your little *army*. I'm here for *the cause*." His eyes pulsed with sarcasm, and a devious smile played on his lips.

"Says who?"

He nodded towards Bergunn and Ylva, who were still speaking to people signing up just inside the tavern's doors.

I scoffed in disbelief. "You are wanted for an attack against the Crown. I don't believe they would have let you in here. The entire Kingdom is looking for you," I retorted sourly.

"Well ..." I felt his fingers slowly work their way up the back of my leg, just behind my knee. "Since you are leading your very own rebellion against this Crown, I don't see why anyone would be particularly *bothered* with *my* presence." His bright green eyes dove into mine, pulling me closer to him. I felt my mouth twist in a scowl, and I worked my axe out of the table, gently dragging it down his chest, stopping once I reached the semi-exposed rune and applied some pressure.

"Well," I narrowed my eyes slightly, feigning a sultry expression. I un-clenched my fingers from his shirt and smoothed it out gently, feeling the solid muscles of his chest beneath them. "You ... are bothering *me*." I smiled as pleasantly as I could before pushing off him with my axe and standing straight. I noticed a clear outline of a bulge had formed on the front of his pants. "Get out," I ordered firmly, my voice filled with venom, as I hooked my axe back in its holster at my shoulder blade.

"I don't know. ... I'm enjoying the positions I've been put in."

"I can see that."

"V," Sindre said my name with such intensity that I straightened my posture at just his tone. I had only turned partially when I bumped into his chest, the scent of cedar and juniper flooding my senses. As I looked up at him, I noticed his brown eyes darken, and a shadow over his face that would strike terror in the heart of anyone who stood before him. I turned back to look at Loki, whose face was lit with a deep interest in this new interaction. "Is everything alright?" There was no emotion behind Sindre's question, just the death stare that consumed his usually kind eyes.

"Everything is fine. He was just leaving," I offered calmly, turning back to find Loki settling into his seat.

"Actually, I'm positive I told you I'm staying," Loki cut in, throwing an arm out to gesture at the crowd in the tavern. "I've joined forces with you lot." His words were taunting, and his wicked smile continued to lock in on Sindre, who didn't seem to be breathing.

"Why?" I spat, crossing my arms across my chest and stepping slightly in front of my friend. When my back rested against him, his posture relaxed.

"Killing a King is a big task," he stated matter-of-factly. "Someone has to keep an eye on you." His eyes met mine, his smile knowing.

"We aren't killing the King. That is not our goal." Sindre declared from behind me, placing a hand on the outside of my arm. "At least not initially. Dethrone him, yes."

"*You* might not be ...," Loki teased, raising an eyebrow at Sindre's hand placement, "but I know revenge when I see it."

Sylve and Askel walked in through the front doors of the tavern, immediately drawing my attention to them. Askel didn't miss a beat as he passed by, nodding at Sindre and me. But Sylve paused, looking between us and Loki, who remained comfortably seated. He nodded at her, a smug smile spreading across his face, and I noticed a small trickle of light begin to form in her palms. I walked over to her, grabbed her hands in mine, and led her past him.

"Stay out of our way."

I looked over my shoulder to find Loki's hands raised in an innocent gesture at Sindre's threat before Sindre whistled at Brax, who followed after us.

"What is *he* doing here?" Sylve asked, hands trembling—out of fear or rage, I couldn't tell.

"He says he's fighting with us," I answered, gently squeezing and releasing her hands in mine until the light faded.

"Bullshit!" She looked furiously toward where Loki was sitting.

"Well, of course, it's bullshit. But that's what he said," I reiterated. "There is nothing we can do about it without causing an unnecessary scene." Sindre sat beside Sylve while Brax crawled underneath the table and lay across my feet.

"He needs to leave," Sindre insisted quietly, placing his forearms on the table. He soon noticed what I was doing to Sylve's hands and changed his focus. "Are you okay?" he asked, putting a hand on her shoulder. She shook her head and brought her focus back to us, pulling her hands from mine and balling them in her lap.

"I'm fine. Sorry," she answered, nodding toward Sindre, who turned his attention back to me.

"He can't be here."

"We can't make him leave," I reiterated. "That is a conflict we don't— can't afford to start right now."

Sindre pinched the bridge of his nose between his fingers in frustration. "This already creates an entirely new issue on top of the one we are facing," he added.

"Just for *us*. Well, just for *me*. I need you guys to stay out of it." I looked between the twins and was met with angry glares.

"Fuck you if you think we are just going to let this guy walk in here and take you when our backs are turned," Sylve hissed under her breath. Sindre motioned at her with his thumb in solidarity.

"That's not going to happen," I reassured, pushing myself back from the table to create some space and ease the tension between us. "He mentioned before that his magic doesn't work on me—whatever that means. BUT, I would assume he can't just make my ass disappear without a fight." Suddenly, four wine-filled goblets were plunked down in the middle of the table, Jerrik towering proudly above us and motioning for each of us to grab one, which we did. I guzzled most of the wine before continuing. "HOWEVER, his abilities do work on *you*, and he *will* kill you. So, I need you guys to please stay out of this, at least for now." I pleaded with the twins.

"No way," Sindre interjected. "We can take him if we have to." He glanced over in Loki's direction before looking back at Sylve, who nodded in agreement.

I gaped in disbelief at their confidence. "No!" I slammed my hand down on the table, startling Jerrik. "He is a fucking God. Don't!" If the heat of my stare could forge weapons, I could have supplied our entire camp with crisp swords and axes. "Please," I added

"Who's a God?" Jerrik asked playfully. "The four of us could take on anyone. How Godly can someone be?" He laughed but soon stopped when he took note of our serious expressions.

"Loki is here," Sindre informed.

Jerrik nonchalantly took another swig, peering over his cup at the crowd. "Where?" he asked as he lowered the cup again. When Sindre pointed him in the right direction, he winced. "Uh-oh ..."

"What?" I asked, pulling my hair up into a ponytail to try to cool the warmth settling into my face and chest.

"Well, ... you see ..."

"Out with it, Jer!" I grumbled, loosening the leather strings at the top of my tunic to get more air on my skin.

"I didn't know who that was when he gave them to me." He put his hands up and slowly pushed his goblet away from himself. We all looked at Jerrik, then at our goblets, before looking back at him.

"You got these ... from him?" Sylve asked cautiously. Jerrik pursed his lips tightly, closing his eyes in defeat. Sindre pushed his drink away shaking his head.

"Hey, someone offers me free wine saying how it's this special *Asgardian* type, I'm taking it and asking questions later." We stared at him incredulously despite him defending himself the best he could.

"Asgard's finest," Loki's voice purred into my ear, making me jump. Sindre held out his hand to stop Sylve from standing at Loki's sudden appearance. The heat, now unbearably pressing against my skin, made it nearly impossible not to tear my clothes off. A muddled heaviness slowly crept into my head while Loki continued to speak. "I should have warned you, though. I apologize." He leaned over in front of me, picking up my mug and contemplating the contents inside. "Asgardian wine is aged by the Gods and intended to be consumed by them. ... Half a horn might be a bit much for a mortal human."

The twin's eyes bulged at whatever Loki was implying, but I couldn't care less. The heat radiating from my skin sent me into a euphoric state as if I drank five times more wine than I had, along with a few mushrooms. When I finally turned to Loki, he was already sitting beside me and staring intently. He lifted his hand—though I swore I saw three—and gently tucked a stray strand of hair behind my ear.

"You all will be fine," he announced to no one in particular. "You will thoroughly enjoy tonight with little to no after-effects come morning." He flashed his stunning, crooked smile before standing and addressing the entire tavern. "WHY DOES IT SEEM SO SOMBER IN HERE? STRIKE UP THE MUSIC! LET US CELEBRATE IN THE NAME OF THE GODS FOR GOOD FORTUNE AND GUIDANCE AGAINST THOSE WHO WALK THE PATH OF EVIL!" He then turned, grabbed my mug off the table, and raised it high. Most of the warriors in the tavern followed suit, and somehow, music filled the air, and dancing broke out almost immediately. Jerrik slammed his thick fist down on the table and stood.

"Yes! A last huzzah!" he roared in agreement, taking Sylve's hand and pulling her to the center of the room. Ylva came over and grabbed Sindre, shooting me a sly smile as she pulled him away to dance, leaving Loki and me unattended. I looked over at him slowly, and all the worry and irritation that I expected to be present was nowhere to be found. I contemplated him for a moment. He stepped off to the side, pulled a man up from his seat, and spun him into the crowd before turning back to me with a wild smile on his face, his eyes filled with mischief, his scarlet red hair cascading over his shoulder as he bent at the waist before me, offering his hand.

"A dance?"

"Oh, you're *asking* this time?" I responded sarcastically, crossing my arms over my chest.

He raised an eyebrow at me. "Would you prefer I have my way with you *without* asking?" I felt the faint gathering of warmth in my cheeks at the insinuating look on his face, then shook my head, slapping my hand into his.

"Fuck it."

# Thirty-Six

I couldn't tell how much time had passed when Sindre's arm grabbed onto mine and began to lead me toward the stairs, pausing at the bottom. We waited there for a moment until I looked up at him in confusion, prompting him to smile at me pitifully before he bent over and picked me up, wrapping a strong arm behind my legs and back. I didn't feel the need to protest since I naturally relaxed into his arms. I tucked my head into his neck, nuzzling into his hair, smelling the hint of cedar enveloping his golden locs.

"Where are we going?" I asked quietly, hugging my body to his as he adjusted his grip.

"To bed. You need to sleep off this *Godly* wine you've clearly consumed too much of," he explained softly. I could feel him smile against the top of my head.

"Why can't I sleep down there?"

"This is precautionary."

"I can—"

"I know you can handle yourself." He leaned down slightly, tipping me to the side to unlock the door. "This just gives us more time to jump in if Loki decides to try you on for size."

"Ha!" I threw my head back with one hard laugh. "That would be the LAST thing he ever did!" I declared drunkenly.

Sindre chuckled lightly in response as he kicked the door closed behind us. He set me down gently and placed his hands on my shoulders to steady me before pulling down the linen on the bed. I leaned against the wall and loosened my pants from around my waist, trying my best to pull my legs out of the fabric, but from the sound of Sindre's laugh, I must have done a poor job. Once I had wriggled free from my pant legs, I attempted to loosen my corset but grunted in frustration as my drunken fingers fumbled with the strings.

"Let me help," he offered, reaching out and gently turning me around to prevent me from making the tangled mess worse. He freed me from my corset prison and threw it on top of my pants, walking over to the bed and lifting the covers. I ripped my tunic over my head and followed him, leaving my undergarments exposed. He turned back to usher me into slumber and paused, noticing my lack of clothing. His eyes slowly caressed the curves of my body unashamedly. When our eyes met, I saw a fire in his that ignited a similar flame deep within me, creating a tingling sensation between my thighs. In just a few breaths, that yearning grew insatiable.

I slowly closed the distance between us, letting my mouth hover near his, my hand cautiously running up his chest, uncertain of the path I was taking. As I gazed into his deep brown eyes, I found the same longing reflected back at me.

Without a second thought, I slid my hand around his neck and pulled him to me, our lips meeting in a rush of drunken passion. He slid an arm around my lower back, pulling me to him before he bent over and picked me up, his hand grabbing onto my ass as I entwined my legs tightly around his waist. Sindre took a few steps forward, and my back hit the coarse straw of the bed, sending my head spinning with the sudden change of direction. My back arched towards him while my hands moved from around his neck down his chest and began struggling with the drawstrings of his pants in a desperate attempt to remove them. Between frantic kisses, I felt his grip release from my hair and his hand grasp at mine, which was struggling between us.

"Hey," Sindre whispered, pushing his forehead down onto mine, withholding me from kissing him again. "Hey, no," he said, his breathing ragged.

"What?" I muttered onto his mouth. "Wha—"

"No," he repeated gently, guiding my hands out from between us before securing them above my head. "Not like this..." My eyes fluttered open only to be met with a tender gaze. Sindre was shaking his head at me, a heart-stopping smile on full display.

"What do you mean?" I asked, my eyebrows knitted together in confusion, letting my body go limp under him as the passion between us deflated.

"This isn't right. If this is what you want, you need to be sure."

"I *am* sure!" I cut in, reaching to kiss him, but he playfully pushed me away with his head.

"I'd rather you not be under any influence. ESPECIALLY a delusional God's influence," he admitted quietly into my hair, gently kissing down my jawline before returning to hover above me.

"I'm not ... I'm—" His reminder was a slap of reality, which was also intensely sobering. I shut my eyes hard and shook my head, embarrassment replacing the arousal that had consumed me a few moments before. "Gods, ... I'm sorry." My head flopped back in defeat as he released his grip on my hands above my head and carefully climbed off me. I swung my legs off to the side of the bed and sat up, rubbing my face aggressively.

"It's okay," Sindre offered playfully.

"Oh, Gods. ... I can hear the pity in your voice." I stood and followed him to the door. He snickered quietly and stepped out of the room, stopping and turning back towards me. Sindre held out his hand, and when I looked down, I saw a small knife in it.

"I didn't see one on you." He winked at me before leaning in to gently kiss my forehead. "Goodnight, V." I smiled down at the knife, knowing I'd sleep better having it near me, regardless of whether I had drunk the whole tavern dry or not.

"Thanks."

He nodded and walked back down the hallway toward the staircase leading to the hundreds of people sleeping on the first floor. Just before I stepped back to close the door, something caught my eye below. Loki was sitting on a table, staring up at me, or by the wretched glare on his face, staring up at Sindre. I held up my knife to show him and pointed it down in his direction as a warning. I grinned as he scoffed and shook his head right before I closed the door and locked it.

# Thirty-Seven

The shutters in my room were left open overnight, so when the morning sun appeared, the light streaked across the room, landing directly in my eyes and waking me promptly. I stretched out the slight ache in my arms and back before sitting up. Despite expecting a headache, I woke up without one and felt more rested than I had in a very long time. I faintly remember Loki saying something about the drinks he provided us, but I shook off the thought, focusing on what the day would bring.

I catapulted off the bed and stepped into the small bathroom, splashing water over my face and neck before braiding one thick plait down the center of my head, followed by two smaller, tighter ones on either side, tying them off and letting the ends flow freely down my back. I walked back to my pile of clothes, digging for the kohl stick I kept in a small satchel, and paused, contemplating how my clothes were strewn on the floor. *Sindre. Oh hel.*

I closed my eyes in resignation and let my hands fall into my lap. All I could hear replaying in my head was the pity in his voice at my lust-driven embarrassment. I knew he was going to want to talk about last night. Depending on how events go today, I'll have to find an excuse to NOT talk about it. I dismissed my thoughts and returned to the bathroom, running the black kohl stick from one temple to the other over my eyelids, then followed up with a thick line under them as well.

After stowing the kohl stick back in my satchel, I pulled on my black pants and a white tunic. I then secured my Raven's corset around my waist along with the matching armguards, weapons, and tool belts. A knock on the door broke my focus, and a knife slipped out of its holster, clattering onto the floor. Sighing, I picked it up and walked over to answer the door, only to find no one was there. I was about to close the door when I noticed a folded red garment on the ground with a creased piece of parchment resting on top.

~ᚱᚾᚹᛁ~

Loki's name was written in runes on the topside. I would never admit it out loud, but I *was* interested. I bent over to pick up the package and closed the door, looking around for the redheaded God to no avail. I unfolded the note with one hand while holding the red garment in the other and read:

*If you want change, you need to invite chaos.*

I tossed the parchment onto the bed and held out the raiment in my hands, letting it unravel and fall to the floor—a red cloak with a silver brooch that had what I now know is Loki's symbol embellished in its center. An accompanying red kohl stick fell to the floor. I bent over and picked it up, catching a glimpse of myself in the small, mirrored glass in the bathroom.

I looked the same as I usually did for raids. ... The same war paint, the same hairstyle, the same weapons. Well, that's not entirely true. I have significantly more weapons now than what I routinely pack for raids. Uneasiness fell over me, turning my stomach slightly. My throat tensed up, and I felt an uncomfortable warmth spread throughout me. The clothes I wore felt too tight, too warm, too restricting. I clenched the cloak in my hands.

*What if I fail today?*

Bryn would have died for nothing, with nobody to claim retribution for him, and Calder—he will turn Sol over to Skirra, and all of the people I know, all of the people Bryn fought to free, will be turned over to their barbaric regime. Frith will have to self-sustain without our help from the outside, and the risk of Sol finding out about the settlement will increase.

I looked at my reflection and wiped away a tear that rolled down my face. That will be the final tear I shed for the fate of the Kingdom, the final tear for this life we might leave behind. If I want to secure victory today, I will have to do something *different*, and that is exactly what I plan to do.

I ran the red kohl stick down from the top of my forehead, over my eye, all the way to the bottom of my jaw, repeating the stroke on the opposite side. I flung the red cloak over my shoulders, securing it with the brooch provided, and headed for the door.

When I stepped out, Sindre stood there, his fist in the air as if he was about to knock on the door.

He stepped back in surprise. "Oh! Good morning." He looked me up and down, a small smile curving the corners of his mouth.

I planted my hands on my hips in annoyance. "What? What are you smiling at?" I asked defensively.

"You look intimidating," he teased, gesturing to the side for me to pass.

"Good." I nodded confidently, leading our way toward the stairs. "So do you," I added over my shoulder.

"I appreciate that." He chuckled, following me down to the first floor.

He *did* look intimidating. Every inch of his god-like frame was clad in battle armor Jerrik had crafted for the Ravens. That and the obscene number of weapons he could fit across the expanse of his back would make anyone wonder if they even stood a chance against him. His hair was pulled up in his usual half-up half-down style, and his war paint was applied heavily beneath his eyes, extending in sharp lines toward his temples, with another diagonal streak across his cheeks.

"I like the red—it adds a nice touch," he said.

I paused for a second. "Thanks." We reached the open floor of the tavern, and the last warriors were walking out the door. Everything in the room had seemingly been returned to its rightful place. "Wow. Is everyone already out of here this early? Isn't it a little soon?" I turned to ask Sindre, but he lightly placed a hand on my back to keep me moving out of the front door.

"Ragnhild and his group made it to Exris about an hour ago. He decided to get an early start. We will be heading to the castle shortly."

"Alright then." I stepped outside and found Rune next to the entrance, ordering a bystander to move some crated supplies to a new location. I walked over to her and softly placed a hand on her shoulder. She turned sharply in annoyance before realizing it was me and relaxed once more. "I can never thank you enough." I pulled her in for a tight embrace, and she reciprocated with a firm squeeze.

"No thanks necessary. I wish you would have told me what you knew earlier. I could have done more to help." She pulled away from me with a mixture of sorrow and uncertainty on her face.

"I wish I could have," I whispered, squeezing her arm warmly. "You'll keep an eye on him for me?" I asked, looking at Brax play with a child down the road.

"Of course. He will be here when you return. ... I'll be seeing you," she stated, her eyes searching for confidence in mine. I nodded and turned from her, following Sindre to the back of the building where our horses were housed. We turned the corner and found Sylve sitting atop Arvak, her twists pulled into a ponytail that reached down the length of her back. Her ensemble of choice nearly matched Sindre's but with an added bow for good measure. The white kohl she used was painted over her eyes and most of her forehead, with additional black kohl splattered around them. When she noticed us, she smiled brightly, a deadly warrior who can still bring light to any room despite the situation.

"Today is the day," she stated confidently, "the day we will remind those in power of the strength of the people they preside over." She guided Arvak out of our path so we could get to our own horses. "He will regret the day he forgot to take us into consideration," she warned, winking at me.

"Gods, I love you, Syl," I breathed out in awe before securing the saddle straps around Grani. The all-black horse was giddy this morning. I'm sure he could feel the tension and fear that had overcome the townspeople. He has always been sensitive to Bryn's moods. If Bryn was upset, you could guarantee handling Grani would be difficult for anyone other than him.

"Are you ready for today?" she asked from behind me.

"More than," I responded swiftly, hauling myself up over Grani's back and settling into my seat. I looked over at her, and she nodded confidently.

"Is that new?" she asked, indicating at the red cloak that draped over Grani's back. I shrugged.

"I didn't realize I forgot mine in the first place. Someone let me borrow theirs," I offered assuredly.

"Suits you," she added before pressing Arvak forward, with Sindre promptly following with Alsvid. I pushed Grani forward and silently continued behind them, letting them lead me to the front of the growing group of warriors. The Elders awaited our arrival, each nodding at us in greeting.

"It's good to see our numbers have grown," Ragnhild said, inclining his head toward me.

"A welcomed surprise," I agreed calmly, trying to maintain my confidence for the battle ahead.

"Are we prepared?" He asked, turning his back to me and leading his horse toward the open road ahead of him.

"Yes," I answered.

"Let's get on then." He nodded toward Thora, who put her fingers to her mouth and whistled, catching Jerrik's attention a few carts behind the front line. His head shot up, and a nervous look flashed across his face as he grabbed the horn from around his back and blew into it.

"WARRIORS!" Ragnhild's voice projected down the street, bouncing off all the shops and houses lining it. "It is better to fight and fall than to live without hope!" A hearty cheer came from the crowd. "We hold our heritage and ancestors sacred; we vow to defend our people and our family to the death. We will sacrifice so others may live free!"

The Ravens and some of the Frithians joined in to speak our oath in unison. "We have sworn to uphold the Raven Banner, to follow the ways of the North, to always act with honor and bravery, to be ever true!" We all placed our closed fists over our chests. "By the Gods, I have so sworn! By my honor, I have so sworn!" The hundreds of warriors sounded out their war cries together, filling the streets and the city with confidence and pride. "TO THE CASTLE!" Ragnhild yelled out, ushering his steed forward and initiating our trek to Sol's town.

# Thirty-Eight

We reached Sol's town in a few hours and paused to restructure our positions. With the castle now in view, the Elders fell in place next to each other. Ragnhild waved me to his left, with Askel falling in on my other side and Ylva next to him. Meanwhile Bergunn, Thora, and Liv flanked Ragnhild's right side in that order. Sylve and Sindre were placed behind the Elder line among the main Ravens. A procession of horse-drawn carts, with more warriors traveling inside, were stationed behind them.

I noticed Kalyani moved her horse behind Sylve's, the two of them nodding slightly at each other. Kalyani caught my gaze and offered me a tight smile in support. I could see her son's confidence and energy in her eyes, now encompassed by black kohl in the shape of a raven, with a smudge of white ash between them where a bindi would usually be, perhaps a tribute to a fallen partner. She had a bow secured around her chest with one or two axes at her side. Her long dark hair was braided, resting over her shoulder and down her chest from underneath the head wrap she wore, a vision of resilience and grace that grew my confidence. *This is the right thing to do. … This battle is worth fighting.*

I looked past her and caught Jerrik's attention as he pulled his cart up behind her. He had his hair half pulled back, allowing his curls to fall neatly on his shoulders. His eyes were outlined with black kohl, forming two sharp lines that extended to his temples and met at the bridge of his nose. He brought his fingers to his lips, kissed them, and waved in my direction. I playfully caught his kiss and pressed it over my heart with a closed fist. Having them all here with me meant everything. *I only hope they knew how much I loved them.*

All of a sudden, a streak of scarlet red hair caught my eye near the back of Jerrik's cart. I craned my neck to get a better look, and my assumption proved true—Loki was there, his arms lazily draped along the edge of the cart. His hair was braided in the same pattern as my own, with black kohl smudged under his eyes and connecting streaks down his cheeks. My stomach tightened at the sight of a thin line of red kohl down one side of his face, starting from his hairline, over his eyelid, down his cheek, and coming to a stop at his jawline. He remained seated while the warriors around him lifted long wooden pikes into the air. *They were working as if they were unaware of his presence.*

I turned away from him and shifted my focus to what the warriors were doing. Each cart stood its staff high into the air, anchoring it in place and pausing momentarily to honor the Raven's banner secured to the top, gently swayed by the midday breeze. Ragnhild cleared his throat, and a respectful silence fell over us as we all turned to him.

"By the Gods, I have so sworn. By my honor, I have so sworn," he stated confidently. A unanimous 'thump' echoed across the warriors as our fists struck our chests in unison. He then turned toward the castle and ordered us forward. Our final few miles lay ahead, and we chose to walk this path with honor. We did not stop to explain our cause to the townspeople. Instead, individual Ravens were tasked with informing people of our purpose as we passed while the rest of us pressed onward.

We were nearing the castle, close enough to see that the drawbridge was raised, cutting us off from accessing the inner city. We halted a few yards from the rise, taking note of the Royal Archers who had their bows drawn along the top of the wall.

"SHIELDS!" Askel commanded, reaching beside him to grab the small round shield from its mount and holding it in front of his chest. I swiftly followed orders, arming myself with my own shield. The shields weren't large enough to cover us entirely. They have proven to be more helpful as a fighting tool by using it to strike an unprepared opponent, and if they blocked a few arrows along the way, we'd consider that a bonus.

"ARCHERS, READY!" Liv ordered. Our second and third formations equipped their bows and pulled their arrows taut against their strings. Ragnhild held up his hand, holding our attack at bay for a few seconds more.

"We are here to stop the infiltration of the Skirrians that stand among you now!" he announced loudly across the open field between us and the castle gates. You could see some of the Royal Archers readjust themselves uncomfortably as if they hadn't expected to be called out. "These unnamed masked warriors that have shown up unannounced have been sent by the Skirrian King with King Calder's blessing! They are here to merge with our Kingdom and implement their views and ways of life," he continued confidently. A few of the Royal Archers looked between each other. I squinted to see if I could identify the Skirrians from the Royal Guards and realized all of them were wearing masks. There was no way of telling who they were exactly. An odd feeling overcame me—perhaps a mixture of unease and dread—and settled heavily across my shoulders.

Either we were too late, and they had replaced all of Sols' warriors, ... or they knew why we were coming. I looked over at Askel, who seemed every bit as ready to break down this bridge with his bare hands. Sindre's words came rushing back from the night before.

*"Askel took Sylve and caught up with them before they left Exris and ... sent them with a message."*

As the unsettling realization hit me, Ragnhild's words muffled in the background. My head shot up just as he was about to signal the start of our attack.

"WAIT!" I yelled, rushing Grani forward and turning sideways in front of the Elders and battalions beyond them. "Wait!" I repeated, raising my hands in the air. "They are *all* wearing masks!" I explained loudly. "Whatever warning that was sent with the stray guards last night has given them time to prepare. They have outfitted ALL of the warriors in masks." Lowering my voice, I spoke only to Ragnhild. "We can't start this without knowing who our enemies are. We aren't here to kill our own people." He peered around me towards the warriors in question, his eyes narrowing before turning his attention back to me.

"We cannot waste any more time with inaction, Veronica," he offered solemnly. "We risk the lives of all who reside in this Kingdom if we wait."

I looked over my shoulder, watching how some guards shifted uneasily from one foot to the next, looking at their comrades for reassurance. An idea then came to mind—a last-ditch effort to preserve the honor of those kept in the dark by the Crown they serve. I turned Grani to face the wall, holding my shield loosely at my side.

"We know you have been ordered to keep your identities hidden! Your loyalty to your duties demands you to follow orders without question!" I yelled out to them. "TAKE THE MASKS OFF AND FIGHT FOR SOL'S HONOR IF YOU BELIEVE IN YOUR OBLIGATION TO THE CROWN! If you don't believe what we say to you today, … look into your comrades' eyes and know what side you've chosen!" We watched a few warriors look around while others remained focused, unmoved by our words or threats.

"WE ARE HERE TO REMOVE THE SKIRRIAN THREAT!" Ragnhild followed, raising his hand high. Our archers lifted their bows, aiming toward the men and women on the rise. "WE WILL REMOVE YOU IF YOU STAND IN OUR WAY!" Just before he gave the signal one of the warriors on the wall ripped off his mask, dropped his bow, and drew an axe. His voice was faint, and we couldn't make out what was said before the archer swung his axe at the female warrior next to him. She narrowly dodged the attack and pulled out her own weapon. This single act started a chain reaction of warriors ripping their masks off and going on the offensive against their former allies.

"ARCHERS!" Ragnhild called out sternly, his hand slicing through the air toward the wall. "FIRE!"

"No!" I tried to raise my hand to stop the attack, but it was too late. I watched as hundreds of arrows sailed and rained down onto the wall. I turned to Ragnhild with disbelief.

"This could be the fight of your life. … It's time to come to terms with the casualties of war, Leif." He ordered me to fall back in line, and I did, reminding myself of why we are here, … what we are fighting for, … and *the retribution I am here to fulfill.*

"SHIELDS!" Ylva screamed from down the line, noticing a handful of archers who remained unbothered by the chaos along the wall taking aim at us. I brought my shield above my head and ushered Grani forward, running past the incoming arrows with the other Elders. We circled around, riding back toward the wall from between our supply carts, when an explosion sounded from behind the giant wooden bridge, flames licking past the top of the gate as it fell open.

Scarlet red hair streaked through the air. Loki was riding the drawbridge as it collapsed onto the ground, sending tremors under our feet. He slowly straightened his posture, dropping the chain that secured the bridge just a few moments earlier.

"PUSH FORWARD," Bergunn ordered, sending our front lines through the entryway Loki had just provided. Horses thundered past him, and his hair whipped back from the speed at which we infiltrated the castle grounds. I stayed frozen in a combination of awe and irritation until someone passed in front of me, seemingly taking Loki's presence with them because he disappeared completely once my view cleared. I shook off the distraction and spurred Grani forward through the opening, immediately veering left and running toward the castle barns.

As I scanned the growing mass of fighting warriors, I watched Sylve leap from her horse to take on four Skirrian warriors at once with her rope dart. Kalyani and Jerrik were close behind her, eliminating any other enemies who dared to interfere with her fight. Surprisingly, the Royal Warriors of Sol removed their masks and joined our fight while the Skirrians kept theirs on. *Why they chose to do that instead of taking them off and blending in, I'll never know.*

I turned away from the main battle and sped down an aisle of produce carts. The royal barns came into view a few meters ahead when three Skirrians stepped into my path. I could easily clear my way if just one had shown up, but taking the risk of running one over and facing the others with an axe still left both Grani and me vulnerable to a wound that would likely incapacitate us. I was about to pull Grani back to dismount when a familiar voice yelled from behind me.

"MOVE OVER, KID!"

I turned quickly and found Ylva powering through the center of the aisle on her horse with Sindre flanking her on the opposite side. I obeyed her command and continued forward, guiding Grani off to the right so Ylva could take the lead. As I pulled out my axe, I noticed Sindre mirroring my movement. Ylva released her leg from the wooden peg that was secured to the side of her horse, and swung it behind her, using the momentum to push herself upright as she grabbed her bow from over her shoulder. She notched an arrow, pulled back, and let it fly, hitting the middle warrior dead between his eyes. The look of shock flashed across the other two warriors' faces, and they both lowered their shields in surprise. Without hesitation, Sindre and I swung our axes through their throats as we passed them.

I rode into the barn, dismounting mid-stride, and swiftly urged Grani into an open stall, hoping nobody would notice his out-of-place presence amid the chaos outside. Securing my shield on my back, I hurried over to the secluded side entrance I typically use to enter the castle. Sindre and Ylva were both waiting there after hiding their horses down an alleyway.

"What are you guys doing?" I asked in a hushed tone, walking past them to open the door. I was surprised that it wasn't locked when I stepped inside. The pair followed closely behind me.

"We are coming with you," Ylva stated plainly, tightening the straps around her wooden leg before pulling her axes out, keeping them ready in both hands. Her silver hair was pulled into two long braids, one on either side of her head. She wore no war paint on her face. However, the tattooed line from her lip to her chin and the lines running from the corner of her eyes to her ears were now accompanied by a new tattoo on her forehead—a '*V*' sprouting from her hairline and pointing down toward the space between her eyes.

I shot a look over my shoulder at Sindre, who only responded with a quiet chuckle. We neared the end of the darkened hallway that led us to the main foyer and paused, peeking around the corners to ensure we could cross the large expanse without being seen.

"Okay," I whispered, nodding at them. "We go up the stairs and take a left down the first hall. There are too many meeting rooms to count, so we will have to start there and work around the castle grounds." They nodded in understanding and readied themselves. I took a steadying breath and ran, the two of them keeping close behind me. We all halted when two figures came into view in the middle of the staircase before us.

"My, my, Leif. What have you done this time?" Ulrik sneered eagerly, his eyes glowing with what he thought was an opportunity to beat the shit out of me—*a traitor*—as retribution for my ability to say every disrespectful thought that came to my mind. I scoffed to myself, forcing his eye to twitch in annoyance.

"Traitor!" Ylva spat, her voice dripping with disdain as she stood beside me. My gaze shifted to the man beside Ulrik, a surge of heat flared in my chest—Tormod, the rat, standing proudly beside Ulrik at the brink of Sol's complete devastation while Bryn was dead. I clenched my fists so tightly my nails were digging in my palms.

"Oh, this young man?" Ulrik asked sarcastically, stepping to the side so Tormod took center stage. "He has been extremely helpful in preserving this Kingdom, alerting us to the start of a potential rebellion. ..." He clasped his hands behind his back, stalking around Tormod and eyeing me as he did, his brutal scar shining across his face when he passed the oil lamp on the wall. "Leading us to where the traitor resides ...," he paused, looking at me with a taunting smile on his face before continuing, "helping us ask the right questions." I could feel my anger pounding through the muscles in my hands. I knew they were shaking. An urge screamed at me to grab a knife and send it into his genitals.

"Why?" Ylva asked the question through a clenched jaw. Ulrik bowed mockingly, giving Tormod the room to answer.

"I'm loyal to the Kingdom and my King," Tormod declared, looking down on us with disgust. Sindre and I scoffed at his claim.

"Is this a newfound loyalty?" Ylva asked. I didn't look back at her, but I could hear the petty smile that was evident in her tone.

"I've always had my priorities aligned. Sol has always come first."

"If that were true, you would have outed us a long time ago," Ylva countered.

"No, what he meant to say was he's loyal to his *cowardice*. The same cowardice the Crown honors at the center of all of this," Sindre stated, his hand moving to the hilt of his sword. Ulrik lifted an eyebrow, a scowl forming on his face—*the same scowl he wore when I ran my mouth, knowing he couldn't do anything about it.* If he thought I was terrible, he just realized that my friends could be worse and much more difficult to take down. Ulrik cleared his throat, taking a step down the stairs.

"Ah, the same cowardice that *Odin's Ravens* display by hiding an entire settlement? What was it called again?" He paused and turned toward Tormod, feigning his need for assistance in identifying the one secret we wanted to maintain during this entire rebellion. "Oh, *Frith*, isn't it?" He turned back slowly, a devious toothy smile split across his face as he continued down the stairs. My heart clenched at the sound of that word on his tongue.

"No, ... you ..." Ylva breathed out raggedly.

"And after this little *inconvenience* is dealt with," Ulrik interrupted, waving his hand toward the noise outside the front doors, "our first order of business will be making sure this *hidden city* knows whose Kingdom they reside under."

"Piece of shit!" Ylva spat. She took off toward the stairs, and I sprinted after her. I knew her only goal was to get to Tormod, but she would need to get past Ulrik first, and I was going to be her buffer. I charged straight for him while his attention was locked on Ylva. When he finally noticed me, I tackled him onto the stairs, grabbing the front of his tunic and pulling him with me as I rolled down them. I heard a separate grunt as we landed on the floor—the sound of Ylva colliding with her target. Ulrik unsheathed his blade from its scabbard, and I rolled away, barely avoiding his knife as it plunged into the ground beside me. I scrambled to my feet just as Ulrik mirrored the motion, pulling an axe from behind his back.

"Oh, I'm going to *thoroughly* enjoy this," he snarled at me. I reached for my short swords as he lifted his axe in the air. He was about to take a step towards me when another axe caught his from behind and twisted him away from me violently. Sindre had somehow slipped behind Ulrik and was now towering over him, sneering as he secured their interlocked weapons with only one hand.

"Is that a *promise*?" Sindre challenged. My stomach twisted with fear at how deadly he looked at that moment. With Ylva and Sindre holding Ulrik and Tormod at bay, I knew this was my only chance to get away. Wasting any more time with Ulrik could ruin my chances of finding Calder. I bolted up the stairs, passing behind Ylva just as she flipped Tormod onto his back, her knife slicing through the muscles behind his knee. She glanced at me and gave a nod of approval.

"We've got it covered down here. We'll catch up," she assured before turning back to the man-turned-prey, whose eyes widened in terror at the blood lust in hers. I shot a quick glance down at Sindre, who seemed to be taking his time in playfully disarming Ulrik as if he were buying me time to gain some ground. He caught my eye and gave me a warning look before returning to the deadly dance he led.

I left my entourage and raced up the final flight of stairs, taking a sharp left down the first hallway before coming to a slow jog. Most of the meeting halls' doors were left open, and each room I peeked into looked as if it had been abandoned mid-meeting. Pieces of parchment were still laid out across the tables. After checking the first few rooms where I thought Calder might be, I stepped into another and saw a map strewn across a table that caught my attention.

As I walked closer, I realized it was a map of the Kingdom, the different terrains and wooded areas clearly marked between the towns. My eyes followed a red line drawn across it, starting at the castle, going through Exris, then Lykke, and cutting through Willingman Wood. The red line encircled the area just past the woods and up the incline towards Mount Eir—Frith's exact location. *That bastard not only told them about Frith's existence but even went as far as delineating our travel route to lead them straight to it.*

I snatched the map off the table and ripped it into multiple pieces before throwing it into the smoldering fire in the room. I returned to the table and shuffled through the exposed pages, grabbing anything that was or could be related to Frith and adding it to the growing flames. I didn't care if they had memorized any of it—even if this was wasted energy, I would do it again. I had to protect the Frithians, and if Sindre or Sylve were here, they would have done the same thing. The sound of hushed voices and the heels of boots echoed from down the hallway, drawing nearer.

I quietly unhooked my axe and shuffled to the open door, waiting for the right moment to attack. ... *A little closer.* ... *NOW!* I leaped from the room, swinging my weapon where I thought the person would be, and barely missed Mazen, who ducked out of the way just in time and ripped the silver mask from his face, his eyes bewildered.

"Veronica?" he asked, surprised to see me. His expression became cautious when he saw I noticed Erikka standing behind him. My breath caught at that exact moment. Mazen slowly drew his sword from his side, positioning himself in front of her. She was wearing the same red dress from the day Bryn died. I was instantly trapped in memories—flashbacks of Bryn's execution flooding in, her cold demeanor toward me and the emotionless stare as her father ordered the execution of my Afi, and the way she proudly followed him out of the arena, red fabric and lace trailing like blood behind her. Stuck in a haze of memories, I mindlessly reached for my second axe when Mazen's voice snapped me out of the void I was in.

"Veronica, ... please don't do this." His tone wasn't pleading or begging—he was warning me. I looked into his eyes and saw the determination in them, and I knew this wasn't a fight I could win. "The Skirrians turned on us and have been trying to kill her," he stated, turning his ear sideways to listen intently for any sounds down the hallway.

I glanced at Erikka and noticed her disheveled appearance—hair tied back into an unusual ponytail with strands that were pulled out of place and fell sporadically around her face. She looked as if she had just stood in a wind tunnel. I finally brought myself to look her in the eyes. I saw uncertainty and a hint of fear, but most importantly, ... I saw Erikka, not Princess Kron. Maybe that is why I lowered my weapons. A small sigh of relief escaped her as she leaned against the wall. Her hands rested on her knees, and her head fell between her shoulders as she caught her breath. I looked back at Mazen, only now noticing the blood splattered on his weapons and clothing.

"It's not mine," he stated, keeping his eyes on mine.

"I didn't think it was," I replied. "Where are you going?" I asked, looking past them down the empty hall.

"Just ... away at the moment," he admitted. "They know every inch of the castle at this point." I glanced at Erikka, who met my gaze briefly before looking away. Mazen noticed the exchange and looked between us. "What?"

"Take him to your spot," I suggested softly. Turning back to Mazen, I said, "I don't know where it is or how she kept it from me all these years, but there is a secret tunnel somewhere." His head jerked up, and his eyebrows furrowed.

"You've had a secret room this whole time?!" he questioned loudly. Erikka quickly shushed him whilst looking down the hallway.

"I didn't think about it!" she hissed under her breath. "I'm sorry." The sound of more approaching footsteps sounded from behind them, and Mazen immediately turned, centering himself in the corridor for battle. Erikka pushed herself off the wall and started toward me but stopped when she saw the dual axes I held. A group of five men came running around the corner towards us, yelling things I couldn't make out.

"Erikka ..." Mazen said as looked back over his shoulder toward me, his eyes looking for an answer to a question he didn't need to ask.

*Will I help them?*

*I don't know. ...*

"You might need to run to that hiding spot of yours ... and don't come out." He turned back, swords drawn, and charged at the men, his shoulder colliding with two of them before regaining his stance and exchanging attacks with both at once. He didn't seem to be struggling. In fact, it looked as if this was a training routine with how easily he engaged them. But when a third jumped in, the pressure on him increased. He shot a nervous look in Erikka's direction when one of the Skirrians ordered the two stragglers to seize the Princess. They turned and slowly began stalking toward her. The look on her face was sheer panic, seeming as if she was trapped from both directions, and her enemies were going to exploit that to their advantage.

When the closest Skirrian drew their longsword to attack her, my body moved on its own. I blinked, and the next second, I was in front of Erikka, catching their sword in the beard of my axes. Despite using both axes to block the attack, the impact slammed Erikka and me back into the wall. She grunted behind me, using her arms to brace the back of my shield.

I pulled down on the sword, but it didn't budge. Instead, the warrior wrenched it from my axes and reared back, preparing to strike again. I looked over to find the backside of my weapons lodged in the wall beside us. *Gods, how hard was this person swinging?* Quickly, I tightened my grip around the wooden handles and pulled my knees to my chest, kicking him square in his just as his sword reached its peak height, causing him to stumble backward and drop his weapon on the floor.

I turned and tried to rip both my axes out of the wall but only dislodged one. I abandoned the other and swung my freed axe into the second warrior, who was advancing toward Erikka. I used the momentum my swing created and spun in a circle, kicking up and across the Skirrian's jaw, sending him sprawling to the floor. With a few seconds to spare, I turned to face Erikka, her eyes wide with shock and pushed my shield into her chest.

"Keep a tight hold of it here and use it to block attacks. It also works great as a weapon if you need one," I ordered quickly. She nodded in understanding and tucked a loose strand of hair behind her ear as her wobbling hands struggled to find a strong grip. When I turned around, I immediately dodged an oncoming strike by dropping to the ground and rolling off to the side. I unsheathed one of my short swords to prepare for their next move. Erikka caught the brunt of the attack, grunting as she stumbled back, tripping on the train of her dress, and fell to the floor.

I watched as the warrior's eyes lit up with bloodlust. He reared back to attack again, but I dove over to Erikka, rolling in time to plunge the tip of my sword into the ground on the opposite side of her neck, barely stopping the enemy's blade from slashing her throat wide open. *That was a close one.* A grunt came from down the hall, and an axe whizzed over us, embedding itself into the enemy's abdomen. Erikka and I shot up to see Sindre running down the corridor with Ylva close behind.

Sindre was about to help me up when he noticed a second enemy on his feet, readying to attack. He switched course and bee-lined for him, blocking an attack with his shield and wrapping his arm around the warrior's, disarming him so quickly that I nearly missed it. One punch to the gut, another across the jaw, and the Skirrian crumpled to the ground, unconscious. Sindre glanced over toward Mazen, who seemed to be holding his own, then hurried back to me, ignoring the Princess still splayed out across the floor. He nodded to Ylva, and she ran over to help Mazen without hesitation.

"Are you alright?" he asked.

"Yeah, but I can't get my axe out of the wall." I nodded towards it as I turned and stood over Erikka, straddling my feet on either side of her. I grabbed the mass of fabric that was part of her dress that tripped her earlier and cut the end off using my knife, throwing the excess aside. I stepped away, withholding the urge to help her up. She awkwardly rolled onto her stomach, maneuvering around the shield, and got to her feet.

"Thank you," she offered through shaky breaths. "You didn't have to." Her icy blue eyes were tearful, a lonely sadness lingering in them. She stood there, fragile yet trying to appear confident, the bottom of her red dress shredded at her ankles, our Raven's shield held close to her like a lifeline. I quickly turned away, taking my axe from Sindre's outstretched hand as I passed him. Ylva helped Mazen up from the floor, kicking the dead Skirrian bodies out of the way. Mazen extended his hand, intending for Erikka to take it. I stepped to the side to let her through, noticing that Sindre had gone back for her, placing a supportive hand on her back as he guided her over to Mazen.

"Where are you guys headed?" Mazen asked, nodding toward me in gratitude for helping him. Sindre and Ylva didn't answer, looking at me, still unsure if they could trust him.

"Calder," I answered plainly. His eyes bore into me as if searching for something to say that could deter me or, perhaps, he was willing to send me in the right direction.

"What do you mean?" Erikka cut in. I ignored her and kept my eyes on Mazen as he continued to think. "Veronica!" She grasped my arm and pulled me to face her. I felt Sindre's presence solidify behind me as Mazen gently tried to pull Erikka back, but she refused to budge. Instead, she locked her eyes on mine. "*Why* are you looking for him?" she repeated sternly. I tried ignoring her, tried keeping my expression neutral, but my eyes started to burn at the thoughts racing through my mind. She tightened her grip, shaking me again. "Veronica!"

"BECAUSE I'M GOING TO KILL HIM!" I yelled, ripping my arm from her grasp. Her eyes remained wide but softened with realization.

"You can't do that..." she warned quietly, dropping her hand to her side.

"I can."

"No! *You* can't," she repeated sternly. I turned my head slowly, clenching my jaw to keep myself from screaming in frustration. I took a deep breath through my nose and straightened my spine.

"I will, and if you wish to evade the same fate, ... you should think about what you are going to do with the crown when I hand it to you," I threatened, stepping past her, Ylva and Sindre remaining close behind me.

"Hey!" Mazen called out. "The last I heard, before all of this started," he waved his hand at the dead men on the ground, "he was supposed to be in the throne room. I can't guarantee anything, but -" I nodded and took off in that direction, with my friends in tow. As soon as we turned the first corner, Sindre stopped us.

"We should probably keep a low profile from here on out," he suggested, signaling for us to move into a raven formation. He took the lead position as I filed in line behind him with Ylva close behind, all of us hugging the wall as we made our way to the throne room.

"Are we going to let her *live* after all this?" Ylva whispered to me.

"That depends on how she handles the shattered pieces of this kingdom," I responded curtly.

"Isn't that going to defeat the entire purpose of *everything* we are doing? *Waiting* to see if she will follow in her father's footsteps instead of cutting her off at the ankles?" I didn't respond because Sindre hushed us from ahead, signaling that we were coming up on a group of warriors. He held up six fingers, indicating the number of enemies around the corner.

He turned back to us. "Is there another way around to the throne room?" he asked in a hushed tone.

I shook my head. "Unless we track all the way back to the entrance and go up the stairs on the backside of the castle. But who's to say there aren't more of them on the other side too?" I explained quietly.

Sindre peeked around the corner to analyze our options and gasped softly. "What the—" He turned back to us, "They disa—" He paused again, noticing something behind us that prompted him to draw his sword. Ylva and I turned to see a group of six warriors standing a few feet away. We quickly mirrored Sindre's defensive stance, pulling out our weapons. A familiar voice spoke from behind us, diverting my attention away from the group. I stepped behind Sindre, pressing my back against his while waiting for the man to appear.

"Well, I see we've found some rebellious mortals," Vali jeered, walking nonchalantly around the corner we were just monitoring. He noticed me and a devilish smile crept across his masked face. "It's an honor to make your acquaintance, *no name*." I didn't respond, feeling Sindre's back flex in annoyance. "Why have you graced me with your presence today? Is there something *I* could help you with?" He gave short bow, keeping his gleaming silver eyes locked onto mine.

"Would asking you and your buddies to jump off the top of the rise be too much?" I asked sarcastically, earning a chuckle from Vali.

"As much as I'd love to satisfy you, a few of them are here to take over your Kingdom and would not listen to *my* command to do otherwise." He waved toward the warriors. I looked over my shoulder, past Sindre's, and noticed four of them beginning to advance toward us.

"What a shame," I retorted. Behind me, the Skirrians attacked Sindre and Ylva, and I charged at Vali, swiping my swords diagonally across his chest. Vali casually evaded each strike of my blade, moving a step back with each maneuver, leading me further down the hall and away from my friends. Once I realized what he was doing, I stopped, but it was too late. He seized my wrist, and nausea ripped through me, making my head spin slightly as I fought to keep him out of my mind.

"You intrigue me," he said, smiling murderously. "I have the craziest feeling that you may have forgotten what I am. I mean, you were on the right track the last time we spoke—taking more interest in Loki, unfortunately—but I was the one offering you all sorts of information." Ylva and Sindre's grunts and the sound of colliding metal grew louder behind us. I turned back and saw Sindre run his sword through a Skirrian's abdomen, heaving the body over his shoulder and throwing it into his comrades.

"Look at me," Vali ordered. My head snapped back towards him without any control. He tilted his head, scrutinizing me before locking his gaze on where his hand remained around my wrist. "I think I might be able to help you after all," he offered slyly.

A weird sensation washed over me as if I had turned into sand and was being pulled away by the tide, back into the ocean. When it stopped, everyone was gone; only distant fighting could be heard. I looked around us, and Sindre and Ylva were nowhere to be found. It was just Vali and me, somehow ending up in front of the throne room doors.

"Wha—" I began, but Vali cut in.

"If it is *revenge* you seek, you should have started with that." He dropped my arm and gestured to the door. Skepticism gnawed at me. Never mind how, but *why* had he brought me straight to the King when he had been working with him for months? Vali turned his back to me and started to walk away.

"Wha— Why?" I asked cautiously, readjusting my weapons in my hands.

He paused, turning to look at me over his shoulder. He reached up to remove the wolf mask from his face, and it disappeared in his hand. His sharp features were finally revealed, and he was stunning. "Revenge is sort of my thing," he answered confidently. "I'll be seeing you." He winked at me and vanished without a trace, leaving me dumbfounded and confused.

I looked around once more. No one was on duty outside the throne room where the King should be. *No, he should be fighting, but instead, he had locked himself away like a coward.* I stared at the grand wooden doors, Yggdrasil carved into them, the tree splitting in the middle when they opened, with a sun etched in its center. *This was it. Calder dies now,* even if I have to take him with me. *If I'm not the one left standing in this room, no one will be.*

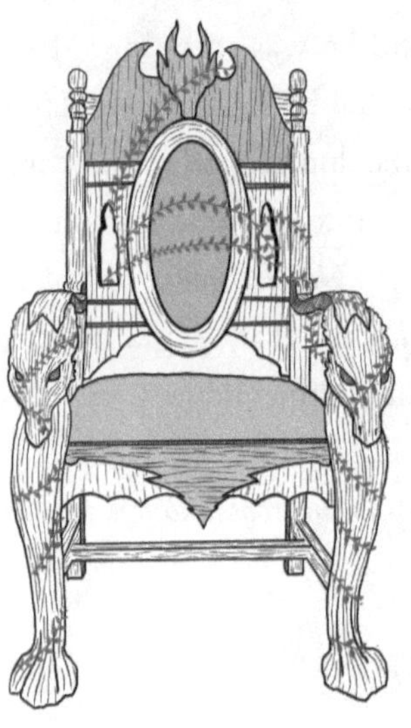

# Thirty-Nine

I took a steadying breath and sheathed my short swords. I needed my hands available to react to whatever awaited me on the other side of those doors. As I reached out to grab the intricate metal handles, I froze. An odd yet familiar sensation came over me as I heard Sindre's distant voice in my head, *"Don't you DARE go into that throne room alone! "*

I retracted my hands and stepped away, realizing I could be making a fatal mistake if I charged in without intel. I walked a little down the corridor and stopped at the floor-to-ceiling windows, peering at the stone wall surrounding the throne room. From where I stood, I couldn't see inside, but if I broke a window open I could possibly scale around to the balcony on the north side.

I unhooked my axe and readied myself, rolling my shoulder in anticipation of breaking the glass. As I lifted my weapon to strike, a tapping noise caught my attention. I looked down and noticed a tree growing in the courtyard below. A branch reached up towards the bottom of the window and continued to gather in front of me, the glass creaking against the building pressure. I moved away quickly as the sound grew more intense, throwing my arm over my face when the window shattered, sending shards of glass raining down the branches that now infested the hall. A chilled breeze funneled in, making it known that night was nearing. I lowered my arm and found Loki standing at the window's ledge. His legs hadn't entirely returned to his human form. Instead, he was covered in bark from the waist down, keeping him connected to the tree he conjured.

"Why am I not surprised?" I muttered, rolling my eyes in annoyance.

He smiled that crooked smile that always tightened my stomach, and his eyes devoured every inch of me, blood included. "Is it possible to fall in love with the same soul twice?" he asked, holding out a hand.

I ignored his question and raised an eyebrow at his gesture. "What?"

"I figured I could at least help you get where you need to go." He nodded toward the throne room. "But with the way my abilities have proven *unhelpful* in persuading *or* restraining you in previous situations, I have a hunch you might need to *accept* my help for my magic to work with you," he suggested, leaning up against the opening with his arms crossed.

"I can get there myself just fine, thank you," I spat, stepping over to the ledge, passing by the tree branches that removed themselves from my path. I looked at him, realizing that his raised eyebrow at how his magic reacted to me suggests that he might not be withdrawing them out of courtesy. Maybe he wasn't controlling them at all.

"As you wish," he stated supportively. He remained where he was as I hooked my axe behind me and stepped onto the stone ledge. There were a few footholds and handholds I was able to use to make my way around the building ... until the protruding column of the fireplace blocked my path. I carefully leaned back, trying to get a view of the wall ahead, but I couldn't quite see around the obstruction. Loki cleared his throat, and I let out a labored sigh, turning slowly to look at him. He had adjusted himself to be adjacent to me, angling his face obnoxiously close to mine.

"You know, ... I could help you get around this ... hump," he suggested, raising his eyebrows at the beads of sweat forming at my temples. "It could be a real energy saver."

I clenched my jaw to stop myself from swearing at him, looked back at my obstacle, then back at him. "Okay," I conceded, holding out my hand.

"Ah–ah!" He pulled his hand away, crossing his arms across his chest. I grasped back onto the wall and shot him a furious glare. "Actually, … I need you to *ask* me." My mouth dropped in disbelief. I glanced down at the ground two stories below, considering my options. The throne room overlooked a bailey that the warriors hadn't reached yet, so no one was below us. *Nobody would know.*

"You know, I think I might just jump from here."

"Oh, come on!" He laughed. "It's for the theory about my magic." He waved his hand in the air and then waited for me to speak. I took a deep breath and put on my best face.

"Would you mind helping me get to the balcony, oh, *God of Mischief?*" I asked, batting my eyes at him.

He stuck his tongue into his cheek and scoffed, tilting his head at my sarcasm. "Of course, meek mortal *human.* As I have nothing more interesting to do, I would be thrilled to help you." He held out his hand, offering a foothold along the trunk of the tree. Once I accepted, his hand solidified into a notch of wood. He gave me a genuine smile as his torso disappeared into the bark, followed by his face. I was left alone on the side of a tree that began to move. I looked down to see the roots crawling along the ground, tearing up dirt, grass, and flowerbeds as we made our way to the balcony. A strong breeze blew the red cloak out behind me as we moved. "Let the chaos begin," Loki's voice emanated from the tree despite him not being visible.

The windows came into view, and the first thing I saw were two guards stationed on either side of the balcony, their eyes widening at the sight of us. Loki centered us where we could see two additional guards flanking the door where I had stood moments earlier. Calder had turned his attention away from the fireplace and slowly walked to the opposite end of the wooden table. He was calm. Only a slightly raised eyebrow gave away any emotion at what he saw before him.

I unhooked an axe from behind me, preparing to jump down, but Loki said, "I can do better than that."

I tightened my grip as the tree rapidly grew, its branches thickening and curling around the balcony rails. More branches and vines intertwined before me, sealing me into a similar cocoon to the one Loki created when he breached the castle months ago. A sudden rush of motion jerked me forward, and the sound of crashing glass exploded around me. The branches unfurled, revealing the inside of the throne room, and I watched as Loki's vines wrapped around each of the Skirrian warriors in the room, constricting them until their heads popped. He then extended another limb for me to step down on, dropping me at the opposite end of the table from Calder. The vines retreated from the room's walls but remained entwined in two places: at the balcony's edge and around Calder's throne.

Calder cocked his head to the side as he watched me dismount from my perch, an arrogant smile on his face. He wore a red silk tunic, loosely buttoned to reveal a dragon tattooed on his chest. His crown glittered as the departing sun shone through the windows. Seeing him standing here so smugly triggered a visceral reaction. My hands began to tremble with rage as my stomach twisted with anticipation. I began twirling my axe in my hand to keep my mind focused.

"So, ... working with the enemy after all," he stated, casually pouring himself a mug of mead.

"If you can't beat 'em, join 'em, ... just following your shining example," I retorted, struggling to contain the whirlwind of emotions stirring in my chest. Calder nodded, taking a long pull of the liquid, finishing it, and placing it down neatly.

"I'm curious," he started, "did you come here *alone*?" He looked around the room as if waiting for someone else to magically appear—something that wasn't entirely impossible.

"Did you want an audience this time?" I asked sarcastically. "I'm sure I could round one up for you. I know a few people who would find great pleasure in watching this," I added, mirroring his movements as he began to circle the table, keeping my distance from him.

"As do I," he replied, a smirk on his face. I unhooked my second axe and held both ready in my hands. He eyed my movements but didn't advance toward his own weapons, choosing to keep his hands empty. "Did you happen to see Ulrik on your way here?" he asked nonchalantly.

"I did. He's been taken care of."

Calder clicked his tongue in disappointment. "Such a poor excuse for a chieftain. Brynjar would have been preferable if we could've just seen eye to eye." He looked away from me, folding his hands behind his back as he walked past the end of the table, assessing the damage to his throne.

"Don't … say his name," I warned, tightening my grip on my weapons.

"Who? Ulrik or Brynjar?" he asked innocently, turning his back to me completely. A bout of anger flashed through me, and I launched myself on top of the table, running across it, and leaped at his back, axes in mid-swing above my head. Calder spun, pulling his own axe from a hidden spot near his chair, and intercepted me, catching both my axes and throwing me off to the side. I rolled over my shoulder and popped back up on my feet, one axe still left in my grasp. The other axe was hooked around his, which he grabbed and balanced in his free hand. His crown didn't even move an inch out of place. "Is something bothering you?" he asked smugly, an evil grin taking shape across his lips.

"I've got a list," I growled through a clenched jaw, debating if it was worth taking out another weapon. "If you thought so highly of Bryn, why did you murder him?" I challenged, opting to draw one of my short swords.

"I'm sure you already know, but I'll indulge you." He took a step toward me, and I braced myself. "He was smart—not smarter than me, but close enough. Even during the war, his strategies could have been as good of an option as mine. I'd find myself considering them from time to time."

"I'm bored," I cut in. A muscle ticked in Calder's jaw, a sign of visible rage that also made the outline of a vein surface along his forehead. "I don't care about your ego trips. I've been forced to listen to them for years. You killed Bryn because you are a COWARD!" I spat. "And now the entire Kingdom knows your plan to bend and fold under Skirrian pressure. We won't stand by and let our home fall." I lunged for him with my axe and blocked his counter with my sword. The blades hissed as they skimmed along each other.

Calder pressed his attack, following one after another, eventually hooking his axe with mine and twisting my arm behind my back. Despite my best effort, I had to relinquish my axe to avoid his second strike, barely raising my short sword in time to catch his axe with it. He tugged my sword towards him, driving a knee into my abdomen, and sent me sprawling to the ground without my weapon. *Gods damn it!* I knew he was good. *I thought I knew what to expect, but it's as if he could anticipate my every move.* He used my sword to stab at me, penetrating the ground just under my arm, catching my cloak, and pinning me in place.

"I killed Brynjar because of *you*," he sneered, pointing his axe at me. I unsheathed my knife from my lower back and swiped at him just as he turned to walk away.

"LIES! You were afraid of the sway he had over the Kingdom! You knew *everyone* would side with him! Everyone *loved* him!" I shouted across the room. The fingers of one hand fumbled to loosen the brooch that anchored my cloak over my shoulders.

He didn't respond immediately. Instead, he paused, contemplating my words before unlacing his sleeves and rolling them up his tattooed forearms, scarred from battles he fought before my time.

"This Kingdom would have never turned on me if it weren't for you," he reiterated, ignoring what I said. "I had already broken him before he returned to you with the news," he explained, rolling his neck to loosen his shoulders. My breath caught in my chest as a weight began to settle there, stopping my attempt to free myself from my cloak. "I threatened to destroy everything he cared about, ... his estate, his city, his *remaining* family." He nearly growled the last word, causing the hairs on my arms to stand, a warning of imminent danger. "He was ordered to control the *youth* he presided over, ... break the news to them in a way to ensure a smooth transition. The fewer disturbances, the fewer lives I would take." He laughed, shaking his head as his eyes found mine. He pulled out a knife and pointed it at me. "I threatened to kill *you* if an uprising were to happen. He made it clear that it wouldn't."

My thoughts went into overdrive, and I froze where I lay on my elbows as Calder stalked over to me.

*You DID kill him!*

*If you hadn't persuaded him to fight, he would still be here!*

*You killed him!*

*He's dead because of YOU!*

Tears stung the brim of my eyes as my thoughts raged within me, giving Calder the time he needed to wrap his hand around my throat and force me to the ground as he straddled me.

"I was coming to get *you* the night we took Brynjar," he snarled between clenched teeth, squeezing my throat relentlessly. The pain snapped me out of the chaos in my mind. I tried to slash at him with my knife, but he swatted it away easily while his fist closed around the handle of his own blade, stabbing it down through my wrist and pinning it to the wooden floor beneath me. I screamed in shock, the agony clearing my mind instantly. "But where were you, Veronica?" He crushed my head against the floor, increasing the pressure of his grip on my face. "Off somewhere in a *hidden settlement*?" he seethed in frustration, raising his fist before battering the side of my face.

"Maybe killing Brynjar was a mistake." I brought my knee up towards his groin in a last-ditch effort to get him off of me, hitting my target and forcing a groan out of him. In turn, he dropped his entire weight down onto my abdomen, knocking the air out of my lungs as he grabbed my free arm and pinned it to my side, grinding his knee into it against the floor. "I should have killed you in that arena ... right after his head met the floor," he admitted into my ear. "But I do have to say, ... watching a man break has always been a pleasure of mine. I will never forget how Brynjar broke when I showed him exactly what I have done to you over the past twenty years."

I began to thrash beneath him, screaming curses as I struggled. Nothing I did could move his weight off me. Eventually, my strength faded, and my ragged breathing and burning tears were the only signs of discourse left. I glared at him as he looked down on me with disappointment. His face turned my stomach. There were no thoughts running through my head, only hatred and loathing radiating from every point where I was pinned to the ground. So, I spat in his face and watched as he turned a bright shade of red, trembling with rage.

"I am going to kill you," I whispered through gritted teeth. He scoffed at my words and adjusted himself, cracking his knuckles lazily.

"That might be the most offensive thing anyone has ever said to me. To think that you honestly believe you will bring me to my end ... by yourself?" He motioned his open arms around the room. "I won't even need a weapon to kill you," he stated triumphantly, bringing his fist barreling down into my face. My vision went black, and distant twinkling lights flickered in the distance before Calder's face reappeared. Then his other fist crashed into my opposite cheek, snapping my head in the opposite direction. The distant lights flashed before my eyes again until my vision cleared just enough to see the red clouds streaking across the orange sky just outside the balcony.

Another hit.

Darkness, then Calder.

Another hit.

Darkness.

Hit.

Red clouds.

Hit.

A woman with glowing golden eyes.

Another hit.

Darkness, then Calder.

Hit.

The woman with glowing golden eyes and long blonde hair reached out to me.

Hit.

Sunset.

Hit.

Darkness.

Hit.

The woman, her hand was outstretched toward me. I could feel myself reaching for her; the fingers on my pinned wrist were aching.

Hit.

A disembodied voice—a woman's voice. She sounded like me but, at the same time, also like a stranger. "Seize."

Hit.

"Your."

Hit.

"Power."

I felt my fingertips brush against the woman's, and suddenly, my vision returned just in time to watch my hand dissolve into a cloud of black smoke, followed by my arm, and an odd sensation washed over me. The room darkened, and I felt myself become weightless as my entire body dissipated and lifted into the air. I felt something pass *through* me, pulling through my presence slowly as if wading in honey. My vision was blurry, but I could still identify a glint—Calder's crown. He remained on the floor but turned to watch in horror as I moved.

Once I felt I was vertical again, I easily identified and moved to the shadow cast by his throne. Though I felt powerless over what was happening to me, the simple desire to rematerialize once I was in the shadows brought me back to myself, whole again and ensconced in the Crown's Seat—Calder's throne. The branches and vines that continued to strangle the throne grew closer to me, anchoring themselves into the floor. They reached further as if in response to the power I had just discovered.

I clenched and unclenched my fists a few times, looking over myself to see if what just happened was real—*and it was*. I glanced to my right and opened my palm, the branches reacting to retrieve my short sword from across the room, placing it in my hand. I stood slowly, just in case my coordination had been affected before stepping away from the chair and facing Calder. I could feel blood trickling down my wrist as I drew my second sword with my other hand. Calder scrambled to his feet, snatching the smaller knife that was left lodged in the floor, and stood to face me, his eyes wild with disbelief. I spat the blood that had gathered in my mouth at his feet.

"Killing Bryn ... was your final mistake," I announced, my voice now carrying a deadly edge that hadn't been there before. A hint of that strange woman's voice lingered at the edge of mine, something only I seemed to notice.

I advanced on him, my first strike blocked by his smaller weapon, forcing him to use his forearm to defend against my second blow. He groaned in pain and spun away from me. Knowing that he wouldn't last long without weapons, he catapulted over the table and grabbed an axe that had been left there earlier. I stalked toward him, pure adrenaline coursing through me, my thoughts quiet and focused, oddly clear for the first time since Bryn's death. Calder quickly tore off the end of his tunic and tied it tightly around his injured arm, where blood poured from the open wound in bursts.

I took two quick steps and brought my swords down on him. His axe's blade rode down the edge of the first sword, driving it into the second, while he thrust his elbow into my back, trying to shove me aside. Instead of resisting, I leaned into his shove, turning my blade and swinging my arm backward as I spun off of him, grazing his abdomen. I followed through with the motion, spinning out and planting my feet wide to face him again.

Calder clutched at the fresh wound, inspecting the blood on his arm, then readied his axe again. "You can't kill me," he laughed. "Not alone," he reiterated, moving towards a longsword that was mounted on the wall.

"I'm not alone," I announced confidently; the scent of his blood flooding my nose and overloading my senses, locking me in on him. *I need to kill him.* Nothing else mattered until I held his head in my hands. The branches responded intuitively to my thoughts, slithering across the floor and up the wall until they reached Calder, snaking up his legs and stopping his pursuit of another weapon. Another branch whipped off the wall and secured his armed hand out to the side. He thrashed against Loki's unyielding hold.

I took my time walking over to him, sheathing my swords back into their scabbards at my waist. Ducking under his extended arm to stand in front of him, I stared directly into his eyes, relishing in the fear I found. "Do you know what has just become *my* new pleasure?" I asked quietly, stepping closer and bringing my mouth to his ear. "Seeing men in power *fear me.*" I stepped away from him and noticed the sound of rushing boots gathering outside the door as it rattled violently, followed by pounding and yelling. I heard Sindre yelling for me on the other side, but I ignored it. "Not yet," I stated aloud, almost mindlessly. As if I commanded them, vines climbed across the ceiling and covered the door, sealing it shut.

"You can't kill me!" he spat. "They will have you hanged!"

"That's why *I'm* going to do it," Loki's voice answered just before he appeared behind Calder. Before he could turn around, Loki's arm speared through the center of his chest, surprising even me at the abruptness of it. Loki's bloodied hand reached for the brooch that still secured the red cloak around my shoulders and ripped it off, pulling it back and depositing it in the king's chest. "I'll see you in Hel, my friend," Loki said, patting Calder's shoulder reassuringly as the vines withered away, releasing him and letting him fall to his knees on the floor.

I turned away and walked over to the longsword that remained mounted to the wall, removing it and playing with its weight in both my hands. I returned to where Calder lay gasping for air, clutching at his chest. I passed behind him and kicked him in the back, sending him sprawling forward onto his hands and knees, his crown clattering to the floor. Raising the long sword above my head, I brought it down onto the back of the King's neck. Only cutting halfway through, I had to swing a second time to fully sever his head. His body crumpled to the floor as his head rolled, coming to a stop with his frozen stare on me. I let the weapon drop from my hands onto his limp body. I crouched down, picked up his crown, then his head by the hair, bringing it to eye level.

"I hope you can hear me ... and I hope my face haunts you for all of eternity in the afterlife," I whispered. I could have sworn I saw his eyes widen at my words, but my attention was drawn away by the cracking of the wooden doors behind us. Loki withdrew his vines from them, and they flew open. A group of warriors I recognized piled in—the Elders, Sindre and Sylve, and even Jerrik, entered the room cautiously with a handful of Sol warriors, Mazen included. Erikka followed, standing in the center of them all. Silence fell over the room as the gravity of what they saw hit them. I stood there, holding the King's head in one hand and his bloodied crown in the other, my gaze locked on Erikka. Her face was devoid of any emotion.

I walked over to her slowly but confidently. All the warriors surrounding her shifted uneasily, unsure whether to apprehend me or allow me to approach her. Mazen held up his hand, motioning for them to let me pass. I stopped in front of Erikka, raising her father's crown and placing it on her head. She didn't flinch when a drop of his blood rolled down the side of her face. I shoved his head into her stomach, holding it there as I leaned in close and declared.

"Long. Live. The Queen."

# Spotify Playlist

*The Bargain with Fate Series (By: Becca Anne)*

"What a Wonderful World" By: **2WEI, Ali Christenhusz, Edda Hayes**
"Wind Guide You" By: **Jeremy Soule**
"If You Should Fall" By: **Craig Armstrong, Cecilia Weston**
"Skraplandschottis" By: **Vasen**
"Drown" By: **Bring My The Horizon**
"Tourniquet" By: **Evanescence**
"Are You Really Okay?" By: **Sleep Token**
"Feel Something (With I Prevail)" By: **ILLENIUM, Excision, I Prevail**
"Delusion of Saviour" By: **Slayer**
"The Devil" By: **Rok Nardin**
"Sound of Madness" By: **Shinedown**
"SunKiller" By: **Spiritbox**
"Welcome Home" By: **Coheed and Cambria**
"Warriors" By: **League of Legends, 2WEI, Edda Hayes**
"Kill The Crown" By: **2WEI**

*Acknowledgements*

Finally!! Book two is out and I can feel complete again! Splitting *The Bargain with Fate* into two books was a hard decision to make. When TBWF and TAOF was one book it made sense, but the SIZE OF IT. My Gods. It was a risk I didn't want to take in possibly scaring off readers, especially with it being my debut.

I appreciate every single one of you who gave this story a shot and stuck around to see the next installment. My hope is that everything now seems a bit more put together than where we left things after TBWF. Although I felt like it worked were I chopped it in half, I was devastated to lose all of the Loki scenes that were in the second half of the manuscript. THANK YOU for returning to the Raven's and if you want to leave a review of your experience, that would be incredibly appreciated. Especially because Indie books depend on them as a lifeline.

NOW, on to all of my love, thanks, and appreciation for yall's unwavering support. Tristan, Sandra, and Anne! I will always be grateful for you guys just sitting with me while I try to walk you through scenes or kinks in my story.

To my amazing editors, Leanne and Amarie. I know we have been working on this second installment for quite some time, but it is finally over, and we can move on to the next! I also apologize for how much work I gave you both, but you have done a phenomenal job and this story wouldn't be what it is without you. Amarie, I LOVE you and your brain! You make me a better writer, and even if that's because of the immense guilt I feel for being so grammatically incorrect, it still counts!! And I appreciate you working with me so patiently through this learning curve.

Thank you to my Beta readers, Keith, Amber, Paula, Sandra, and Tristan. Your feedback and critique is always helpful and really gets me to think more about the story elements, where I want it to go, and how I intend to get there. Sometimes writing a story is so much fun but you forget that each little scene needs to have a purpose and an impact, and you guys kept me on track!

Thank you to all of my wonderful wonderful sensitivity readers! Neisha, Sruthi, Amarie, Kesar, Gulnaz, and Sarah. Your feedback is greatly appreciated. Thank you for holding me accountable and teaching me knew things along the way. Keeping TBWF series a safe space for everyone is my top priority, and you guys never let me down in any way! Thank you! Thank you! Thank you!

Shiloh!!! Thank you for coming back and helping me get everything together for TAOF. You are a life saver!

I have GOT to thank all the artists I have worked with so far for TAOF because they are all phenomenal to work with and are incredibly talented and deserve all of the recognition for bringing these characters to life. Ivy (Ivy_gwendoline on Instagram), Jake (@_artjake_ on Instagram), Nalou (@nalou_arts on instagram), and Paulina (@palsonart on Instagram). You are ALL so amazing and I wish nothing but the best for all of you and your creative, talented minds. If I could hug all of you I would!

Finally, I want to thank you, the reader, for trusting me with your time and energy. I can only hope you enjoyed your TAOF experience. Whether you love-read it or hate-read it I hope you enjoyed it and had a good time.

# *Glossary*

**Aesir:** The group of Gods of the principal pantheon of Old Norse religion.

**Aesir (Magic):** The ability to use elemental powers to enhance their physical abilities and weaponry.

**Afi:** Old Norse word for Grandfather.

**Alfheim:** Home of the Light Elves.

**Algiz (Rune):** Protection rune that also represents defense, and prosperity: Branded onto Loki's left chest.

**Angrboda:** Second wife to Loki: A Jotunn: Mother to Hel, Fenrir, and Jormungandr.

**Arlan:** Boat maker: Neighbor and friend to Brynjar and Veronica.

**Asgard:** Home to the Aesir Gods.

**Askel:** Name means 'cauldron of the gods, protected by god': An Elder Raven Council member.

**Bergunn:** Name means 'from the fortified hill or castle and unn means love': An Elder Raven Council member.

**Brynjar:** Name means 'warrior in armor': Veronica's grandfather : An Elder Raven Council member: Blood brother to Ragnhild.

**Byleistr:** Brother to Loki and Helblindi: Son to Laufey and Farbauti: A

Jotunn.

**Calder:** Name means 'cold and harsh waters': King of Sol : Erikka's father.

**Chamois:** Species of goat-antelope.

**Dark Elves:** Thought to be the same as dwarves and burn if exposed to the sun. Can cause human disease or heal it.

**Draugr:** The undead army of Norse mythology. Resembling zombies more than vampires, possess superhuman strength and are able to grow in size.

**Dunga:** Old Norse insult: a useless company or fellow.

**Dwarves:** Small misshapen creatures that live underground. Said to have crafted the finest weapons and jewelry, including Mjolnir.

**Eir:** Norse goddess/valkyrie associated with medical skill.

**Erikka:** Name means 'feminized word for ruler': Princess of Sol : Veronica's childhood friend.

**Exris:** The kingdom of Sol's trades town.

**Farbouti:** Loki's father: Consort of Laufey: A Jotunn.

**Fenrir:** Child of Loki. The father of Skoll and Hati. Is foretold to kill the god Odin during the events of Ragnarok.

**Fossegrimen:** A water spirit and creature who plays the fiddle with incredible talent and can be coaxed to teach the skill. Found in water-falls/moving water.

**Frith:** A hidden city where the ravens take the freed Skirrian thrall to live and establish their new lives.

**Glut:** First wife of Loki: Fire Giantess.

**Gjallarhorn:** A horn associated with the god Heimdallr and the wise being Mímir. The name is Old Norse for "hollering horn" or "the loud sounding horn". The horn is described as "ringing" and could be heard throughout heaven, earth, and the lower world.

**Gudmund:** Name means 'god is protecting': Sylve and Sindre's father.

**Gungnir:** The spear of the god Odin.

**Halle:** Name means 'heroine; derivative of Hallr means rock': Veronica's mother: Daughter to Brynjar.

**Hel:** Child of Loki. Goddess who rules the underworld and presents as being cruel, harsh and indifferent to the concerns of the dead and living.

**Helblindi:** Loki and Byleistr's brother: Son of Laufey and Farbauti: A Jotunn.

**Helheim:** Home of Hel and the dishonorable dead.

**Hemming:** Name means 'changing shapes'.

**Huldra:** Wardens of the forest that were beautiful and seductive. Had cow tails and bark along their backs. Will lure men into the forest and keep them as slaves or lovers.

**Jerrik:** Name means 'king forever': Raven member: Best friend to Veronica, Sylve, and Sindre.

**Jormungandr:** Child of Loki. A giant sea serpent whose body was so long it wrapped around the entirety of Midgard and bit its own tail.

**Jotnar:** Giants of Norse mythology that have powers that rival the gods and embody chaos. Enemies of the gods despite being descendants of them.

**Jotunheim:** Home of the giants.

**Kalyani:** Name means 'Auspicious, Excellent, Fortunate': Mother to

Raoul and Hemming: Newest member of the Ravens'.

**Kraken:** An aquatic monster that is said to dwell near the shores of Norway and Greenland. Depicted as a gigantic octopi or squid.

**Kron:** Name means 'crown': King Calder and Princess Erikka's last name.

**Kynda:** Name means 'kindle'.

**Lagom:** Name loosely translates to 'not too much and not too little, just right'.

**Laufey:** Loki's mother: A Jotunn Goddess: Name roughly translates to leaves or foliage.

**Light Elves:** Much like the gods of Aesir and Vanir, and could cause human disease or heal it.

**Leif:** Name means 'descendant': Veronica and Brynjar's last name.

**Liv:** Name means 'protector of life': An Elder Raven Council member.

**Loki:** The god of mischief: Sigyn's husband.

**Lykke:** Name means 'happiness'.

**Mare:** A monster that gave people bad dreams at night by sitting on them in their sleep.

**Mazen:** Name means 'to make' OR the Arabic version means 'rain cloud': Personal Royal Guard to Princess Erikka Kron.

**Midgard:** The human realm. (Earth).

**Muspelheim:** The realm of fire and home to the fire giants and demons.

**Narfi:** Son of Loki and Sigyn: Twin to Vali.

**Nidavellir:** Home of the dwarves.

**Niflheim:** The realm of frost, ice, snow, and mist.

**(The) Nine Realms:** Niflheim, Muspelheim, Asgard, Midgard, Jotunheim, Vanaheim, Alfheim, Svartalfheim, Helheim. The nine worlds in Norse mythology are held in the branches and roots of the world tree Yggdrasil.

**Nokken:** An ancient water spirit who shape-shifts into a beautiful man to lure women into the water and drown them, or into a white horse to lure children onto it's back to take them into a body of water to drown them.

**(The) Norns:** Deities in Norse mythology responsible for shaping the course of human destinies. They are powerful maiden giantesses (Jotuns) who had the important task to help Yggdrasil stay green and healthy.

**Nott:** Goddess of night.

**Nyhus:** Name means 'new house': Sindre, Sylve, and Gudmund's last name.

**Odin:** The Allfather: Husband of Frigg: Father of Thor, Bladr, and others.

**Odin's Ravens :** Secret viking group that raids Skirra to save the enslaved thrall and offer them a life of freedom, without the Sol government knowing.

**Osera:** The continent that Sol and Skirra are found on.

**Ragnhild:** Name means 'advising in battle': An Elder Raven Council member: Blood brother to Brynjar.

**Ragnarök:** The final destruction of the world in the conflict between the Aesir and the powers of Hel led by Loki.

**Raoul:** Name means 'as wise as a wolf': Eldest son to Kalyani.

**Ran:** Goddess of the sea.

**Reisa:** Name means 'raise'.

**Rune:** Name means 'secret': The Dark Sun Tavern keeper.

**Seidr:** Actions ranging from shamanic magic (spirit journeys, magical healing, magical psychiatric treatment), to prophecy.

**Sigyn:** The goddess of victory and fidelity: Loki's wife: Mother to Narfi and Vali.

**Sindre:** Name means 'one who is small and trivial; also means the sparkling one': Best friend to Veronica and Jerrik: Twin brother to Sylve: Member of the Ravens.

**Sisu:** Name means 'arctic nature has given us guts'.

**Skadi:** Goddess of winter.

**Skirra:** The "enemy" kingdom that the inhabitants of Sol fought a war against to earn their freedom: Name means 'scare'.

**Skuld:** The fate of the future.

**Sleipnir:** Son of Loki: Became Odin's eight legged horse.

**Sol:** The home kingdom of our main characters.

**Sol:** Goddess of the sun.

**Stillridge:** A city in Skirra that the Ravens target on their raids to rescue the thrall.

**Svartalfheim:** home of the dark elves.

**Sylve:** Name means 'she who holds the strength of the sun: Best Friend to Veronica and Jerrik: Twin sister to Sindre: Member of the Ravens.

**Sylph:** Air spirit.

**Thora:** Name means 'fem variation of Thor': An Elder Council member.

**Thrall:** Slave.

**Tormod:** Name 'derived from thor and *mod* means mind, wrath, courage': Member of the Ravens.

**Troll:** There are two types of trolls : large ugly trolls that dwell in forests and mountains, and small gnome-like trolls that live underground.

**Trond:** Name means 'to thrive and grow': Giant Veronica fights in Book One.

**Trygg:** Name means 'trustworthy or faithful': Jerrik's last name.

**Urd:** The fate of the past.

**Valerian:** Veronica's fighting personality: A root used to help aid sleep.

**Vali:** God of revenge who was created solely to enact revenge upon Loki after he killed Baldur.

**Vali:** Son of Loki and Sigyn: Twin to Narfi.

**Valknut:** Old Norse symbol composed of three interlocking triangles.

**Vanaheim:** Home to the Vanir Gods.

**Vanir:** The second pantheon in Old Norse Religion, who value nature, mysticism, wealth, and harmony.

**Verdandi:** The fate of the present.

**Veronica:** Name means 'victorious woman': Female Main Character.

**Veslingr:** Old Norse insult for a coward or annoying person.

**Volva:** A seeress who was honored and sought as a wise woman, healer, prophet, oracle, and priestess.

**Yggdrasil:** The world tree that connects the nine realms.

**Ylva:** Name means 'wolf'.

**Ymir:** A hermaphroditic giant and the first creature to come into being: Ancestor to all Giants and Gods.

*About the Author*

Born with a creative fire that never wavered, Becca Anne emerges as a first-time author passionate about reshaping ancient tales into vibrant narratives. At her Hill Country home, she shares her life with a devoted husband and a charming menagerie of animals, all cared for under the umbrella of her animal rescue. This sanctuary not only speaks to her love for animals but also symbolizes her dedication to positively impact the world.

Beyond the realm of fiction, Becca radiates empathy and compassion. A member and staunch advocate of the LGBTQ+, mental health awareness, and supporter of BIPOC communities, she uses her literary prowess to prioritize diversity and inclusivity. Her commitment to fostering understanding and acceptance reflects her deep-seated belief in the power of unity and love.

With each word she pens and every life she touches, Becca weaves a narrative of compassion, acceptance, and hope. Her artistic and altruistic endeavors merge seamlessly, painting a portrait of a soul whose light shines brightly, within her community and beyond.

*Sneak Peek*

Here is a sneak peek at book three in *The Bargain with Fate* series.

## The Twist of Fate

**The following text is not final and is subject to change.*

Loki flicked his arms out – a habit I've noticed he has prior to using his magic – before holding out his open palm between him and Sindre. "Fire," he said simply. A flame appeared in his palm and he began casually tossing the small ball of fire around. Suddenly the flame grew, connecting both of his hands before solidifying into a long sword. "Weapon."

"You make it look easy," Sindre huffed in annoyance. "I can assure you I'm thinking of weapons."

"You need to visualize what your power looks like. Bring it to life, and then mold it into what you need," Loki instructed, splitting his long sword into two short swords, one in each hand.

"Wouldn't it look like Sylve's?" Sindre asked, perplexed.

"Maybe, maybe not. But your power is there – I felt it when you attacked me in that castle's dungeon. So, all you need to do is feel it, too." Flames ignited along Loki's back, snaking down his arms, and forming a bow of fire. He turned towards me and as he pulled on the string, an arrow formed, notched in place. Turning towards the tree he conjured, he released the arrow, sending it past the tree into the darkness beyond.

After a few moments of concentration, a small point of light flickered in Sindre's palm, just as bright as Sylve's, before disappearing. I gasped in excitement, and Sindre nodded, satisfied.

"Great, now you know what it looks like. Now, form a weapon." I noticed Loki's voice dropped into a low, dangerous growl, a hint of malice lacing his words. It seemed Sindre did too with the way his body tensed.

"He was just able to conjure his magic. He's not going to be able to do everything in such a short time," I contested.

"He needs to. You all need to. Form. A. Weapon." Loki sprouted an evil grin, his piercing gaze never wavering from Sindre.

"Loki," I started. "We're done." I tried to walk towards Sindre to usher him back to the house with me. One second Loki was standing a few feet away, and the next he had a death grip on my arm.

"I wonder if your power only surfaces when it comes to her?" Loki mused, an unsettling curiosity in his eyes. "I have only felt your essence in times of distress, so I wonder if it's a matter of triggering it to make it come out in full force."

I attempted to pull away, to no avail. Instead, he yanked me close, his hand pressing firmly around the side of my neck. "What are you doing?" I asked in disbelief, my anger rising.

Sindre took a step towards us, but a root erupted from the ground and looped around his wrist, securing him in place. He glanced at the restraint before rolling his neck to look at Loki.

"Why would humans ever let their guards down when confronted with the existence of the Gods?" Loki jeered. My heart was pounding rapidly against my chest as I realized how helpless I was against him. I could kick and claw, but any struggle would only humiliate me further.

"If this is an attempt to push me, it's not going to work," Sindre replied coolly.

Loki leaned down towards me, his lips grazing my ear and trailing down my neck. I gasped softly, caught off guard. My stomach fluttered before twisting in embarrassment. I kept my eyes locked on Sindre's as Loki spoke.

"If I were human, or even a demi-god, and I – along with a particular friend of mine – acquired the attention of not one, but *two* Old Gods, I sure as hel wouldn't invite one of them to live with me."

"You insisted on staying," I seethed through clenched teeth.

Loki pressed into the nape of my neck, whispering, "And when you send me away again, who'll protect you from him?" My eyes fell to the ground, realizing Loki's plan – to force Sindre's powers to surface, ensuring more people could fight Vali.

"I thought you said I'd be safe with you around," I muttered under my breath.

"You care about your friends, don't you?" he asked quietly as he stepped in front of me, his back to Sindre, and gripped my shoulders. "Help me help you."

I took a deep breath and closed my eyes, bracing for what came next. "Okay."

"Good girl." He flashed his crooked smile as two roots emerged from the ground, winding up my arms and holding me in place without tightening around my skin. I shifted a little and they allowed me to move freely and escape if I wanted to. *Maybe this was a good idea.*

Loki strolled past Sindre, who swiped at him, his efforts futile. Loki stopped, standing twice as far from me as he was from Sindre.

"Let this be your first lesson," Loki announced as flames coiled down his arms to form another bow. "Never trust the Gods."

"You won't hurt her," Sindre laughed.

"Why do you think that?" Loki asked, cocking his head. "I could kill her now, and start this cycle anew. If she reincarnated once, I'm sure she'll come back again. In the meantime, I could rid myself of the thorn in my side that is Vali before seeking the next Sigyn. Maybe I'll even find the Norns and ask them about the specifics of our bargain."

My stomach sank as I realized he was right. Why had I put ANY trust into Loki when in reality he *could* just kill me and start over? Find someone who is willing to play along with his original plan? Suddenly, the roots around my arms felt ten times tighter despite hearing the voice of reason in the back of my mind reminding me I can just swat them away and free myself.

Sindre's face darkened when he noticed my growing fear.

Loki pulled his bow, a fire arrow forming. He aimed it at me and released it. The arrow whizzed past my head so fast that it lifted my hair off my shoulder. My breath hitched and my eyes widened in disbelief. *Did he just shoot an arrow at me?*

"Stop it, Loki!" Sindre snarled, straining against the tree roots wrapped around his wrist.

"Make me," Loki challenged, a nefarious grin forming along his mouth. His bow dissolved into flames and reformed into a small knife. He flipped it into the air, catching it and throwing it at the ground between my feet.

I kept my expression neutral, hiding my unease. It seemed to work on Loki but the moment I met Sindre's eyes, something in him snapped and he struggled violently against the root.

"If you hurt her, I will kill you, and I won't need magic to do it," Sindre bellowed, his jaw clenched.

Loki smiled sinisterly and said, "Yes, … yes, you will."

9 798330 495979